ISBN: 978-0-9764441-1-4

Cover Design by: N'Digodesign.com

Printed in the United States of America

Getting Up
and
Getting On

By

MBridges

LOF Publishing

Praise for *Are You Satisfied, Yet?*

Voted Best New Author of 2005 &
Best Romance Relationship Drama of 2005

*"This cast of characters will definitely keep
tongues wagging...."*
—RAWSISTAZ, 4 stars

*"The characters are believable, the issues are
real...."*
—Wanda E. Moorman, 5 stars

*"Definitely recommend(ed)..an intelligent,
intriguing read...."*
—APOOO Book Club, 4 stars

*"The writing compels you, invites you in and then
seduces you...."*
—Sydney Molare,
author Small Packages, 5 stars

"A dramatic tale that will pull you in...."
—Shelia M. Goss,
Bestselling author of *My Invisible Husband*

~ ~ ~

Other titles to watch for:

Life Happens
Extenuating Circumstance
An Angel's Face
Leaving Autumn
I Am
Too Deep for Tears
My What Nots

Acknowledgements

My thanks goes to God for giving me the gift of putting pen to paper and breathing life into the characters inside my head and making them real enough for others to see, too.

To Kenyatta Patton whom without my characters may never have made it into book form. Your belief and faith in my writing is always the adrenaline shot I need when I'm running low on perseverance. Your supply of encouraging words and support is endless.

To Toni, Janice, Bertie, Ms. Jae, Raphel, LaTonya, Lolita, all of you who read this manuscript and were happy to do so. Your opinion means alot and is valued beyond measure.

There are many others who read my first book and enthusiastically requested the next story, then the next... and the next—far too many people for me to name individually but I want each of you to know that without your love and support I can do nothing. My appreciation of you goes beyond words—even for me. God knows what He is doing when He places certain people in your life. Individually I've needed each of you and collectively I can't do without you.

I pray that this story entertains you as much as the first one did and makes you repeat the question—"Do you have anything else I can read?"

The answer will always be "Yes!"

Thank you endlessly...

Profusely...

Profoundly...

*This book is dedicated
to all the readers who asked
"What happened in California?"
This is how it went...*

Chapter One

S he could see the twinkling lights of the city below her. Content, she sighed, sipping at her wine. Resting her head against the cushion on her lounge chair, she sung along with the music streaming out from the living room through the patio door she'd left open.

There will be mountains that I will have to climb
And there will be battles that I will have to fight
Victory or defeat, it's up to me to decide
But how can I expect to win, if I never tried

"*I just can't give up now*—" she started on the chorus before realizing that she sung alone. The vocals of Mary, Mary no longer accompanied her. Confused by the interruption, she turned in her chair to see Sheila strolling through the patio doors.

"I only paused it, don't worry. Whatcha got up for tonight other than the usual, *I'm just going to enjoy some peace and solitude* crap?"

In response, Betty Jean rolled her eyes before turning back to her view of the city. "I'm perfectly content to—"

"Just sit here." Sheila said the last few words in unison, having heard them for the past several months. She poured wine into the glass she'd brought with her from the kitchen. With a sip from her glass, she took a seat across from Betty Jean.

Neither woman spoke for a moment. Sheila sat staring into her glass searching for the words she wanted to say. They'd been in California for nearly eight months and aside from a handful of times when they first arrived, Betty Jean refused to go out with her. It wasn't that Sheila was a party horse, she wasn't. She just didn't like the way Betty Jean was burying herself. As far as Sheila knew, Betty Jean hadn't dated since their move and *Sheila knew.*

"Come with me to the Chicken Shack," she said, abruptly breaking into both their thoughts.

"I don't know. I don't feel like booty shaking tonight," Betty Jean said, frowning at the thought of going to a club. She didn't feel like shouting to be heard, being bumped into, ground against, leered at or lied to and she couldn't seem to get her friend to understand. She really was content just sitting at home.

"Is that the only excuse, I mean reason, you have for not wanting to come with me?" Sheila raised a brow, asking the question into her glass before sipping again.

"Yeah, I guess." Betty Jean's reply was wary. Why did she get the feeling she was walking into a trap? She got a vivid image of the last time she went out at Sheila's urging and she shook her head, trying to back away from any potential snares. "I'm just not feeling the noise of a nightclub."

"So, no dancing and music?"

"No."

"Okay, cool." Sheila grinned and her eyes lit up with mischief. "The Chicken Shack is a poetry house. Kinda Love Jones-type ambiance. Since the loud music and dancing are your only objections, you have no reason not to go. It's going to be fun." Sheila stood, draining her glass.

"Come on, Sheila," Betty Jean groaned, closing her eyes.

Sheila stared down at Betty Jean, shaking her head. "I love you, Betty Jean. You're one of the best people I know, so I have to tell you this," she paused, uncharacteristically hesitating to say what was on her mind. Regaining her seat, she reached for Betty Jean's hand. "You can't stop living. Now before you go shaking your head, let me talk. You aren't living, baby, you're existing. You go to work, you come home. That's it. You wouldn't give anybody the time of day if you were wearing two watches. How long are you going to mourn, Betty Jean?"

"Mourn?" Angry, Betty Jean snatched her hand away. "Stop talking crazy. What the hell am I mourning?" She rose, pulling her robe closed. She padded angrily across the deck, going towards the house, on the pretense of getting ice.

Sighing, Sheila rose to follow her.

Betty Jean wasn't getting away from her so easily. Now that the subject had been broached, she was going to see it through. *In for a penny, in for a pound*, she thought before saying, "Mourning for yourself. The loss of Ezekiel. Hell I don't know, Sweetie. I only know it's barely seven-thirty in the evening on a Friday and you're wearing your bathrobe. Unless you're going to work, you're always in that damned thing and to tell you the truth, I half expect you to show up in it at Hurstwode and Donovan one day!"

Pulling the freezer door open with more force than was required, Betty Jean reached for an ice tray. "Damnit, Sheila, what's so spectacularly wrong with me wanting some peace and quiet?"

"Having peace and quiet and pulling the covers up over your head aren't the same thing. Are you certain which one you're doing? There's just no way in hell you're going to convince me that this is what you want. Your bathrobe on a Friday night. *Every Friday night.*"

"Well, it is." Betty Jean turned to face her friend. "All I have right now is peace and quiet and it's all I want. No bullshit. No drama. No headaches—"

"No life. No Zeke," Sheila cut in. She pretended not to see Betty Jean flinch. "Why are you letting him win?"

Frowning deeply, Betty Jean said in a low voice, "I'm not."

"Yes, you are," Sheila said, pushing through her guilt. The two of them had grown close and the last thing she wanted was to hurt Betty Jean. But watching her zombie her way through life was hurting. She couldn't sit back quietly and let it happen anymore.

Betty Jean's trembling fingers couldn't remove the cubes from the tray, so she slammed it upside down on the counter. The sugar bowl rattled and she stopped, staring at it. She dropped her head, closing her eyes for a brief moment. "I haven't let him win anything." She tucked a long strand of hair behind her ear. The action echoed her vulnerability, but Sheila plunged on.

"Okay, fine. Call him." Sheila removed the cordless phone from its cradle, extending it towards Betty Jean. "Call him. See if he's sitting at home lost, confused, barricaded against life. I'm your only companion, Betty Jean, and I'm scared of moving out and leaving you alone. This time next month I'll be in my own place, then what? You can't stop living 'cause I guarantee you, he hasn't. Hurt feelings and all, believe me, he's rolling on. Don't be afraid of being hurt again. Hell, be afraid of hurting somebody else this time around! Let somebody else shake and tremble at the mention of Betty Jean's name.

"Sweetie, you had the courage and strength to leave Zeke. Now I'm just saying it's time to get up and get on with it. You have a new life. A fresh beginning. Stop sitting at the start line and join the damned race." Placing the phone on the counter, she touched Betty

Jean lightly on the shoulder. "It's fine to listen to your gospel music, but hear what it's saying. There's a message in it. You have to try, Betty Jean and sitting here locked in your safe, lovely house, away from the world and the living is not trying. It's giving up." She left the kitchen, pausing to restart the CD Betty Jean had been listening to and Mary, Mary filled the room again.

"There's a new poet doing a reading and signing autographs. I forget her name, but her book is *Too Deep for Tears*. It's a collection of poetry and short stories. Hell, with the title alone, I'm interested. I'm getting dressed and going to check it out. You're welcome to come along." Her voice faded as she turned a corner and Betty Jean stared down at the phone.

She still knew his office number by heart. His cell phone number was a little sketchy, but she knew with a little thought and concentration it would come to her, as well. She thought of Sasha and shuddered. He'd rot in hell before she called his cell phone. The last time she dialed that number she got a whole earful of something she didn't want to hear.

Music suddenly blasted from the back of the house roaring from Sheila's bedroom and Betty Jean jumped at the unexpected noise. Rap music screamed from the Kenwood speakers and she recalled Sasha screaming Zeke's name. The woman rapping was telling some man to kiss her ass and Betty Jean found herself concurring with the sentiment, Ezekiel Johnson could rot in hell just the same, even without her calling his cell phone! Sweeping the ice tray into the sink, melting ice and all, she left the kitchen. Racing to her own bedroom, she hurried through a shower, mentally searching her wardrobe for something to wear.
**

Sheila was right, Betty Jean thought, the poetry house did have a Love Jones type ambiance. It was dimly lit with small domed candles on each table. Only the small circular stage offered any real light and even that was shadowed. They'd heard two poets already and was waiting for the evening's star attraction to come out on stage.

"How about another round?" Sheila asked, looking around for the waitress.

"I've had my eye out for the waitress for the last few minutes, but it's such a crush in here I don't spot her until she's fading back into the crowd again. I keep getting pulled into the performances. She'll slip my mind until it's too late to catch her attention." Betty Jean looked around smiling, glad she'd come out for the night.

"Speaking of having an eye out. That guy over there—" Sheila leaned in towards Betty Jean about to point, but was interrupted by the poet who'd come onto the stage.

The woman stood for a moment, until the house was completely quiet. Then lowering her head, she perched on the edge of the stool that was placed in the middle of the stage.

"*Cravings.*" The voice sounded husky and seductive and the few patrons who had lowered their conversations, but not stopped talking, fell silent. In a hypnotic trance, all eyes turned towards the stage and the petite woman, lured by her voice.

"*I seek your arms around my waist.*" She breathed slowly into the microphone until her voice filled the room, replacing the air.

"*I crave your lips upon my face. I want your scent on my hair.*" The woman ran a hand slowly through her cropped curls, sucking in her breath sharply. She exhaled the next two lines in a rush of sensual sound. "*I need you here. I need you there.*"

"*Temptation, that's this strong, in itself could not be wrong. Loving you all night long.*" The woman speaking smiled slowly, nodding her head in agreement to the lured suggestion. "*To you I should belong.*"

Her smile suddenly faded and she frowned, rising from the stool. Her voice was harder when she commanded, *"Don't shake your head to cause me grief,"* but there was a whisper of fear in her eyes. She wrapped her slender arms around her body, hugging herself. *"Just hold me tight and then release."* She flung her arms wide with the word. *"Do all the things your heart feels. Touch my soul and make it real."*

She sat again on the stool, first sagging in gratified contentment, then stretching long and straight on the stool. Her words came faster. *"Arch my back, make me cry, let me know that I'm alive. Love me till I think I'll die."* The word echoed through the room and she paused surveying the entranced audience before adding in a breathless whisper, *"Then sigh, content and satisfied. Look at me through lids half shut."* Her own were half closed and heavy lidded of a sudden.

"I think I love you, but—" She was shaking her head in the negative. Despair was written clearly in her expressive features and the audience waited, sharing her heartache. *"Arms so strong should bare my name, not just a minute's pleasure from a timeless game. Kiss me deeply, like the ones we stole."* A sweet smile spread across her face, a strange mixture of strength and weakness. *"And once again lay claim to my soul."*

There was a brief moment of stunned quiet as the crowd regained itself that was followed by thunderous applause. The poet smiled shyly, took a sip of water and launched into another piece. Fifteen minutes later, Betty Jean sat back in her booth with a hand to her chest. "She was incredible. I liked all the poetry this evening, but *that* was performance art. She has such wonderful control of her voice."

"I'm going to get an autograph later," Sheila said, absently searching the crowd for the man she'd seen earlier. All through the poet's set, his attention had been on Betty Jean. Now Sheila couldn't find him. A shame, too, because even from a distance, she could tell he was a hotty. Pushing him from her mind, she gave her attention back to Betty Jean. "So, what did you think? Worth getting out of your bathrobe for?"

"Worth getting out of my bathrobe for," Betty Jean conceded, laughing.

"Exactly, the reaction I was seeking," a male voice cut in from just behind Betty Jean's left ear and she stiffened, her eyes wide.

Sheila stared across the table at the man she'd seen in the crowd. Up close, as promised from far away, he was a handsome devil. There was something familiar about him, though, she was certain she'd never met him. A name might slip her mind, but damned if she'd forget a face like that, especially when it was attached to such a body.

"Amaretto Sour, I believe." With an exaggerated flourish he placed a glass before Betty Jean. "Courvoisier with a splash of Ruby Red grapefruit juice for the leggy one."

When Sheila lifted an eyebrow at his words, he held up his hands in mock defense. "Don't blame me, I'm only repeating what the waitress said. *Amaretto Sour for the Cutie in Blue and Courvoisier with a splash of Ruby Red for the leggy one.*"

"Why didn't you repeat the Cutie in Blue part when she got her drink?" Sheila playfully sucked on her straw, a breath away from flirting with the tall stranger.

"Because," he explained, seating himself beside Betty Jean in the booth, "I'm saving her for myself."

"And the lesbian waitress can have me, is that it?" Sheila asked laughing, reluctantly tapping down her attraction. He'd made his choice when he slid into the other side of the booth.

To this, the man merely hunched his shoulders, a grin stretching across his features. "I don't judge. Women are beautiful, sexy. I don't blame your kind." Sheila gave him a look and he laughed out loud only teasing. "Sorry, but I spotted Cutie in Blue first." He pulled his attention from Sheila back to Betty Jean's stunned face.

He doesn't remember me, she thought wildly. He'd hunted her down back home, sprouting all sorts of nonsense about connecting with her and wanting to get to know her better, but less than a year later and he didn't even recognize her.

Betty Jean took a long swallow of her drink, grateful the bartender had a generous hand with the alcohol and decided to go along with it. If Byron had forgotten her, so be it. If he wanted to pretend that they were strangers, she could, too. Hell, they were! It would be no real stretch of the imagination to act as though she didn't know him. She could forget him just as easily. No, great trick that would be, she mumbled into her glass, taking another long drink.

Sheila raised an eyebrow at Betty Jean's nearly empty glass. It was not like her friend to suck down a drink, but she tactfully refrained from making any comment. The table's newest arrival; however, had no such qualms.

"I don't usually drive women to drink until after we've dated," he joked. Having observed the two women since they first entered the club, he didn't think she was a lush. He smiled inwardly. This woman was having a really strange reaction to him. Either their chemistry didn't mix at all or he was missing a piece of the puzzle. His smile grew. He liked enigmas. And this one looked like it was wrapped up in a bit of mystery, too. Double the goodies.

Betty Jean didn't even try to keep the nastiness out of her voice. "I guess you just have that kind of effect on me."

"Want to be able to blame anything you may do on the alcohol, hun?" He winked at her, goading her further and she nearly kicked him under the table. The only thing that stilled her foot was that the move would be really awkward with him sitting beside her in the circular booth and she might strike Sheila by accident. Then she'd have to explain why she was playing footsy under the table.

"I'm grown. An adult," she said, completely contradicting her last thoughts that proved the contrary. Adults didn't kick people under the table. "I don't need an excuse to do anything. And if I were to do something, I wouldn't use alcohol for my reasoning. I'd want to be clear headed. That way, later I wouldn't have difficulty remembering anything I'd done," she snapped.

Eyebrows raised above the rim of her glass, Sheila tried to understand the hostility emanating from her friend. She knew Betty Jean was a little bit off men at the moment and she didn't blame her, but damn! It wasn't like her to attack like she was doing now. She usually just displayed cool disinterest and politely refused any offers to exchange numbers. Why she'd want to do that to the fine bit of goodness sitting next to her was beyond Sheila's realm of comprehension, though. It was all she could do to keep from eating him up with her eyes. He'd chosen the left side of the booth to sit his fineness in, not the right.

Betty Jean reached for her pocket book, belatedly thinking to pay for their drinks. She didn't want Byron's charity. He stopped her with a wave of his hand. "They're on the house."

"Why?" Betty Jean demanded. Her look, completely pugnacious. "Are we the one millionth customers at the Chicken Shack?" she asked sarcastically. No, thank you. I've learned how unwise it is to let a man buy me a drink in a strange night club."

He turned his head to stare at her and her stomach flipped a little recalling the touch of his lips on her thigh. A touch he obviously didn't remember. Suddenly, a smile came into his eyes and pulled at the corner of his mouth. He continued to stare at her, but there was a subtle difference in his gaze and she began to feel uneasy. Why was he looking like that, like he knew something she didn't? What was he thinking? Was he remembering something? She frowned. "Stop staring at me," she snapped, turning her head. Bastard.

He stared at her a moment longer before looking back at Sheila, who laughed as she sipped her drink. "Right about now you're wishing you'd have went for the leggy one, hun?"

He should have, but he was a man of principle. He did like Leggs. She was sexy, tempting as sin. Wild, he could tell. There was a taunt in her eyes when she looked at him. A tease on her full lips, but as much as he liked a good taunt and a little tease, he'd spotted Cutie first.

Smiling, he slid from the booth, bidding them both good night.

Chapter Two

Following Betty Jean into the living room, Sheila stepped out of her three inch mules and tucked her feet beneath her on the couch. "So, what the hell was that all about?" she asked without preamble. "Why'd cutie get the rough end of the stick?"

"Cutie's lucky I didn't have a stick handy," Betty Jean growled raking a hand through her hair. "I have half a mind to find one and go back to the club. Introduce myself correctly."

"What am I missing here?" Sheila asked. Betty Jean rose from the couch, walking into the kitchen. The house had a large open floor plan with the kitchen as the center of activity. It was designed so that the person cooking would not miss out on all the fun being had in the living room. The two rooms flowed together and were separated by the bar. Sheila could have kept her seat on the couch and still been able to easily converse with Betty Jean, but she chose to follow her towards the kitchen instead. She plopped down on a barstool. "Have we met him before? He looked vaguely familiar, but for the life of me I don't know why. I'm almost sure I've never met him before, but he has that look. Like if you see a celebrity on the street or meet someone's relative and you get that *don't I know you* thing going on." Sheila frowned trying to place the stranger.

"You want some crab legs?" Betty Jean asked reaching into the refrigerator.

"I want some answers. You already know I'm not going to sit here and let you eat those crab legs by yourself. As a fact," she said leaving her stool to retrieve a deck of cards. "We're going to play a little gin, eat a little crab and you're going to tell me a little story."

Sighing, because she knew it was inevitable, Betty Jean added crab boil to the water in the large pot she'd placed on the stove. "Let me get out of these clothes first before I'm forced to spill my guts."

"Of course," Sheila said smiling, turning to go to her room and change, also. "I don't want you to have any excuses, sorry, *reasons* to stop talking right when it starts getting good."

Betty Jean smiled as she exited the kitchen, taking a hallway opposite of the one Sheila had taken. She was accustomed to Sheila's slip of the tongue between excuses and reasons and no longer even bothered to respond to the bait. She'd also grown accustomed to their chats. When either of them had something to discuss or talk about they usually did it over a deck of cards and food. They considered it cheap therapy and joked about needing a session sometimes.

The night had turned out to be relatively nice, she thought, considering she'd been ignored by a man who had set her blood on fire and swore he'd never forget the experience. Briefly, she recalled their night together on her first trip to California months before. Closing her eyes she could feel his breath on her hips, then her thighs, all over again. Just like she'd felt when he looked at her tonight. *Perfection*, he'd said to her in French before dipping his head to taste her. She shook her head, clearing the vivid images. She frowned, waving away his flowery words. She wouldn't be upset, she told herself. If she had been just another faceless woman to him, it was just as well because he'd only been used to serve her purpose at the time, anyway.

She'd forgotten all about him as soon as he left her hotel room.

If not then, certainly by the time she'd flown home, she convinced herself.

By the time he tracked her down, weeks later, she barely knew who he was, she out and out lied.

**

"You're kidding." Sheila laughed snapping one long crab leg in half. She removed the meat, popping it into her mouth. "Are you sure that was him?" She frowned thinking. "That would explain why he seemed so familiar to me!" Sheila nodded her head, but her tone was still doubtful. "Damn, you said he looked good, but damn. You did not give your description of him justice." Again she frowned. "Are you *sure* that was him? You said, as I recall, *he's a nice looking young man*," she copied Betty Jean's voice perfectly. "*That* however was not a nice looking young man. *That* was an *ought to be a sin to look this way* fully grown man." Sheila frowned. That still didn't explain what she felt looking at the stranger, Byron. She'd felt a sense of recognition, a connection that she could not explain. She still felt it. Invisible strings pulling at her like spider webs.

Betty Jean stopped sucking her finger to glare at Sheila. "Of course, I'm sure. I know who I slept with even if his memory is faulty. I still can't believe he could forget about me so completely. It was good, too. Shit," she said laughing. "*I* thought it was good at least!"

"You put your thang down on him, girl?" Sheila laughed, dipping her crab meat in the bowl of butter before putting it in her mouth.

"Yesterday, I would have said girl, yes, all loud and proud and sure," Betty Jean said chewing. "Now, I'm just like I don't really want to talk about it," she said low and rapidly. She hunched her shoulders like she was trying to evade a camera crew and they both laughed.

"See? Had you been videotaping like I've been telling you to do, you'd be able to go back and see what
you did wrong. You could be like *stop the tape, that's it,
right there! Right there is when I lost him! I should of
been going down, when I was going up. Yep, that's the
moment when he forgot all about me.*"

"Nasty ass," Betty Jean teased throwing her used
napkin across the table at Sheila.

**

For the third time that morning, Betty Jean picked
up the cordless phone and for just as many times, she
only got as far as pressing the number one. She held
the phone for a few seconds with her thumb hovering
over the second digit of the number she knew she didn't
need to dial. Sighing heavily, she pressed the end call
button instead and returned the phone to it's resting
spot on her chest.

Nearly two weeks had passed since the incident at
the Chicken Shack, but she still couldn't get it out of
her mind. Ironically, it was not Byron's betrayal that
plagued her, but Ezekiel's. Her ex was back in the south
where'd she'd left him, but Byron's ability to dismiss
and erase her from his mind so completely kept a litany
of the things Ezekiel had told her running through her
head and she worried that he may have been right.

She'd meant nothing to Byron.

She wasn't a twelve year old child and she didn't
align sex with love, but his actions reaffirmed that she
was alone and uncared for again. She didn't know why
she wanted to call Ezekiel. She wasn't certain if she
wanted to curse and scream at him for not having his
act together or hope when she called he did have it
together, that he changed and she'd be able to give
him another chance.

Again, Betty Jean sighed. She rolled to her side in
the bed cradling the phone in her hand. Glaring down
at it, she pushed it across the bed with enough force
to send it sliding to the floor. Having landed on the

thick throw rug and not the wooden floor, the phone landed quietly. Betty Jean was anticipating the thud of the phone when it hit the floor and frowned when it didn't come. Pulling herself to the other side of the bed, she peered over the edge barely lifting her head from the mattress. She flung an arm down from the bed. Retrieving the receiver, she placed it flat on the floor. Pulling back as far as she was able to while keeping the phone flat, her arm shot forward, sending the phone careening to the other side of the room. Satisfied with the amount of noise the rejected phone made crashing into the closet door, she pulled herself back across the bed to her original location.

Damn him, she thought trying to erase Ezekiel from her mind. They were good together. If he could have simply kept his pants up, they would be together now lying in bed and listening to the rain on the roof.

But *no*. Instead, he cheated and ran around on her so much, she ended up betraying him with a man who didn't know her from Adam. Or Eve for that matter, she amended the thought.

She flopped over onto her back and stared up at the ceiling she thought she'd sleep under with Ezekiel. She hadn't spoken to him since she'd moved to the West Coast nearly a year ago. Sometimes she wondered who stood in her place. Carla? Sasha? Someone new? Did *whomever* have the same Ezekiel she couldn't tame? The same one that loved her to no end, but refused to do right by her or the new improved version? The new Ezekiel. *The XP model?* She mused cynically.

Turning her head, she watched the rain falling against the window through half closed eyes. Did whomever she was have an Ezekiel that knew how to say *"No, thank you, I've someone waiting at home for me?"* Grabbing a pillow, Betty Jean placed it over her head and screamed into it's billowy softness. She was tired of lying around worrying about Ezekiel, what might have been, should have been and never would be. Aggravated, Betty Jean hurled the pillow across the room.

She could not go on this way. Sheila was right. She did need to get on with her life. Glancing at the window one last time, Betty Jean climbed from the bed. She needed to do some shopping and didn't feel like waiting out the rain. Besides, the way it had been coming down all morning, it didn't appear to be letting up any time soon. One corner of Betty Jean's mouth lifted in a humorless half smile. It didn't matter. Let it rain. It would fit her mood. The lyrics to Brook Benton's Rainy Night in Georgia came to mind and she hummed them to herself on the way to the bathroom.

**

Betty Jean made a mad dash across the crowded parking lot where she'd spent the better part of five minutes searching for an available space and into the pleasantly aromatic coffee house. She wanted a strong cup of cocoa, a cherry filled donut and a moment's reprieve from the rain that alternated between annoying drizzle and downpour.

It was mid afternoon and, just as she suspected, the morning's showers had not subsided. She was pleased to have completed her errands and was anxious to reward herself. She intended to slide into one of the corner tables at Java Jack's and fall into her poetry book.

She'd hardly had any time to indulge herself since purchasing it. Work was hectic and she'd been putting in extra hours. The free time she'd had was better spent on laundry, grocery shopping, cleaning her house or some other mundane chore. Her new book had been forced to take a back burner to life's more pressing demands, but not today. Today she would sit, read, relax and enjoy being among people. Turning from the counter, she surveyed the room then smiled to herself. There was one corner table left.

She'd just barely sat down, sighing in relief, when a male voice exclaimed, "I thought it was you, but I've seen so many apparitions of you over the last year, I couldn't believe it! But I parked my truck anyway and son-of-a-gun if luck wasn't smiling on me!"

She froze, looking down into her steaming cup of cocoa. Watching the cream melt, she shook her head in disbelief. If there was any truth in mythology, Loki, the God of Mischief was working overtime. Which was fine, Betty Jean thought, she just wished he'd find somebody else to focus his interest upon. Seated before the intruder who stood at her window seat, Betty Jean still managed to look down her nose at him, as she inquired about what he wanted.

The brilliant smile from moments before vanished and the tall man frowned down at her. The two of them simply stared at one another, until Betty Jean began to gather up her things. In confusion, his frown deepened. "Are you leaving, already? You haven't even touched your cocoa." He peered quizzically at her still steaming cup.

"I don't know," Betty Jean huffed. "Are you staying?"

"I intended to when I first saw you come in, but I get the impression that you wouldn't be too thrilled with the pros—"

Betty Jean's white teeth flashed in a feral smile as she cut into his sentence. "I'd forgotten what a really bright guy you are. Quick to catch on." When he remained in her presence, Betty Jean rolled her eyes, adding, "Or maybe not."

Seating himself across from her, he touched her lightly on the arm. "What's wrong, Queen Bee? Why the animosity?"

Betty Jean jerked back, narrowing her eyes. "So, your short term memory is shot to hell, as well as your long term? Is that what you're saying?" she asked referring to their episode at the Chicken Shack, which he'd apparently forgotten all about.

"No, that's not what I'm say—" he broke off. "What's going on here, Betty Jean?" Byron demanded, his confusion rapidly turning to bewildered anger. "I haven't—"

She cut him off again. "So, you *do* know my name." Her eyes widened in imitated surprise.

"What? Why are you—" he began again, then stopped, looking around the small coffee house, almost rising. His voice was lowered to a whisper when he turned back to her. "Is he here? Is that's what's going on?" He hadn't seen anyone else when he spotted Betty Jean running across the parking lot, but maybe he'd been ahead of her in the rain. Then, too, he'd had to find a parking space. The guy could have materialized then and he just hadn't made a connection between him and Betty Jean. *Hadn't he seen some guy out in the parking lot?*

"Is who?" She frowned. Who did he think was there with her? The answer occurred to her and she frowned deeper, sucking her teeth over the absurdity. "Zeke— Oh, what would be the point in telling you his name again. Surely it's not significant enough for you to remember it. What is?" She waved the question away with her hand.

"Look, Betty Jean, I—"

"You what?" She interrupted him again, snatching her arm from beneath his hand, determined not to hear what he had to say. "Oh, I get it. Now I understand why you so suddenly recall having met my acquaintance and can clearly state my name! You even remember calling me, Queen Bee! You want a repeat performance of our first meeting, don't you?" She leaned slightly across the table, smiling seductively. "A little cream? A little sugar maybe?" Skimming her finger across the top of her mug until it was covered in thick, frothy cream, she flicked the white foam across the table where it landed with a soft plop across the front of Byron's tan polo style shirt.

In disbelief, Byron's head snapped down to look at the melting mess on his shirt. He could not register the action and was baffled further still when she squeezed the filling from her donut, squirting him with its cherry sweet goodness. "Knock yourself out! *Cream and sugar*, just like you were hoping for," she said throwing the empty donut shell across the table at him. With grime satisfaction, she saw it stick to his shirt for a second before plopping to the table, then his lap.

Grabbing up her book and car keys, she rose from the booth and exited the building too mad to even care about the stares that followed her. Nosy ass people should mind their own business anyway, she fumed. She hadn't been loud. There wasn't any reason for the whole establishment to turn and watch her walk out the door. If she hadn't given Byron his desired cream and sugar right there at the table, none of the other patrons would have been the wiser. She and Byron would have gone completely undetected.

She marched across the parking lot searching for her car, oblivious to the rain. Why was she so mad, anyway? What had she expected? Undying love from a stranger? Maybe not, but at least something that made sense. Right now nothing did. She had a one night stand with a man who hunted her down and contacted her even after she told him it was the last thing she wanted. Claiming he couldn't get her out of his mind, he extorted a lunch date from her boasting about how he'd not only collect on it, but was looking forward to it. Such devotion. Then a year later he couldn't pick her out of a line up one night, but would run out in the rain to verify he'd seen her a couple of weeks later. Not a lick of sense. Unless she had been correct at Java Jack's and he'd only wanted what she'd given him before. In which case, it was good that she'd given it to him. Turning in circles, she scanned the parked cars wiping her hair from her face. *This*, she thought, was his fault.

She'd been happily indulging herself when he showed up. Then, running from him, she turned herself around and somehow exited the wrong door at the coffee shop. Now she couldn't find her car. On top of everything else, she was soaking wet. A state she'd managed to avoid all morning. And of course, right on cue, the annoying drizzle became a downpour.

Spotting what she hoped was the lamp post she'd parked near, she cut between the vehicles, still mumbling to herself. Nearing the lamp post, she paused. Not only had she discovered her car, but so had Byron. She cursed the luck that made him spot her in the first place, including the night they first met at Rufio's.

Chapter Three

Again, what do you want?" She stopped walking a few feet away from where he casually leaned against the door of her Infiniti.

"I'd say the lunch you promised me, but after the cream and sugar incident, you'll understand if I don't." He tried to jest, but it was received by a straight face.

Rolling her eyes, Betty Jean looked away from him. Curse his eyes for being so good looking. Even covered in the goo she'd thrown at him and drenched from the rain, he was still too handsome by far and she wanted to get away from him before he found a way to make her forgive him. She blamed her reaction to the fact that she hadn't been with a man for about eleven months. That and, though he'd forgotten, their night was still engraved on her memory. Even if, right now, she was loathe to admit it.

"If you'd step away from my car, I'd like to leave now." She tried to sound haughty, but it was hard to pull off with rain water running down her face.

"Sure, but you can't leave." He smiled, politely backing away from the driver's door.

Quickly, she let herself into her vehicle, slamming the door before he could say another word. She'd put the key in, started the ignition and was about to put the car in reverse when Byron tapped on the window. Impatiently, she brushed hair from her face, as she turned to glare out the window at him.

Pointing towards the window he motioned for her to lower it.

Frowning deeply, she shook her head.

Smiling, he nodded his.

Raising what looked suspiciously to be Betty Jean's purse, he walked around to the passenger side of the Infiniti and waited.

Betty Jean lowered the window just enough for him to squeeze her purse through the opening. Bending until his face was centered in the window, his smile broadened and it was his turn to shake his head in the negative.

"Sorry, I can't just hand it over, ma'am. I need to be certain it belongs to you."

Staring at him hard, she considered letting him have the damned thing. Her face reflected her thoughts, causing Byron to raise a dubious brow. "Do you truly have time for the DMV?"

"I can always replace it online." She shrugged carelessly, looking through the window.

"There's bound to be cash and credit cards in here, too." He shook the purse a little, as though he could hear the mentioned items rattling around.

"Money...there's more where that came from. Credit cards can be canceled and replaced." She lifted an eyebrow in anticipation of his next counter.

"Open the door. I'm getting really wet out here." She hesitated and he added, "You won't get this back until you do and I'm going shopping at IKEA with your credit cards if you don't."

With great reluctance displayed in her every move, she raised the window and unlocked the door. Retrieving a towel from the back seat, she wiped the excess water from herself before tossing it across to Byron, who caught it grinning.

"Why IKEA?" she asked, in the driest tone she could manage.

"I need a new table for my office at home." He was still smiling inanely.

He looked so ridiculously pleased to be in her company, she felt herself softening towards him and she thrust her hand out, palm up. "May I have my bag, please?"

"Again, you'll have to appreciate my reluctance and refusal to just fork it over. It's the only leverage I have." He used the damp towel to wipe off the leather bag. "Take me to my truck. It's that Black Suburban over there." He pointed with his chin to the truck parked four rows over from Betty Jean's, on the end.

Betty Jean glared at his high handed manner, but followed his instructions none the less. She just wanted her property returned and him out of her car and out of her life. She could sense the drama lurking within and didn't want to deal with it. One minute he was half in love with her and next he was an Alzheimer patient. Silently, she shook her head. She had enough on her plate, thank you very much for asking, but no thanks.

Lost in thought, she pulled to a stop along side the Suburban. Before she knew what he was about, Byron leapt from the vehicle saying, "Pull into my slot when I back out. Then get in my truck." Her purse was tucked neatly under his arm.

Deciding not to think on the wisdom of her decision too much, Betty Jean again, followed his instructions. "Where are we going?" She asked when they exited the small shopping center. Her purse was still held captive, wedged between Byron's left side and the driver's door.

"I told you. I need a table from IKEA." He glanced across at her, smiled, then turned back to the road.

"You can't be serious?" She was in the presence of a mad man. She dodged a bullet with his memory loss bullshit the other night, but Loony was going to get her anyway. Mentally, she shook her head. Her mama told her about jumping in the car with men she didn't know.

"Of course, I can. I need a table for my office. You need to tell me how I managed to drop in your esteem since the last time we spoke, so—" He continued to look at the road letting the sentence hang in the air. "We're going to kill two birds with one stone."

"I'm not going anywhere with you," she said hearing the lunacy of her own words, as she was in the process of zooming along at his side as she spoke. Feeling herself blush, she added belatedly, "Not looking like a wet cat."

After a quick glance in his rear view mirror, Byron switched lanes in traffic. He went up a few blocks, made a right then entered a really nice subdivision. Betty Jean pressed her lips together in a thin line. Where the hell was he taking her? She'd ask, but she was too afraid she already knew the answer. Looking around at the large houses and sprawling yards, Betty Jean decided not to be impressed. Hadn't he told her he'd been a jack of all trades? It was not surprising that he'd done well for himself.

She read the street signs as they passed them, but he twisted and turned so many times, she'd still need a ton of bread crumbs to find her way out of the maze of houses. As the thought struck her, she narrowed her eyes in suspicion. Maybe that was his plan, to get her so turned around and confused, she wouldn't be able to run away from him if the need came. Definitely a mad man move she thought, narrowing her eyes at the side of his head.

With renewed interest, she stared harder at the signs and surrounding landmarks. Nearly five whole minutes went by before she pointed triumphantly out the window. "Kettle Lane! I knew it! This is the third time we've passed this street! Why are you driving in circles?" Damn if she was going to go quietly.

"Sorry," he said, not sounding as though he meant it at all. "I was enjoying your company and wanted to prolong it. Didn't realize you were reading the street signs."

Betty Jean stared at his profile for a few quiet seconds. What was he playing at? Was he trying to confuse her? One day, it's as though they never met, then the next he's back to behaving like the man she knew in California a year ago. He said he had some questions, which was good because *she* wanted some answers!

Before she could think of what to say first, he pulled into the circular drive of a beautiful two story house. Huge palm trees followed the curve of the drive on both sides, making for a tropical canopy, adding additional elegance to the stately home.

"Come on," he said reaching for the door handle.

"I'm not getting out of this truck."

Her voice held enough firmness to stay his hand on the handle. He turned and they both observed the other in mute contemplation, broken first by Byron. "Why are you doing this, Bee? Why are you acting so strange?"

"*I'm* acting strange, Jekyl and Hyde? Why are you running through the rain kidnapping me and calling me Queen Bee like the name meant something to you, when you looked right through me devoid of recognition before?"

With each word she spoke his look of consternation intensified. "Before? Before what? Before when? What are you talking about?"

Great, first he couldn't remember who she was, now he couldn't remember not remembering! Through clenched teeth, she said, "I'm talking about a couple of weeks ago at the poetry house."

To this he raised a questioning brow, as though she should continue.

Completely vexed by now, she slapped her hands down on her thighs. "Are you trying to tell me you don't recall what happened at the Chicken Shack?"

"It's been a while since I've been there to be perfectly honest with you. No, I can't say in great detail what happened the last time I was there." He opened the door, climbing from the vehicle's cab. "Come on inside." He slammed the door on her look.

He was lying.

She couldn't put her finger on what it was exactly that told her, but she knew he was lying. He had her going at first, but once she mentioned the Chicken Shack by name something changed in his expression. Just like that night at the club. And again, he masked it before she could figure out what it was and her temper rose to confront the issue.

She opened the passenger door, asking, "Why are you playing with me, Byron?"

He dropped his head and walked back to the truck. "I'm not playing with you, but—"

"But what? I don't look stupid enough, yet?" she attacked.

"I'm not trying to make you look stupid, Queen Bee. In fact —"

"Then why did you act like we never met? Were you interested in Sheila and trying to down play what happened between us?" The thought had occurred to her before, but she hadn't liked feeling the jealously that came along with it, so she'd let it go. Now she wasn't so certain she'd been wrong and depraved.

He frowned. "Sheila?"

The question in his voice nearly pushed her over the edge. "I am violent by circumstance, not nature," she warned. "Yes, Sheila! T*he leggy one*, remember?" She threw her hands up in exasperation. "It's the Chicken Shack all over again, I swear!"

"I wasn't at the Chicken Shack, Bee. Not with this Sheila person or anyone else. I haven't been anywhere near that place in a good couple of months. Maybe even closer to about six or seven months."

Her mouth fell open in disbelief. Snapping it closed, she looked him up and down. "Well, someone doing a damned good impersonation of you was there and they just happened to sit at my table and talk to me." His lips twitched at her comment and she secretly dared him to laugh and that circumstance she just warned him about was going to take place.

Grabbing her hand he pulled her from the truck. "I've been out of town for about a month or more, so I can assure you, it wasn't me." He tugged when she resisted. "Come on inside, I'm sure I can prove my innocence and clear this whole thing up."

Entering the house he led her to a comfortable sized den. There was a black baby grand piano sitting on an elevated portion of the floor and before it sat a small bench. There were two overstuffed, soft leather chairs in the room and a man sized sofa. On the walls and in frames on the table and sideboards were hundreds of family photos. The room looked nice and cozy, exuding comfort and warmth. It had a lived in, welcoming feeling with all the smiling faces peering down at her and Betty Jean folded her arms across her chest to ward it off. Damned if she was getting cozy.

"I'll be right back," he said, sprinting out of the room.

She stood in the center of the floor trying not to look around. She didn't want to know anything about this man and it would be hard not to glimpse something of the man with so many personal items in the room. Turning, slowly she took in her surroundings. There was a well worn Little League baseball glove under a glass dome and she smiled in spite of herself. *How cute.* It was cushioned and domed, holding a place of honor as though it had belonged to Willie Mayes or Hank Aaron and not just a little boy. And she knew it belonged to simply a little boy and not some legendary ball player, because *Byron* was engraved in black letters on the base of the dome.

The glove case sat on the end of a long sideboard along with dozens of other personal things. There were books that looked like they'd been read a million times or more that stood between book holders, book holders that were clearly a shop class project and numerous photographs. The first photo to the left of the case was of a woman Betty Jean guessed to be Byron's mother. The two favored greatly and Betty Jean thought he had her eyes.

The photo next to it was of a smiling little girl with long ponytails. Betty Jean could see the resemblance between the girl and Byron and wondered briefly if she was his daughter. She picked up the photo closest to her on the table just as Byron walked back into the room. She glanced down at the picture in her hand without really seeing it, having alternated her attention from the pictures back to Byron. She was replacing it to the sideboard when it registered and she frowned. Automatically, her hand brought the photo back up to her eyes. She looked at it, then back at Byron. A moment later, she repeated the action.

"Why are there three of you in this photo?"

He smiled crossing over to her. "I'm only here." His fingers brushed the boy in the middle of the three-some. "That's Ayron." He pointed to the boy on his right. Indicating the smiling boy to his left, he said, "That's Cyron."

"There's three of you," Betty Jean said again, staring dully at the picture.

"Well, no," Byron insisted. "There's Ayron, Byron and Cyron. Triplets - one fraternal and a set of twins. Cyron being my younger twin." He emphasized the word younger, seeming to enjoy an inside joke. "But there are three of us, as my mother could surely attest, not just me. See there?" He pointed again at Ayron. "His eyes are hazel. Lucky dog. There are slight differences between Cyron and myself, as well, but nothing significant. We're identical. *Almost.*"

"Almost? Why *almost*?" she asked, imitating the way he'd said the word. "You're either identical or not. There's no almost."

"I see. And do you have a twin?"

"No."

"Then, as I was saying, Cyron and I are *almost* identical twins. I have him by nearly an inch," he said smiling and replaced the photo to the side board. "Or at least, I did when we were fourteen. Needless to say, we'll never know now if I still do or not."

He was still smiling over his inch. Betty Jean who was still reeling from the revelation of triplets failed to catch his meaning and suggested, "Couldn't you just stand back to back and be measured?"

"How's that going to help?" Byron asked, suppressing his smile as best he could.

"Then you'd know who's the tallest."

"Tallest?" He shook his head at her error. "Ayron, Cyron and I are the same height and weight. Six four." He closed one eye, thinking. "Two hundred forty pounds...I think."

"You said you had them by nearly an inch when you were fourteen and hadn't measured to see since."

"No. I said I had Cyron by nearly an inch and I did. But Ayron refused to cooperate, so he didn't get measured. He refused to participate in a number of things Cyron and I would think up. He probably did it himself later though. I'm sure he'd have wanted to know. But I wasn't referring to our height, anyway. That's always been the exact same."

"But if you've always been the exact same height, what inch are you tal—" Comprehension dawning, Betty Jean looked at him with big eyes. Her mouth formed an O and her look changed to one of mild curiosity. Her eyes dropped to the crotch of his pants and she raised a considering brow. "I'd never thought of that."

Byron grinned. "A gym locker room filled with fourteen year old boys would."

Chapter Four

Curled up and cozy in the overstuffed chair in Byron's den, Betty Jean laughed again. Byron was regaling her with stories from his youth. It appeared that if a bit of adventure could be thought up, it had come to one of the boy's mind at one point or another. They gave a surreal meaning to the words *been there, done that.*

"So, each of you broke a window on the same day?" she asked, wiping tears from her eyes.

"Yep, another brilliant idea of parenting gone wrong. Mom figured we got into so much trouble together that left to ourselves we'd not be so mischievous. The day before we were under foot all day and kept getting into trouble, so the next morning, *the day of the incident,*" he said sinisterly, "she separated us. We were each to find something to do that did not involve the other two. How she thought three devils running loose individually would be less trouble than the three combined, I may never know. Maybe she was working with the delusion that two of us had a leader and without him, whichever one it was, we'd be okay. But like I said, another brilliant idea of parenting gone wrong. There was no divide and conquer amongst us boys. Even if we didn't act as one, our paths were entwined as she soon found out." He laughed a little and Betty Jean raised her eyebrow in encouragement for him to continue.

"In retrospect, I guess mine was the stupidest, which would explain why it went wrong first. After trying, unsuccessfully I might add, to play a game of catch by myself the usual way. You know, tossing the ball straight up in the air and catching it?" He demonstrated the motion with an invisible ball a few times. "Well, that got boring pretty quick and Mom couldn't stand us bouncing the ball off the side of the house. Besides that, I knew Cyron was round back that way and she wanted us to stay clear of one another, so that was out. Anyway, I got this great idea to play catch for real. You know, throwing it horizontally?" He swung his arm out in a pitch.

"Oh, no." Betty Jean laughed into the sleeve of her borrowed sweat shirt.

"Oh, yes." He smiled.

"That game is a lot easier when there's someone on the other end to catch the ball."

"Yeah, I know now, but we were about nine or ten then. Hell, I was superman! I threw the ball down the length of the back yard, but before I could zip down there to where I imagined I'd be waiting with glove in hand, my parents bedroom window caught the ball instead. But before Mom could get to the scene of my crime, we could hear glass falling again. There was a path that led up the side of the house from the garage to the back patio area. The garage wall that faced the path had two large windows on it. There were these really pretty little window boxes with potted plants on each one that ran the length of the windows. Sort of picturesque. Mom and I skidded around the corner, me from the backyard, her from the house, to see Cyron trying to rise from the debris of potted plant, glass and windowsill.

"He was playing on my dad's motorcycle and tipped it, which was one of the reasons my dad had admonished us repeatedly about messing with the thing. His weight plus the weight of the bike sent it to its side and that wasn't a good spot up against that window frame and all. Well, the guy that repaired it figured there must have already been a hair line crack in one of the windows, or something, for it to just give away the way it did. According to Cyron, it held for a moment, but the more he struggled trying to rise... The bike pretty much had him pinned. Well—" Byron shrugged, lifting his hands.

"Was he hurt?"

"By the fall through the window or my daddy?" Byron grinned, laughing at the memory.

"How did Ayron break his window?"

"Throwing a book at my sister who was agile enough to duck out of the way. My mother and I had barely reached Cyron and was brushing glass off of him when we heard the tingle of glass again. That may have been the first time in my life that I can remember hearing my mother curse. Now I'm not saying she never did before, I can't recall, but that's sure my earliest memory of it. Her running back towards the house, cursing like a sailor!"

"Your poor mother."

"Oh, don't you feel sorry for her. Dad was her champion, make no mistake. We all caught it that night, even Julie and Daddy rarely saw pass her dimples to the tail and pitchfork!"

"Don't tell me your sister was hell on wheels, too? You boys involved her in your mischief?"

"Involved her? Jules was usually the master mind. The ring leader in our little circus. That's her picture over there." He pointed to the fireplace mantel at the cherubic face of a young girl no older than ten. "She's younger than we are, but Jules followed us boys everywhere we went. She didn't care. If we could do it, she could do it." He smiled fondly at the framed photo, adding, "And she usually did it better." His smile grew. "But I'll deny it vehemently to the end!"

Betty Jean noticed that the girl in the photo she'd seen earlier wasn't Julie and asked if the girl was his daughter.

"My cousin, actually. One of the few females in the family. We're a brood of men." There was unmistakable pride in his voice. He shook his head. "I've never been married."

"Since when are fatherhood and matrimony synonymous?"

"With me they couldn't be any other way. My mother would be horrified. I could hear her now, *No wife, but a baby. A baby that's going to grow into a child that has to wonder how come they have two homes.* My dad wouldn't say much, but I would know he was disappointed in me. He preached about that sort of thing once we boys started dating. He'd think I hadn't listened to a thing he'd said my whole life. He'd be hurt and I couldn't live with that. But even aside from my good son routine, it's personal, too. I don't want to miss a second of my child's life. I don't want to come over on Friday surprised that the baby can sit up. I don't want to watch my child grow up in a series of photographs and weekend sleepovers. Photographs are to remember a moment, sort of like holding that time in your hands when you touch them. They can't make you part of a moment just by holding them, though. I want to be part of the moment. I want to know what's behind the smile." He shrugged, not the least bit uncomfortable with his topic.

"Parenthood would be just as binding and sacred as marriage to me. I want to cuddle my wife beneath the sheets while my child sleeps in her arms." His words were painting a very clear image of what he someday wanted and he was watching her intently.

Blinking out of the spell woven by his words, Betty Jean sought to steer the conversation away from babies and marriage. "Why are the majority of your photos so old? I mean some *are* old, like your grandparents pictures, but I mean old like from your childhood. You hardly have any current photos of you and your family." Betty Jean sat up a little to look around the room. There were a lot of pictures around the room, but very few were current or of adults.

"It's like I said, you hold that time when you hold a photograph. I like seeing what we were, where we came from, that sort of thing. I love that picture of Jules, bad as the devil, but so sweet and innocent. She's smiling like that because she just finished doing something she didn't have any business doing and got away with it. No one even suspected her." He held up a hand, chuckling. "Let's just say it involved a roman candle, a white sheet and the neighbor's dog one infamous fourth of July."

"The neighbor's dog?"

He waved her off. "He wasn't hurt." He shrugged his shoulders, looking at her. "I like seeing me and my brothers when we were super heroes. Still carefree and posing as one another on a whim," he said grinning. "That picture over there is of my grandparents, taken at their sixty fifth wedding anniversary. It's sitting next to a picture of them from the day they first married. See how he's still looking at her, after all those years? That's my grandmother over on the sideboard next to my cousin. She was twenty five in that photo." Betty Jean smiled as he spoke, telling her about his family and occasionally stopping to point someone out. It was easy to imagine his stories as the photos reflected the words.

He was right, too.

His grandfather *did* appear unyielding unless he was looking at his wife. Julie definitely had the look of a wolf in sheep's clothing and it was really obvious that his parents were crazy about each other. She was almost embarrassed looking at the photos of the two of them. She felt like she was intruding on a private moment, like she should go back out of the room and close the door behind her. She could see that though they were triplets, it was something behind the eyes and beneath the smile that made them each different and stand out as individuals as they laughed from various frames.

"Did you ever fool your parents?"

"If we kept quiet and didn't speak, Mom couldn't tell or at least she'd act like she couldn't. I never knew if she was sincere in her discovery to find she was talking to the wrong son or not. Dad didn't care who was who as long as everybody did what they were suppose to do, but we couldn't fool him one bit. We'd stand quiet and straight faced, the same as two mirrors, but he'd look at us really hard, turn his head a little to the side, like so. Like he was seeing us from a different angle and sure enough he'd pick us right out. Every time, without fail."

"You sound like you come from a loving family," Betty Jean said sincerely.

"Yeah, it was pretty nice growing up in my family. Family is good." He was lost in melancholy until the dryer buzzer rang out a moment later. "Sounds like your clothes are finished." He rose from his seat, stretching.

Alone in the room, Betty Jean rose stretching from her chair. She circled the room looking at the various faces of Byron's kin. As an only child, she was slightly envious of the multitude he seemed to spring from. She'd lost her parents nearly a decade before when she was barely an adult. Sometimes she wondered if she would have taken so much crap from Ezekiel had she had a mother or sister, a cousin or girlfriend, hell anybody there asking, "*Have you lost your mind, girl?*"

Shaking Ezekiel from her mind, she smiled warmly as Byron came back into the room extending her dried clothing. "Thank you." She was suddenly self conscious. Hugging the warm clothes to her, she fled the room.

Returning a few minutes later, she stood in the doorway with her hands clasped before her. "I guess I'd better go. The sun's out and everything," she stammered unnecessarily, as light was streaming in through the windows behind the baby grand.

"What about IKEA? Aren't you still coming with me or am I taking you to your car?"

"I'd probably better go get my car," she said softly.

Byron turned towards her. "You never told me what Cyron said to you that had you so upset." He came closer. "What must I apologize for?" He stopped walking when her nose was just inches from his chest. *Strange*, but she didn't remember him being so tall. His question had been so softly spoken, Betty Jean imagined she had to strain to hear it. It was the psychological interference that was causing the strain, though, not the softness of his voice.

Looking into his wide chest, her thoughts faltered and collided. What had she been saying? From within her murky mind the answer came that it was not she who'd spoken, but he who waited her answer.

He touched her chin, lifting her face. "Should I say I'm sorry?"

"For what?" She mouth the words, staring into his eyes.

Saying nothing, his head bent and he captured her lips in a kiss. The months between his kisses faded away and Betty Jean melted into his arms as though the lapse hadn't existed.

When he finally pulled back from her, he stared down into her eyes and a slow smile came to his face that stretched into a wide grin. "Well, I won't apologize for that. I had to wait a long time for it. I wanted to know if I needed to apologize, make excuses or beg for my brother's pardon regarding anything he may have said or done while you thought he was me."

Betty Jean blushed thinking how she snapped at Sheila. *I know who I slept with.* Apparently, she didn't. "I wasn't upset about him getting out of line or anything like that. He seemed to be a little less reserved than I recalled you being. A bit smart assy maybe, but other than that your personalities were alike, I guess." She hunched her shoulders in observation. "I thought he was you. I was angry that you didn't remember me when everything about our encounter is still so clear to me. When you said you couldn't forget me, the last time we spoke."

He laughed a little, pleased she remembered their last conversation and she poked him in the ribs. He grabbed her finger, laughing. "I'm ticklish and vengeful once roused, so stop." His voice changed and he said, "I can't believe you thought I'd forgotten you. Woman, I could pick you out from fifty yards away running through the pouring rain," he bragged.

**

It was nearly eleven in the evening when Betty Jean unlocked the front door, letting herself into the house. Sheila was circling into the living room from the kitchen with a bowl of popcorn. She placed the bowl in the center of the coffee table and picked up her rented movie. Crossing over to the DVD player she dropped the disc into place, saying over her shoulder, "Do you see what you've done? I was so overcome with worry I canceled my plans tonight to be here in case you needed me." She turned with her hands on her hips, frowning. "Not even a phone call."

She stood staring at Betty Jean and a smile pulled at her lips. "Well, well, well," she said as Betty Jean crossed the living room. "I'd say look what the cat drug in, but you look more the cat in the cream than what he carried in."

Betty Jean had already cut through the living room and was down the hall towards her bedroom. Without turning, she raised her voice to be heard. "Most likely you stayed home tonight so you could get the story in full detail while it was still hot off the press. Overcome with worry my foot." She turned into her room saying louder, "What movie did you get? Not another Denzel flick, hun?"

Sheila retrieved her popcorn. Walking to the edge of the hallway Betty Jean had disappeared down, she leaned against the doorjamb. "There's nothing wrong with Denzel," she said munching.

Betty Jean poked her head into the hall. "We've been through this before. It's not that something's wrong with DW. I enjoy watching his fine ass just like anybody else, but how many times do we have to watch Mo Better Blues, Training Day, Fallen or any one of his other flicks?" Her head disappeared back into her bedroom and she emerged moments later in an old tee shirt, a pair of boxer shorts and socks.

Passing Sheila, she took a handful of popcorn and removed the bowl from Sheila's arms at the same time. Carrying it to the couch, she placed it on the center cushion and settled herself on the floor.

Sheila stepped across the arm of the couch, folding her legs beneath her. Filling her hands with a generous amount of popcorn, she used her tongue to spear kernels and maneuver them into her mouth. They chewed in silence for a while. Betty Jean was lost in the day's reflections with a slight smile on her lips. She reached for more popcorn, oblivious to Sheila's glare.

Sheila snatched the bowl away, pulling Betty Jean's attention to her. "Get out of my damn popcorn! Whomever he was should have bought your ass dinner!" She placed the bowl in her lap, picking at the few bits left in the bowl. She raised her eyes to Betty Jean's still patiently smiling face and rolled them. *Cow*, Sheila thought with affection. Betty Jean knew she was about to pop with nosiness.

Betty Jean leaned her face into the bowl. Disappointed, she sighed. Snatching it up, she walked back into the kitchen to pop another bag. Four minutes later she walked back into the living room with a fresh bowl of buttered popcorn and two cokes. Sitting across from Sheila on the couch she placed the bowl between them. She twisted off the top of one of the bottles, smiled when she read *you are a winner* and handed the drink to Sheila. "As a matter of fact, he did buy me dinner and we put a table together afterwards. And I must tell you, I think I'd rather pay for the shipping and handling of an assembled item than deal with IKEA. *Easily assembled*. Ha!" She dug her hand into the bowl, grinning over Sheila's stunned silence. "I said all that to say, I'm not hungry. *My ass* was fed. I just wanted some damn popcorn."

Sheila pressed play, starting the movie. Betty Jean closed her eyes, shaking her head. She was correct. It was another Denzel Washington film. One they'd seen at least four times in the last couple of months. Twenty minutes into the show, she put her hands up in surrender. "I give up, officer. I'll come out quietly. I'll tell you what you want, if you just please stop the movie. I know everybody's lines, officer. I can do a one woman stage play of the movie, officer. Please make it stop."

"What?" Sheila asked, pausing the movie.

Laughing, Betty Jean bargained, "I'll tell you everything that happened today if it'll keep me from sitting through this movie. *Again*."

Sheila smiled and stopped the DVD. Turning, she gave Betty Jean her undivided attention.

Chapter Five

.

It was nearly three in the morning and sleep eluded her still. She'd been lying in the darkness gazing up at the ceiling since one thirty. The house was quiet all around her and she couldn't remember ever feeling so alone.

Her day had been filled with revelations. Running into Byron, discovering he wasn't just a twin, but a triplet, as well, then finding out about him as a person, about his family. They'd had a thoroughly enjoyable day together, but it still ended as all her days since her arrival in California ended - with her alone.

She was tired of staring up at the ceiling each night with no purpose in the action other than to be staring up at it. There had been no other reasons to be on her back. She hadn't been held or touched since Ezekiel and that last time had hardly counted there on her living room floor amongst the boxing tape.

Byron's kiss had been so sweet, she closed her eyes briefly in reflection. He'd found cause to press his lips against her a number of times during the day. His lips brushed her shoulder, her temple, her hands and her cheek. Once even the tip of her ear lobe she smiled recalling, but he hadn't kissed her again. Not like he had when he was discussing marriage and babies. Thinking of marriage and babies soon turned Betty Jean's mind to Ezekiel again and she sighed. They'd discussed getting married and having a family, too.

Except when Ezekiel spoke of the same things Byron had, he was not abstract in his thinking.

When Ezekiel Johnson spoke of love and the future, he was speaking to her, about her, not someone who was still a distant enigma even to himself. Byron's musing touched her, but only because he was saying all the right things. All the things she wanted. He wanted them, too, but he'd been speaking in generalizations. He didn't know her like Ezekiel did. He didn't love her like Ezekiel did. She'd seen and heard what she wanted to hear. She'd let herself get caught up in the moment and believe that he alluded to her. But she was back to her senses now and knew he hadn't been implying or suggesting anything. He'd only been talking about what he hoped to find someday in the future with somebody. Not her specifically. Not like Ezekiel.

Curling on her side, Betty Jean hugged her pillow close. She was not going to cry, she told herself firmly. A tear slid down her cheek a bare moment later. Instead of wiping it away she turned her face into the pillow and let her heartache flow at will. Why couldn't she stop thinking about Ezekiel? If time healed all wounds, exactly how much time was going to have to go by before she could get her life back? How long would she hurt and ache behind this man? She shook her head from side to side in the pillow, completely aware that she was the very picture of wallowing in misery and didn't care.

She'd bet Sheila hit it right on the nose when she said Ezekiel had moved on without her. He most likely hadn't bothered to look back, either. She'd left and he picked up and moved on. Gone and goodbye. If she called him right now he'd probably have to pull out of somebody just to answer the phone. Almost immediately she asked forgiveness for her ugly thoughts. She was feeling mean spirited and nasty towards him because of his ability to proceed with his life when she was stuck in some sort of vacuum that sucked at her strength and will every day. Spewing venom wasn't going to make her feel any better, she chided herself, but hid an insolent smirk that beg the contrary in her pillow beneath her wet cheek.

A blue flash appeared in Betty Jean's peripheral vision and she turned her head sharply to investigate its origin. She and Sheila had two separate phone lines. Sheila's line only rang in her bedroom, but Betty Jean's extension was the main line and serviced the entire house. Betty Jean customarily turned the ringer off on the phone in her bedroom, but the call indicator light flashed blue when the phone rang, as it was doing now.

The light on the phone flashed once more before Betty Jean reached to answer it. Wiping her face to rid the dampness from her cheeks, she answered softly. "Hello."

"Hey, I'm sorry for calling you so late." The male voice was just as soft and low as hers had been.

"No, it's okay." She rolled to her back, taking the pillow with her to hold between her upturned knees. Her legs were freshly shaved and the soft cotton of the pillowcase felt smooth and cool against her skin. "Is everything, okay?" She tried to inject a sleepy quality to her voice so he wouldn't know she'd been wide awake.

"Basically, yeah. I guess."

"Doesn't sound like you're too convinced of that," she said giving up her pretense of half sleep. There really wasn't any point in it anyway, seeing as how he obviously hadn't had any luck counting sheep, either. By all rights, he should be sound asleep, but he was wide awake and placing phone calls, no less. Who was he to judge?

"I just wanted to call and let you know how much I enjoyed your company today. It was really nice. See-ing you again and getting to spend some time with you. It's something I've been thinking about for a while,

you know? It was nice to finally get to do it today."
Blushing into the phone for a moment, Betty Jean
didn't know what to say. He spoke again, saving her.
"Why weren't you asleep?"

"How do you know I wasn't?" she teased into the
phone feeling like a school girl suddenly.

His voice was deep and warm in her ear. "Because
I've woke up beside you before. I know what your voice
sounds like fresh from sleep. I knew you were fake at
hello."

She laughed, knowing he did a parody of a Jerry
McQuire scene. "Was I that bad?"

"Maybe not to the untrained ear, but I know fake
sleep when I hear it." He wanted to tell her how her
voice went through his mind every morning that he
woke up since meeting her, but was wary of scaring
her off. He wanted to keep things light and casual until they were both ready. Maybe he heard her voice in
his ear every morning, because it was rare for him to
go to sleep without thinking about their night together.
It made sense that if he went to bed with her on his
mind, he'd wake up in the same condition. *With her on
his mind.* Instead he laughed and tried to sound like a
sage on the subject. "It's what women do to discourage
booty calls. You answer the phone all *hello* and try to
sound breathlessly semiconscious. Dead give away of
being awake. Sure sign of an amateur. Broken sleep
does not get answered on a sexy *you just woke me.*
Broken sleep gets answered like *somebody better be
dead or dying.*"

"That's terrible!" she said covering her mouth on a
laugh. "You can't answer the phone like that! What if
someone really is dead or dying?"

"Most times somebody better be at three in the
morning or you're going to get the curse out. Unless of
course it's a booty call."

"And is someone dead or dying tonight?"

"Yes."

"Who?" She was surprised by his answer. She'd anticipated a negative response or for him to say something like, *only me without you*. Something corny to make her laugh, not affirm the question.

"Thankfully, no one I know personally, but someone, somewhere. People die every second of every day. Do you know how many people have departed since our conversation started? Quite a few. But to report a tragedy was not the reason for my call tonight."

"So, is this a booty call?" She was smiling confidently and enjoying her flirtation, because she knew it wasn't. He just wanted to talk to her. Besides, booty calls didn't waste time talking. Did they?

"Not tonight, pretty lady. I just wanted to call and make goo-goo eyes at you."

"How are you going to make goo-goo eyes at me over the phone?" The expression made her smile.

"I'm not certain. I've never really figured out how to do it, but it can be done. Every time one of us was on the phone and something needed to be done that's what my mom would say. She'd say, *Stop making goo-goo eyes at that little fast tail girl and come help me*." He mimicked a woman's high pitched tone and Betty Jean's hand flew to her mouth as laughter erupted. Him using that voice was the mental picture of a bull in a china shop. It just shouldn't happen. He waited for her to stop laughing then said softly into the phone, "I miss you, Bee."

Breathless, she said nothing, but the pressure she was applying to keep the pillow in place between her knees went lax and it fell across her chest, lightly smacking her in the face.

"I just left." There was no lingering laughter in her voice.

"I've been missing you for two hundred ninety seven days. When I last left you I wanted to turn around and beg you to give me a chance. I settled for going back later and leaving my card with the front desk clerk.

But I started missing you when you held the door open for me to leave. It was a really long walk to the elevator that morning."

"I don't know what to say," she confessed her thought aloud.

"Good. You don't have to say anything, then. I know you had some unfinished business when we met, but since you're here alone I assume it's finished now. I don't want to rush you into anything or ask for too much, too fast. I just want a chance that's all and with you here now, *alone*, maybe you'll see fit to give me one."

Again, Betty Jean was reminded of courting as a schoolgirl, sneaking on the phone late at night to whisper sweet nothings to some knuckle head or another and she closed her eyes, smiling. "So, *this* is how you make goo-goo eyes over the phone?" she asked and he laughed.

**

"You look like hell," Sheila said coming into the kitchen the next morning. She had on yellow shoes, a yellow hat, yellow gloves and a bright sunny yellow dress. She was a fresh burst of light in the kitchen.

"Well, aren't we a little ray of sunshine this morning." Betty Jean sprinkled cinnamon in with the eggs and milk already in the bowl. She set the cinnamon on the counter before reconsidering and sprinkling in a dab more. She woke up feeling good, a bit tired around the edges, but good nonetheless and she felt like making French toast. Maybe it was the schoolgirl feeling she'd gone to sleep with. Belle used to make her French toast in the mornings.

"I woke up *too* crabby. I have to go to church today. I am feeling really raggedy and churlish. Maybe some of the spirit can refresh my own, you know?"

"Yes, girl, I do," Betty Jean replied secretly thinking she was going back to bed like the heathen she was. She liked to think she gave her Father His due, but it wasn't in her today. She would worship on her own and read a little of the Good Book, but she wasn't up to visiting His house. He was more than welcome to visit hers, she smiled privately.

Pulling off her gloves, Sheila snagged a slice of the turkey bacon Betty Jean had on a plate. Chewing the bacon, she sat down at the kitchen table and Betty Jean placed a glass of orange juice before her.

Eyeing Sheila's hat, Betty Jean curled in her lips to keep from smiling. It still managed to slip out and she couldn't stop herself from asking, "Why on earth do you have on that hat? And more importantly why do you even own such a thing? Can you see from under that brim?" Betty Jean asked bending down a little to look at Sheila's face.

Removing the pins that held the hat in place, Sheila frowned at Betty Jean snapping, "*I told you I'm crabby.* I thought a pretty hat would make me feel better." She fingered the hat's design unaware that her bottom lip was sticking out. "That's why I'm heading to church. My nana used to tell me that if you had something too heavy to be cured by a pretty hat, you best take it to the Lord 'cause wasn't nobody else going to be able to help."

"Wise woman."

"In fact, my nana gave me this hat last year when I went to visit," Sheila said absently.

It figured as much, Betty Jean thought amused. The big floppy hat smacked of someone's grandma. She turned back to the French toast. "You want some of these?"

"Two or three, please."

Only after Betty Jean took her seat at the kitchen table and they both had steaming plates of food in front of them did Sheila speak again. "This is my last Sunday morning here and I must admit to being a little sad about it. This could be the root of my crabbiness. I think I'm pouting."

"*Oh.*" Betty Jean reached across the table, squeezing Sheila's hand.

"I know we'll still see one another, but I got accustomed to having someone to talk to and I liked having company without having to entertain anyone or leave the house. I've always lived alone so these warm fuzzy feelings about companionship are new to me," she said reaching for syrup. Shrewdly, Sheila observed her friend before adding, "I don't know if I'm going to lose any sleep over it though."

When Betty Jean merely raised an eyebrow confused by the statement, Sheila said, "Doesn't look like you got too much sleep last night. Were you up thinking about my final weekend, too? You got this raccoon thing going on this morning." She did two quick circles in the air, indicating Betty Jean's eyes.

"Well, thanks," Betty Jean said dryly. As a fact, she hadn't had much sleep. Maybe an hour or so, nothing more. She was still chatting on the phone with Byron when the sun came up. They'd talked, laughed and giggled away the last few hours of the night.

"Did you sneak back out last night?" Sheila asked in a scandalized whisper.

Sucking syrup and butter from her finger, Betty Jean shook her head wide eyed.

Sheila narrowed her eyes in scrutiny, but Betty Jean only smiled. "I know I missed something," she said pointing at Betty Jean with her fork. A few drops of syrup fell to the plate before Sheila lowered the fork to eat again. "But it's okay. Keep your little funky secrets."

Betty Jean laughed. "Why do my secrets have to be funky?"
**

As it turned out, Betty Jean went to church that morning after all.

"Well, if this wasn't worth the fried chicken dinner after the service," a familiar voice drawled from behind the two women. Warmth bloomed in Betty Jean's chest and she turned smiling. The eyes that met hers were wide in feigned surprise. "I didn't know mean hell cats went to church."

Betty Jean's smile faded and she frowned peering closely over her shoulder at the man in all black seated in the pew directly behind her. Sheila turned to scowl at the man bothering them. Her mother was a firm believer in the church being a good place to find a potential mate, but for herself, she really couldn't stand men who tried to pick up women in the church house. Especially, those that couldn't even wait for the service to end.

The man in black smiled dangerously. Arching a brow, he said, "*The Leggy One,*" in a tone too sensuous for the Lord's house. Sheila smiled in recognition no longer intent on dressing him down. Betty Jean's face blazed in embarrassment. "What?" He noticed the change in her expression. "Wasn't who you thought I was?" He was smiling at Sheila, but Betty Jean was pretty sure his comment was directed at her and her embarrassment blazed higher. He gave them both a knowing smile. "We'll speak after the service, ladies."

He nodded his head towards the elderly woman who sat to his left in the pew, who had been giving him the evil eye since he first opened his mouth. Retrieving his Bible, he slid back in the pew, raised his hand and said, "Praise! Praise!" on cue with the rest of the congregation.

Chapter Six

Moving up a step in line he bent slightly saying in a low voice, "For a moment, you were pleased to see me. Admit it."

Betty Jean rolled her eyes then looked across to Sheila who only smiled, suddenly becoming very interested in the morning's program. So, she was to brave the lion's den alone, was she? Betty Jean's eyes narrowed on Sheila's bowed head. So be it. "I admit to being pleased, but it had nothing to do with you." She hunched her shoulders in a dismissive shrug. "For a moment, you looked like someone I knew. Must have been the lighting."

"Lightning, you say? Quite right. I expect it to strike you at any moment."

Sheila suppressed a giggle behind a cough and a mumbled comment about the slowness of the servers, but Betty Jean shot her a glare anyway. "Don't encourage him," she instructed.

"Don't listen to her." He stepped between the two until they were a quaint threesome. He brought Sheila's hand to his lips and kissed it. "Please," he smiled into her amused eyes, "encourage me." He wiggled his eyebrows and Sheila, giving up all pretense of being on Betty Jean's side, laughed out loud.

Great, Betty Jean groaned inwardly. She could see this person, this imitation Byron, was going to be a thorn in her side. They hadn't even been properly introduced yet and already he was nettling her. Obviously, he'd figured out what the misunderstanding had been at the Chicken Shack and planned to enjoy himself about it. Asshole. She rolled her eyes. The statistics were right. There *is* one in every crowd.

Just yesterday she was wondering what she would say to him in apology for her rudeness, but he could forget it. She wasn't explaining anything to him and the last thing she'd do was apologize to some egotistical jackass, she huffed. Nearly as out of breath as if she'd said the words aloud.

She was going to have to apologize to Byron when she spoke to him again. He was nothing like his brother. Twin or not. Their similarities only extended externally. And it was plain that conceit over the external had rotted the internal in this one. Oh, no, they were nothing alike.

Sheila laughed again trying to extricate her hand from his much larger grasp. "Are you going to let me have that back?" She smiled beautifully, indicating her hand.

"Oh, you're going to have to do better in the way of persuasion than a beautiful smile, Missy." His look was so hot, Sheila unconsciously fanned herself with her program.

Betty Jean shook her head, not bothering to hide her look of disgust. How'd the Devil get into the church? She cut her eyes sideways at Byron's twin, who fit the part of Satan in her mind and was already perfectly attired for the role.

Sheila lifted a brow. "You keep it up and I'm going to think you're flirting with me."

"You keep resisting and I'm going to think I'm doing it wrong. Cutie In Blue has already done a number on my self confidence with her open hostility and un-warranted dislike, as though her mishap was my fault."

Betty Jean's head snapped up at his barb only to discover he'd turned his back to her, making her a third wheel on his and Sheila's twosome.

"Cutie In Blue was the one you were after that night, not the Leggy One, remember?" Sheila pulled her hand away from his as they moved up in line. "Here or taking it to go?" She looked around his back to Betty Jean. There were picnic tables set up under the trees for the congregation to enjoy the chicken and potato salad dinner the church was serving to raise money.

In answer Betty Jean glared at the broad back that blocked her view and Sheila told the church's organ player who was acting as server to box her food. With dinners in hand the trio crossed over to the church secretary, who was playing cashier for the five dollar a plate event.

He gave the matronly woman a folded bill. "This is for all three plates, Miss Ella. Keep the change as a donation."

When they stepped outside, Sheila looked up at the handsome man. "I'm not accustomed to men I don't know buying my dinner."

"Especially when our money would have been a contribution to the new building, *if* we had been allowed to pay for it our selves," Betty Jean cut into her flirt. But there was no logic behind her remark.

"You could have still given your money for the cause." He hunched his shoulders. "You didn't see her fighting to give my donation back, did you? You ever hear a church say, no, no, we have more than we need, hun? You could have still given. You're the one who chose to keep your purse closed, just because you weren't buying a dinner."

Thinking of the half of Ben Franklin's face she'd glimpsed in Ms. Ella's hand before it was placed in her little box, Betty Jean's own face reddened, because he was right. She could have still paid her contribution. She was so intent on him irritating her, she'd forgotten to even open her purse just like he said. Betty Jean walked off towards her car without replying.

He watched her walk away, then turned to Sheila. His generous lips stretched into a smile. "Cyron de Monbleau."

"Sheila Cooper." Once again, he placed his lips to the back of her hand and Sheila smiled. "I'm beginning to think you like doing that."

"*I'm* thinking you're beginning to think you like it, too." He grinned hugely at the tongue twister. They stood staring at one another. Finally, Cyron asked, "Is this where we exchange phone numbers?"

"Who said I'd give you my number?" Sheila resumed walking, following the direction Betty Jean had taken. "You wanted the Cutie in Blue," she reminded him from over her shoulder.

"I've been advised that I should have went for the Leggy One instead." His voice came from just behind her and Sheila suppressed a smile.

"You left me for the lesbian, remember?" She kept walking.

When she reached the car she placed her food on the back floorboard, then slammed the door. She was reaching for the door handle to let herself into Betty Jean's car when he spoke again.

"I really would like to see you again, Ms. Cooper." He spoke formally without the usual bantering style she was beginning to expect. Sheila looked up to see him standing midway between where she'd left him and where she stood.

She walked half way back to him, folding her arms across her chest as she went. "I don't really do well as a second choice."

"That's understandable." He closed the distance between them. "I'm not asking you to be second to anybody. She," he jerked his head towards where Betty Jean sat in the car waiting, "did catch my attention at the Chicken Shack. I won't even lie about that, but like I said that night," he hunched one shoulder, "I simply saw her first. I saw her walk in and merely kept an eye out for her. Truthfully, I didn't see you until I was already heading that way." The look he gave Sheila would have made a less experienced woman blush. Sheila only looked insulted. Cyron smiled. "Don't know how in the he-, heck, I could have missed you, but—" He shrugged, trailing off. "I knew I made a mistake, though, as soon as I sat down at the table. I saw you and thought, wrong side of the booth, buddy, but it was too late then. Anyway, I can sense I'd be walking in my brother's footsteps and I've no desire to do that."

"Your brother?" Sheila asked innocently. "We haven't been in town for too long. Less than a year. We don't know a whole lot of people. What makes you think you're walking in your brother's wake?"

"It's a long story," he said in dismissal. "Right now it'll suffice to say I've been mistaken for them before and have beard the brunt. I know the signs. A de Monbleau has crossed her path, but it wasn't me."

Sheila's eyes narrowed a bit and she shook her head slowly. "Still don't know about this. Say something that will make me want to give you my number."

He looked at her for a moment then smiled. "Give it to me because you know you want to." He spoken in flawless French and a slow smile crept across Sheila's face.

Okay, she was intrigued, if not impressed. She was lying. She was very impressed. "Should I slap your face?" Sheila asked flirting.

"Should I teach you the language of love, instead?" He meant the question in various ways and ninety percent of them were showing in his eyes.

Sheila reached into her purse retrieving a pen. She grabbed his hand writing her number in bold black strokes across his palm. "It remains to be seen who'll teach whom what." She turned to leave. She didn't know any other languages, but she could have his big, sexy ass speaking in Tongues. She meant that in as many different ways as he'd meant his question. "You better do something with that before you sweat it all away," she called over her shoulder walking back to the car.

Cyron pulled his eyes from the retreating figure in yellow to his hand, which, sure enough, was already beaded with moisture. What could be expected when one dared to touch the sun? He smiled, pulling his cell phone from his pocket. He wanted to enter her number before he lost it.

**

"Say it before you burst open."

Needing no further encouragement, Betty Jean asked in a wail, "Why! What could you possibly see in him?"

"Six feet four inches of gorgeous? You can't be serious." Sheila's mouth fell open in shock. "*What do I see in him*? Hell, what do *you* see in him?"

"Nothing! Nothing redeemable, at least. I don't even know what you find attractive about that man."

"You're kidding right? What did you see in Byron? And I know damn well you found him attractive so don't even bother denying it. A blind nun would find him attractive."

"Byron? *Please*. What does Byron have to do with this? He is nothing like *him*. Nothing," she added emphatically. "The resemblance stops at the physical and even that is just barely." She stared straight ahead at the road. "I don't even think they look that much alike." Sheila ignored the blatant lie. "Maybe they're fraternal."

"Have you seen Cyron since the Chicken Shack?"

"No," Betty Jean responded automatically. "Thank God."

"Then why are you so hostile towards him? Did Byron tell you some evil twin story that you failed to pass on to me? Is it going to be like on the soap operas when one twin is completely normal and the other is Psycho Bob in disguise?"

Betty Jean's no was given somewhat reluctantly. "Well, except for your last question. You can never know for certain and I don't know how well disguised Bob is right now." She stopped for a red light, frowning deeply. They sat through the light in silence. When the signal was once again green, Betty Jean removed her foot from the brake sighing. "I don't know why he gets under my skin the way he does, but girl—" She cut her eyes at Sheila and laughed. "My hand is itching to smack him one. He's so smug. You ever just meet someone and instantly you want to strike them?"

"Well, I'm glad you refrained."

Betty Jean made a rude noise. "Just barely."

"Just barely is good. So, is it a good healthy clash of personalities that just happens sometimes, a genuine bone deep hate or a passionate dislike and you really want to jump his bones?" Sheila asked seriously.

Not wanting to dismiss any of the possibilities out of hand, Betty Jean drove in quiet contemplation for a few minutes weighing her options. "Sadly, I think it's mostly the first one."

Sheila laughed. "Sadly, hun?" Betty Jean did sound pretty mournful about the outcome.

"Yeah." Betty Jean sighed. "Had it been one of the other two you might have reconsidered."

"I don't know, girl," Sheila warned playfully. "He was speaking French to me."

"So. What's that mean?"

"It means as fine as he is, *you* may as well be speaking French, too, telling me to leave him alone. I can't figure out what either one of you are saying to me. At least with him I'm a little intrigued and more than a little willing to find out."

Betty Jean laughed. "You didn't ask him to translate did you? That'll open up a new can of worms."

"I offered to slap his face if he was being fresh."

Again, Betty Jean laughed. "Good. Anything that looks like that should be slapped every once in a while on GP alone."

"GP?"

"General purpose, girl." Betty Jean pulled into the driveway of her home. "General purpose."

Sheila grinned. "Actually, you know someone who looks just like that, too. Maybe you should try slapping his face on GP."

"Who?" Betty Jean was big eyed with interest.

"Byron, silly." Sheila's hand was on the door handle.

"You wish," Betty Jean said climbing from the car. "Byron looks way better than that black suited devil you were talking to! He's obviously the cute one."

**

"Sheila!" Betty Jean called from the kitchen. "Your phone is ringing!"

Reaching for a towel, Sheila stepped from the hot tub on the deck, where she and Betty Jean had been enjoying a soak. Wrapping the towel around herself sarong style, she stepped into her water sandals before entering the house where she all but ran to her room to snatch up the ringing phone.

When she came back into the living room, Betty Jean handed her a frozen Margarita across the bar. She took it sipping, shaking her head into the phone. "Actually, we seasoned some meat and were about to put it on the grill."

She listened further. "Hold on, let me check." Pressing the mute button, she looked into Betty Jean's curious face. "Do you feel like having company over?"

"Of the irritating kind?" Betty Jean asked before she thought to stop herself. In reflex, she hunched her shoulders. "I don't care, but I'm not sharing my steak."

Sheila smiled and returned the phone to her ear. Crossing the dining room, she headed back towards the hot tub. Just as she was about to step outside her voice tingled with laughter and Betty Jean rolled her eyes to the sky light in her kitchen.

"Tell him to bring some ice," she said loud enough to be heard. "Lord knows I'm going to need a few more drinks by the end of the night." She added the last part just a bit more under her breath.

**

An hour later there was a knock at the door and Sheila moved seductively through the house from the patio to answer it. Betty Jean smiled to herself, tickled by Sheila's behavior. You'd think the walls were made of glass and he was already looking at her, Betty Jean quipped amused.

"Hello," Sheila's voice rang out cheerfully as she addressed the man who stood on Betty Jean's front porch cradling two grocery bags in his arms.

He smiled back, just as cheery as she. "Hi!"

Neither of them moved and Betty Jean sucked her teeth. "Stop gawking at one another and come inside!" she called out from the kitchen counter where she was cutting onions to put on the grill.

"Queen Bee? Is that you in there hollering at people?" he asked, stepping inside the house.

Queen Bee? Betty Jean's head snapped up to observe their visitor.

Sheila noticing Betty Jean's slight elevation in status from Cutie in Blue, as well, raised her brows in surprise.

"I'm sorry to gate crash, but I invited myself." He walked over explaining when a confused Betty Jean entered the living room. "Is gawking the same as goo-goo eyes?" Byron asked. Relaxing, Betty Jean laughed, happy to see him.

Still in the dark about what was occurring, Sheila made to close the front door and was stopped by a muffled expletive. She jerked the door open again and came face to frowning face with the same face that was smiling in Betty Jean. She stared from the man in the doorway to his identical image in the living room and back again. No wonder Betty Jean had been so pissed at the Chicken Shack. They did look exactly alike. Given the same circumstances, she would have thought she'd been forgotten by the man, too.

No wonder she was always so irritated with Cyron, Sheila thought further appreciating the situation. It was rather disconcerting now that she'd experienced it for herself. Maybe they should wear name tags or something.

"May I come in?" Cyron asked with a touch of sarcasm when Sheila stood in the doorway continuing to stare at him.

"I just let you in, didn't I? Aren't you over there in the living room?" Sheila's own tone was just as sarcastic, but she still didn't move aside to allow him entrance. The two men looked exactly alike. She tried to pull her eyes away and stop staring, but she continued to search his handsome face for clues to the miracle of his birth.

Sighing, Cyron finally brushed past her and into the house. "An egg split," he explained as he passed, his tone arcane.

Frowning at his back, she closed the door and followed him in to join the others.

Chapter Seven

"Are you upset by my sudden and uninvited appearance?"

Betty Jean shook her head sipping at her drink. Byron was manning the grill and she was keeping him company. Sheila and Cyron had disappeared to their own little corner of the back deck, so both couples were afforded a semblance of privacy.

"I'm pleasantly surprised."

"Good." He smiled. Her hair was swept up into a ponytail and he longed to kiss her neck, but they'd moved so fast the first time he was willing to wait and show patience now. Things would move along at a more leisurely pace, at least until she demonstrated she wanted otherwise.

"Don't let my burgers burn, man!" Cyron called from across the deck, breaking the spell.

"Let me do this, baby boy!" Byron called back.

"Baby boy?" Sheila whispered to Cyron smiling. It was hard to imagine the big, strapping man in front of her as a baby anything. She supposed he wasn't always so large, but all she had to go by was what was in front of her and that was a lot.

"I was the last one out."

She wrinkled her nose, striking Cyron lightly on the arm. "That's gross. Don't give me mental images I can't get rid of," she admonished.

"Well, I was," he said rubbing the spot she'd hit. "Byron had his foot in my back, I'm told." He raised his voice to be heard over at the barbecue pit.

"There was none of that going on, son. Like dad said, you probably heard someone say line up for work and moved to the end to the line."

"You're terrible," Betty Jean said laughing.

"Are we telling war stories?" Cyron asked with an unmistakable gleam in his eye. They'd been referring to their childhood memories as war stories ever since they were grown. It was the general stuff of family. Braces, eyeglasses, no date on a Friday night, a favored nickname used for ridicule, the age you stopped wetting the bed. The things of youth you just want to forget about, but the people you grew up with refuse to let you. Childhood anecdotes always seem funnier when they're told about a sibling and they never fail to be some embarrassing story that had been buried for a reason. One past humiliation revealed always led to the exposure of someone else in retaliation, until a full fledged war would break out resulting in everyone's dirty laundry being aired.

"Actually, we're pulling the steaks and hamburgers off the grill," Byron said in an effort to change the subject. Their father had a few colorful opinions concerning him, as well and the last thing he wanted was to get Cyron started in on them. No one could be more vicious when telling war stories. He remembered everything they did as children like he had been taking notes. The only person worse than Cyron was Julie.

Cyron uncurled his long limbs, rising from where he and Sheila were seated in the lounge chairs. Pulling Sheila to her feet, he held her hand in his as they crossed the deck to enter the kitchen.

Byron smiled at Betty Jean as he piled the meat on a plate she held.

Inside, Cyron smiled also and Sheila raised a questioning brow at his humor. Lifting the salad bowl from her hands, he began to briskly toss the bowl's contents. "By's outside smiling to himself thinking he's saved because I came inside."

"Saved from what?"

"Me telling some of his stories. I'm not the only one dad had something humorous to say about. There was three of us boys and he dished it out in thirds, believe me. Everybody had an equal portion." His eyes were glowing from warm memories and two Heinekens when they fastened on her.

"You keep it up," Sheila wet her lips, repeating her words from earlier when they'd spoke at the church, "and I'm going to think you're flirting with me." Her eyes were focused on his lips, but when they claimed hers in a tender kiss she was still taken by surprise.

He placed the bowl on the counter with his left hand and pulled her closer placing his right hand in the small of her back.

His kiss began softly as he slowly placed his lips upon hers. His mouth was open slightly and he both licked and sucked at Sheila's mouth simultaneously. Gently, he pulled at her bottom lip. Sheila closed her eyes sighing into his mouth. This man knew how to kiss. He knew the secret behind a gentle stroke and she wondered what it would feel like lying naked beneath his touch.

He gave just enough in his kiss to make her want more. He was controlled in his technique and she longed to shake him up a little. His soft kiss made her knees a bit weak, but she would not be mastered so effortlessly. Opening her mouth beneath his, she placed a hand to the nape of his neck and deepened his kiss.

It was still soft, but the strokes deepened and were sustained longer. Cyron's kiss had become their kiss with Sheila joining him at the helm.

Finally, pulling away from her, Cyron stood with his eyes closed for a moment, breathing through his open mouth. His hands were at her sides anchoring her hips and he squeezed a little, enjoying the feel of her. "That was nice," he said, at last.

"Mmm." Again, wondering what being touched by him while naked would feel like. She looked into his eyes and knew it was inevitable. She was used to hot, sweaty, nasty love that was better than any aerobics routine in her mind, but something in his kiss told her she was in foreign territory dealing with Cyron de Monbleau. Later, she would figure out if she liked uncharted waters or not, but for now she was on board.

"You thinking something I want to know about, Leggs?"

"Not likely," she said backing away from him. She retrieved four plates from the cupboard and he took them from her, placing them on the table as Byron and Betty Jean came in from the deck.

The evening passed enjoyably and it was with some regret that Betty Jean called it to a close insisting she needed to get some sleep. She had to go to work in the morning and she was already running on her reserve batteries. All she wanted to do was fall into bed, she was saying as they walked towards the front door. Byron halted in his steps, smiling widely as though he had been invited to join her and she shoved him in the back, laughing.

"Keep going. You caused me to lose enough sleep last night."

"Ha! I knew it!" Sheila trumpeted from the front door. "You can't keep secrets from me."

Byron stretched out his arm pushing Sheila onto the porch to join Cyron who was the first to step outside. He closed the door on her surprised grasp. Turning he leaned his back against it and pulled Betty Jean into his embrace. Her arms were folded in front of her, but she let her head rest against his chest. His arms felt nice around her and he smelled faintly of barbecue smoke.

"Are you glad I came by? Are you sure you didn't mind my unannounced visit? I called my brother just as he was heading out. He mentioned a Sheila and I recalled you had, too. I figured it would be too big a coincidence to have two Sheila and Betty Jeans new to the area. Then of course, when he described your car, I knew it was you. But again, did you enjoy my company tonight? You were glad I was here?" Byron asked the question for the third time that evening, trying not to be too obvious in his bid for affection.

Betty Jean smiled and nodded her head. "I would have attacked your brother otherwise."

"Is that so?" He laughed. "Well, that might not be such a bad thing. You attacked me once and I liked it. I'm sure he would, too."

"You know that's not what I meant. Besides there wouldn't be a point in attacking him that way. I've been there and done that," she said looking him slyly, up and down.

"Now that's not true. Just because we all look alike doesn't mean we're alike. We have our own styles or at least Rochelle, thought so."

"Rochelle?"

"This girl we knew way back in the way back. Her birthday wish was the de Monbleau brothers in three D. Literally, three D and she said we each had a different method and she could tell who was who when she had her eyes closed."

"I won't even ask if you're serious or not, but shame on you for telling that story."

"Shame on me? Rochelle told it at the last class reunion."

"Last class reunion? How many have you had two? Three? How old are you?" Betty Jean asked pulling away from him.

"Five in dog years."

"Five in—" Her voice trailed off and she frowned. Finally, her brow cleared and she said, "You couldn't have just said thirty five?"

He hunched one of his shoulders, a habit she noticed his brother also had and pulled her back into his arms. "This would feel so much nicer if you'd put your arms around me, instead of against me."

Realizing she was clenched up like a fist, Betty Jean force herself to relax and doing so, she slid her arms up and around him. She closed her eyes, sighing in contentment. She agreed with Byron, this did feel nicer.

Leaning against the porch rail, Sheila stared up at the night sky. "Diamonds on velvet," she said softly.

"What's that?" Cyron asked tracing her jaw line with his finger.

She looked at him smiling. "That's what nana, my grandmother would say about a star studded night like this. Diamonds on velvet."

"Would she say that you look really pretty standing underneath them and some man would want to kiss you?" he asked coming closer until there was no space between them and the top of his head blocked the stars and sky from her view.

He'd spoken very softly, very slowly and Sheila was scared to breathe. Afraid she'd miss something. There was a tiny little defiant Sheila within her who was going into hysterics telling her to snap out of it, but she couldn't. Danger, danger, danger! defiant Sheila warned in hysteria. He placed both hands on either side of her face and pulled her gently towards him. He was aptly named. Sheila surrendered to him thinking of the mythical sirens that lured ships to their destruction.
**

That night Betty Jean dreamt she was a wild horse.

She was tall and graceful with a long, flowing mane that whipped out behind her when she ran. And run she did. Over fields and meadows. Streams and valleys. With the wind on her limbs she could taste freedom.

How sweet, how sweet.

Never having felt a bridle or saddle, she trotted, pranced or raced however she chose. Smiling in the innocence of sleep, Betty Jean hugged her pillow. It was the first time in a long while that she felt the peace that only the truly free could experience.

Betty Jean's smile faded and her hand moved from beneath her pillow to her throat as if to remove some unseen object. Betty Jean's lids flickered as they fought to open and rid her of the dream turned nightmare.

Behind Betty Jean's eyes, inside her mind where all thoughts dwell and merge, both the conscious and the unconscious, she was still the beautiful mare, but she no longer ran freely. No wind rushed in her face, curling it's fingers through her mane. Instead a rope pulled at her neck, cutting and burning her flesh. She strained, bucking and fighting against it, but whomever held the rope, held fast. Though she fought hard, a stronger hand pulled against her.

The mane that had flown out majestically behind her when she raced in the breeze was tangled and twisted around her as she struggled to see who sought to bind her. She whined and neighed. Raising up she kicked at the sky, but the rope held firm.

Sheila burst into Betty Jean's bedroom to find her sitting straight up in the middle of the bed desperately pulling at her throat. Flicking on the light switch, Sheila assumed her best Hank Aaron stance. She had a bright pink scarf tied around her head and was wearing the Victoria Secret Angel tee and boy shorts from page thirty two of the current catalogue. She had a wooden bat grasped firmly in both hands and raised to her right shoulder. She was ready to swing for the fences.

"What's wrong? What's wrong?" She looked around frantically for signs of an intruder. Seeing no one she lowered the bat and walked over to the bed. She touched the other woman on the shoulder. "What's wrong, Betty Jean?"

Still struggling against the fear of her sleep, Betty Jean was incapable of coherent speech. She looked wide eyed at Sheila, but her eyes were wild and unfocused. Her hands no longer pulled at her throat but lay at her sides, still and useless.

Sheila removed her hand from Betty Jean's shoulder and stood staring at her. Betty Jean's eyes were filled with terror. Knowing Betty Jean was seeing beyond the walls of her bedroom, Sheila felt the hairs on her arms rise and prickle with goose bumps.

Half afraid to shake her, Sheila said, "Betty Jean!" in the sternest voice she could muster, scared as she was. Tears smarted in her eyes and she called Betty Jean's name snapping her fingers hard beneath her nose. "What's wrong?"

Betty Jean's eyes began to blink furiously and she collapsed to the mattress with a cry of distress. "My God!" she cried weeping.

"What's wrong?" Sheila asked again, sitting on Betty Jean's bed and wiping her hair from where by sweat or tears, it was stuck to her face.

"My God," Betty Jean repeated into the mattress.

"You take your time." Sheila stroked her back softly in comfort. "Take all the time you need, Sweetie, to pull yourself together." She sniffled. "Don't take too much time though, BJ, 'cause you're scaring the shit out of me." The last of her sentence was barely coherent as Sheila, too, began to cry. She held Betty Jean, covering her back. "What's wrong?" She wailed with genuine concern.

A few minutes later, after pulling herself together for Sheila's sake, Betty Jean told her about her dream. When Sheila told Betty Jean about her near trance like awakening, Betty Jean nodded. "I know. I could hear you talking to me, but I was somewhere between reality and the reality in my dream. I could hear your voice, girl, but somehow mentally I was still a horse."

In spite of herself, Sheila laughed. Holding up one hand, she pinched her nose with the other in an effort to keep from snorting. "I'm sorry," she finally got out, "but that tickled me just then. *I was still a horse.*" She chuckled trying to pull herself together then laughed again. "I guess that would explain the God awful noises you were making that woke me up."

"I screamed or something, didn't I?"

"Well, no." Sheila was trying hard to keep a straight face. "Not exactly."

"What do you mean not exactly?" Betty Jean eyed Sheila suspiciously.

"You were making this really high pitched noise. A scream, but not quiet a scream, I guess." She shrugged. "It could have been neighing now that I think about it. I guess you were still a horse." She tried to say the last part with a straight face, as well, but she failed half-way through her sentence. "The horse whisperer," she added on a snicker.

Betty Jean laughed a little, too. "Oh, shut up. You were no help. You asked me what was wrong about fifty times!" She slapped at Sheila, who managed to evade the hit.

"What was I supposed to say when I burst in here ready to kick box with an intruder and I find you trapped in the clutches of a dream, instead? And just for the record, I ain't never seen no shit like that before in my life. And trust me, I've seen some shit."

"You could have asked if I was all right or shaken me or something."

"Nana said never shake a sleep walker and like I said, I've never seen any damn thing like that before. You should count yourself fortunate that I didn't push you outside, then call a priest and hold a séance or an exorcist, shit. Secondly," she said before Betty Jean could speak, "there wasn't any point in asking if you were all right when I could plainly see, you weren't. Your head was all but spinning around on your neck. I was waiting on the green vomit!"

At that Betty Jean laughed, too, conceding the logic.
**

Later that week over lunch, Sheila asked, "What do you think caused that dream? Who do you think it was who threw the rope around your neck?"

"I couldn't see their face." She forked up more salad, waiting for Sheila to sip her soda before adding casually, "My mane was in the way."

Sheila laughed inhaling coke and choked. She was undecided on whether to breathe, laugh, cough or swallow her drink. Her face burned and her eyes were watery before she managed, "You did that on purpose, evil cow."

"That's what you get for finding humor in my fears." Betty Jean grabbed one of Sheila's french fries. Lathering the fry in ketchup, she bit it in half.

Sheila dabbed at an imaginary spot of coke on her blouse with her napkin, saying, "Your fear isn't that you're a horse." She laughed a little, then tried to frown. "Damn it, that's just funny, but I digress. Your fear is losing your freedom, having it taken from you in some capacity and I haven't laughed at that. I feel that way myself sometimes, that's why I quietly fade into the background when men start getting too attached. Time to exit stage door left, to quote a favorite of mine."

"You know, you really had me fooled sprouting all this wisdom on dream interpretation, right up until you quoted Snaggle Puss."

Chewing around a mouth filled with cheeseburger, Sheila frowned at her. Her hand flew up to cover her mouth. "There's nothing wrong with Snaggle Puss!"

"It's time to let the cartoon network go, Sheila."

"No, it's time to let reality television, tabloid talk shows and What Won't I Do For Money shows go and put cartoons back on mainstream television for our children." She took a deep breath and inwardly, Betty Jean groaned. Inadvertently, she'd tapped one of Sheila's pet peeves and she could see her climbing atop her podium for a sermon. "Remember Saturday mornings with Gargantua, Wile E. Coyote, Fat Albert *and the gang.* Even that damn bill no one was ever going to pass that sat on the steps of congress and sang? *I'm just a bill, on Capital Hill.* Remember? What happened to all that? We need television like that again. Not the crap they have out now. Exploiting human ugliness."

"Exploiting human ugliness?" Betty Jean asked dubiously at Sheila's extreme words.

"Well, that's what it is." Sheila sipped her coke. "People eating bugs, being stranded on islands, buried in insects, marrying strangers, all for money and an eager audience to watch the degradation. Please!" She waved off the spectacle with her hand turning sideways in her seat to cross her legs. "I long for simpler times, that's why even at the ripe old age of twenty—" She caught herself, cutting her eyes at Betty Jean. "That's why in my *maturity*, I still love the cartoon network."

Betty Jean smiled. "In your maturity? We're about the same age and I don't really think that twenty ni—"

"Dangerous territory, Betty Jean. Really dangerous territory." Sheila's eyes narrowed in warning when she cut into Betty Jean's sentence. "We're not about to start talking about my age and don't be saying we're about the same anything. I'm not confessing to anything over twenty three."

"What's so golden about twenty-three?"

"They have more sense than twenty-one, but not as many miles as twenty-five and not as close to thirty as anything over twenty-six. Now let's get off this unpleasant conversation and back to the singing constitution cartoon thing."

Betty Jean laughed. She loved messing with Sheila about her age. It was a sure way to get her riled up.

Satisfied with the small ribbing she'd given her, Betty
Jean looked skeptical. "They don't air the singing bill
spots anymore." There was a tiny blossom of hope that
they did. She used to love his little amendment songs.
She stamped on the hope, though saying, "I know you
don't get *all that* on the cartoon network. Gargantua
and singing bills. That's programming from the six—"
She stopped and smiled when Sheila's eyes narrowed
again. She was going to say sixties or seventies, but
thought better of it. "You just watch cartoons, because
you like cartoons."

"No." Sheila shook her head at Betty Jean. "I just
saw an opportunity to bitch about a particular injus-
tice and took it."

"It's unjust that they don't play the same shows
that they did in our youth?" Sheila gave her a look and
Betty Jean rolled her eyes, correcting her question.
"The shows that they played in *my* youth, okay, happy
now?"

"Yes, but that's not my point. The point is that they
can put cartoons on regular television for the children.
It's unjust that kids are being robbed of their seven-
teen years to be a kid."

"A little billy goat?" Betty Jean laughed at her own
joke.

Sheila ignored her. "Let 'em laugh and have fun as
long as possible. Have you even seen any of today's
cartoons? Children are watching Pokemon with a
straight face. X-Men. Yu-Gi-Oh. All of it. It's not funny.
Just animated war games. I say let children laugh at
Bugs Bunny. Give them back their cartoons for now.
Fantasies about destroying the planet can come later
when they're old enough to appreciate them. Once life
has given them a reason to dream a little dream or
two."

Betty Jean sat in amused silence. She wanted to
egg Sheila on further, but she didn't want her riled up
for the rest of the afternoon. She'd stop to tell anyone

who would listen about her cartoon fetish and the need to see children laughing over them again. She'd be passing out petitions to demonstrate in front of the network studios. Betty Jean hid a smile behind her drink, deciding to risk the chance of getting Sheila started again. "There's always books. We should all read a little more."

"Then there's that," Sheila agreed, absently.

Betty Jean knew she was carefully wording her petition and sought to change the subject. "Why are we talking about cartoons?" She looked at Sheila, sipping her tea.

Chewing her food, Sheila shook her head frowning. "We aren't." She made a show of swallowing. "I was being wise, quoting wisdom, your words, not mine and you were being a *wise ass*, my words, not yours, about my age or lack of it." Sheila smiled, reaching for her drink. "I was letting you know you weren't the only person afraid of having their freedom taken away and you were letting me know Snaggle Puss should not only *not* be quoted, but should become a thing of my past, like he so obviously has become to you."

"Are you finished?" Betty Jean picked up a hot wing from her plate. Biting into it, she wrinkled her nose at the spicy heat of the sauce.

"Also," Sheila went on, "you didn't give me a chance to say you shouldn't be afraid to let Byron in, of getting close to him. He seemed like a really nice guy the other night. Unfortunately, not as cute as his brother." Betty Jean opened her mouth to protest, but Sheila held up a hand shaking her head. "No, it's okay. It happens. One twin is usually the cute one."

Betty Jean frowned at her, but moved on. "So, you think Byron's the one holding the rope in my dream?"

"I think it's a whole lot of people and things on the other end of that rope, but I think you believe it's Byron. You had the dream after spending time with him over the weekend. Maybe he got close and you feel like you liked it too much. Being hurt again scares you, under-standably and that fear manifested itself in your dream. In a sense your freedom has just recently been won. A part of you may see Byron as a threat to that, if things get serious with him. Which in all likelihood, it will." Sheila laced her fingers together, using them as a rest-ing place for her chin. She propped her elbows on the table and smiled at her deductions.

Betty Jean looked at her with smiling admiration. "Why aren't you out psychoanalyzing people for a liv-ing and getting paid for it, Dr. Cooper? You're always so insightful and dead on when you're helping me work my way through something." Betty Jean was complete sincerity.

Sheila was just as sincere in her response. "Be-cause they insisted that I have some sort of degree and a license to practice first." Sipping her drink, Sheila waved her hand in dismissal.

Chapter Eight

Saturday morning Betty Jean woke early from a sound sleep by a thirst that demanded attention. Grumbling, she flipped over on the mattress and reached for the water glass that customarily sat on her nightstand. She lifted the glass and her arm sprang up a few inches. Briefly opening one eye, Betty Jean shook the glass, confirming its lack of contents.

She sighed and pulled herself from the bed.

She'd been out with Byron the night before and while she planned to be up early to help Sheila move, she hadn't planned to be up this early. Dark thirty, she said under her breath, as she looked to the window in her bedroom.

It was barely six o'clock, way too early to be awake on a Saturday. Bleary eyed, she walked slowly down the hall. Her hair was in her face and she brushed it away with the back of her hand.

Exiting the hall, she entered the living room and paused. Standing perfectly still, she wondered at the movement that had caught her attention. Turning slightly to her right, she released an audible breath. Continuing on to the kitchen, she yawned. "Why are you sitting here in the dark?"

"I haven't been here that long." Sheila's voice came from the corner of the couch.

"Length of time had nothing to do with the question." Betty Jean yawned again, opening the refrigerator. She retrieved a bottle of Evian before walking back into the living room. Unscrewing the cap, Betty Jean drank deeply. Lowering the now half empty bottle, she clarified. "The question was *why*."

"I was at Cyron's," Sheila said and Betty Jean sat down on the couch, sensing that there was no quick answer to her inquiry. When Sheila said nothing further, Betty Jean raised a brow. In the soft light filtering in from the various windows she could just make out her friend's troubled countenance.

"I was over at Cyron's lying in his bed, half asleep and just as snug as could be, then I asked myself what on earth I was doing there. I crept out without waking him. I mean, it's only been a few days since he and I met," she recapped unnecessarily. "Everything's great."

"Well, hell, why are you saying it like it's a death sentence or should he be beating you by now or something? You guys are two good people or at least you are." Betty Jean smiled when Sheila did. "There's no reason why the two of you together wouldn't be great."

"This isn't me, Betty Jean. You know that song? *I'm like a bird, I'll only fly away. I don't know where my soul is. I don't know where my home is?*" She hummed a little bit, rushing through the lyrics and Betty Jean nodded her head, wondering where she was going with her question.

"Nelly Furtado, right?"

Sheila nodded her head in affirmation. "That's me. I fly away. *I don't need nobody telling me the time.*"

Betty Jean smiled a little, recognizing the words from Erykah Badu's *Certainly*. Reaching for Sheila's hand, she gave it a squeeze. "Stop with Sheila's greatest hits and talk to me, please. What's wrong? And say it without involving Motown."

Sheila turned to look at her and Betty Jean could see tears glittering in her eyes. "I've never met anyone like him before, girl. I've never connected with anyone like this. He just makes me feel like—Like I—" She stumbled some over what she was trying to say and she closed her eyes.

"When we're together," which they had been every night since their meeting, "I feel calm. You know me, I don't stay put for too long. I can't be with the same man for too long, like most women. There's just too much drama in that mess. I get in, I get out. I keep it light. No deep feelings. No attachments. And I prefer to only see men who think the same way. Once a guy catches feelings for me, as they used to say, I catch the first thing moving away from him." She ranted some more about her phenomenal ability to cut ties and run, using various songs to illustrate her point and Betty Jean sat quietly sipping her water and listening.

Either from lack of breath, complaints or songs, Sheila stopped speaking and Betty Jean stepped into the void left by her silence. "So, what's so terrible about feeling calm with Cyron and *catching feelings* for him?" She wanted to say, *other than the fact that it was Cyron*, but refrained. She'd take shots at him later when Sheila was better prepared to defend him.

"I've been in situations before where I hit it off with some guy and we were all hot and heavy, but as soon as that fizzled out it was time to move on. I don't know how to say this right, but - I don't get cozy." She frowned in aggravation. "I sure as hell don't let anyone get cozy with me, but Cyron—" She stopped again, shaking her head at a loss for words.

"*Nobody's supposed to be here?*" Betty Jean couldn't stop herself from naming the Deborah Cox song that fit the situation perfectly. She could see why Sheila did that all the time. It was really handy and summed up a situation nicely. She grinned, proud of herself.

"Exactly! No damn body's supposed to be here and already he's all over the place. Settling in and getting all cozy and comfortable."

"Maybe it's just a physical thing. Maybe it'll fizzle out soon, too and you won't have to worry about getting your heart caught up and involved. Didn't you and Spencer date seriously before it became just about sex with you two?"

Sheila rolled her eyes. "I've never dated anybody seriously. I've always been full of shit. I tell men flat out and up front that I don't do the lovely dovey shit and not to get too attached to me. He'll only end up with his feelings hurt."

"What did Cyron say when you told him that?" Sheila pursed her lips. In the semi lit room of rising morning, Betty Jean thought she could see a blush and stated the obvious. "You didn't feed him your usual bullshit, then?"

"It's not bullshit."

"Protective gear, then, or whatever you want to call it. You never let anyone see the real you? The real Sheila that isn't playing at being tough. The sweet, sensitive, vulnerable you and Cyron's trying to peek behind the curtain, hun?" Betty Jean tried to be encouraging. "Maybe once the sex cools, he'll lose interest or you will." She shrugged, never completely understanding Sheila's desire to stand alone and independent in the world. She was single right now, but customarily Betty Jean was a woman who liked being in a relationship. She liked the idea of belonging.

"He doesn't have sex."

"Excuse me?" Betty Jean was pulled back from her own reflections.

"Cyron stopped having sex about a year or so ago."

"Why?" Betty Jean asked incredulously. Her own sex life had been dragging as of late, but it wasn't because she'd chosen that route. It had been thrust upon her by her current situation. She wasn't in a relationship and had never gotten into so called casual sex. A single man who looked like the de Monbleaus should not have a problem finding a willing partner, though, and it was doubtful he'd have a problem with the casual part.

"I don't know." Sheila shrugged, but Betty Jean got the feeling that she did know. "Something to do with being tired of frivolous sex and just giving his body to any woman that caught his eye. The meaninglessness of the act was overriding the pleasure of it or so I understand." She shrugged again. "He's looking for a mental connection, I think. I don't know, shit. He's protesting the rise of AIDS among the African-American community and a whole bunch of other unnecessary mess he went on and on about. Just suffice it to say, he doesn't have sex." She frowned, mumbling. "Should have left his black ass alone right then."

Betty Jean sat blinking at the shock of Sheila's words.

"He's said he's not having sex again until he's looking in the face of his wife."

"That's admirable," Betty Jean said because she couldn't think of anything else to say. What happens if he never gets married?

"Yeah, but without the sex—" Sheila said, breaking into her thoughts.

"He's going to see right through your smoke and mirrors to the real Sheila," Betty Jean cut in finally grasping some of Sheila's problem. "Like you told me, there's nothing to be scared of."

"I never said there was nothing to be scared of."

"You did!" Betty Jean said in surprise. Sheila usually remembered everything. "Remember quoting Snaggle Puss?"

"I said you shouldn't be *afraid* to let Byron in. I didn't say don't be scared of the process or what happens after he gets inside. Hell, yes, be very, very scared! Fear makes you cautious. Believe me, there's plenty to be scared of!"

"Then why did you—" Betty Jean began only to be interrupted by Sheila who answered the anticipated question.

"I told you everything I said, because it was *you*. It *is* good for someone to fall in love. It's fantastic for someone *else* to meet someone who sends them into a whirlpool of unfamiliar feelings. I was gaily standing on the sidelines watching as love should be watched, as a spectator. I was on the side of the field, not even thinking of suiting up and joining the game." She shook her pretty head looking woefully at Betty Jean beside her. "Cyron is getting into my head, if not my bed and I don't think I like it at all."

    **

"How about here?" Cyron asked, rearranging the sofa, yet again.

Sheila stood in the middle of her living room, shaking her head. "No. I don't like it," she said deciding and Cyron collapsed into its dark blue embrace, stretching his legs out. "I like it better now." She came to stand before him.

His eyes were still closed when his hand reached out and his fingers closed around her wrist. Tugging gently, he pulled her off balance and she landed in his lap. Sheila turned until she was cradled sideways in his arms and laid her head against his shoulder.

"How about now? Did it get any better?" He kissed the top of her head.

"I could get use to it." Sheila laughed. Realizing that there was more truth than jest in her words, Sheila leapt from Cyron's lap.

Startled by her abrupt departure, Cyron sat up staring. "Was it something I said or something you said?" He replayed their few words in his mind.

"What?" Sheila frowned in distraction, feigning renewed interest in the lay out of the room. "I think I want it in the middle of the floor, so I can put one of those sofa tables behind it. Maybe set some flowers and candles on the table, you know?" She barely paused for breath as she rambled on discussing her decorative ideas for the room.

Cyron sat watching her, then leaned back against the cushions. He stretched his arm out across its back and listened patiently a little while longer. "Come here,

Leggs?" Focusing on the mini blinds samples in her hand, she pretended not to hear him. "Leggs." His soft, sensuous voice reminded Sheila of lips on her spine and she moved further away from him, deeper into the living room.

Where Betty Jean's living room faced towards the front of the house, looking towards the front yard, Sheila's afforded a beautiful view of the back yard. She turned to the circular wall of windows, loving the view. One of the reasons she'd chosen her house was because of the windows. "Maybe I'll use wooden blinds or bamboo. Something different," she added, thinking.

"Leggs?"

"I'd leave the windows uncovered altogether if it didn't look so, I don't know. Blank."

Again, Cyron stretched out his long legs and called to Sheila. He added a please and a sappy line about being too tired to get up and come to her that finally won her acquiescence. She crossed the room to stand before him once more.

Cyron patted his thigh for her to have a seat, but she looked at him, hesitating to take it. "Come on. I'm that kind of guy. Big and cuddly. I like to talk it out. I'm a talker. Come on," he coaxed smiling and she settled herself upon him for the second time that afternoon.

"Why'd it take me three days to get in touch with you?"

Sheila was looking down at her hands and Cyron touched a finger to her face, turning her attention to him.

"Are you walking on me, Leggs?"

"Walking on—" Sheila began in confusion, shaking her head. "I'm not—" She stopped again, not feeling too good about lying to his face. She *had* been trying to put some distance between herself and this man who insisted upon tantalizing her senses. In just over a week he had her wondering about what it would be like to be with him. Not in the sexual way that she usually referred to being with a man, but in the real sense of the word.

Until that morning, the only furniture she'd been able to find that she liked was her bedroom set. They'd spent most of their time since Sheila's move from Betty Jean's house as they'd spent it before, either out or at his house. They'd spent a few hours at the Chicken Shack after work on Tuesday, bought their dinner from a little Italian place they discovered and went to his place to eat. Everything had been going along just fine. He was telling jokes as usual and she was laughing, enjoying herself as usual in his company, then out of the blue it struck her. *I wonder what it would be like to be with Cyron.* The traitorous thought sprung from some unknown place within her and Sheila had known true fear.

She didn't want to know if he could make her cum or not. She didn't care if he had six inches hanging between his legs or a whole foot. Just then, she'd been looking at him laughing, wondering if his son would have his eyes or how strict he'd be with his daughter.

She wanted to know what it would be like to *be* with him. To wake up next to him every morning. To scramble his eggs and fight over counter space in the bathroom. She wanted to know his politics. Who'd he vote for last election and why? Did he laugh more than he frowned? Because he looked like he did and she wanted to wrap herself around him and be there laughing with him always.

She wondered about his likes and dislikes and wanted to know each and every one of them like they were her own. She wanted to know what fears scared Cyron de Monbleau in the dark and vanquish them for him. She looked at him laughing and thought it was the hand of fate she'd felt that first night when she'd seen him across the room at The Chicken Shack. He looked so familiar to her, because his face was etched on her soul by God and her heart recalled it, even if she didn't.

She'd been blown away by the depth and strength of her feelings and she spent the remainder of their evening meditating on her thoughts. When she left for home that night, she hadn't spoken to him again until he showed up at Hurstwode & Donovan Friday afternoon on some bogus errand for his brother. He'd stepped into Betty Jean's office for a hot two seconds before coming back out and harassing her into having lunch with him on Saturday.

She told him she was furniture shopping and he volunteered to tag along, using the excuse that his Escalade truck would be perfect for the excursion. Having no real reason for her avoiding him or at least not one she'd tell him about and knowing she missed him anyway, she agreed. His Escalade had only been an excuse to go shopping with her though, because he looked aghast at the furniture salesman's suggestion that he bring his truck around to the loading dock. Instead, he paid the delivery men to deliver her furniture. She didn't know how much he gave them, but her furniture left the warehouse when they did.

Now, just as she feared, after spending more time with him, her thoughts were becoming wayward again. She'd spent the last few days going through Cyron detox, now she was back to where she'd started. Feening like a junkie. *I could get use to it*, she repeated the words and the tiny Sheila within her was shaking her head. Hell, it looked like she already *was* used to it, she reprimanded herself privately.

"I've been busy with the move, that's all," she lied to the hands in her lap.

"We just brought in the first pieces of your furniture or rather, they just brought it in, but Leggs, we unpacked your clothes and brought in your things from storage last weekend. What could you have that's kept you busy since Tuesday night?" He touched her face turning it towards him. "You're walking on me? Why?" She remained silent, causing him to urge, "Why have you been avoiding me?"

Sheila opened her mouth, then closed it dropping her gaze to her lap again.

"Poor, Leggs." He traced the curve of her face with his finger.

"What?" Confused, she frowned. "Poor Leggs, what?"

"Never getting too close." He completed his sentence as though she hadn't interrupted. She tried to rise from his lap and his arms tightened around her waist. "Now I see why those legs are so long. They have to put as much distance between you and whatever gets too close for comfort as they can."

"You don't know," Sheila snapped. She was not so easily read! "This time two weeks ago you didn't even know I existed." She twisted, but he held firm.

"So, is that what's bothering you? If I knew that you existed two weeks ago?" he asked in bewilderment.

"No. Yes. No," Sheila said rapidly hopping from one side of the fence to the other and back. "That's not what I'm saying. It is, but it isn't." She looked into his quizzical gaze and cursed. "Damnit, yes it is."

She attempted to rise again and Cyron stopped her. "I like to touch when I talk things out. I've found that when you can't find the words," he laced his fingers with hers, "your other senses can supply them for you sometimes. Come here. Turn." Sheila's back was now positioned comfortably against his chest. When she was facing away from him, he put his arms around her. "Now tell me what's going on with you. Pretend I'm a big ole soft cushy chair, you're alone in the room and talk."

She sat stiffly for a moment, then relaxed against him. "I feel like I'm caught in a whirlwind, Cyron. I talk to you and I feel like I've known you my whole life. I feel stark naked in your presence and it scares me because I don't generally connect with people like this

and - And I don't even know you. Not really," she added
feebly, knowing in her heart that she was only telling
a half truth. Even in her big ole soft cushy chair, alone
in the room, she was lying. It would make no difference how long she knew him. Once either of them got
too comfortable, she'd be in the wind.

"What don't you know about me? What do you want
to know? I'm an open book."

"I want to know *you*, Cyron," she said softly and he
squeezed her to him. "I want to run from what I'm
feeling and find some jackass to prove me right when I
say that no man is worth the drama he'll put me
through."

Cyron remained silent, merely kissing the shoulder
her halter-top revealed to him. He wondered who hurt
her so deeply and wanted to assure her it would never
be him. He'd told her he'd been celibate for a while,
but he hadn't divulged the complete reasoning behind
it. He'd been tired of just satisfying his body. He was
getting older and the time had come for him to put
childish games behind him. He wanted to find someone he could be real with and expect the same thing in
return. He didn't have sex because he wanted to make
sure he had something real and solid connecting him
to a woman and not just what she made him feel when
he had his pants down.

Truthfully, he'd surprised himself since he started
his little search. He'd seen a lot of women in the past
year who would have assuredly ended up in his bed
and he was dismayed to see that a number of them
didn't have a brain between them. It would have been
good sex. He thought again about one or two of the
women and corrected himself. It would have been *great*
sex, but nothing more. Some of them put up a good
front, but after one or two conversations he could see
clearly that there was no substance. He wanted more
and had cut out sex to eliminate the confusion when
he found it. Sheila was the first, and only woman, he'd

met who even seemed worth the effort of the hunt. He
saw plenty of women who appealed to him sexually,
but Sheila just *appealed* to him. There was no physical, mental or emotional. She just felt good to him.
The right way. Every way.

She was intelligent and funny with a sense of style
that even his mother would envy and that was saying
a lot. He could see that a temper lurked beneath her
cool exterior and her mouth was more sarcastic than
even his. He laughed with her a lot and she seemed to
understand him without him having to explain himself. Every day he spent with her made him look forward
to the next time he'd see her. It made him a little nervous, too, that their relationship was moving so fast,
even without sex between them.

He thought he'd have some time to meet someone.
Maybe take some time to get to know them, *really know
them* and then hopefully, feelings would develop and
so forth. Then they would take it from there, but this
thing with Sheila took off like a rocket ship. There was
no adjustment period for him either and he was kind
of glad that he wasn't experiencing his fears and concerns alone. Maybe they took off like they did because
of the lack of sex. Without it he was able to see the
woman before him and he liked what he was seeing. A
year ago he wouldn't have hesitated to take the beautiful, sexy woman in his arms to bed, but he may have
missed something in his haste.

He held her and was assaulted by her perfume. He
sighed, closing his eyes. Maybe if he'd already had sex
with her, he wouldn't feel so ripped open and exposed
himself when she looked at him. Instinctively, his arms
tightened around her, proclaiming his last thoughts a
lie.

He thought again about what she was saying and
decided not to comment. There was nothing really that
he could say that would put her mind at ease. His
mother always told him that with women actions spoke

a hell of a lot louder than words. He'd keep his mouth shut and hope she kept her eyes open. Kissing the back of her neck, he squeezed her again.

Chapter Nine

"**M**s. Carlson, you have a call on line one," Sheila said professionally into the phone. Unless, they were alone, Sheila was never overly familiar with Betty Jean. To most of the staff at Hurstwode and Donovan, she was nothing more than Ms. Carlson's ever efficient assistant and Sheila wanted to keep it that way. The last thing she needed was people in her business.

"Who is it?" Betty Jean's voice inquired from the intercom.

"You wouldn't believe me if I told you. The other end of the rope perhaps," Sheila replied ambiguously, before sending the call through with no further warning.

"This is Betty Jean Carlson," Betty Jean said tentatively into the phone just before an irate male voice exploded in her ear.

"You could have left a forwarding number or address, *Ms. Carlson.*" Indignantly, he stressed her name.

Betty Jean sat silently, frowning slightly in concentration. *It couldn't be*, her mind raced zeroing in on the voice. She hadn't heard it since leaving for California, but she was nearly certain it was him. But was it? She strained to hear, though he was no longer speaking. She sat back removing the glasses she occasionally wore when working on her computer. She put one end of them in her mouth, sucking on it slightly, as she thought.

"This is a long distance call, you could say something."

Betty Jean smiled in full recognition. Only one person complained like that. "How are you doing, Mr. Grailton?"

"Don't give me that care and concern BS. That jackass you left me with is driving me to the poor house with his idiotic handling of my affairs."

"You're not happy with Vincent Sanders?" She was truly concerned. No one had ever complained about Vincent before. He was good at his job and got along with all sorts of people, one of the reasons he did so well. His disposition and drive were the reasons why she'd chosen him to take over the hand holding of Gerald Grailton.

"Vincent Sanders? Who in the world is Vincent Sanders?"

"Vincent Sanders is the man I introduced you to before I left. The man we had lunch with so you could meet. The one I turned over your accounts to," Betty Jean said patiently into her headset. Rolling her eyes to the ceiling, a smile spread across her face. It felt good to touch base with her old client again. Even if he was a little eccentric and sliding dangerously close to being a lot eccentric, to being blatantly unbalanced, she thought, smiling with affection.

"Oh, that sop? I banned him from my presence barely a week into your departure. He was two or three stuffed suits ago. Thank God my business is concluded with that firm and the private dick I hired was able to locate you."

Betty Jean laughed, flattered that he'd gone through such extremes to find her. She had to admit she'd missed the old man's grumbling.

"One of the incompetents that I had to suffer through reminded me of you a little in the beginning and I thought I'd be okay, but I was wrong. She was cute as a button and looked really nice in her little suits, but she was only playing dress up. She was no Betty Jean. I fired her thinking what I needed was another you and then I got to thinking, hell, why not you? So, here I am ready for you to take me back."

"I'd be happy to bring you over to Hurstwode and Donovan, Mr.Grailton. We may have to wait, to keep you from losing any significant money." Her mind was working furiously trying to find a way to squeeze him into her already tight schedule and knowing it would be quite an accomplishment on her record with the firm if she did. Gerald Grailton had an extensive port- folio.

"Call me Gerald, woman and grab your coat. We're going to lunch to discuss my finances. I'm in the limo parked at the curb downstairs. And hurry Betty Jean, it's not polite to keep an old man waiting."

**

Betty Jean returned from lunch two hours later. She walked in swinging her purse from two fingers with an amused smile on her face.

Sheila watched her approach with a raised brow. Scribbling something on a piece of paper, she gave it to Betty Jean when she passed her desk.

Pausing, with her hand on her office doorknob, Betty Jean glanced down at the note then back at Sheila who typed as though Betty Jean had already been dis- missed from her mind.

"Twenty-five, fifty, and seventy-five? What's this?" she addressed the top of Sheila's French coiffure.

"Prescription strengths for Viagra." Without raising her eyes from the correspondence she was typing, she smiled.

"Really cute." Betty Jean was about to enter her office when Sheila spoke again.

"Someone who doesn't require assistance from that little blue pill was thinking of you."

"What?" Betty Jean paused at the door. "What do you mean someone was thinking of me?"

In lieu of an answer, Sheila rose from her desk. Walking over to Betty Jean she opened her office door and pointed in. "*Someone* was thinking of you."

"My goodness." Betty Jean stepped across the threshold and into her office. "Oh, my." She turned in a full circle to look around her, feeling like she'd stepped into Wonderland. Her office was filled with flowers. It looked as though someone had bought out not only one florist, but two.

There were carnations in vases, single long stemmed roses in various colors and some in bundles. There were flowers in boxes, cups, vases and tissue paper. Even a few teddy bears holding floral arrangements. She saw tulips, chrysanthemums, gladiolas and snap dragons. Those were just the ones she knew by name. There were more brilliantly colored blossoms that she didn't recognize, but they were all beautiful.

In awe, she turned to Sheila who smiled back at her. "Who did this? Byron?" Betty Jean asked, dumb struck by the sight of her office.

"I don't know." Sheila was about to explode with glee and excitement. She hurried to close the door behind her and all but danced in anticipation of her story. "They started arriving almost as soon as you left. In fact, if you passed someone in the elevator or in the lobby carrying flowers, they were probably yours. I put the one with the note in it on your desk. You should have seen the expressions on all the delivery men's faces! Priceless! This one guy came three times!"

Betty Jean looked at her desk where at least eight vases stood and back to Sheila who propelled her forward. "See?" She indicated the single white rose that laid in green tissue paper in the center of her desk. There was a small envelope tucked into the tissue. "Read it! Read it!" Sheila said, snatching up the envelope and offering it to Betty Jean who took it with fingers that trembled lightly. Who would empty a flower shop for her?

"Read it! Read it!" Sheila chirped at Betty Jean's side, as she untucked the flap in the envelope.

"*Just thinking of you,*" they said in unison.

"You read this?" Betty Jean looked accusingly at her assistant.

Sheila was unabashed. "Girl, someone was trotting in here every two seconds with a flower delivery for you. That one was the last to arrive," she said, pointing a well manicured nail at the white rose that held the note. "Hell, yes, I peeked! You can't possibly blame me! You think it's, Byron?" she asked, still excited.

"I guess." Betty Jean dismissed Sheila's nosiness. "There's only one way to find out." She placed her purse in an empty desk drawer and pressed a button on her desk phone. Digital dialing filled the air, followed by ringing.

"You have him on speed dial?" There was humor in Sheila's voice.

Betty Jean sniffed a pot of daisies to hide her blush. When Byron's machine answered, she hung up. Looking at Sheila, she hunched her shoulders. "I suppose it's a mystery until tonight."

"Hmm," Sheila said, in thought.

"What?" Betty Jean bent to smell more flowers.

"I have about two weeks worth of soap operas to watch." She frowned, calculating.

"*And?*"

Sheila started off across the office to return to her own desk. She answered without turning. "*And* I'm trying to determine the best time for you to call me with the scoop. You got drama, too, but the CBS daytime lineup—" She left her statement hanging uncompleted, closing the door.

A moment later Betty Jean's intercom buzzed. She took her nose out of a flower to press the speaker button. "Yes?"

"How's nine-thirty or ten o'clock? I should be done with The Young and the Restless by then."

Betty Jean laughed, disconnecting Sheila.

**

Passing through the house on skips and twirls, Betty Jean paused to spray perfume lightly in the air.

Viventy

She closed her eye, inhaling deeply. It was her newest fragrance and she loved it.

Walking over to the bar, she mixed herself a Tom Collins. Lifting the glass to her lips she sipped at the drink. Byron had called saying he was on his way and she fairly glowed with eagerness.

They hadn't been intimate since their one and only encounter, but she was going to change that. It was all well and good that they were taking things slowly, but if they slowed down any further they'd be standing still. They were two adults who found each other physically attractive, had good chemistry together and liked each other's company. There was no reason to continue to delay their intimacy.

She had been beginning to wonder if he ever intended to touch her like that again, but her insecurities and doubts were gone. After inheriting her little flower shop she knew he was thinking about them, too and she worked to make the night magical.

After work, she and Sheila labored to fill a box she had in her office with rose petals. One of Betty Jean's associates stuck her head in the door to say good night and ended up sitting on the floor helping them. When their box was filled, she industriously retrieved another one from the copy room and stayed to assist in it's filling, too.

Carol was one of the firm's corporate lawyers.

She was fun and likable with a sharp wit and great sense of humor. Betty Jean liked her at first sight. Encouraged by her friendship with Sheila, Betty Jean welcomed the other woman's kindness. Having other women to talk to and share life's experiences with was an uncommon luxury for Betty Jean, but she found herself adapting to it rather nicely.

Betty Jean sat in the Lazy Boy rocker and pushed the recliner back. She sipped her drink again wondering if Carol made use of her rose petals, yet. In return for her assistance, she requested some petals of her own. She was going to bathe in them with her husband, Paul.

Betty Jean knew at least three men at the office who wanted a chance with Carol, but she always responded in the negative, reminding them that she was happily married. In any case, Carol always waved off their sincerity as corporate games and politics. But sometimes she'd say something like *Can you see the one that proceeds the four in my dress size?* But that was only her dark humor speaking. Carol often joked about her size, but that's all it was, joking. She had enough confidence in who she was to give some away and still have enough left over to be slightly conceited. A derogatory statement would generally be followed with one like, *Or maybe they just have a softness for deep blue eyes.* She'd then bat her long lashes to draw attention to her own. No, Carol had no qualms about her size. As she liked to say when she was paraphrasing Sheila, she *worked* it.

Betty Jean smiled visualizing Carol imitate Sheila. On occasion the three of them had dinner, went bowling or shot a game of pool over drinks. They got along well and Carol was forever teasing Sheila. It felt good to see the shoe on the other foot. Sheila was always teasing Betty Jean about one thing or another and usually had the ambush prearranged so that Betty Jean walked into the trap, but wouldn't be able to respond in time. With them, Sheila always ended up with the last word, but Carol was great retribution. She stayed on her toes and was a good match for Sheila.

The doorbell rang and Betty Jean took her time walking to the door. Her hair was loose around her shoulders and she fluffed it a bit with her hands. She pulled the door open with a seductive smile. A sheer black gown with slits that gave a nice peak at her butt covered her body. The sheer gown had a velvet vine of roses crawling across it that exposed more than hid the lush spots on her body. A matching sheer black robe that did absolutely nothing to hide any part of her body from view hung off her shoulders.

The draft from the door waved her scent beneath his nose. He responded like a bull to a red flag. Betty Jean told him not to worry about bringing anything and for once he'd listened. He was glad, too, as there was nothing to keep him from grabbing her.

He put an arm around Betty Jean's waist and jerked her to him out the door. His arms were wrapped around her and her feet never touched the porch. His kiss was hungry as he backed them into the house. Once inside, she wrapped her arms around his neck and pushed the door closed with her hand as it circled up around him. Still holding her off the ground, Byron made their way to her bedroom. If he noticed the rose petals that carpeted his steps, he gave no sign of it.

Betty Jean's room was lit by four candles that stood in tall stands on either side of the bed and two at the foot of it. Red roses shone brightly on the black satin sheets she bought for the occasion.

Finally, releasing her, Byron began to unbutton his shirt and Betty Jean pushed his hands aside. He stared into her face and she bent her head to the task. Byron's hands came up to knead her shoulders gently, then slipped her robe off. His eyes heated further at the sight of her in just her gown and he bent to kiss, then lightly bite, her shoulder.

Betty Jean inhaled at the unexpected pleasure pain of his caress and closed her eyes as a soft gasp escaped her lips.

His lips moved to her neck, trailing hot kisses down from her ear to the base of her throat. His shirt hung open finally and he slipped it from his arms, then folded one beneath her knees just as they turned to jelly. He swooped her up and onto the bed.

Amidst the rose petals, he kissed and caressed her until her nipples stood out like buds and she dripped her own sweet nectar. He refused to come to her until she nearly cried in desire for him. By the time he entered her warmth every fiber in her body was taut, eager and alert, screaming at him for attention. Attention he was more than ready to supply.

Their passion was more powerful than their first time together had been. He was just as good as she remembered. Time had not exaggerated his skill and technique. However, this time when he switched languages and whispered foreign words in her ears, she didn't even attempt to decipher them. She just closed her eyes and gave herself up further to his touch. At the last, he held her tightly to him breathing a soft *Mon Dieu* in the hair at her neck. She smiled. *That*, she understood even without translation.

Chapter Ten

W hat's a man have to do to buy you dinner?"
The question brought flashes of Cyron to mind
and Sheila pushed the images away in annoyance. Smiling her most flirtatious smile, she raised
an eyebrow. "I don't know. What's a man want to do in
order to buy me dinner?"

She lowered her voice suggestively and the man
standing before her desk visibly relaxed. He'd been trying for weeks to work up the courage to approach the
dark beauty. Her sensuous response encouraged him
and he held out his hand in introduction.

"Michael Roundtree."

"Sheila—" She hesitated then decided to leave it at
that. Unlike Cyron, this man wasn't getting any further
with her than she wanted him to get. Admiring the
way his designer suit showed off his body, she smiled
to herself. For what she had in mind, he didn't require
her last name.

She was going to exorcise Cyron from her head.

The idea came to her so suddenly she was momentarily stunned by it. Then the seed planted, began to
grow and her smile grew with it as she made her decision. She was going to rectify her previous mistake.
She'd been one on one, spending all of her damned
time with Cyron exclusively. That was her problem,
why he was able to get in her head so much. No one
else was in it.

She needed to diversify her attention.

She was sure that would put Cyron back at arm's length where he belonged. She didn't need anything deeper than the shallow end of the pool where she was firmly standing. She'd been standing there for years with no intention of going towards the deeper end. Looking at Mr. Roundtree, she could tell he'd only tread where she wanted him to. He was no threat to her peace of mind. She could control him easily. Not like Cyron. He prodded her mind again and she felt the faint fingers of budding guilt. None for her premeditated usage of Michael, but an odd sense of betrayal of Cyron's trust.

She wasn't married to Cyron de Monbleau, she thought defensively as though the suggestion came from outside of her own head. She could do what she wanted, with whomever she wanted. It wasn't her fault Cyron was trying this other level shit wanting to *know the person*. Maybe she didn't want that. Maybe she never would, she countered frowning.

Michael smiled, misinterpreting the sudden crease in her brow. He assumed her mind had gone blank, like when someone suddenly asks you your own phone number and for a split second you have no idea what it is. "Can't remember your last name?" he asked, guessing at the cause of her frown.

"Do you need my last name?" Sheila asked with the heat in her eyes turned up to full blast and he stared into them transfixed, before slowly shaking his head no.

"I thought I could handle you when I first walked over here. Up close, I'm not so sure," he said on a smile, but Sheila knew he was only half joking. She was too much for him. She could see it in his face. He was nothing like Cyron, the traitorous thought came again.

"Few people can." She smiled to reassure him, squelching down Cyron's presence again.

"I'm just a shy country boy at heart. Raised up on the family farm." He smiled, showing even white teeth. "Are you going to be one of those big city girls my daddy warned me about?"

"Oh, I'm sure *somebody* warned you about *somebody* like me a long time ago. Mike." Playfully, she gave his name it's own personal sentence with heavy emphasis on the *k*. Taking in the name brand suit that she knew couldn't be bought off the rack, the designer was strictly tailor made, she smiled slowly. If he was from down on the farm, country damn sure wasn't country anymore.

He smiled at her comment. "It took me weeks to stop being a coward and ask you out."

"And are you asking me out? Mike." She continued to flirt blatantly.

He liked the way she played with that k. Smiling, he nodding his head. "Yeah, I am, Miss Sheila."

She rolled her eyes. "Surely, not that, please. I'll feel like I'm about a hundred years old if you Miss Sheila me all night. *Miss Sheila.*" She tried the sound of it on her own lips, then shook her head in distaste. "No, doing. Mike. You have anything else you could call me?" She could have been speaking to a clerk in a department store requesting to see the same sweater, but in a different color.

"Like what?" He smiled, trying to relax in her presence.

Leggs is nice, she thought, letting Cyron barge into her head again before she could stamp him down.

She shrugged her shoulders, looking coyly at him through her lashes. "I suppose we now have dinner conversation... What can Mike call me other than Miss Sheila?"

Stepping off the elevator, Betty Jean noticed the young man standing at Sheila's desk and sighed. At this rate, she was going to end up working another twelve hour day. In no hurry to encounter more work to add to the pile on her desk, her feet lagged as she approached her office.

On closer observation, she didn't recognize Sheila's companion from the staff at H & D. Her pace picked up some as did her ears and she passed the two of them with a soft hello. Entering her office, she raised a brow and shot Sheila a *what the hell are you doing?* look.

Later, when Sheila walked into Betty Jean's office with a small box of files she said, "I don't want to talk about Cyron," before Betty Jean could even form a question. "I'm single, grown and able to do anything I want. I'm totally free. I don't need to date one man, get all super intense and attached, only to end up broken later. No offense, girl, but I don't dream about horses and ropes around my neck."

Betty Jean's look darkened and she bristled at the comment, but tried hard not to take offense, as instructed. She hunched her shoulders in dismissal. It wasn't her business, anyway. "Ball 'til you fall, Playa Playa." Her voice held just a trace of offended sarcasm.
**

Sheila leaned towards the mirror, tracing the out line of her lips with a dark brown lip liner pencil. The phone rang and she glanced down at it reading the caller ID. Seeing the name on the display, she shook her head, frowning stubbornly. She had a date to get ready for, she didn't have time to waste talking on the phone.
**

Cyron let the line ring until the machine picked up. He held the phone for a few seconds, not knowing what he intended to say. Frowning, he hung up feeling like a stalker.

He wasn't going to chase Sheila down like a dog in the street to get some attention from her. Even celibate he had plenty of women to chose from. In fact, women were approaching him at an unprecedented pace of late, he glowered, full of shit and knowing it.

**

Twenty minutes later, she was halfway out the front door when her phone rang again. There was a brief pause before she pulled the door closed and locked it. She was backing out of the driveway when the answering machine in her bedroom beeped to record a message.

"I just wanted to let you know that I'm thinking about you, Leggs. Give me a call when you get in. Maybe we can have a drink or something together." Cyron sat holding the phone, again not knowing what he wanted to say. He contemplated too long and the machine decided for him. Beeping a second time, it ended his recording.

Cyron hung up his line, wondering what he'd have to do to get Sheila to stop running from him. He thought about calling her cell phone, but declined. If she was purposely not answering her home phone, chances were real slim that she'd answer her cell. His sister, Julie, popped into his mind and he dialed her number, smiling.

Jules was a guru went it came to the female brain. She had her own radio talk show on the subject. True, she gave out more *Girllll, you better clean your house up! Sweep him right off the porch!* and *You didn't need to call me to figure that out. You already know the answer, you just want confirmation!,* than she gave out any real help. She was like a talking advice column and she gave the dish, as she called it. She kept it real for her listeners. She must know something, though, because she had a loyal fan base that loved her every comment, be it *love that man* or *lose that fool* and her audience was growing.

Jules, could tell him what to do about Sheila.

**

"Cut your losses and run, run, run." She bit into a roll. "These are *so good*."

"Do you give the same advice to everyone? The last time I listened to your show you told at least four callers to do the same thing. To get out while they could."

"*The last time you listened to my show*? See? That's wrong, Cy. I go to the Shack faithfully. I tell my listeners to go relax and expand their minds with poetry at your place and to fall into Rufio's when it's time to party and find someone new. And my own brothers don't even listen to my show. Okay, periodically listen," she amended, cutting off his protest.

"Your show is targeted at women. I'm your brother, but I'm still a man. An unhappy man at the moment who wants a real opinion from the guru. Not just *run, run, run!*" His voice was a shrill imitation of her voice.

She hunched her shoulders and used her index finger to push up the glasses that were sliding down her nose. "I call it like I see it. Why waste your time, seriously? If this woman has an intimacy hang up and can't let you in emotionally and is too afraid to get too close to you, well." Her shoulders lifted again. "It's not like you're in it for the sex, right? She's gotta give you something. It's a whole different game being celibate, Cy, you know that. I gave you all the pros and cons of the decision last year. How can she withhold her mind or heart or soul or anything else from you, if her body's not an option? You need everything else in a relationship, because the physical aspect is gone. You need the mental and the emotional. If she can only provide the physical side of herself and nothing else—" she broke off, shrugging again. "At that point, what are you two doing except wasting one another's time? What can you do other than cut your losses and run, run, run?" She repeated her advice, looking at him over the top of glasses that were again sliding down her nose.

Cyron smiled, more at his sister's personality than at her words. Jules was always so direct. It was not her lot in life to mince words. She said what she had to say, then moved on, cheerfully stepping over the mangled carcass of the naive wisdom seeker who unfortunately stepped too close to her razor sharp tongue.

Her wit and not her journalism degree was actually how she landed her dream job. She was a receptionist at the radio station, hoping something would open up for her and she'd be able to get on the air. She had an independent streak as strong as his and Byron's and was determined to make it on her own without depending on being a de Monbleau.

She'd gone to college, then put in her mandatory year at DMB Shipping afterwards. At the end of that year, she was champing at the bit to be away from corporate America. She detested the endless meetings, early mornings and late nights. As soon as she was finished serving her time, as she put it, she went to work for her current station putting her journalism degree to use. Or at least that was the plan. Being an on air personality was her goal, but she didn't think she'd ever finish paying her dues and would be stuck at the receptionist desk forever.

One morning a chance encounter on the elevator changed everything. She was listening to a fellow coworker's home situation and being typical Julie, she told the woman in no uncertain terms what she needed to do. The station's owner just happened to be on the elevator at the time and he'd gotten a real kick out of her solution to the other's problem. Later that afternoon when the previous host of her time slot was arrested on arson charges, *Grilling with Gail*, was canceled and *Julie's Jewels* was born. The station owner put her on the air impromptu style and she was a hit. The switchboard lit up with people seeking one of her jewels of wisdom.

Demonstrating her talent to advise and move on to a new subject with the case closed in her mind, Julie asked, "What time is the movie starting again? Do we have time to get more rolls?"

Instead of answering, Cyron stared at a point just over her head. Seeing his stare, his sister looked behind her at the couple walking through the door. She looked at the woman's multicolored, calf length dress and tall leather boots, nodding her head. The woman's hair and nails were done. The jewelry she wore was understated and accessorized perfectly with her outfit. Julie always noticed and admired women who had themselves together like that. They reminded her of her mother's class and style. Jules was always in blue jeans and a tee shirt. She had no style, no flare of her own. A duckling, not a swan.

She thumbed over her shoulder, turning back to Cyron. "See? You should find you someone like that. Someone with her stuff together. Stop chasing these baggage carrying chicken heads."

"Sheila isn't a chicken head." Automatically, he defended Sheila to his sister. "You think I need a woman like that?" He sat watching the couple that was now being led to a table of their own.

"Mmm, hmm." Jules chewed her food looking around for the waiter.

Cyron picked up his napkin and wiped his mouth, rising from the table he shared with Julie. Her eyes grew round in curiosity when Cyron excused himself then made his way over to the other couple's table.

She hissed his name a few times, but wondering about the impending drama unfolding before her, she made no other effort to stop him from crossing the restaurant. She did, however, trade over to his side of the table in order to get a better view.

"What did you think of the movie? Loved it or hated it? It seemed like a film someone would either love or hate, no middle ground. It was brilliant or a waste of good film?" the man asked, leaning forward in his seat to smile at the woman seated across from him.

She'd read the more exciting version of the film when it was still in book format and secretly thought the movie had been boring as hell. It was a travesty what they'd done to the author's story. If she hadn't known for a fact that the production was based on the book she'd read, she'd have had no idea. They chopped, cut and edited the story to such an extent it was a totally different story. Even the title had been altered. She was being nice, though, so she returned his smile saying the movie was great.

She had just opened her menu when a shadow fell across it. She raised her head to tell the waiter they weren't ready to order, yet, and found *she* really wasn't ready for what she saw in place of a waiter.

"Good evening, Miss Cooper." Cyron's greeting was courteous and polite. Reaching for Sheila's hand, he kissed the back of it. "I saw you come in and knew I had to say hello."

Michael was growing uneasy in the lengthening silence as Sheila and Cyron stared at one another. "Hello, I'm—" he began, but was cut off when Cyron held up a hand to stop him mid sentence.

"Not necessary. No introduction required." Cyron didn't even bother looking at him. "I left a message on your machine tonight. Did you get it?" Sheila pressed her lips together glaring at him, but he waited patiently. Michael cleared his throat uncomfortably, but was ignored. "I wanted us to go out for drinks, later, when you got back in."

He waited expectantly and Sheila's eyes narrowed. Michael, obviously at a loss to what was going on, cleared his throat a second time. When that too, went unheeded, he tried for a third time a bit louder.

"Are you waiting for me to respond to you?" Sheila asked incredulously, when Cyron continued to stare down at her. She was mortified. Cyron was not tripping on her like this. Half the place seemed to be staring at them. She wasn't going to look around to verify if they were or weren't, but she could feel eyes boring into the back of her head.

"When you finish up here, we can—" Cyron began but, Michael made the rolling noises in his throat again determined to get attention. Finally Cyron granted it, turning his head slightly to look down the length of his nose at him. "Do you need a cough drop for that? A mint? A prescription?" With each question his voice dropped and his left eyebrow arched higher, giving him a menacing expression.

Michael swallowed then looked at Sheila who was openly frowning at the man who towered over their table. Feeling at a disadvantage to the other man who was at least four or five inches over six feet, Michael, who wasn't, stood from the table. This in no way put him on eye level with the stranger, but he tried to assure himself it was better than sitting and being loomed over.

"Oh, shit," Jules said from her table, hurriedly covering her mouth. Why did dude stand up? What was Cyron saying? Hell, what was Cyron *doing*? She'd only used the woman as an example of the type he should go out with, she didn't mean for him to go duke it out with her date, though.

Julie's legs bounced excitedly beneath the table, tapping out Morse code in her nervous anticipation. What the hell was Cyron doing over there? Wait until she told Ayron about this, she speculated with twinkling mischief, thinking about her favorite sibling to gossip with. She'd call now, but she left her cell phone in the car and couldn't risk missing anything by going to get it. Damn that Cyron, she should have come prepared!

"Cyron." Sheila tugged at his arm. She tried to stand, too, wanting to pull Cyron away so they could speak in private, but he blocked her exit from the booth and wouldn't budge.

He turned to her, all friendly smiles. "That's not necessary, Leggs. I don't want to interrupt your evening." Michael made a rude noise at the comment and Cyron again turned to stare at him. "You want to sit back down?" Cyron's eyes darted from Michael to the seat he'd rose from and back. When he continued to stand uncomfortably uncertain of what to do, Cyron jerked his head in indication that he should take his seat. When the young man was again perched on his chair across from Sheila, Cyron turned and addressed her. "Like I said, I don't want to interrupt your evening." Cyron paused for a moment to look at Michael who was fingering the tines on his fork. He remained silent and Cyron went on. "I just wanted to come by and say hello. It would have been rude not to, seeing as how I was only a few feet away." Sheila continued to glare daggers at him. He smiled beautifully, bowing slightly at the waist. "Miss Cooper." Formally, he inclined his head, then turned to go back to his own table.

Michael tried to think of something to fill the awkward silence after his departure and said the first thing to pop into his rattled brain. "Cooper, is it?" He nodded his head as if in approval, then reached for his water glass and sipped.

Sheila rolled her eyes on a glare. "You see what happens when you give people your last name?"

He didn't, but smiled anyway thoroughly disappointed in her. "It's never easy, is it?" Nothing was ever easy with these west coast women.

A little while later, Julie and Cyron were leaving the restaurant and he stopped at Sheila's table for the second time that night. Looking at Michael, he said calmly, "This lady is very special to me. Don't hurt her. Don't play with her. Don't give her any shit. You do. She tells me about it. I come to discuss the matter with you personally. That's not something you want, believe me." A slow promising smile slid across Cyron's face and he straightened up again.

He turned and was about to leave when he turned back. "Sheila, if you're going to run from me, my love, and put up barriers between us, you'll have to do better than this." Michael frowned in confusion when Cyron nodded in his direction. "I would never tolerate such disrespect. Not to myself, because I'm a grown man, but I would never let myself be humiliated in front of a woman I wanted." He spoke to her in rapid French, his grandfather's language. Having been the only person present who understood what he turned back to say, Julie's eyes grew large.

He ushered her away from the table just as, "That's who you're all moon faced over?" burst from her mouth. She tried to get a good look at Sheila from over her shoulder, but Cyron rushed her out the restaurant door and onto the street. Appreciating the irony of her telling him to go after the very woman she was telling him to give up, she started laughing with complete disregard to his feelings. He mumbled something beneath his breath and she shrugged, laughing still. He always switched languages when he was upset. All her brothers did. It was an unconscious trait inherited from their father who inherited the habit from his.

Chapter Eleven

The wind threaded its fingers through her hair freeing it from the pins that held it atop her head. But she didn't care. The breeze in her face felt so good she laughed in happy abandon. Betty Jean couldn't remember the last time she felt so alive, so free. Smiling she bent to pluck a blossom from a bed of beautifully colored flowers and her hand became a hoof, pawing at the earth.

She flung her long, graceful head back, neighing loudly. She raced across the meadow but it was not exuberance that made her run. It was fear. She was being pursued across the field, her assailant concealed in the eerie darkness she raced against.

Bits of debris flew out behind her as her powerful hooves struck the earth. The beauty of the day was split in two by the darkness that pursued her. Daylight still shone in front of her and where she ran, but behind her the wicked darkness that flashed blue lightning swallowed the day as it passed. She ran and ran, but could not out distance the spooky storm that enveloped and hid the area it covered.

Fearing her own consumption by the greedy darkness, she ran even faster. From the day turned night a lasso was tossed by an unseen hand and Betty Jean woke up screaming just as the noose dropped from the air, fitting itself around her neck.

Byron was snatched awake and alert in an instant. He sat up pulling Betty Jean to the comfort and security of his broad chest and strong arms.

"More rope?" he asked with the thick sound of sleep in his throat. There was no humor in his question, no intended jibe. In fact, he found absolutely nothing humorous in Betty Jean's dreams at all. It seemed to him that she had them in association to their strengthening relationship and he didn't relish feeling like a noose around anybody's neck, especially not someone he really cared about. He felt that the dreams were induced by her subconscious fear of getting too close, too fast and ending up hurt again. He knew she tried to keep at least an arm's length distance between them so she wouldn't feel trapped, like she was getting too involved.

It felt like she tried to keep their relationship as anesthetic as possible. She didn't want to lose herself in him only to find out when it was too late, that he wasn't worth getting lost over. She was taking it slowly; inching forward to test the water. He understood that and wanted to give her time. As tonight proved, she was trying to overcome her doubts about him. He sighed inwardly, at least she could handle their relationship when she was awake.

He lay back in bed, pulling Betty Jean with him. She rested her head against his shoulder and sniffled. Byron pulled the sheet more securely around her shoulders, then pulled it back briefly to kiss her bare skin. He replaced the covers asking if she wanted to discuss the dream.

She shook her head and a rose petal fell loose, falling across her face and onto Byron who picked it up, smiling. "I didn't think we'd gotten all of these up," he said, squirming on the bed as though some were wedged in uncomfortable places on his body making Betty Jean smile.

"Thank you." She reached out a hand to touch the flat of his nipple. His chest was bare and hairless making the dusky colored nipples easy to see. She kissed the one nearest her, then it's twin, thinking them beautiful.

Byron laughed. "I've never had anyone thank me before, especially when it's me who should be paying homage. I mean, when you opened the door about to fall out of that gown," he stopped speaking and shook his head in appreciation.

She slapped his chest lightly with her hand and he caught it in his kissing it with a loud smacking noise. "I meant for the flowers, perv."

Byron stopped stroking her wrist. Raising a brow in question he tried to see her face and bumped her head from his shoulder. "What flowers?"

Rising up on her elbow, Betty Jean gave him a half smile. "The ones you sent that covered my entire office. The ones that were on the floor and on the desk and every where in between." She kissed him as she named the various locations. His face remained blank and Betty Jean sat up fully, holding the sheet to her chest. "The flowers that I got all these petals from."

"*All* of these?" Byron looked around incredulously.

"And some to give away! In fact, most of the flowers were distributed throughout the building at work. We figured it would be a nice surprise in the morning. Even Carol took some petals and flowers home. You didn't notice the vases of flowers in the living room when you came in?"

Byron gave her a long look. "You're kidding right? There could have been a giant pink elephant with purple hair riding a child's tricycle through the house when I got here and I still wouldn't have seen anything but you. I'm not certain, but I think your outfit was designed with just that intention."

Ordinarily his flattery would have made Betty Jean blush, but this time she stumbled past it asking in growing apprehension, "If it wasn't you, who sent me flowers?"

"I don't know, baby," Byron said seriously. Trying to lighten the mood, he pulled her towards him. "That's why you seduced me? You thought I sent you flowers?"

She resisted his urging to lie back and continued to sit up, hugging the sheet to her body. "Not just flowers Byron, but a flower shop or two. Literally. You should have seen the assortment of flowers. It was unbelievable."

"And you thought I'd sent them." He wished he had thought of it himself. "Was there a card?"

"*Just thinking of you* is all it said. Since we had plans for the evening, I just assumed they came from you. Maybe without our plans," she said shaking her head in growing confusion. "I would still have thought they came from you. Who else would send me flowers?" She was looking deep into Byron's eyes as though she could find the clues to the mystery there.

"Maybe someone you went out with is wanting another chance. Hell, maybe someone would like a first chance and is working up the nerve to ask you out," Byron suggested helpfully, not really caring for either scenario. He didn't want anyone else trying to get with Betty Jean.

"This is a little scary, Byron," Betty Jean admitted as she reclaimed her original position at his side. "I mean there are a lot of psychos out there. Your sweet gesture of emptying a couple of flower shops for me is incredibly romantic, while coming from some loon whose thinking creepy thoughts about me is—" She shrugged. At a loss to express what she felt and not really certain he'd understand anyway, she said simply, "Well, creepy." She snuggled closer to his security.

Byron's arms closed, circling around Betty Jean's lithe form. He hugged her close, kissing the top of her head. "Come on, Sweetie, it's not anything like that," he told her with firm conviction in his voice, but felt little of it in his heart. It unnerved him, too, that someone was sending his Queen Bee a flower shop worth of flowers. But he didn't let his worries show through when he teased, "He's wasting his time anyway."

Rolling over to cover her body with his own, he kissed her neck, throat, then temple. "I'm not going anywhere." He said the words looking into Betty Jean's brown eyes. Her hair was tousled and spread out across the pillows, framing her face in its vibrant shades of deep chestnut to honey brown. "I can see why a man would send you flowers." His lips were just inches above hers when he spoke. "Queen Bee." The endearment for her was a declaration just before he claimed her mouth.

When she reached up to put her arms around his neck, he pulled away breaking the kiss. He wanted to put on a condom now before he got too caught up in what he was doing and didn't feel like taking the time for precautions. Not that she'd let him get away with anything like that. He turned from her reaching for the packet on the nightstand thinking that Betty Jean would surely remind him even if he did get too caught up.

When he turned away a rose petal clung bravely to the center of his back before falling to the mattress to await his return. Its plans were thwarted when Betty Jean picked it up, rubbing its velvety softness between her fingers. She looked at it and some of the desire faded from her eyes. He had the foil pack between his teeth ready to tear it open, when he turned to face her. Betty Jean dropped the petal she held and reaching for the pack, she removed it from his teeth.

Remembering how she put the first one on for him, he smiled in anticipation, growing harder. He reached for Betty Jean and she pulled away, sitting up. "I want to get rid of these flowers, change my sheets and get all this crap out of my house."

The tent in the sheet at Byron's lap collapsed, slowly folding in on itself as he absorbed her words. "I'm sorry."

She knew her timing sucked. "I just saw the petal stick-ing to you and—" she raised her shoulders unable to explain further. Letting her shoulders fall back in place, she said, "I wanted to change the sheets."

Byron sat looking at her for a long moment, grudg-ingly understanding. He kissed her cheek. "We need to eat anyway." Climbing from the bed he stepped into his boxer shorts, glancing at his watch. It was near eleven. "Am I cooking or cleaning?" He pulled his white crew neck tee shirt over his head.

Betty Jean smiled, allowing herself to relax a little. She, too, stepped from the bed reaching for her discarded robe. It was see-through and offered little protection, but she intended to pick up where they left off and wanted to keep the fire stoked. "I'll clean." She imagined herself bending to pick up the petals scattered throughout the house.

Byron faced her raising a brow at her robe. It was obvious the same images came to his mind as well. "I hope it's a lot of flowers and petals scattered around out there."

A few hours later Byron stood uncertainly at the front door, gathering Betty Jean close. They never spent the night together. One of them would always go home. Another tactical ploy of Betty Jean's, but tonight he'd hoped she'd relent. It was a pissy thought, he knew, but he'd thought for sure she'd want him to stay out of fear, if nothing else, and he was a bit disappointed with her reassurance of being fine.

"Okay." He kissed her hand after lifting it from the broad expanse of his chest. "If you're sure you'll be all right."

Betty Jean nodded, smiling. "I feel better since we threw the flowers out."

His arms tightened around her waist, pulling her closer. "Is that all that made you feel better?" he asked, with his lips against her neck.

Betty Jean closed her eyes, enjoying the sensation his mouth was creating. "Mmm, that's nice." She reached up, stroking his head, neck and shoulders.

"You recall what else made you feel nice?" He sucked at the hollow in her throat with his tongue.

"Dinner was perfect," she teased, refusing to say what he wanted.

"Vixen." Byron bit her shoulder lightly. Opening the door, he stepped onto her porch. Betty Jean turned on the porch light and it flickered, going out. Byron kissed her goodnight, then instructed her to close the door and lock it. She usually watched him from the porch, but he wanted to be certain she was safely in the house tonight. He played it down, but he didn't like the mystery behind her flowers either. "Make sure you change that bulb tomorrow." He leaned in for a final kiss.

"I will. I have a pack of bulbs in the kitchen or the garage. Somewhere." She smiled. Already missing the warmth of his body, she hugged herself.

"Inside." He turned to go.

"Goodnight." Betty Jean waved, then closed the door. Byron stood on the porch waiting to hear the bolt turn in the lock. The rattle of the chain being pulled across told him it was safe to leave. Whispering an unheard goodnight in response to hers, he descended the steps of the porch and crossed the driveway to the waiting Suburban.

**

She folded her arms across her chest and sighed. Loud and heavy. Glancing at her watch, she sucked her teeth. It was almost two thirty in the damn morning. An approaching vehicle's headlights lit the interior of her car. Not bringing the person for whom she waited the vehicle kept going, passing her on the street and she glared at it. She'd been up for nearly twenty-four hours, but she'd be damned if she was going to sleep before she gave Cyron a piece of her mind.

Sheila stifled another yawn, frowning deeply. She was going to straighten a few things out with Mr. Cyron. He didn't own her and she wasn't trying to get caught up in no sentimental bullshit, either. She had no sob story of her own, but she'd seen too many intelligent women go down in flames behind *something real* they had with some man.

No, thank you, it was not for her. She kept it light and fun, she thought angrily as her eyes crept closed. She'd been doing it that way for a long time and saw no reason to change it now, just because Cyron wanted to be more than he was. Arrogant bastard.

Where the hell was he?!

She shook her head on the thought trying to clear it, as her eyes were forced open again. She pictured the cute, if unkempt, woman he was with at the restaurant and her eyes narrowed in consideration. Who the hell was *she*? He had his nerve. Trying to check her all in public and threaten her date when he had some teenager riding his coattail! Why was she hanging around Cyron? What had they been doing at the restaurant? Eating? They couldn't have been having a drink, not that child at least. She wasn't getting any if that's what she thought, Sheila added snidely, rolling her eyes out to the night, then smiled.

She sure wasn't! Whomever the hell she was, looking at Sheila with a face full of curiosity, she wasn't getting any of Cyron de Monbleau. Of that Sheila was certain and was truly appreciating his decision of celibacy. She drummed her fingers on the steering wheel in agitation. A celibate Cyron was still desirable, Sheila jealously thought as she drummed. A celibate Cyron was dangerous.

Cyron was probably trying to get into that woman's head right now!

She propped her arm against the door and cradled her head in her hand. Her eyes slid shut again. Her eye lids felt cool lowered against her tired, burning eyes and she let them rest that way for a moment. He needed to get home, so she could really tell him about himself. Out with strange women.

Mind whore, she accused as her eyes swam open, deliriously fighting sleep.

**

"Get in the damn car, Cyron!" Irritated as hell, Julie frowned at her brother. She knew going out with him would be a mistake. He was seething all through the movie he insisted he still wanted to see. She doubted if he could recall one single scene. Especially now. When he said he wanted a drink she should have went home instead of tagging along. Holding the door open, she ordered again, "Get in the car!"

"Did you see him, Jules? That boy?" His words were slurred slightly and she could smell the fumes wafting from him. She wrinkled her nose, waving a hand beneath it. He wondered why she advised him to dump this woman. Clearly, she wasn't any good for him. "Was he fully grown? Did you see him, Jules? Wasn't he kind of short?"

"Yes, I saw him, Cyron. Compared to you, lots of people are kind of short. He was okay. No hoop dreams, I'm sure, but okay. Are you going to get back in the car or not?" He'd insisted on driving pass Sheila's house on the way home and now refused to get back in the car, as it didn't appear she was home.

"Are you gonna go knock at the door for me?" he parried back, leaning heavily against the rear passenger door.

"No," she said through clenched teeth. She pushed up her glasses, glowering at the part of him she could see against her car. She took a deep breath, preparing to make him see reason. "It's past two in the morning, Cyron. It's pitch black out here! Not the middle of the afternoon. No!" She gripped the steering wheel of her BMW tightly. "Talk to her in the morning. Show up with donuts and coffee or something." She leaned across the passenger's seat to peer up at him. When he belched, the wind blew the odor into her car again. She screwed up her face, adding, "When you dry out."

"I'll do it myself." He lurched away from the car in drunken bravado. He seemed to stagger, even though he hadn't really moved yet and Julie leapt from the vehicle, hurrying to stop his procession up the driveway. Unsteady on his feet, he stumbled to his left and Julie took advantage of the moment, shoving him off balance. He landed in the passenger's seat hitting his head on the roof of the vehicle with an audible thuck. "Damn, Jules!" he protested her rough treatment, rubbing at the injured spot as she quickly slid his legs into the car, then slammed the door.

She was pleased when his head lulled against the headrest on his seat, quieting his complaints of abuse. Approaching Cyron's home, she slowed her car noticing the two door red Honda Accord parked at the curb in front of his house. Creeping slowly, she saw the woman from the restaurant asleep behind the wheel.

She shook her head continuing up the drive. She figured it would be easier to get him in the house from the garage than it would be from the front door, considering she'd have to escort him up the path to the door. She could just topple him into the house from the garage entry if need be and throw a blanket across him. At least he'd be in the house. She pressed the remote she'd removed from Cyron's Escalade and the garage door lifted silently.

Deciding she didn't feel like driving home and wanting to be there when the saints came marching into Cyron's skull in the morning, she pressed the remote again. The door lowered, concealing her car in the garage.

Briefly, she toyed with the idea of waking the sleeping woman. Sheila was it? Voting against additional drama for the night, she walked around to the passenger side of the car to assist a semi coherent Cyron.

**

He rolled to his side intending to lie flat on his back, then came to an abrupt stop. A demolition crew was waging war inside his head. Squeezing his eyes shut in protest to the affront on his senses, he half rolled, half collapsed onto his back.

Soft tingling laughter erupted and rang out in his head like the Bells of St. Mary and his eyes opened in wide shock before snapping shut against the light pouring in from the windows. An additional assault on his war ravished and pounding head.

Why the hell hadn't he closed the blinds last night, he wondered wincing at the amount of noise his brain made when he was thinking. The laughter rent the air again and he frowned, but didn't open his eyes again.

Who was in his house?

Sheila?

No. Sheila was somewhere with her date. Besides, he'd remember if he'd spent the night with Sheila.

He could feel every inch of the clothing that touched his body, so he knew his virtue was still in tack, but who the hell had he brought home? He frowned, trying to focus a mind that fought his prodding.

"I swear to God, Ayron, as drunk as a skunk!" he heard come from a room near by and identified his visitor as his sister, Julie. Again, he frowned. Why was she here so early? He brought his hands up using them to scrub at his face, but stopped immediately when stars exploded behind his closed lids. His hands had somehow been replaced with sand paper that sounded like sledge hammers pounding concrete when he touched his face.

More laughter rang out and he winced. Why was she being so loud?

"You should have seen me trying to get that ox out of my car. It was nearly as hard as getting him into it. I started to leave him lying on the garage floor, but I thought about carbon monoxide poisoning and changed my mind. I would have felt bad if something happened to him."

When she began to recount their trip to Sheila's house, Cyron knew he'd better get up before she told Ayron all of his business. He could swear the two of them gossiped more about him and Byron than they did about everybody else they knew put together.

Julie laughed again, causing St. Mary's Bells to dong loudly in Cyron's head and he groaned. Sitting up he held his head in his sand paper hands for a moment then stood carefully, trying to find balance on the deck of his rolling house. Steadying himself, he stretched out a hand for support. He needed to find Jules before she could tell it all. *If* there was any part of his dignity left to save, he grumbled sourly. The way his head felt, Ayron probably knew more about his actions of last night than he did. He had a scratchy void where last nights memories should be.

"That isn't the good part, yet, either, Ay," she said on a breathless giggle. "Sheila was—" she began, but was interrupted when Cyron jerked his phone from her hand.

"Jules has to go now, Ayron. She was just leaving." Cyron replaced her ear with his own, walking from the room to talk to his brother.

"I don't care." She was loud, causing Cyron to glare over his shoulder at her as he retreated to his bedroom. She slid her feet into her mule styled tennis shoes and picked up her car keys. "See you later, Cy. Love you!" She heard a mumbled reply before letting herself out.

Damn, she wanted a front row seat when the woman finally confronted Cyron. She knew she should have waited before calling Ayron. She pursed her lips at the lost opportunity and waited for the garage door to open. As she waited an idea came to mind and she smiled, resembling the mischievous little girl from the picture Betty Jean had seen.

Quietly, she rolled out the driveway and pulled up along side Sheila's car. She smiled at Sheila's sleeping head, then blew her horn rapidly three times. Startled awake, Sheila jumped, bumping her knee against the steering wheel.

Bewildered, she stared around for a moment, trying to get her bearings when she noticed Julie's smiling face in the vehicle along side hers. Sheila frowned deeply at the woman's smug look. What the hell was she doing leaving Cyron's house? Why was she even at his home? Sheila's frown intensified and her mouth became a thin line as they looked at one another.

Up close, Sheila could see that the woman was indeed a woman. She had a young face and her unfortunate choice of blue jeans and a tee shirt only helped subtract years from her general appearance, but she wasn't as young as Sheila had thought when seeing her in the restaurant. Did her fake youthful look attract Cyron to her? Why had this woman spent the night with Cyron? Sheila continued to frown as her questions about the woman multiplied along with her curiosity.

Damn, she couldn't believe she'd fallen asleep outside of his house. While he'd had another woman inside it! Instead of confronting him, she felt like she'd been caught hiding in his bushes or something. Or worse, caught sleeping in her car, she supplied irritably as the woman pounded her horn again. Sheila raised a brow in question of the other woman's behavior and the sardonic smile grew, as she pointed behind Sheila towards the porch where Cyron was just opening the door.

She lowered the window on the silver BMW 745i. She was still smiling cheerily. "I didn't want you to leave without getting a chance to say hello!" Sheila could hear the bitch saying snidely through the Honda window she'd made no move to lower.

She should get out and kick her ass.

Sheila was contemplating just how funny Miss Smiley-Happy would find that. Obviously suspecting danger, the woman waved, then drove off. Sheila considered starting her engine and doing the same thing, but didn't want to look like a coward. She'd come to say her peace and she was going to get it said. Collecting her keys and purse, she climbed from her car and walked to the porch to join a scowling Cyron at the front door.

"Let me call you back, Ayron." He turned from the door, leaving Sheila to follow or not at her discretion.

Chapter Twelve

Not a serious bird watcher, Betty Jean had no idea which species of fowl it was that chirped from the deck railing outside her bedroom window. As she watched, another bird joined it on the ledge. They chirped along companionably for a moment as though catching up on old times before the second bird took flight and was air borne, leaving the first bird alone again.

The bird's head darted around in confusion a few times as though surprised by his friend's departure and Betty Jean sighed. "Sucks, hun?" she asked to her feathered companion. It was her idea to usher Byron out the door every night or insist on leaving his house, but she always woke up feeling a lit bit lonely on the weekends.

The rush of the weekday morning gone, she became really aware of the silence in her house. And really aware of being aware of it and it pissed her off as it was doing now. Part of the reason she didn't get too close to Byron was because she knew she was weak. There was a time when she was strong and felt comfortable in the quiet of her own head, but now she only felt loneliness and the fear of always being that way lurking in the still of a moment. She feared the silence and didn't want to get wrapped up in Byron as a means of drowning it out.

The silence demanded to know if she was ready for a relationship. Ready to put herself out there again to be hurt. Would Byron hurt her like Zeke had or would he come with his own brand of pain and heartache? Would she give and give and it never be enough? Did she even have anything left to give anyone? Would she hurt *him*?

Yes, the silence requested reflection and reflection sought answers she wasn't sure she had and knew she wasn't ready for, even if she did. She knew there would come a time when she had to stand in the silence, face the hard stuff and not be afraid. It was a point that everyone had to reach, but she wasn't ready, yet. The peace she sought when she first came to California still eluded her and she couldn't stand the demands of silence without first finding peace within herself.

After showering and dressing in loose shorts and a printed tee shirt, Betty Jean decided to purchase a bird feeder for her yard and collected her things to leave the house. She picked up the phone to ask Byron or Sheila to come along and maybe make a day out of it, but she returned the phone to it's cradle deciding against it.

She was going to venture into silence today.

Just her and herself picking out a bird feeder or two. She wasn't going to hunt for peace, but if it happened to find her and wanted to spend a little time with her today, she'd welcome it gladly. Arming herself with her weaknesses and hoping that the Powers That Be might allow peace to hang out with her for a few hours, she walked out the door.

**

The Powers That Be had their hands full trying to keep the peace over at Cyron's house.

"Who the hell do you think you are threatening my date likc that?" Sheila roared before Cyron disconnected the call, giving Ayron a rare treat of hearing unfolding drama amongst one of his brothers first hand.

"Don't yell at me in my own house!" Cyron shouted, ignoring the thundering in his head. "You stop by here on your way home?" he asked, seeing that she still wore the multicolored dress and tall boots from the previous night.

"I ought to slap your face." Sheila put her hands on her hips huffing. "Some little scamp just drove away from your house after having spent the night and you accuse me? Mr. I-Want-To-Get-To-Know-A-Woman First."

"Scamp? Who the hell—" He stopped. Had he brought someone home after all? Jules was evil enough to let him get that drunk, too. But then he recalled that he had on all his clothes when he woke up on his bed. Even if someone had been there with him, they hadn't done anything.

"I know you aren't going to defend her because I called her a scamp?" Sheila glared at him in shocked challenge and Cyron asked who in guilty confusion. "I know damn well you know who I'm talking about. The woman from the restaurant last night. The one you left with. The one who just drove away from your house looking like she not only had the cat's meow but enjoyed, it, too. Damnit that's who!" Sheila stared at Cyron with her hand on her hip barely registering that this was not what she was supposed to be angry over.

She was supposed to be reading him the riot act over last night's presumptions and threats. She was not his for him to come barging into her dates and making scenes. And what had he said to her in French, anyway?

She'd rehearsed her speech on treasuring her independence and was supposed to be laying down the law according to Sheila Cooper's way of life. A way of life that did not include getting emotionally involved with people and placing her heart and sanity on the line. But damn what she came to talk about last night, the woman with the young face was what she wanted to talk about this morning and realizing the shift in her priorities only made her angrier. Here she was caught up in bullshit and drama!

"What the fuck is going on, Cyron? The last thing I need is to be dreaming about becoming a horse!"

He frowned at her irrationality, trying to figure out her recent interest or distaste, he couldn't figure which, for all things equine! He said, honestly, "The only person here when I woke up was my sister, Julie—"

"Your sis—"

"I had one or two drinks last night, but I doubt if I brought anybody home. You seem kind of adamant about it though." He hunched his shoulders to clear his drink shrouded mind. He continued not having heard Sheila's attempted question or seeming to notice her frown. "I went to the restaurant with Julie, too." He stopped there frowning in recollection. "It was *you*," he pointed an accusatory finger at Sheila's chest, "who was out of line. You're worried about who was over here, where the hell did you sleep last night? I know you weren't home. Were you with Armani boy at his parents house? Who the hell is he, anyway? Where were you?"

"She's your sister?" Sheila asked, losing some of her own thunder.

"Even if she is," he said evasively, "that wasn't your brother you were with." He lowered his voice to stop the sledge hammers from pounding in his head.

"Wait." Sheila held up her two hands, gesturing for a stop. She closed her eyes, shaking her head before opening them again. She pointed her long finger with it's square tipped, burgundy painted nail at Cyron. "We are not talking about me. We're trying to clarify the identity of your companion."

He raised a brow before turning from her. "Really?" He headed towards the kitchen talking over his shoulder as he went. "Why don't we clarify the identity of *your* companion. Identify the person who you were company for last night."

"What?" She frowned, not liking what she thought was being implied. She followed closely on Cyron's heels. So close, in fact, he nearly ran her over when he swung to face her again.

"That made sense, but fine, I'll clarify my question. What's up with you, Leggs?"

Shoved off the road of attack, Sheila's defense was less aggressive. "What?" Her eyes dropped to his shirt front, but with great effort she raised them to his face, meeting his eyes. She folded her arms in front of her and glared her displeasure, rolling her eyes in exaggeration. "Nothings up with me. Should something be up with me?"

"You tell me. We have a good time, then you push me away. You come back. We chill, then you run from me. For every two good days you give me, I'll have to eat shit for four."

Her eyes widened then narrowed at his language and tone. "Why are you bothering with me then, Cyron? If I'm giving you the run around and making you eat shit?"

"Because I happen to think the time we spend together is worth eating shit to get." He almost smiled, but it fell a little short. "Look, Sheila, I know I'm a little older than you are and—" He stopped when she raised her eyebrow, questioning his dubious choice of words and he frowned. "Yes, only a little bit older. How many birthdays do you have left with a two in front of *it*? I thought so," he said when her brow cleared, but she remained silent. "What I'm saying is, I know what's out there, Sheila. Games and bullshit and I should know because I spent a lot of time out there creating it back in the day. In my youth, hell, up until about a year ago, I didn't care too much about anything or anyone besides myself. In the process I lost a few good women. It was good. It was an eye opener. I lost enough of them in my life to recognize them early. You're a good woman, Leggs."

"I know that," she snapped. "I don't need confirmation. I don't *need* any of this."

"Any of what?" he asked, taken aback.

"Any of this, *let me take care of you* crap. This, *lets be more to one another* crap. *Let's be in love and spend every second of every minute together, so we never forget how truly special the other person is* crap. Come here." She beckoned to Cyron sarcastically. "Let me look in your eyes and see if I see forever."

He ignored her last comment. "I never said I wanted to spend every second of every minute together and I sure as hell never said I was in love with you."

Sheila switched to the offensive at his words. "What's wrong with being in love with me?"

"Other than the fact that you clearly aren't ready for me, yet?"

"*Aren't ready for—*" she repeated his words, choking on her anger. Shoving past him, she marched back the way they came and Cyron called behind her.

"See? That's what I mean. Not ready, yet. Still running marathons. Still distancing yourself from anything real. Who hurt you, Sheila?" His last question was a taunt and Sheila whirled around to face him flinging her purse that was sliding down her arm to the sofa as she passed the living room hall. It landed with a bounce from the force of the throw, then hit the floor with its contents spilling out.

"Understand something, Cyron. I don't get hurt. There's no sad and touching story behind my aloof manner. No battered, scarred heart scared of reaching out. I've got no wounds to lick and I like it that way. So fuck you. I don't need *this*." She encompassed their entire situation with a sweep of her hand. "I don't want to get to know anybody and I could really do without anyone trying to get to know me. That shit is always a hassle. I've seen so many people go down in a hail of bullets trying to love someone. It's not worth it. Emotional bullshit. Dragging your heart along to every relationship. Hell, having to even have a relationship! Nothing deeper or more meaningful than sex is worth the bother. It's not even that important."

"And since I'm not going to have sex with you, I'm not important at all. My company, my heart, my feelings, my life, me... I'm not important."

She felt low and her head hung slightly. "I didn't say that." She couldn't say that. It would be a lie. His feelings, his heart, his life....those were all the things she wanted to come to know and understand about him. Stubbornly, she swallowed the words. Let Cyron think what he wanted if it would get all this emotional, lovey, dovey mess out of his head.

"So, Armani's important because you can have something physical with him?"

"I damn sure didn't say that."

"Trouble in paradise already?" She didn't say anything and he sighed. "What the hell are you saying, Sheila? I'm confused as hell and you aren't helping it any!"

"This isn't about having sex or not having it. It's about me and what I want." She hunched her shoulders. "Or don't want."

"You don't want me?"

"I didn't sa—" she began.

"Don't say it, Sheila. I'm serious, if you say, *I didn't say that* again....Look—" Cyron tried to calm down when he realized he was nearly shouting again. "Maybe we're just in two different places in our lives right now. I've done all my playing around and trying to stay brief and elusive and unattached. I want more than that now, more than the bullshit that's out there. I want something more than a woman's legs wrapped around me and that seems to be all you're interested in or capable of giving. What else is there to you other than that hole?"

At his words, Sheila turned and walked over to the couch in the living room. Stooping she picked up her lipstick, wallet and the loose coins that had fallen from her purse. Shoving them back in, she made to rise.

Cyron watched her wishing he could stop her from leaving, wishing he knew what to say, but he was angry and still slightly hung over, if not a little bit drunk and being charmingly persuasive was beyond his realm of simple abilities.

"You going to go tell him you came by to defend his honor?" Apparently being an ass wasn't. Ignoring him, Sheila scooped the last of her belongings into her purse and stood. Placing the strap on her shoulder she headed for the door. Crossing the room rapidly to reach the door before she did, Cyron turned the knob pulling it open.

"Yes, run, run. Be free little birdie!" He swished his hand back and forth as if fanning smoke through the door and out of the house.

Ass. She passed him.

She wanted to point out that birds didn't run, they flew. If he was going to be a smart ass he could at least get his metaphors correct, but she had nothing else to say to him.

Stupid ass. She walked down the driveway with slow dignity.

Her head was held high and her nose was in the air when Cyron slammed the front door.

Ass. She was silently seething.

**

Betty Jean sat in the middle of her living room floor reading the How To instructions on assembling her bird feeder. She'd purchased two. One for the front yard and one for way in the farthest corner of the back yard. She wanted the far corner of the yard that she could see from her bedroom window. That way she could see the birds in the morning, without being chirped awake by them.

The house was quiet. Betty Jean was surrounded by the silence of her home and was okay with the thoughts in her head. No conversations to hold, no television playing or radio blasting. Nothing, but the noise of her own thoughts and she was rather enjoying the solitude. She hadn't picked up the phone to call anyone. She didn't need to break away from her worries and concerns. In truth, there weren't any to hide from at the moment.

On the way to purchase her bird feeder she sung along with the radio, humming when she didn't know the words or couldn't hit the note with the song's artist. She took her time walking through the store selecting her feeders. She was calm and unhurried and enjoying it mightily. The thought struck her as she read section B of the instructions and she smiled a little in realization. She hadn't felt so liberated in years.

Humming, she tapped her foot to an unheard beat trying to decide what color to paint the birdhouse styled feeder. Maybe later her anxieties and fears would come out and torment her, but for now with sunlight pouring through her living room windows and a tune in her heart, she was content and in the presence of peace.

**

It had been three hours since Sheila left Cyron's house and she was still pissed off. Music blared from the Kenwood speakers surrounding her living room, but it didn't help to improve her mood. Changing into her running shorts and tennis shoes, she snapped off the stereo by remote, grabbing her keys.

She was going to the park and run. She was going to lose the anger she was feeling on the track before she broke somebody's neck. She recognized the irony between her choice of stress reliever and Cyron's parting words. *Run, run,* she mimicked, making a face.

Ass. She closed the front door with unnecessary force.

Chapter Thirteen

Byron followed Cyron into the kitchen. Stopping at the bar, he straddled a stool. "So, why didn't you get Jules to take you to your truck before she left?"

Cyron reached into the refrigerator extracting two bottles of Heineken. "I threw her out before I realized I needed a ride." Removing the top he passed one to Byron who took it swallowing.

Lowering the bottle, he asked, "And Sheila?"

"Look, if Julie already called you with the details, say so and stop playing around. I'm not really in the mood for that shit right now." He'd gone back to sleep for a while after slamming the door behind Sheila. The repair work that was being done by the crew in his head was completed and the pounding had stopped, but his mood had not improved.

"I'm not worried about your moods little brother, so there's no point in biting my head off," Byron said smiling. "Hey, remember that time the old man turned the hose on us out in the backyard when you, me and Ayron were going at it?" He asked, changing the subject as the memory came to mind.

"Yeah, I remember," Cyron said, rubbing at his stubbled jaw. "Funny, I can't remember what the hell we were wailing on one another for, though."

Byron chuckled a little. "Me either. All I remember is two of us were going at it and the other one was trying to break it up, then he got hit and all hell broke loose." His smile grew. "I guess the old man was right about that, too. *You'll beat each other black and blue over something ridiculous that you won't even be able to recall when you look back on this stupid shit.*" He imitated his father's deeper voice.

Cyron laughed, too, taking a swallow of his beer. "When did you ever know Brandon to be wrong about something?" They both sat in appreciative silence for a moment, thinking of their father. "We need to go for a visit some time. It's been too damned long since we were all together. Everybody. The whole family."

"Mom and dad haven't stopped traveling in two years. *They* need to come for a visit. Seems they've been gone since dad retired."

Cyron hunched his shoulders. "Hell, that was the game plan remember? Every time mom wanted to go do something and dad couldn't spare the time to get away, he'd say, *that's just another stop to add to our retirement tour.*"

Byron laughed, remembering. "He'd say it like they were some rock band or something. *Their retirement tour,*" he repeated chuckling.

"I guess he meant it though."

"You think he really had a mental list of all the places mom wanted to see?"

"Hell, it looks like it. Where haven't they been in the last couple of years?"

"Here," Byron said, lifting the beer to his lips and drinking.

They were quiet for a moment thinking of the parents they loved and missed.

"Anyway, man." Byron shook his head, ridding himself of the sudden melancholic mood. "I only asked about Sheila because I would have chose my girl to spend a little time with, not my brother."

"Sheila's my girl?"

"She's not?" Byron was surprised. The way the two of them had been glued together lately, he was caught off guard by the skepticism he heard in Cyron's voice.

"Even if she was, she probably isn't after this morning."

"What happened this morning?" Byron asked, with his eyebrows raised.

Cyron took a small sip of his drink before answering. It was after two in the afternoon and he knew he needed some food more than he needed the Heineken he was drinking, but he sipped again. "I threw her out, too. Right after Jules hit the sidewalk, I hefted out another." He smiled a little, saying, "I'm piling 'em up at the curb, looks like."

Byron laughed, seeing Cyron's grin. "So, today's just your day to boot women out of your house or what?"

"Hell, I don't know man. No, wait, yes I do." He pointed at Byron, narrowing his right eye to a slit. "Jules was giggling with Ayron—"

"Oh." Byron smiled, nodding his head in understanding. He'd been the topic of Jules and Ayron's lovefest plenty of times himself.

"Sheila was just driving me crazy," he said on a suppressed belch.

"Is she coming back?" Byron asked, because he knew what she meant to Cyron.

"Don't know." Cyron hunched his shoulders. "Don't know if I want her to, either."

"Is that right?" Byron asked rhetorically. Cyron said nothing else and Byron knew the subject was closed, at least for the moment, so he changed the subject away from Sheila. "Where's your truck?"

"I'm thinking it's at the Chicken Shack." Cyron ducked his head sheepishly.

"You think?"

"Last night is a long story, By. Call Jules, she knows where it is." Cyron left the kitchen, heading back down the hall.

Five minutes later, Byron walked into Cyron's room where he found him sitting on the side of the bed lacing up his tennis shoes. Pulling the phone from his ear, he said, "Jules wants to know why you didn't get ole girl in the Honda to give you a lift."

Cyron frowned up at him and Byron grinned. "She said if you don't answer her question, she won't answer yours. You can find your truck on your own."

Cyron raised his voice to be heard by his sister. "I could always just go look for it. It can't be in too many places."

"She said go ahead and see if you can find it and don't waste time going to the Chicken Shack."

"I sent Sheila back to the man she spent last night with," Cyron gritted out angry. Bryon's eyes widened over the unexpected tid bit of information, but he remained quiet. "Now get out of my damn business and tell me where my truck is," Cyron hollered, irritated.

A few seconds later, Byron hung up the phone. "She said you're an ass and that Sheila spent the night at your house last night."

"My house? How? Where was she? When was she here?" Cyron demanded mad at his sister. He just finished saying he didn't feel like playing and here she went.

Byron hunched his shoulders against the tide of angry questions. "Don't know. She hung up," he said leaving the room with Cyron behind him.

"So, where's my truck?"

In front of him, Byron smiled. "At the Chicken Shack."

**

It was nearly seven o'clock before Betty Jean heard from Byron.

"Hey, beautiful," he said into the phone making her smile.

"Hey, handsome," she teased in response.

"What are you doing?"

"Finishing my class project for the day."

"Class project, hun?"

"Yeah, I bought a couple of bird feeders for my yard this morning and I've been assembling them."

"Look at my, Queen Bee." She could hear the pride in his voice and she blushed.

"Are you teasing me?" She still wasn't familiar enough with him to always know when he was joking with her or not.

"I can't be proud of you without teasing?"

"Yes, I suppose so." Betty Jean smiled shyly at his chastising.

"Are you going to come over and put one out in my yard?"

"You are teasing me!" She laughed, narrowing her eyes in accusation.

"I'm not," Byron said laughing. "I really do want you to put a bird feeder in my yard. Why can't I want to look at the birds, too? Feed 'em a little seed to help them out in the lean months."

Betty Jean laughed. "The lean months, Byron?"

"Mmm, hmm," he said, enjoying the sound of her laughter. "Do you have any plans for tonight?"

"Not really. I might run by Block Buster Video or something," Betty Jean replied, lying flat on the carpet. She'd been hunched over her task most of the day and her back ached a little. She propped her legs up on the couch cushions and smiled at the surprising comfort of the position. No wonder Sheila was always hanging from the couch like a giant possum. "What time are you going to work tonight?"

"Actually, I'm already on my way in. Fennel called in sick, so I'm bartending till two."

"What exactly do you do at Rufio's? Last weekend you worked the line, a couple of weeks before that you were at the door and register, tonight it's the bar."

"I told you. I work all of Rufio's positions. I can even DJ as well as Diamond the guy whose getting paid to play the sounds," he bragged.

"So, no set position for you. You work wherever they need you at the moment?"

"Yes, ma'am, that's the deal. Wherever I'm needed that night, I shall be," he said as evasive as ever regarding his role at Rufio's. He was sure Betty Jean wasn't after his money by now, but he still wanted to hold off on telling her.

He wanted to be just Byron for a while longer.

His ownership of the club usually led to questions that only led to more questions. Eventually, he'd be on a path he didn't like to tread. Opening a spot like Rufio's took a substantial amount of funds. Through various endeavors, he and Cyron had come up with the bulk of the money to open their respective spots, but DMB Shipping, his grandfather's company that Ayron now ran, had helped a bit. Ayron was the only one of the four de Monbleau children to ever feel at home behind the confines of a desk. Even Jules preferred her talk show to the helm of one of the largest shipping companies in the country.

The de Monbleaus could literally use money for toilet paper and still die wealthy, but the siblings each lived off the money they earned independently of the company and each of them earned a pretty good living, but DMB had been at the root of their success. Even if only round about, but Byron liked to be as low key as possible. He'd grown up in a house where his father believed that each man was responsible for himself. What the family had was unimportant, it was what each person was individually that mattered.

The wealth of his family's holdings was incredible, but that wasn't Byron. Byron was an ex-model who hoarded his earnings until he could open the type of night club he wanted. He was still a de Monbleau. He loved his family and was extremely proud of them, but he didn't go around trumpeting their history and assets.

He had Rufio's and the club was doing better than ever. Even his second club, R2, that he was able to open without aid from his family, was holding it's own in Los Angeles. He opened it's doors six months ago and had been running back and forth between the two cities, holding it's hand whenever necessary.

He was sure he'd tell Betty Jean about all of this one day, but his confession wouldn't come tonight. Turning into the club's crowded parking lot a valet ran out to meet him. "I'm going to talk to you later, Queen. I've got to get inside."

"Okay, that's fine," she said and was talking to dead air.

She continued lying on her back for a few minutes longer before sitting up to complete her feeder. Afterwards, she'd go get a movie then come back and fix herself something to eat. Her stomach rumbled protesting it's place in line and she pressed a hand to it, changing her plans.

She'd go get a movie, pick up something to eat on the way home, come back and maybe finish her bird feeder. If not, she'd have something to do tomorrow. Either way, she was going to get something to eat.

Maybe a slice of cheesecake from the deli, too, she thought as she stood stretching the knots from her back.

**

Sheila sat in the middle of her bed staring moodily at the television set. She ran over six miles, but it hadn't done anything for her disposition. She was nearly certain nothing would work to improve it until she crunched a hole through Cyron's neck. Who the hell did he think he was saying she wasn't ready for him yet, like she was a piece of fruit? The ripe fruit picker person?! She said aloud, then folded her arms across her chest, the very picture of adolescent outrage.

And then, too, what was that mess he said about her wrapping her legs around someone? Oh, yeah, she nodded as she latched on to the memory. *That seems to be all you're capable of doing.* And that shit about her hole! Crass, is what he was. A crass ass, she mumbled enjoying the sound of it.

And she was not nearly his age! Wasn't he almost thirty five or something like that? She was barely twenty seven. Or eight, she fumed, even lying to herself. Either way, she hadn't seen thirty yet and he was trying to make them the same age.

Sheila looked at the phone. She wanted to call Betty Jean, but she didn't want to inflict her bad mood on anyone else. Then she figured Betty Jean would welcome the chance to help her rake Cyron over the coals. She dialed her number, but hung up when the machine picked up.

**

Cyron sat at the bar nursing a bottle of mineral water. Tonight's poet was a young man who'd been on stage a few times before and he was pretty good, but Cyron didn't hear a word he was saying. He was busy trying to push Sheila from his mind and she was stubbornly refusing to go.

**

He sat outside in his little rented car, three houses down and watched her when she left. He smiled at the way her hair danced in her face with the evening breeze. She had pretty hair. He'd been thinking about her hair when he sent her the flowers. He imagined them now all over her house and he felt good. Everywhere she looked, she'd see his flowers and think of him, just as he always thought of her.

Chapter Fourteen

In no rush to answer the knock at her door, Sheila took her time drying her wet hands on a dishtowel before crossing to the front entry hall. Another knock sounded, followed by the doorbell and she sighed, unlocking the door.

He smiled when the door swung open, but it froze on his face when he saw the look on hers. "Sheila, I—"

"You're what?" she prodded, raising an eyebrow. "Already making me regret agreeing to see you?"

The victim of a strong willed single mother, he ducked his head embarrassed like he always was when a woman confronted him and stared him down. "I just wanted to say I was sorry, that's all. I had no right to get angry and say the things I said to you the other night."

Sheila stood in the doorway staring at him. Almost reluctantly, she stepped aside allowing him entrance. She wanted to tell him he had ten seconds of her time, but decided against it. She would not be a total bitch. She'd give him a sincere opportunity to make amends. Opening with, "You're over an hour late," probably wasn't the least aggressive thing she could have said, but she shrugged mentally in nonchalance. Apparently she wasn't in the mood for bullshit and falsities.

"Yeah, after the way I'd acted I didn't know what to say," he admitted. "I'd used up all my nerve calling you. I fully anticipated you hanging up in my face when

I called. Heck, it took a week for me to accept I was even wrong. I've never treated a woman, so abruptly. My mother would be gravely disappointed."

Softening a little, Sheila conceded that what he'd done hadn't been all that bad and if she wanted to be really charitable, she'd confess that she was just as much to blame as he was. She'd been ugly last Friday night, as well, letting her mouth get away from her as usual.

The fact of the matter was, she did like him. At least a little and she would enjoy seeing him again. She'd been glad when he called the day before saying he wanted to come by and talk. When he slammed his car door on her in a huff that night after telling her off, she was sure he was a lost cause and all her chances were gone. She hadn't given a rat's ass at the time, but then he called.

Tired of her week long snit and hungry for a change of attitude, she agreed to let him stop over. Maybe by mending a fence or two, she'd feel better. Like her old self.

"I just met you. I was out of line to try and demand something out of you. Your business is your business."

"You could know me a thousand years and still be out of line to demand something of me," she shot back instantly. Since he already seemed to know the rules regarding her business she didn't mention it and wouldn't as long as he understood exactly what he'd just said. Her business was just that, *her business.*

"Maybe," he hunched his shoulders, "but then, too, maybe you got mad because you don't know what you're doing or what you want." He'd spoken calmly, but she could detect the underlying anger coursing through his words. "Just like a lot of you city women."

"So, this is how you apologize?"

"Actually, the more I think on it, *Ms. Cooper,* the less I think I have to apologize for. I mean really, what the hell did I do? I merely reacted to an uncomfortable situation—"

"By making it worse," she cut in, fed up with playing nice. "I have no control over the actions of a loon, okay?" she said venting her anger. "Instead of recognizing that what do you do, but blame me? Like I asked him to come over to our table and embarrass you like that. If you think he was out of line with you, you should have said something when he was still standing there. Then you have the audacity, the gall," she said, releasing her full temper, "to tell me to find someone else to play games with, along with a few other choice words and just drive away. You left me standing there with not so much as a kiss my butt, Cyron and if you think you can just walk in here and—"

"Who?" he interrupted, frowning.

"Who what?" Sheila's stared at him with eyes blazing, unaware of what she said during her misplaced rage.

"What's my name, Sheila?"

"Why?" Suspicious of the request, she narrowed her eyes. Folding her arms across her chest, she refused the request. "I know your name."

"Then why did you just call me, Cyron? Who's Cyron, the hulking behemoth from the restaurant?" Sheila remained mute and the man before her shook his head. "You're right, this last name stuff is ridiculously complicated, isn't it? Look, I'm sorry for losing my temper and for storming off last week, that's all I wanted to say. And I'm really sorry for slamming my car door in your face and not escorting you home properly. That was out of character for me and I apologize again."

She shrugged. "I had my own car." He looked at her for a moment saying nothing, then shook his head again. He turned to leave and Sheila reached out a hand to stop him. "Come on, Michael," she began, but he shook his head at her words.

"People are always talking about men who don't know what they want. Men who have game. I've heard that shit all my life. Men this, men that, but it's a whole lot of you women out here fucked up in the head, too. I haven't met one sane female since arriving in California. Not one that wasn't full of shit and playing games." He left out the door, closing it behind him.

**

"Are you feeling like company tonight, baby?" There was a slight pause as she considered the work spread out before her. Her desk at home had nearly as much paperwork covering its surface as the desk at her office. Misinterpreting her hesitation, he asked if something was wrong. "I mean, I know I've been really busy with work lately and a lot of women can't handle my schedule too well, but I want you to be able to talk to me, Queen. If you need more of me than I've been giving, let me know. Don't back away from me silently, only opening your mouth when you say goodbye."

"Okay, whoa!" Betty Jean removed her glasses, rubbing her nose where they rested while she worked on her computer. "You sound like you need a few sessions on a couch," she said teasing. "Been given up on one too many times, Byron?"

Ignoring her attempt to lighten the mood and put him at ease, he remained serious. "Once or twice I've had to choose between what I was trying to accomplish; the life I wanted to live and a woman who I was interested in. I've done enough with myself now to prove I'm my own man and not just my father's son, so I can sit back a little bit if I really had to."

Betty Jean was speechless over his unexpected oratory which was just as well because Byron wasn't finished speaking. He'd only paused briefly to collect more of his thoughts and catch his breath. "I have a destination in mind of where I'm going with my life and the kind of woman I want by my side when I finally get there. True, I lost out on a few women that I could have made something happen with, but there's only been the one that I'd regret losing and that's you. I watched the others leave without a backwards glance or tingle of anything other than the hunch of my shoulders. A few had been important to me, but none were important enough to make me slow down. But if I need to give you more time and attention, let me know. Talk to me, okay?

"I won't come to a complete stop right now, not for anybody, because, like I said, I have a destination to reach and a time line to do it in and I can't apologize for that. Hell, I *won't* apologize for it, but I'm willing to go on cruise control for a little while to keep you interested and at my side. Hello?" he asked, when a few minutes passed in silence.

Her voice was soft. "I'm still here."

Thinking of the circumstances surrounding their meeting and what a fool he thought her ex was for not being in tune with her and seeing to her needs, Byron urged gently, "Talk to me, Queen. What's up with you?"

"Nothing, Byron. Honestly. I've just been up to my neck in alligators lately. And taking a little me time," she added, truthfully. "This is really the first time I've been truly alone in years and it's taking some getting use to. I've been in California for almost a year, but Sheila's been here with me. Before that Ezekiel and I lived together for six years. It's been a while since it's been just me and after what I tolerated these last few years, I need to get to know me again. I haven't had to listen to the silence in my head or in my own house. I've just been sitting listening to it lately; listening to me, trying to get accustomed to it all again. That's all. I've just been looking for Betty Jean," she ended simply.

"One of those searches you have to mount alone, hun?" He wished he could go along to help. But he understood the search for one's self and knew there was nothing he could do, but be tolerant and wait it out. Basically, the same thing he'd needed from the women he'd just been telling her about. "Am I out of luck on seeing your pretty face tonight?" he asked, steering the conversation back around to it's original position.

"I would love to pass an evening with you, my lord," she said adopting a thick English accent that made him laugh.

"Good. I've got the perfect thing to help you relax."

"What?" Her eyes narrowed.

"What time do you get off work?"

"I'm at home, nut. Didn't you just call my house?"

"Like that matters. It's after seven and you're still busy. You work longer hours than I do most days, but I was referring to the work you're doing right now. What time are you calling it quits?"

Betty Jean looked around her cluttered office. "Can you pick up a pizza on the way here? I'm starving."

"I'm on my way, Extra Cheese and Onions," he said calling her by her usual requested toppings. He knew she liked her pizza with a thick crust and everything in the place on it with extra cheese and onions covering the whole mess. He liked his pizza to properly clog the arteries, as well, but it was nice meeting a woman who wasn't afraid to enjoy food for a change. He knew a lot of stick thin women who wanted to be even stickier. He liked that Betty Jean liked eating.

"Don't forget some cokes. I'm out."

"Will do." He paused on a thought. "Or does that mean I will forget? Okay, will not do or whichever is the correct response. Call the order in and I'll pick it up on my way, that'll be quicker. We can't have you over there starving."

"More like, we can't have you at the pizza place, pacing and growing impatient."

"Either way, as long as we're both happy." He laughed because there had been some truth in her comment.

A few seconds later, Betty Jean hung up the phone laughing, too. She liked that about Byron. He could almost always make her smile. She left her office pulling her tee shirt over her head, intent on showering before Byron arrived.

Stepping into the glass shower, she adjusted the water adding more heat until it steamed, fogging the glass. She thought of Byron and smiled again. A woman could always take care of her damned self. It was nice to have a man who wanted to do it, but it could be done without one. Just like any man could take care of any woman. But to find one that could make you laugh when nothing was funny or make you see pretty blue skies when the blackest clouds hung overhead with more rolling in... now that was something.

She'd take giggling under the covers with a poor man that made her happy over sleeping down the hall from a rich man she hated, any day. But all of that would come in time, she thought lathering soap on her thigh. For now, she needed to work on Betty Jean and be able to maintain her bliss alone or in a crowded room. She stopped suddenly, wondering if she'd inadvertently stumbled across the truth during her musings.

Was Byron poor?

Well, not *poor,* she amended but could he be a paycheck to paycheck type guy? Was that why he never gave her a serious answer when she asked about his work? Was Rufio's just barely paying the bills? She'd seen his house, but that meant nothing. She knew a lot of people who lived above their means and struggled everyday because of it. Could that be why he always seemed to be at Rufio's? People who didn't make that much money and spent freely had to work extra hard just to make ends meet.

She continued thinking as she bathed and her mind went from one wild notion to the next. Was that why the other women left him? Because of his financial situation? That was sad. He was still a good person. If they couldn't appreciate Byron the person, without seeing his financial bottom line their own finances must not have been all that great. For herself, Betty Jean earned a six figure salary. She could afford to be with a poor man that could make her laugh. She paid her own bills.

What happened to his earnings from when he modeled? Had he been like so many others unaccustomed to wealth and spent it all? Betty Jean shook her head at the senseless waste. Finishing her shower, she stepped from the cubicle patting the water from her skin with a soft towel. Reaching for a bottle of baby oil, she rubbed it in still thinking, then she shook her head again.

She could not worry about someone else right now. She was the work in progress at the moment. Byron would just have to wait his turn.

**

He was contemplating going over and knocking on the door when the big Suburban swung into the drive. For the second time in a week, he watched the unknown man climb down from the SUV and head towards the porch. Tonight he carried a pizza box in one hand and another box was tucked under his arm. Squinting in the darkness and the distance, he couldn't make out what the second box contained.

In irritation he started his car, revving the engine unnecessarily before peeling off.

"What was that?" Betty Jean stood on tiptoe trying to see around Byron's broad shoulders. They watched in unison as the little car turned the corner. It was leaning dangerously close to being on two wheels as it turned.

"Whomever it is, is going to tip over driving like that." Byron kissed her quickly in greeting.

"Tip over? Was that an SUV?" Looking innocent, she fought back a smile.

"Very funny." Swatting her on the behind, he entered the house.

"What cha got in the box, Pops?" She took the pizza from him, but was referring to the box he still held under his arm.

Byron smiled hugely, giving nothing away. "You'll see."

**

"Where are you, Betty Jean?" Sheila asked aloud as the phone went unanswered.

Betty Jean giggled again. "I have to answer the phone."

"No, you don't." Laughing, he flicked the arm on the arrow again causing it to spin madly.

"The phone!" Betty Jean giggled trying to catch her breath between pants. "My arm—"

"Stop whining," he ordered playfully. "Left hand yellow."

"I can't!" Laughing, she stretched out her hand.

The phone rang shrilly in the background of their entangled limbs, desperately pleading for attention.

Sheila sighed, wanting to hang up the phone, but wanting Betty Jean to answer more. She hung on hoping at least for the answering machine.

Collapsing on top of Byron while trying to reach a green circle, Betty Jean laughed pushing her hair from her face. Before Byron could stop her, she grabbed the phone from the coffee table.

"Hello." This was said on a giggle as Byron's hand circled her ankle.

"Hello?" Sheila said in breathless joy. She was home! She was home! She was home! Her mind sang happily.

"Hello? Stop it!" Betty Jean laughed. "I'm trying to answer the phone." Byron continued to playfully manipulate her leg and she shrieked, dropping the phone.

She was home and she was occupied. Sheila's joy faded as she hung up the line. Betty Jean wasn't going to be a sounding board or distraction for her tonight.

Inspiration struck and Sheila picked up the phone again dialing by memory the number of a favored pick me up. This phone rang also, but Sheila wasn't distressed. When the baritone voice came on the line asking her to leave a message at the beep, she did.

"Give me a call when you get this message. I'm thinking about heading south for the weekend, baby." She used her sexiest voice for the message.

She hung up, hugging the phone to her chest. She'd go spend a little time in her old stomping ground and wouldn't know Cyron from Byron come Monday!

Chapter Fifteen

"Good morning!" Light hearted, Betty Jean breezed past Sheila's desk Friday morning.

"Better for some of us." Sheila eyed Betty Jean speculatively. "Is your car outside?" She asked as Betty Jean entered her office.

"Yes. Why?" Betty Jean poked her head back out the door. "Washing and waxing, like a true assistant? Like Peter Fillerman's assistant?" Betty Jean smiled when Sheila narrowed her eyes at the mention of Mr. Fillerman's over zealous assistant.

"You know that man is more squire than anything else. I'm thinking about giving him a new desk nameplate for Christmas with the necessary adjustments made, but I wasn't talking about him anyway. I was wondering if you drove your car in or just floated to work." Sheila turned back to her file cabinet. "Now I see you merely rode in on your broom."

Betty Jean laughed a little enjoying the daily battle of wits they played. "Remember on the Electric Company when they'd do the Adventures of Letterman skit?"

Sheila looked at Betty Jean frowning slightly, from both the memory search and the unexpected left field question. "Yeah," she answered cautiously. Suddenly her face lit and a huge smile spread across her features as she recalled in full detail. "Yeah, I remember," she said getting excited about the childhood recollection. She used to race home to watch The Electric

Company on PBS, preferring it to Sesame Street. She never did like that bird.

"Girl, yes." She put her hand on her hip wondering vaguely what brought the show to mind for Betty Jean. "The bad guy would steal or change a letter out of a word to make it say something different and Letter Man would have to figure out which letter was changed to fix the word and make it right!" Triumphantly, she smiled. The kid in her was all excited and ready to watch the show. Had Betty Jean bought some of the shows on DVD? Lord knows they were putting every other show under the sun on disk. "What made you think of that? It's on DVD?" Sheila asked still smiling.

Betty Jean's smile grew. "I don't know if it's on DVD. I'd have to check for you. I was only thinking of it because you implied that I was a witch a moment ago. I replaced the W with another letter and wondered if Letter Man would get here in time to stop me from saying it to you." She closed the door quickly on Sheila's reply, certain her assistant was about to rotate a few letters of her own.

She pushed away from the door laughing. She'd never gotten one up on Sheila before. It felt good. She didn't dance over her small victory, but she did shake her booty a little on the way to her desk.

"Don't be in there dancing jigs and shit," Sheila's voice advised from the intercom just as Betty Jean was sitting down at her desk. Looking at the phone, she smiled and turned on her computer.

**

It was another rotten day.

He'd been trying to balance his books all day, but he'd done it four times so far and had come up with four different figures. He'd had to go to the liquor store because his order didn't arrive. The store clerk tried to convince him he hadn't made an order that week, but that was absurd. How the hell could he run a night spot with no alcohol? And on a Friday night, too!

Some of the poetry at the Chicken Shack tended to be really deep and thought provoking and some of it was just depressing as hell. Deep thinking and depression made people want to drink booze and he didn't have any. But fine, it was *his* fault.

When he tried to put the change from the bank in the club's safe he succeeded in nearly slamming his hand in the safe's door. He'd snatched it back, but not completely in time and he still managed to give it a hit that resulted in a trip to the emergency room.

Now he was half stretched out across his living room couch, chewing on painkillers. The last two fingers on his left hand were in splints. Dr. Too Damned Young, who tended his injuries, insisted that his fingers weren't broken, but Cyron had his doubts. What did someone wearing braces know? *He* knew his fingers hurt like hell. Just like they were broken.

He frowned at the muted television and flipped channels with the remote. There was a knock at the door and his head swiveled towards it. Curling his lip, he turned his head away as the knock came again. A few moments later the lock turned in the door and he cursed. Too many people had keys to his house. He was going to have to demand the keys back or change his locks.

"Cyron?" He heard her call softly from the door, but remained silent. Maybe she'd go away. "Cyron, are you in here?" The living room light came on and he sighed. No chance she was going away now that she found him. "Why are you sitting in the dark? What happened to your hand?" She crossed the room to stand over him, waiting for an answer.

"Because it's my fucking house and I smashed it in the safe," he growled, answering both questions at once with his right arm slung across his face to shield it from the lamp's sudden glare.

"I know you are not cursing at me Cyron Anthony de Monbleau," she said primly.

"Jules, go home and leave me the hell alone." Grumbling, he waited for his pain pills to kick in. Taking the lid off the prescription bottle he still held in his right hand, he popped another pill into his mouth.

"Is your hand hurting you a lot?" Jules ventured with concern, seeing his grimace.

"That one wasn't for the pain in my hand. The pain has moved a little lower." He stared directly at her and she got the feeling she knew how low it had gone and whom he was referring to.

"Why are you so cantankerous lately? Is it because of Flawless But Crazy?" The name she'd given Sheila.

"Seriously, Jules, do you have a reason for being here?" His face was covered again as he tried to dismiss her.

"I called the shack and they said you had an accident and left. I wanted to see if you were okay—"

"Why? So you'd know what to tell Ayron?"

She continued on as though he hadn't spoken. "And you weren't answering your cell phone—"

"I turned it off, not wanting to be bothered by anybody," he cut in again, hinting. He was still belligerent but his words lost their heat when they started to slow and slur from the medication he'd taken.

Again she ignored him, finishing her statement. "So, I decided to pop in and see if you needed anything."

"Other than for you to go away?" It had been over an hour since he'd taken his first two pills and the effects were becoming obvious as Jules stood watching him drift away.

"I'm going big brother." She looked down on him. His arm was still across his face, but his eyes were closed and his lips were slightly parted. Handsome devil, she smiled, removing the pill bottle from his lax grasp.

She retrieved a blanket from the closet and laid it across him, shaking her head. Whoever she was, Flawless But Crazy was sure running her brother ragged. She adjusted the blanket, so that his injured hand was free of cover, picked up the remote and turned off the television set.

Lifting Cyron's arm from his face, she softly kissed his cheek. He moved in his sleep a bit and she was straightening away. "I love you, Sheila."

Her glasses slid down her nose a bit and her eyes opened wide, as her hand flew to her mouth in surprise at the revelation. Cyron was in love with Sheila! Both their parents had lectured them all on love, the rights, the wrongs, the dos and the don'ts. Love was not a toy and the words didn't come lightly. If Cyron was saying he loved Sheila, in his sleep and drugged up no less, then he meant it. Cyron was in love with Flawless But Crazy, Sheila!

Wait until she told Ayron!

Julie sprinted from the living room to the guest bedroom. She was spending the night!

She couldn't wait for Cyron to wake up, so she could grill him!

She couldn't wait to talk to Ayron! Cyron was in love!

Throwing her purse in a chair, she landed across the bed on a dive, reaching for the phone on the nightstand.

**

"Do you know where we are?" Carol raised her voice a little to be heard as Betty Jean nodded, giving her car keys to the valet. "They aren't going to let me in here! Have you seen me? Cute as a button and about as round. Not exactly height and weight proportionate. Only tiny waists and cute little butts like yours, get through those doors. And not even then if you're a troll."

"You aren't a troll." Betty Jean bounced and snapped her fingers to the music on her way to the door.

"Honey, I never said I was." Carol laughed, noticing that they weren't going to the end of the line, but were walking to the front of it. She also noticed the ugly looks they were getting and she slowed her pace a fraction. She looked good in her outfit and wanted to give the crowd a chance to see her. She was a plus size girl who blossomed into a plus size woman and all kidding aside, she liked her body and was comfortable in it.

"Hey, Grimace." Betty Jean smiled and hugged the burly guard in the deep purple tee shirt.

"Brown Sugar Baby, how you doing?" He returned her friendly greeting, happy to see her.

"Fine now!" she flirted. "This is my friend, Carol. We came to party with you guys tonight!"

"That's all right, then." Nodding his head, he smiled at Carol. "You looking good, Blue." Carol's eyes matched the color of her outfit perfectly. He held out his hand for hers and she shook it smiling, also.

"That's exactly the effect I was going for, *Cowboy*," she replied, detecting what was left of a southern twang. "Blue on blue."

The big man was suddenly all teeth as he nodded his head, pleased that she noticed his accent. "That's all right then." Obviously, his favorite phrase. He was looking at Carol, intrigued. "Left Alabama a long time ago."

"Not completely." She smiled. "You can take the boy out the country and all that..."

"If we're all finished noticing one another, we're going to go inside now." Betty Jean was still bouncing to the music, ready to get on the dance floor.

"Don't be mad, baby girl, 'cause you might not be the hottest thing in the joint tonight." He was speaking to Betty Jean, but was still looking at Carol with interest.

"Good! I need a break!" Betty Jean laughed and grabbed Carol's arm to pull her along.

They were seated at a RESERVED booth and a waitress took their drink orders. A few minutes later they were sipping Amaretto Sours and checking out the scenery.

"Damn, this drink is strong," Carol said, smiling. "I love a bartender with a generous hand. All right, spill it!" She turned to Betty Jean, her eyes twinkling with mischief.

"Spill what?" Betty Jean asked slightly distracted as she searched the crowd. Then her face cleared and she smiled.

"Who'd you have to sleep with to get us the VIP treatment!" Just then Carol's attention was turned when a tall, handsome man who looked better suited for a football field than a bar, approached the table. And she was glad she'd cleaned up the wording of her question, because by the smile on his beautiful lips, she was certain he'd heard what she asked.

"Good evening, ladies. I hope everything is fine. Are you enjoying yourselves?"

"We only just arrived, but so far everything's fine." Betty Jean sipped her drink.

"It's my first time here. It's great!" Carol chimed in, moving to the music that blared from the speakers surrounding the club.

"Well, we hope it won't be your last." He smiled fully at Carol and she thought she'd swallow her tongue, he was so gorgeous. And the way he wore his clothes...he looked so good he was dangerous. Did she say he looked like a football player? Maybe it was the muscle she couldn't help but notice, but up close, his face was worthy of a camera. Gorgeous, didn't do him justice at all. She couldn't wait until she got home tonight. Paul was going to get it, she thought smiling.

Someone motioned to the divine creature and he turned to go, excusing himself. Carol was just thanking her lucky stars he hadn't heard her comments to Betty Jean when the man bent and kissed Betty Jean on the lips. It was sweet, but quick and he pulled away. "I have to go. I just wanted to be certain you were being treated like a VIP." He turned and winked at Carol letting her know he had indeed heard her comment.

"That scrumptious piece of juicy is Byron?" Carol put a hand to her chest, watching him as he faded into the crowd. "How do you get up and come to work every morning?" She was still looking into the crowd even though he was gone from sight. "Where have I seen that face? He was hot, but I had this de ja vu type reaction going on, too."

"No telling," Betty Jean shrugged. "He's been to the office once or twice to pick me up for lunch and he used to model, so it could have been anywhere."

"*He used to model,*" Carol imitated Betty Jean's nonchalance. "And now I'm riding his dick. His gorgeous penis. Scrumpchie, Umpchie, Deliunchie, he's so good looking." Carol shuddered like a chill had gone through her. "How can you stand it?"

Betty Jean shrugged, smiling. "Paul is cute."

Carol nodded, agreeing. She sipped her drink. "Yes, Paul is cute, but Paul isn't *that*." She pointed into the vicinity of Byron's disappearance. "*That* is just simply ridiculous. Why should anyone be allowed to look like that and walk amongst us mere mortals?"

Betty Jean waved her away. "Once you've had someone fart on you in his sleep, the glow dims a little, you know?"

Paul came to mind and Carol laughed. "For real! He's only human after all, hun?" They both laughed enjoying their night out.

"Dancing or only in your seat?" a man asked at Carol's elbow and she looked up surprised. She hadn't seen his approach and was slightly startled by his presence.

"Watch my drink." Carol slid her glass closer to Betty Jean and was out of the booth following a trail to the dance floor.

"Designated drink watcher for the night or can you dance a little, too?" A rather young looking man asked Betty Jean a few moments later and she smiled, rising from her seat. They could order fresh drinks when they returned to the table. She took his hand in hers and led him onto the dance floor where she kept him dancing for over an hour.

**

"What's the deal? Why are you still on the West Coast?"

"You never answered my call. I wasn't going to just pop up on you."

"Woman, get your sexy ass to the airport. Your flight is leaving in less than an hour. I booked it online for you. Let's go! Let's get hot! We're wasting time talking!" he said full of pep, into the phone.

Sheila smiled. See? She didn't need Cyron's shit! Some people knew how to live in the moment and have fun. Spencer didn't want anything from her, but a good time. Nothing deep and consuming or scary, she added frowning, shaking Cyron from her head. "I have to pack some things."

"Fuck that. Anything you don't bring, we'll buy. Don't miss that flight Sheila!"

"I'm calling a cab now." She sat up, tossing the bag of chips she was eating aside.

"Move it, Sexy. I'll see you in a little bit."

She hung up the phone smiling. She was going to kick it with Spencer for the weekend, shout at a few old friends and have a glorious time in her old town without nary a thought of Cyron entering her head. She couldn't remember the last time she thought about him anyway. Yes, it was going to be a glorious weekend!

Chapter Sixteen

The weekend sucked.

The only thing saving it from being a complete catastrophe was the fact that she hadn't spent any of her money on the damn tickets that had flown her in and out of Hell. She hadn't lost money on top of everything else. If she never again saw the so called *Third Coast*, it would still be too damned soon!

What the hell was going on with all the men in her life? Honestly, was there something in the water she should know about? Maybe the city, both cities, needed to check into it. Hell, the whole world should check their water supply. It could be a growing epidemic of dementia running loose and amuck!

He was surprised she'd called from out of the blue. What was wrong? She didn't seem herself. She could talk to him. She could come home to him. Home. Since when was Spencer home? Spencer was great sex. Spencer was a used to be. He wasn't her future, just a pleasant distraction to her present sometimes or at least he had been. She didn't know what the hell had happened to him. He'd changed since the last time she'd seen him. He recanted his casual acceptance of their relationship.

He started reminding her that she was the one who broke it off with him back in the day. That he never stopped caring for her. He just knew she needed some time and he took it as a sign that the time had come when she called. He was on her nerves so bad by mid Saturday, she called one of her girls and spent the rest of the weekend at her place, catching up on old times and new news.

**

Cyron fared no better over his weekend. It started out early Saturday morning when he woke to a splitting headache, a throbbing hand, a mouth as dry as the desert sands and that same pain in the butt to which he'd fallen asleep singing in his kitchen.

"Did you lose your house? Have you been foreclosed upon?" he asked, leaning in the doorway. "Do you need me to front you some cash? Is that why you keep hanging around me? Jules, I'll buy you a house if you just leave me alone and go back to yours. If you still have one."

"You'll buy me a house, if I go back to my own house? Is that a crack on my cute little brownstone? If not it doesn't make sense." She rambled on as she scrambled. "I don't need a lot of space, it's just me. And you and Byron have more than enough space for me when I need to move around a little." He made a noise in his throat and she shot him a look over her shoulder. "Does Sheila know you wake up surly?" She slid eggs from the skillet onto two plates.

"Damn." Cyron grumbled obscenities walking over to the table. He raised one long leg across the back of his chair and sat down with his elbows on the table and his head in his hands. His injured fingers stuck out against the side of his head. "We aren't going to start the morning off like this, are we? I don't want to talk about Sheila. I haven't even had breakfast, yet."

Placing a platter of bacon and beef sausage on the table, she raised an eyebrow over his bent head. *He hadn't had breakfast, yet*. If it hadn't been for her, there wouldn't be any breakfast. He was whining, so she ignored him. "Why not if you love her?"

"What?" Cyron lifted his head, pinning Julie with a look.

"Heads up." Quickly he moved his elbows out of the way and she set a plate before him. Continuing the discussion, she said, "You heard me."

"I didn't understand you."

"I understood you. Loud and clear."

"Stop talking in riddles and say whatever the hell it is you have to say," Cyron snapped.

Julie handed him a glass of orange juice and two pain pills. "Here. Take these. Pain must be why you keep biting my head off. So, go ahead and take them before I forget my good intentions and curse your ass out." She said all of this smiling sweetly and Cyron took the pills from her hand.

Scooping eggs and grits into his mouth Cyron glared at his sister. A few minutes went by before he asked, "What makes you think I'm in love with Sheila?"

Julie hunched her shoulders, biting into her toast. "Besides the fact that you've been a jerk since seeing her with someone else?"

Cyron raised a brow in warning. "Yes, other than that."

She chewed slowly and Cyron frowned, impatient for her to swallow and continue her explanation. She continued to chew and his frown deepened. Her bite of toast hadn't been that damned big. With the tip of his finger he pushed her orange juice glass closer to her hand.

Jules smiled, finally swallowing her toast unassisted. "You told me so last night." She succeeded this statement with a huge mouth of food.

Cyron stared at her agog. "I said what? *When? When* did I say I was in love with Sheila Cooper? *When!* Was I under medication at the time? Not those little pansy pain killers that don't work, either, but real medication?! I'd have to be insane to—"

"Stop shouting at me!" Julie swallowed, forcing down her eggs. "You know what? I'm leaving. I stay the night to see if my brother will need me in the morning, seeing that he's all hurt and injured and what do I get for my sacrifice? Nothing! *Nothing*! I tell you."

"An award for acting?" Cyron asked, indicating her dramatic performance. Jules was up from the table in a flash, exiting the kitchen. Cyron was right behind her. "I'm sorry, I'm sorry, I'm sorry," he chanted catching up with her just past the kitchen entry. "I'm sorry, Jules. My hand hurts," he lied, and she smiled, knowing it. He tried to look pitiful, like he was in pain. He grabbed his left hand and held it lightly in his right.

"Why is it so complicated, Cy?" She bit into her toast when she was once again seated before her breakfast. "You love her, then love her." She shrugged. "Why are you tripping?"

"Why am I tripping? This from *run, run, run*?"

"That was before you said you love her." She waved her hand in dismissal. "Different rules apply. There's the before you fall in love rules and the too late, you've done it now rules."

"Okay." He chewed thoughtfully. "The difference, in condensed form please."

"Well, it's like...not in love? Good. Cut your losses before it's too late and you make a fool of yourself. In love already? Oh, well, in for a penny, in for a pound. You might as well throw caution to the wind and go all out because it's a given that you will make a fool of yourself."

"I was in the first boat, now I've got an oar in the second?"

"Exactly. I knew you'd get it. Except for the oar part. There's no oars when you're up Shit's Creek." He laughed and she smiled, swallowing orange juice. "Now you have to do the in for the penny, in for a pound part and tell Ms. Thing how you feel about her."

"Not going to happen."

"What! You're not going to tell her?"

"Nope." Cyron continued to eat. "She made her choice. You saw her. I don't have time for that kind of mess. That woman should have been wearing track shoes instead of boots the other night. She's running full speed away from me."

"Stop her then."

"How? You saw her, Jules! She was out with another man. Some insignificant little nothing in an Armani shirt. Pretentious ass pimple—"

She frowned over her plate. "That's nasty, Cyron."

"Anyway, she made her choice."

"Did she tell you she wanted that other guy?"

"She didn't have to tell me anything. I saw it!" His voice rose, he was getting angry again. "I don't care what I feel for her. I can squelch it down. She made her choice when she went home with Armani, then had the effrontery to come over to my damn house still wearing the same old dirty dress and defend him. And question me! She wanted to wave it under my nose and be sure I knew why she hadn't been home that night. They're welcomed to one another."

"When did she go home with him?" Julie folded her arms across her chest, not willing to let the matter drop.

"Hell, that same night, Jules. I guess. When she got here the next morning she still had on that shit from the restaurant, didn't she? That's not like Sheila. She loves clothes too much to be in the same thing two days in a row. She just stopped by here to rub my face in it, that's all and let me know what she thought of me."

"Probably so, but she didn't get here Saturday morning. When we got here from staking out her place, she was already here." Julie tried to rise and clear the table of their used dishes, but Cyron grabbed her arm, staying her hand.

"What do you mean, she was already here?" He was looking at her intently. Man, if Jules was pulling his leg.

"When I drove up, she was already parked in front of your house. She was asleep in her car. That red Honda. I guess she was conducting her own little stake out and ending up crashing out instead. By the time, I got your drunk ass in the house, I'd forgotten about her. When you threw me out the next morning, she was still asleep in her car. I was nice enough to wake her for you."

"Which is why you kept blowing your horn," Cyron concluded, sitting back and putting two and two together.

"Ding, ding, ding, ding, ding! And the prize for Slowest To Catch On goes to...drum roll, please." She pretended to open an envelope.

"Yeah, very funny." Cyron rubbed a hand down his face. "She slept out in her car. In front of my house." He was in disbelief. "That's why she was still in those clothes."

"Yep and if her sleeping in her car doesn't say something about the way she really feels about you, I don't know what does. I mean, I don't know why exactly she was asleep in front of your house, but come on... that's not indicative of a person who doesn't care. Even if she only stayed to curse you out...because I know I would have, but still...it shows you mean something to her, right?"

"I talked about her for coming straight from dude's house to mine." He stared down at his plate, barely hearing his sister.

"You're an ass," she said explaining his actions. Hunching her shoulders, she added, "It's forgivable," as an after thought.

He looked at her as though just remembering she was there. "Get out." Getting up from his chair, he hurried down the hallway to his bedroom.

"See? You're an ass!" Jules called smiling as she reaffirmed her previous opinion. She piled the dishes from the table into the sink and wiped off the counters. She would clean up completely, but her brother told her to leave his house and being the obedient sister she was, she would grant his wish. He could clean up the mess himself later. Smiling still, she let herself out.

Cyron dialed the first of many unanswered calls to Sheila. He'd even gone by her house a couple of times, but it was pretty obvious that she wasn't there. Her house had that empty, nobody's home look.

He stood on her porch late Sunday afternoon wondering where she was.

**

"Did you enjoy your trip?" Betty Jean asked over lunch.

"Don't get me started, girl." Sheila rolled her eyes. "The best part of it was my visit with Max, one of my old girlfriends. And even that wasn't too hot. She bitched her way through the whole weekend." Betty Jean raised her eyebrows, encouraging Sheila to speak more. She shrugged. "She's tripping right now. Nothing too major, I guess. Just being Max. Her cousin joined the military sometime last year and apparently, Max and cousin's baby's mama, don't get along too well."

"This had her bitching all weekend? Why?"

Again, Sheila lifted her shoulders. "I think it was little Ebony's birthday or something. It was either this past weekend or the one coming. Or the one before I got there. Hell, I don't know. I only know she had a birthday and Baby's Mama wouldn't bring her by so Max could see her or something to that effect. As Max is close to her cousin, she was kind of close to his kid, so she had her all the time. She's a real little cutie, too. I met her a few times with Max." Sheila hunched her shoulders, dismissing it all as trivial.

Betty Jean agreed. "So, what's so drama filled and major about that? She'll just have to wait until her cousin—"

"Thomas," Sheila supplied.

"She'll just have to wait until Thomas goes home on leave or something."

"That's a problem, too. Thomas has not been home since enlisting. Max is sure he's just avoiding his little girl's mother. According to Max ole girl is a real piece of work whomever she is."

Betty Jean shook her head. "I can't say I'm all over-come with sympathy. That's why people should be very careful about who they choose to have children with. Now two people who can't stand one another are stuck together with a child or at least the girl is stuck, since you said he's gone and hasn't been back."

"I'm not too certain what the relationship between mother and father is. I guess it wasn't too bad, be-cause like I said, until he went into the service he had his little girl all the time. Max would watch her some-times if he had something to do, that's how I've seen the little girl before. I think the conflict is between her mother and Thomas's family. I don't think they like her too much."

"Well, I wouldn't want people who didn't like me around my child either. Especially, without the father being around. No telling what they could be saying to that child about her mother."

"Anyway, Max is trying to think up a scheme to bust her little Ebony Doll out of bondage. I told her to let it ride until her cousin gets back, but it's looking pretty heated. She wanted to go over to the woman's house this weekend, but I talked her out of it. I don't even know what I said to her, but I changed her mind, at least for a little while. Which was my only goal. Save it until after I'm gone. I'm not getting caught up in that bullshit. I have enough of my own already." Sheila shook her head, swallowing more of her coke. "I know

Max, though. She's going to do something pretty soon. Probably something really stupid, too and old girl is going to have to cut her."

Betty Jean raised an eyebrow. "Cut her? You are really tripping. Where's the dialect coming from?"

Sheila smiled, crunching into her taco. She ate, saying, "Girl, it's coming from being hold up with my ghetto hoochie friend, Maxim. She's always talking about having to cut someone. I doubt if she even owns a knife or knows how to use one on anything other than a steak, though."

"How does she plan to liberate her little cousin?" Betty Jean was curious.

Sheila waved the question off, but answered anyway. "She was talking about going up to the day care center and picking her up. She used to do it all the time, so they know her up there. It shouldn't be too hard to walk in, get the little girl and walk out. I mean, Ebony knows her, so there shouldn't be anything too suspect about it."

"That's bad business there." Betty Jean shook her head. "Sounds suspiciously close to abduction by relative."

"I think she just wants to hang out with her, but would take her home afterwards." Sheila shrugged again. "*I think.*"

"So, your weekend consisted of espionage and secret plots to abduct minors?"

"Hell, yes! It looks that way, doesn't it?" Sheila smiled, liking the image of herself as Jane Bond. She sipped her coke again. "But when the reporters contact me, I plan to look into the cameras and say, I told her to leave that little girl alone!" Betty Jean laughed at Sheila's assumed deadpan expression. "Shit, I can't go to jail. I'll have to sing like a damned canary. I'm too cute to keep from being Big Wilma's bitch."

"Not to mention the jail clothes. You'd either be in orange or stripes all the time," Betty Jean added helpfully, still munching.

Sheila froze with her hand halfway to her mouth. "Not even playing, okay? We never joke about such things. Me, wear the same thing over and over again, blending in with everyone else? Oh, hell, no! I'd rather be Big Wilma's bitch!"

They laughed in unison, continuing their lunch.
**

When she pulled up to her house after work, Cyron's big, black Cadillac Escalade EXT was blocking her drive way. He was seated on the truck's tailgate and she sat in her car staring at him. Cyron smiled and she considered driving away. She smiled, too and her intentions must have shown in her face because he shook his head at her. Rising from his seat, he walked towards her. Sexy as hell in his dark blue jeans.

Squatting down by her car door in the middle of the street, he peered in through the tinted glass. When she only sat there, he tapped at the window. Sheila lowered it and his smile grew. "How are you doing, Leggs?"

"Better if I could get into the driveway I paid for. Could you move your truck?"

"I would," he said squinting at her, "but then you'd park inside the garage and lock yourself in your house before I could stop you."

"That's probably true." Sheila looked over at her driveway. "What do you want Cyron?" She didn't feel like playing around. He ignored her after making her leave his house. What else could he possibly have left to say? Did he want to tell her again how she only knew how to wrap her legs around a man? Spencer came to mind and she pushed the thought aside, blushing.

Cyron could kiss her ass. She wasn't embarrassed about liking sex. Anybody who didn't simply hadn't had it done right. She wasn't suffering from that problem and wasn't ready to push away from the table just because he had his hand up, saying *none for me, thanks.* His problem, was not her problem and it wasn't going to be either.

"Get out the car."

"Excuse me?"

"Get out of the vehicle." Each word was spoken separately and carefully.

"Why?" She was already getting angry.

Cyron opened the car door and reached across her, releasing her seat belt. "Please."

Sheila stood from her car, sighing in annoyance and Cyron pulled her into his arms. She was hauled up close, his hands were in her hair and he was kissing her like Sweet Jesus, she didn't know what!

Never in her life had any man kissed her like that. Sheila felt so weak and woozy when he finally let her go, she thought she was going to be sick. Don't ask how she got her car into the garage of her house, because she couldn't tell you.

All Sheila knew was that Cyron's kisses made her weak and clouded her mind and he kept her feeling light headed for most of the evening.

**

"Hello."

"Advise me."

"What?"

"Advise me. I don't know what to do."

She laughed into the phone. "Have you been following my track record, closely? Did you not read my story, girl? I had to write a book about it! Are you sure you want advice from me?"

"Stop playing. I need counseling. An emergency session is in order."

"Okay." She sobered up. "What's going on?"

"No, no. The phone won't do it. I might cry a little and I'll need support. I'm stopping to pick up ice cream, but I'm already in route."

Half an hour later, Betty Jean answered the urgent knocking at her front door. She looked out the peephole then cursed. The light was still out on her porch. She couldn't see a thing.

"Betty Jean?" The knocking came again and she opened the door. "You were going to leave me out on the porch?" Sheila came into the house. "I saw you look out the peephole."

"You could see that?"

"Yes," Sheila said, shrugging. "The little lit circle goes dark for a second when your head's blocking the light. Anyway, I don't see how you can see anything as dark as your porch is."

"I can't," Betty Jean confessed, retrieving two spoons from the kitchen. Walking into the living room, she gave one to Sheila who was stretched out on the couch, having removed her sandals.

"Rocky Road, hun?" Betty Jean questioned, reading the label on Sheila's pint of ice cream.

"Girl, if you knew the half of it," she said, removing the lid. "I got Peaches and Cream for you."

Betty Jean looked at the container, frowning. "Why?" She looked suspiciously at the container and knew she was correct when Sheila smiled slyly.

"You've been looking good lately, that's all," Sheila replied, a little too innocently to be believed.

Betty Jean raised a brow to let Sheila know what she thought of her innocent act and picked up the pint of ice cream. Folding her feet beneath her, she sat Indian style on the carpet. She'd removed her lid, licked it, then took a large spoon of the dessert. She put the spoon in her mouth and Sheila added, "While I'm on the Rocky Road to Hell, your life is Peaches and Cream."

"What!" Betty Jean exclaimed laughing at Sheila's woeful expression. "You rarely require a session. I always have some problem to hammer out and get over. We should switch containers!"

"You've been doing good lately, BJ. I'm serious about that part. Look! You're out of your robe and everything. You were just a little down and needed a kick in the butt."

"Really?"

"Don't sound like that, it's true. Or I can say you needed something else and you've been getting that, too, from the way Byron is always over here. Either way, it's all good."

"I just needed time to heal, that's all. I still do. I was with Ezekiel for almost seven years. It's going to take a minute to completely shake him off," she said into her ice cream. *Was* she taking too long to get over Zeke? She couldn't lie. Every now and then, he'd sneak into her mind and set up shop before she knew what he was about. One second she'd be light and free, then in the next some song they used to dance to would come on the radio and she'd be right back in his arms, smelling his cologne. Chained to him again. She was stronger now than she had been in a long time, but there were still a few chinks in her armor.

"Oh, Sweetie, no." Sheila shook her head, bracing up on one elbow. "I'm just being a snotty bitch, acting jealous and snide. My own situation is just getting so raggedy. I'm sorry. I wasn't trying to hurt your feelings."

"It's okay," Betty Jean said quietly, as Sheila tripped all over herself trying to apologize.

"No, it's not. I'm sorry. I know your own stroll is far from peaches and cream—"

"I wouldn't say *far from.*"

"And I didn't have to say what I said. I know you've been struggling a lot with everything you've been through and it's been a tough year."

"Yes, it has," Betty Jean said, scooping up ice cream, "but I'm coming through it. I can finally see a light at the end of the tunnel. I don't know how far away it is, but I can see it at least and that's better than last year."

"Amen," Sheila agreed, relaxing back on the couch. "Now if we could just get *my* little light to shine."

"Meaning what?"

"Meaning Cyron was at my house when I got home tonight. We—"

"Really? I thought you guys were kaput."

"We were. We are. We—"

"Didn't he throw you out?"

"Are you going to let me talk, counselor?"

"I'm sorry," Betty Jean laughed, sucking on her spoon. "Please continue." Sheila hesitated and Betty Jean assured her. "Go ahead," she coaxed, nodding.

"You don't have to enjoy this, *this much*, you know?"

"I'm sorry," Betty Jean repeated, putting another spoon of ice cream in her mouth and trying not to smile as she did it.

"Spencer wanted us to try again. He kept harping on it and that's why I left his place. I went there to get away from the whirlwind of crazy that Cyron was making me feel and ended up in a new kind of wonderland."

"I thought you and Spencer were never a couple, *Alice*."

"You didn't ask if we were ever a couple. You asked if we were serious and I said I've never been serious about anybody in my life."

Betty Jean gave Sheila an ugly look. "Semantics and you know it."

"That's still not what you asked," Sheila said in dismissal. "Anyway, I went to get away and ran into that. Now Cyron's back, saying Julie cleared up a misunderstanding he was laboring under."

"Julie?"

"Sister Julie."

"How could sister Julie straighten out a misunderstanding involving you two?"

"No telling," Sheila said sucking ice cream from her spoon. "She seemed better equipped at creating problems than solving them, if you ask me." She was remembering the glee on Julie's face as she pounded on her car horn.

"You met sister Julie?"

"Sort of."

"Sort of?"

"Sort of. Lets just say it left much to be desired on my end and leave it at that."

"Okay," Betty Jean said laughing, "but I think it's a story there."

"Not one that's ready to be told yet." Sheila could think of no way to make her mouth say she'd slept in her car outside of Cyron's house. Damned if she'd look like a crazy. Especially, not after all the streaker cracks she made to Betty Jean that time she chased Ezekiel out of the house stark naked.

"So, what's the problem? You don't want to be bothered by Cyron? He doesn't seem like the type to hang around where he's not wanted."

"No, I want him."

"Then?" Betty Jean prodded.

"I don't have a big crushing sob story of a broken heart or a relationship gone bad. I've seen enough of heartache to stay away from matters of the heart. It's why Spencer and I originally split up. He wanted to date exclusively and I took a hike. I'd seen enough from my girls to know that road led to Dramaville and I didn't want any part of that. He and I would hang out, but that's it. We had damn good sex together. We'd go to a movie, out to dinner, bowling, to shoot pool, anything as long as he played by the rules I set. I'd be there as long as he kept it light and his feelings to himself."

"Which he failed to do this weekend."

"Exactly. I guess the months without me pushed him over the edge and he was ready to confess all again."

"What do you do to these men?" Betty Jean asked suggestively.

"Hell, I can't call it, but it can't be what you're thinking, because Cyron hasn't been to the promise land, yet, remember?"

"The promise land?"

"The promise land," Sheila confirmed her wording, laughing. "Cyron is serious. It's like he's going to *make* me give him a legitimate opportunity. He wants me to open up like some type of flower and let him in."

"What do you think? Are you going to let him in?"

Sheila searched for answers in her ice cream container and hunched her shoulders when none were forthcoming. "I don't want to end up hurt. I don't want to be broken and battered. I don't want to be forced to pick up the pieces and start over again."

She looked up at Betty Jean. "You're a whole lot stronger than I am, Ms. Carlson. I don't have the strength you have. That's why I got so upset with you for throwing in the towel and walking around in your robe all day. You were giving up, not even trying and letting Ezekiel win. If you get beaten, what hope do I have? If someone as strong as you are can be brought down to her knees, what would happen to me? Crushed into the floorboards forever?" She shook her head over what she saw as a very strong possibility. "I don't want to have to cry over anybody, Betty Jean," she said the last quietly, shaking her head. "I would cry a river for Cyron."

Betty Jean sat in silence for a moment wondering what to say. Caring about someone was a can of shit sometimes, she couldn't deny that. But then she smiled, too. It was a unique experience that smelled a little different with each whiff and should be tried at least once. She gave her opinion to Sheila who laughed, too.

"I should open up a big, stinky can of Cyron?" Sheila wrinkled her nose, laughing.

"You should pop the top and dive in. You can't live on the outskirts of love. I have it on very good authority that you can't really appreciate anything from the sidelines. You've got to get in there. Participate. Get a little dirty. Contrary to popular belief, love is not a spectator sport."

"What if I get hurt?"

"You will."

"What?! You weren't supposed to agree with me. You were suppose to feed me some crap about tea and roses and the sweetness of falling for someone, not a *you will*."

"It's all part and parcel, Sweetie. You're going to get hurt, but you hope the good outweighs the bad and you spend more time laughing than you do crying. And then you press on."

"And then I press on, hun?" Sheila asked, testing the words on her own lips, then she raised her spoon in the air like a glass preparing to make a toast. "To pressing on."

"To pressing on!"

Chapter Seventeen

It was after ten when Sheila left and nearly eleven when Byron called.

"What are you doing?" he asked.

"My part to aid society. Keeping the insane from going plain crazy."

"Do you work with small parties or just large groups?"

"I don't know. How small a party are we talking?"

"Society of one."

"How can I be of service to a society of one?"

"I'm lonely. I miss you."

"You always say that," she replied, smiling.

"It's always true. I need a vacation. Let's skip town, ride off into the sunset."

"It's Monday night. Why didn't you think of skipping town Friday?" Betty Jean groaned playfully.

"Friday? You mistake me, woman!" he said, playfully offended. "I want to take a real vacation. I need at least a week in a tropical setting where I can unwind and recharge my batteries."

"If you can afford to take the time away, you should go."

"Again, woman, you mistake me. I said *let's skip town*, not let skip town. See? Without the plural it doesn't make too much sense."

She laughed at his humor, but declined the offer. "And I said if *you* can afford to take the time away, you should go. Implying, tactfully, that I can't. I have an obscene amount of work on my plate right now."

"Are you sure that's the only reason you don't want to fly away with me?"

"Why else would I shake my head at such an offer?"

"Honestly speaking, not everyone can afford plane tickets and a week's accommodations to a tropical paradise on the spur of a moment. If your no was financially motivated I was going to tell you I was going to pay for everything."

"If you called me saying *let's escape for a week to paradise* it would be understood that you were the one footing the bill, anyway. Like you said, not everyone can afford such luxuries. So it would go without saying, if you're the one suggesting....you're the one paying. *Let's go to a movie. Let's go out to dinner. Let's spend a week in paradise.* It's all the same thing."

"We've eaten out on your suggestion before and I still picked up the tab. If the one who suggests is the one who pays, why didn't you pay?"

"Your mother raised a gentleman," she said on a smile. "However, I'm always fully prepared to pay for whatever little expenditure I suggest. My salary is so large it's almost embarrassing. Believe me, I can afford to pay the tab for brunch or fly away for a trip. It's whatever," she bragged flirtatiously.

"I remember when I felt that way about my own income. That it was almost embarrassing," Byron replied quietly and Betty Jean felt a little bad. Why did she bring up money? She'd already guessed he probably didn't have much of it. She didn't know how the hell he was going to afford paradise for two, but figured he hadn't been literal anyway. She was on the verge of apologizing for her tactless comment, when he sighed heavily. "Then it grew even larger and it finally reached the embarrassing stage. You keep reaching for the stars, though, honey, it'll happen for you, too."

"You sneak! You can't turn my own burn against me."

"Your own burn?"

"I've been watching That Seventies Show again." She giggled.

"Pop in a tape, so you won't miss anymore cute euphemisms, pack a bag and let's go to paradise."

"For an entire week?" Was he one of those credit card junkies, in debt to his teeth?

"Yes, for an entire week...or more. Come on, Queen Bee. I need a break. Seriously, I'm wiped out."

"You've been working non stop for weeks." To pay off credit cards?

"Try months. At least a year by now. I want to throw my cell phone in a lake like they do in all those commercials. You ever notice how no one ever seems concerned with tossing away their cell phone? It starts ringing and away it goes. Why not simply turn the thing off? My address book alone is worth a small fortune to me. My phone holds a lot of numbers. I wouldn't want to try and recreate it. Hell, I don't even think I could."

"Then don't toss your phone in a lake."

"Come with me and be certain I don't. Come with me and I won't even need to bring it. I'll leave it sitting in it's charger on my night table."

"I can't. I—"

"You're Betty Jean Carlson and you're a workaholic. Say it with me."

"I won't. It's not true."

"When was the last time you took a break?"

"I've been at Hurstwode & Donovan for less than a year. I got a break in transit from my last job."

"You stepped into those shoes running and you know it. You told me so yourself. There was no breath between quitting and starting. You basically had enough time to get to California and dress for work. Your own words, I think. *A break in transit.* An oxymoron, if I've ever heard one."

"I didn't know you were going to go traitor on me and turn my words against me later."

"Traitor? Me? Never. I'm—"

"And that's a slight exaggeration, too. I had a day or two off, before I went to work."

"Just trying to make you see reason."

"You're trying to twist my arm."

"I'm *trying* to get you on a plane, then on a beach. When was your last break, Betty Jean, seriously?"

"Three years ago," she said quickly.

"Three years ago!"

"I think," she added lamely.

"More or less than three?"

"Leaning heavily towards more."

"And you won't take a break."

"Okay."

"Okay, what?"

"Okay, I will."

"Okay, you will *what*?"

"Take a break. Wow you must really need one. You can't even keep up with our conversation."

"I'm nervous, now. Why the about face?"

"I was just thinking about how long it's been since I was off a schedule and it *has* been too long. *Way too long*, if I can't even recall it. I had to think too hard about the last time I rested. I'm going to put in for a vacation. My anniversary is coming up soon and it would be perfect timing."

"Perfect timing is calling the office from the plane in the morning to say you won't be in for a while," Byron pouted into the phone.

"Come on, stop whining. It'll give us a chance to plan and pick the perfect spot. Not too much tourism," she coaxed. "We can really be alone and relax."

"If I have to wait, I get more than a week."

"I'll give you a month for your patience."

"It's not nice to tease a desperate man."

She giggled. "I'm serious. I'm sure Charles can do without me for a little while. He knows how hard I work. He's the one who came personally to woo me into working for Hurstwode & Donovan. He knows if I call uncle and say I need a break, I really need a break. That and I'm guaranteed four weeks of vacation a year, it's in my contract, and I haven't used any of it since I started."

"All right. We're going to plan a trip then, instead of escaping the correct way."

"Behave."

"I'll try," he promised with no weight.

"Good. Now I have to say goodnight. It's late and I have a seven thirty meeting in the morning."

"Seven thirty? That's kind of early, hun?"

"Depends on which time zone, in which part of the world you're in. The meeting is being done by satellite. We're pulling in big wigs from all over for this."

"Yeah, but you're still on Pacific time, so the meeting's seven a.m. for you. Early as hell." He was complaining like he had to get up, too. Yet another reason he avoided the boardroom. Their day started way too early for him.

"It's not so bad. I'll probably go in about six to pre-pare for the meeting. Have a few cups of cocoa to wake up, that sort of thing. It'll be fine."

"Well, get you some sleep, so you'll be even more beautiful for the camera. Sweet dreams."

"I hope."

**

She slept undisturbed that night.

Her dreams didn't haunt her sleep until two nights later.

In her unconscious world she was again the tall graceful mare that ran with the wind.

In her last dream she was herself reaching for flowers then became the horse. This night it was the opposite. As she ran four legs became two. Her vast meadow was replaced by a thick forest. She ran naked through the trees and brush. The unyielding weald scratched and bit at her bare skin. She was forced to pick her way barefoot through the trees, stepping on sharp stones and thistle.

Hers was the heavy, labored breathing of one pursued.

Every now and then she would look over her shoulder, wildly trying to locate whomever tracked her footsteps. Someone was out there in the darkness. She could feel it.

She ran through the thick forest as best she could, intent on reaching the light that shone palely through the branches in spots. If she could make it to the light, she'd be okay. She tripped and fell, cutting her hands and bruising her knees.

She was nearly to the end of the line of trees. The streams of sunlight filtering throughout the trees were becoming more predominant. Her heart beat faster. She could hear her would be assailant behind her thrashing through the brush in pursuit, but she was going to make it! There was security in the light and she was almost there. Just as she made it to where the forest ended a rope sailed through the air landing neatly around her neck. Betty Jean was jerked off her feet and landed flat on her back on the forest bed.

She struggled to rise and get her fingers between the rope and her neck, but she could do neither. Coughing and gasping, she struggled with the rope as the slack was taken up. The rough fiber bit into her neck and tears came to her eyes.

Her attacker stood above her and she blinked furiously to clear her vision. She would know her tormentor. Before she could see who would turn her victim, her alarm clock rung.

Moments later, she woke on a gasp of recognition.
**

"Are we ever going to talk?" Cyron brushed the side of Sheila's face with his hand.

"What do you want to talk about?" Her head was in his lap. She was lying on the big cushions on her couch, curled on her side. He was putting her to sleep with the soft rhythmic stroking of his hand. He seemed to trace her profile a thousand times. His finger slowly moved back and forth as though mesmerized by the curves of her face. She felt good. Relaxed and calm. The last thing she felt like doing was talking and ruining her tranquil mood.

"I wanted to talk when I came by the other night, but you wouldn't let me. I'm willing to let the things we said in anger to one another go. I want to know if you could do the same thing."

"I already have or you wouldn't be here now. Everyone says something they wish they could take back." She kept her gaze focused on the television set, even through the commercial. She didn't know what was going on with Cyron. She couldn't judge his mood. They'd spent every night together since his apology on Monday and each night he seemed more intense, like he was chewing on something he wanted to say. Part of her wished he'd get it said so they could move on and the other part hoped if she didn't appear too concerned, he'd drop the subject and keep his mouth shut.

"Do I scare you, Sheila?" His question was softly spoken and his finger continued it's lazy journey along her jaw line.

She wanted to lie. She wanted to lie. She wanted to lie. Oh, how she wanted to lie.

She wanted to, but she couldn't.

Her eyes glazed over suddenly and her throat closed up a bit.

It took a little effort to push her yes out. She blinked trying to dispel the tears. Yes, yes, yes, he scared her and this was exactly why. No one ever made her feel the way that Cyron did. She cared about him and it frightened her. If she could be guaranteed she'd never end up as a basket case because of him, all her reservations would fade away. There was no man in her life she couldn't raise her foot and walk across on her way out the door. No man she wanted to feed breakfast to.

No man she couldn't erase from her mind as easily as she could cleanse him from her body, but somehow Cyron had gotten past all her defenses and she found she couldn't erase him from her mind or bar him from her heart. Try as she might to get away, every corner she turned only brought her right back to Cyron. Mentally and emotionally, if not physically, and in her mind that was just as bad. Worse.

"Why? Because you can't run from me or because secretly you don't even want to?"

See? He was always reading her thoughts. Seeing what was real even if she didn't want to show it to him. "Both." There was no point in trying to lie to Cyron. Even when she didn't say it, he knew the truth.

"Sheila, I can't promise that I'll never make you cry, but I give you my word that I will never hurt you. And if you do shed tears because of me, I'll hold you through 'em. I'll never walk out and leave you upset or lonely or hurt. I don't want any other woman. I think you'll be more than enough to keep my hands full. You'll never have to worry if I'm where I say I am or if I'm running around on you. I'll look at other women, because I'm human and it's some really beautiful women out there, but I wouldn't find one that could compare to you and I'd never risk losing you over something that meaningless. As my current situation proves, I want something more than sex. Sex is good, but it's only a small percent of what's real. A very small percent of the whole package and I'm interested in the whole package. I can have that with you. I'm too big to ever think about putting my hands on you. I'd walk out and leave you alone forever before I raised my hand against you."

Sheila closed her eyes listening to his quiet pledge. When he promised to always take care of her and provide for her, her eyes opened and she rolled to her back looking into his face. "What are you doing?" Her question was a breathless sigh of disbelief. She knew what she thought she was hearing, but she couldn't be correct. He wasn't—Her eyes stung.

"I was going to take you out tonight. Amongst the pop and flash of the evening, I was going to convince you to wear this." In his hand materialized a ring. A gorgeous square cut princess diamond in a platinum setting. He held it gingerly between thumb and index finger. He rolled it back and forth between the digits, watching the diamond sparkle in the light from the television.

Sheila said nothing. She stared at the ring, too. Her eyes stung even more.

"But I changed my mind. I decided against the pop and flash, because it'll just be you and me. No fancy restaurants and waiters on the day to day, just you and me. So, I figured I'd start it out the way it would go." He shrugged his shoulders, still studying the ring. "Then I changed my mind about trying to convince you. My mama told me once that when I asked my sweetheart to marry me, if she had to think about it, she was the wrong sweetheart for me. I should then recant the question. She either wanted me or she didn't, there shouldn't be anything to think about. I figure it should be the same way with trying to convince you. You either want me or you don't. So." He took a breath, still holding the ring. "How about it, Leggs? You want me or not?"

Sheila lay there staring at that ring with her stinging eyes, breathing harder as she fought to get air into her lungs. She was going to hyperventilate, she thought wildly or faint or scream or all those things. True, she'd never hyperventilated or fainted before, but she was sure this is what it felt like. Did she have any brown paper bags in the house? She stumbled around mentally, in confused turmoil for a while, afraid to make a mistake, but her gaze never wavered from the ring Cyron held. Her eyes got redder and stung worse than ever.

She felt like she was suspended in time and had lain motionless for hours, but only seconds had passed since his question. "We don't know one another," she whispered.

"My favorite color is burgundy. My lucky number is seven. I detest artichokes and I like to wash new sheets before I put them on my bed. I've never cursed at my mother and my Granny can get me to do things no one else in the world can. I love children, but have no preference for how many I want or the sex. I'd love my daughter just as much as my son. Sick or healthy, I wouldn't care. I'd still be there. I have a close family and I want you to be a part of it. What else do you need to know?"

"We haven't known one another very long, it's only been a few weeks. I don't even know what you were doing, say....ten years ago."

"What's to know? Ten years ago I lived in Spain for a little while." He smiled at her dubious expression. He'd already told her he'd modeled for a while. He went there on a shoot and stayed for over a year. "I have two brothers, one sister. I speak three languages, thanks to my grandparents—"

"What do your grandparents have to do with the languages you speak?" she asked, interrupting his speech.

He shrugged. "My grandparents are from France and it's the only language my grandmother will speak. The Spanish I picked up in school and it just sort of came natural to me. I guess since I already had two other languages in my head."

"You don't look French."

"I said my grandparents were French. That's beside the point though. There are plenty of black Frenchmen, woman. We have crossed seas before, you know." He said, giving her a gentle squeeze before continuing his narrate. "I played three years of college football before a really bad hit took me off the field during a game and I figured out that shit wasn't for me. Byron and I posed for a college sports calendar our school was doing for a fundraiser. He was the quarterback. I was a wide receiver. A modeling scout happened to see the calendar and signed both of us. After I left college, I spent a few years on a runway, until that got pretty boring. Bummed around Europe for a year or two, then came home and started The Chicken Shack. Not really interesting. Typical story, really." Sheila laughed a little nervously at his *typical*. "I've met a woman or two that I could have had something serious with, but it never happened. I just wasn't ready, I guess. I don't know that I've ever truly been in love before now and I've never lived with anyone. Too big a step towards commitment for me. I've been all over the place and done a whole lot of things. I can't complain about my life, but now something is missing and I know what it is. It's you. I want Sheila. I *need* Sheila. My princess. My love." He kissed the top of her head. "I love Sheila."

The tears in her stinging eyes finally spilled over as she slowly raised her left hand. There was no confusion in her heart when he slid the ring onto her extended finger, then captured her hand in his. Pulling Sheila close, Cyron kissed her. He pulled away from her on a noisy sniffle and Sheila gave another nervous laugh at his shining eyes.

"This is my moment. You aren't supposed to be crying!"

"I was so scared you were going to say no," he said letting his breath out in a rush. "Look at that." He held his hand out and it wobbled visibly. "I was terrified you were going to throw me out." He pulled her to him again, kissing her face, her throat, her neck. Any part of her, his lips could reach.

She grabbed his hand, careful of his injured fingers and kissed it. His ring twinkled from her finger and she confessed, "I'm terrified, too, Cyron. What if—"

"I said I *was* terrified," he interrupted frowning. "I'm not anymore. I was only worried that you'd turn me down."

"Yes, but what if—"

"What if we have a great life and live happily ever after?" he cut her off, asking. "Nothing negative, Leggs. From here on out it's you and me, okay? We get to a dark spot, we find a flashlight. Up to our neck in water, we do the breast stroke together, okay?" He looked into her eyes, nodding his head. "Fifty years from now on our what, silver anniversary...or is it the golden, when we're being toasted by family and friends, I'll let you tell me all your *What ifs* then, okay? And we can laugh about them together. Okay?"

"Okay." She smiled through her tears.

A few hours later, Cyron swatted her behind. "Let me up."

"Why?" She was unwilling to give up her comfortable position.

"I'm going home." At her frown, he laughed showing strong white teeth. He stood stretching. "That ring's only a down payment, you haven't purchased full liberties yet." Her frown deepened and he kissed her, drawing her to her feet.

"You're serious? You're leaving?"

Cyron stood staring at her, then he ducked his head. "I know it's super cheesy, but," he shrugged. "I kind of like it that we haven't slept together, yet. I feel a little nervous when I think about you. I feel like I'm sixteen and it feels goods." Self-conscious, he shrugged again.

"I'm no where close to being a virgin, but I almost feel like one around you. All new and green and untried."

Sheila smiled. "So, you think I'll steal your honor if you stay the night? We'll wake up in the morning with blood on the sheets?" she asked, smiling slowly at the picture her words created.

"You think you could keep your hands to yourself if I stay the night?"

"This house has three bedrooms," Sheila hinted.

Cyron pulled her to him, nuzzling her neck. "No way. I get the full torture treatment. If I stay the night, I sleep with you in my arms. A prelude to the rest of my life."

"Are we really not going to have sex until after we're married?" Sheila asked, putting her arms around his neck.

"Why? You can't wait that long?" He kissed her lightly.

She shrugged. "I only took the ring to get at your body."

"Is that right?" He smiled. Cyron tightened his hold on her and deepened the kiss. He was kissing his future wife.

Chapter Eighteen

*W*hen you talk to her, talk to her
like you want somebody to talk to your mama
don't get smart with her, have a heart to heart
with her, just like you would with your daughter

Late Saturday morning, Sheila danced around her living room accompanying the musical talent of India Arie who sang from the Kenwood speakers surrounding the room. Betty Jean knocked several times before finally letting herself in. She opened the door and the music hit her in the face like a wave of heat.

"Sheila?" she called from the entry way. Walking into the living room she was caught off guard when Sheila grabbed her arm spinning her around. Moving Betty Jean's limbs like she was a puppet, Sheila made her dance with her, as she continued to sing:

'Cause everything you do or say
you gotta live with it every day
she's somebody's baby
she's somebody's sista
she's somebody's mama

"Okay." Betty Jean raised her voice over the music. "You better not have pulled me over here this early on a Saturday just to dance with me." She was a little grumpy. Since her last dream she hadn't had too much sleep and it was beginning to show in her disposition. Seizing the remote, she lowered the volume on the home theater system.

"What do you think? Fuschia? Powder blue? Yellow? Or the traditional white? Oh!" She stopped her twirling as a thought occurred. "Mother of Pearl! Yes! Yes! That has all the colors of the rainbow in it." Her voice was singsong and she was obviously filled to bursting with happiness and joy.

Betty Jean smiled, collapsing into a chair. "Mother of Pearl, for what?" She yawned wide. It was nearly eleven in the morning, but she was worn out.

"Why, for the bride of course." Sheila was still speaking in her sing song voice. Betty Jean could picture her as a cartoon Snow White dancing through the forest with her little animal friends. Her tired mind was getting fanciful, Betty Jean thought as she fought to keep her eyes from sliding shut. All Sheila lacked was a little blue jay -

"For the what?!" She sat up erect in her seat, instantly awake and alert.

"For me! For me! For me!" Sheila laughed. Kneeling on the carpet before Betty Jean, she extended her hand and they both stared down at the four carat diamond ring.

"Oh, my goodness," Betty Jean said with a hand to her chest. Normally, she didn't like big rings. They were usually gaudy or looked fake whether they were real or not, but not Sheila's. Sheila's was suited to the shape of her hand and said *chop her finger off and take me, 'cause I'm real.* "It's beautiful."

"Yes, it is." Sheila held her left hand looking at the ring in wonder.

"When did Spencer fly down?"

"What?" Sheila's gaze snapped up from her hand to meet Betty Jean's.

"That's not Spencer's ring?"

"You know damn well this is that lunatic Cyron's ring."

"Yeah, I know. You just looked all weepy. I wanted to divert your attention for a second. Come here." Betty Jean opened her arms. "Are you happy? Are you sure you want this?" she asked hugging her good friend.

"More than my life, Betty Jean. When I first met Cyron at the Chicken Shack my attraction to him was immediate, but you were having issues about him so I told myself to forget about it. Then we ran into him at church and I had the same reaction, but stronger. Girl, I think I've been a little bit in love with Cyron since he first approached our table and I've been mad as hell about it ever since. I fought against it, tooth and nail, but when he asked me to marry him, it all fell into place like dominos. It made perfect sense to me. I'm going to love this man for the rest of my life." She fingered the ring, smiling softly.

Betty Jean sat back smiling, glad for Sheila's good fortune. She couldn't resist teasing, "You sure opened up a can of shit, didn't you?"

"And took a big ole whiff!" Sheila said recalling Betty Jean's words of wisdom.

**

"I can't believe it." Jules sat in the corner of the couch in Cyron's living room, frozen in shock.

"Son-of-a-Bitch!" Byron exclaimed, bounding to his feet to thump his brother on the back. He pulled him towards him, holding Cyron in a tight embrace for a second, before pounding him again.

"I know man," Cyron said, returning the hug. The three brothers had always been exceptionally close. Without a doubt, Byron knew exactly what Cyron was feeling just then. It was cool being a triplet sometimes. He didn't have to search for words of explanation. Ayron and Byron just knew.

"I'm here, too, damnit!" Ayron called from the speaker phone on the coffee table.

The siblings laughed and the thick emotion was dispelled from the room. Julie finally stood, ungluing herself from the couch. She hugged Cyron, saying she was glad for him. She was, but secretly she didn't believe in love at first sight. Those people that knew each other a hot two seconds, got married and stayed that way were the lucky ones. Most filed for divorce before the ink was even dry on the marriage certificate having discovered they should have found out more about one another before I do.

Personally, she'd rather know a little bit about a person before she committed her life to him. But since the impromptu celebration was in Cyron's honor and not hers, she shrugged her shoulders and went with the flow.

**

He saw her pull into her driveway just before sunset. He wanted to rush over to her, but he refrained. He would wait until it was dark, then they could go out on her deck and beneath the moon and stars, he could tell her he loved her.

She'd have her hair down and the moonlight would catch in it. He closed his eyes and visualized the softness of her hair, the smell of it. Taking a deep breath, he glanced at his watch. Tonight was the night he'd finally get to hold her in his arms.

**

"I know. Sheila told me this morning," Betty Jean said unpinning her hair, then shaking it out with her hand. "Me, too, but it was a nice surprise. You know your brother, should I drive Sheila to church the day of the wedding or to the border?"

"Cyron's a good guy. Besides, my dad would string him up if he was playing around. Dad has one brother and three sisters. He said he had to listen to too much crying growing up. He'd see us going out as teenagers and holler, *Don't be making nobody cry tonight.*" Byron was quiet with the memory of his father for a moment before saying, "No, I don't think he'll make her cry. It's safe to drive her to the church."

"Are you coming by tonight?" Betty Jean stepped over to the closet, removing her capri pants and top. When she was naked she went into the bathroom and ran her bath water.

"I'm not sure yet. Depends on what it's looking like at Rufio's when I get there."

"Well, I know to keep my fingers crossed." She added bubble bath and sea salts to the running water.

"Maybe we can get a bite to eat, if you don't mind waiting a bit."

"Will it be before ten this time?"

"Will it matter as long as we eat?"

He had her there and she laughed. "I'm going to read a little and soak in the tub, while you decide on a course of action, Mr. Man."

"Sounds like a plan to me," he said before saying goodbye.

Betty Jean hung up the phone then stepped into her bath water. Grabbing her book, she turned off the cold water, leaving the hot water to finish filling the tub. Lying back in the steam, she opened the book to her page.
**

She was still in the tub an hour later when a knock sounded at the door. Using her finger as a page marker, she closed the book listening. The knock came again and she rose from the tub to answer it.

She was walking pass the table in the front entry hall when the phone rang. "Just a minute!" she called to the front door.

"Hello? Hi!" Her voice registered her surprise. She walked towards the front door. "Did it take me that long to get to the door? You had to call me?"

"What do you mean?" Byron turned down the radio in his truck, so he could hear better. "I'm a few blocks away from you, but I'm not at your door, yet."

Betty Jean had turned the lock and had her hand on the knob when his words stopped her. "You're not at my door?" She turned the lock back. She squinted out the peep hole, but saw nothing in the blackness. Damn, she needed to remember to change that bulb.

"Nope," he confirmed. "Who's at your door?"

"I don't know. I can't see anybody." She was on tiptoe with one hand against the door for balance. "Hello?" she called to be heard through the thick wood.

"Maybe they left," he suggested, helpfully.

"It didn't seem like I took that long to get to the door."

"Maybe it was a false alarm."

"Maybe."

"No one knocked, it was just you anticipating my arrival."

"Maybe," she said again, "but I was sure I heard it more than once."

"Well, keep the door closed and locked until I get there." He could hear the worry in her voice.

"Sounds good to me." Betty Jean rubbed the chills from her arm with her free hand. She looked out the peephole once more, before turning away.

**

He stood in the darkness on her porch, pressed against the door. He'd heard her phone ring. She was close enough to the front door that he could make out nearly every word of the muted conversation. From what he could gather, she was expecting company and not from him. Most likely she was expecting the Suburban driver.

When he heard her call out, he hesitated for a moment. Maybe he'd wait like she asked and she'd send old boy away when he arrived. Hope blossomed when he heard her turn the lock, but it was dashed seconds later when it was turned back.

With the second click of the lock, he'd moved quickly aligning himself with the door, so she'd not see him if she looked through the peephole. He'd changed his mind about seeing her tonight. He didn't want to share her attention.

When he felt her move away from the door, he sprinted down her driveway, being careful to stay in the shadows. He'd just climbed back into the rental car that he'd parked at the end of the block, when the lights from the expected SUV lit the street.

Scrunching down in his seat, he watched with envy as the other man exited his vehicle and approached Betty Jean's house. Soon, her front porch was flooded with light that was pouring out from the open door way. He was irritated, but tried not to let it show as he turned the key, starting his engine.

He'd just have to come visit some other time.

**

"You're sure it was him?" Sheila asked looking up from the bridal magazine she'd purchased on the way over. Betty Jean was hosting an intimate shindig for her and Cyron and she was supposed to be helping. So far, she'd only sat at the bar and looked through her magazine turning up her nose at most of what she was reading. For some reason, Betty Jean's horse dream popped into her mind and she'd asked about it.

She expected Betty Jean to say the usual. That her assailant was still unknown, since the masked identity was one of the things that remained the same regardless to the other shifting details of the dream.

Betty Jean hunched her shoulders. "I didn't see his face or anything, but I'm pretty certain it was Ezekiel."

"Why are you dreaming about Zeke?"

Betty Jean frowned. "I'm not dreaming about Ezekiel! I mean, I am, but I'm not, but listen. I've given it some thought and I think he represents my fears and anxieties. The closer I feel to Byron, the more in depth the dream. I guess subconsciously my mind is trying to warn me not to get too comfortable, to remember what Ezekiel did to me."

"That doesn't make sense." Sheila frowned, closing the magazine. "I still say the first dream was about losing your freedom, somehow. Basically, all of them have been a variation of the same theme. Losing your freedom. There's no hidden warning to stay away from Byron. Maybe Ezekiel, but not Byron."

"Okay, Miss Defender of the Unjustly Accused," Betty Jean said in response to Sheila's sharp tone. "Taking the sister-in-law role to heart, are we?"

"No, it's not that. I just don't want you to read something into your dream that may not be there. Byron cares about you and you care about him. I'd hate to see both of you lose out because of Ezekiel Johnson. He's not worth it. He's probably off somewhere gaily destroying another woman's peace of mind. Stop letting him rob you of yours. The dream's about your fear of getting too close again and losing your hard fought for freedom. It has nothing to do with your ex."

Betty Jean shook her head. "It did. He was there."

"You said you didn't see his face—"

"I smelled his cologne."

"You did what?"

"Liz for Men. I smelled it. When I fell and he was leaning over me, I smelled Liz for Men. Then the alarm went off and I woke up, but trust me. It was Ezekiel."

"You can't smell in a dream!" Sheila gave her a quizzical look. "Can you?"

"I did."

"Well, maybe so, but that still doesn't mean leave Byron alone or feed him with a long handled spoon. It could mean run to Byron to escape that fool."

"I don't want to run to anybody. I want—"

"You know what I mean. You—"

"I only know what you said. Run to Byron. I want to stand up to the demons in my head. I existed before Ezekiel Johnson and I'm trying really hard to not just exist, but *live* without him. I'll admit, it's damned hard sometimes, but I can't quit. I can't run to Byron. I can't run to anyone, if I ever plan to stop running. My weaknesses will follow me wherever I go. No." She shook her head again, stirring the marinade she was preparing. "If I ever run to a man, I don't want it to be because I'm running from another one. Or even from another's memory."

"You just make sure you don't let a good man go because of something someone else did. If you do that, you're still allowing Zeke to hurt you and he's done enough damage."

Betty Jean sucked the marinade from the tip of her finger. It had just the right amount of tartness for the fish dish she was serving. "I'm with you on that. Believe me, Ezekiel can't harm me any further. I just need to recoup and rebuild. Is Julie bringing a date, do you know?" She turned the subject.

Sheila stared at her hard for a moment at the mention of her sister in law. She shrugged her shoulders and opened her magazine, again. "If she can find a warlock that's free for the evening, I suppose so."

"Are we once again doing word play with The Letterman?" Betty Jean asked, knowing that warlocks dated witches and witch was only a Letterman rescue away from being bitch.

Sheila raised a brow. "Either that or I can just cut to the chase and stop implying my opinion about dear sister Julie."

Betty Jean laughed at Sheila's dry tone and facial expression. "Now, now. Let's play nicely, children," Betty Jean teased.

"I'll play nicely." Sheila flipped the page with such force it tore at the top.

"She cannot be that bad." Betty Jean tilted her head to the side and put her hand on her hip.

Sheila raised her head, lifting her brow again. *You'll see*, it said.

Chapter Nineteen

She's not that bad." Byron pulled into the drive, turning off his engine.

Julie gave him a sideways glare folding her arms across her chest. "You'll see." She turned her attention to the window again.

"I have seen. And I like her. She's one of the realest people I've ever met. She has legs that end at her throat. A quick wit and a cute face. She makes Cyron happy, too. I think Cyron did well." He smiled in approval.

"I guess." She was still looking out her window, but seeing only her own reflection in the glass and nothing of the world beyond it.

Byron sighed. "Damn, you're such a spoiled little brat. You always have been."

"What?" Incredulous, she snapped her head back around to face Byron.

"You heard me. Brat. Brandon's Brat." He taunted her like he'd done when she first earned the childhood nickname and Julie wished suddenly that she'd driven her own car. She'd put the gear in reverse right now and go home. "I can't believe you'd try to rain on Cyron's parade. Dark thunder cloud of a brat." He shook his head.

"You didn't see what I saw. What Cyron saw with his own eyes. I'm just saying he should tread lightly and with care. Take his time a little, that's all."

"Dark thunder cloud."

"Shut up, Byron! You don't know!" Flouncing back with a pout, she folded her arms against her chest in an angry cross.

"Don't know what? That Cyron, my brother, is in love? That he's never felt this way about any woman that I know of. *Ever.* That he wants to be with her because being without her makes him crazy? That—"

"Seems being with her doesn't do much for his sanity either," Julie cut in, grumbling.

"Maybe," Byron conceded. "But it's a different kind of crazy."

"You are not about to sit here like I'm six years old and explain love to me." Jules turned her head to the window again. He was tripping, for real. Trying to explain love and relationships to her like she didn't have her own radio talk show on the subject. She was the guru not him.

"Stop sitting here acting like a six year old who needs it explained to her, then." She remained stone faced and Byron shook his head at her negativity. "I'm going inside. You can follow when you're out of your snit. I want you to have a smile on your face when you step into that house, okay? Or just sit in the car. It's your call. I'm taking my keys, though," he said pocketing his key ring. "I don't want to come out here later and have to find a ride home." She still didn't say anything and he smiled. Extending his hand, he offered her his cell phone. "Want to call Ayron?" he offered innocently.

"You aren't funny." She smiled a little. She knew he was being sarcastic, but the comment still pleased her. She'd been caught. Everyone knew Ayron was her favorite shoulder to cry on. They were triplets, but Ayron had always been her big brother. She turned to look at Byron. "I already tried. He's not at home. I haven't been able to reach him all day."

"I know." Byron's smile deepened. Julie frowned. What did he know that she didn't? Still smiling, with his secrets in tact, he climbed from the truck slamming the door on Julie's narrow eyed stare.

"Wait!" She leapt from the truck to follow him up the path to the front porch. "How do you know I couldn't get in touch with Ayron?" she hissed, hurrying to keep up.

**

"It was difficult to look at Julie de Monbleau and see the vixen Sheila described. Since her arrival half an hour earlier, she and Betty Jean had gotten along well. They shared quite a few interests and liked some of the same music. Betty Jean could see herself hanging out with the slightly younger woman and becoming friends.

She insisted on helping Betty Jean with the food and the two of them were in the kitchen laughing together when the couple of honor arrived.

"Congratulations!" Byron exclaimed, opening the door and pulling Sheila into a big hug.

"Thank you," Sheila said beaming and stood on tiptoe to kiss his freshly shaved cheek.

"Get away from my girl, man." Playfully, Cyron stepped between Sheila and his brother. Turning Sheila, he dipped her, kissing her giggling mouth.

"I'll take this." Byron removed the bottle from Cyron's hand. "Nice," he said observing what he knew was a thousand dollar label.

"How many times does a man get engaged?" Breaking away from Sheila, Cyron smiled and stood her up right.

"Hopefully, just the once." Wiping her hands on a dishtowel, Julie walked over to kiss Cyron's cheek. She turned with a tight smile. "Sheila." She gave her a small hug. Very small.

"Julie."

"I'd forgotten you two haven't actually been introduced have you?" Cyron said, looking from one to the other.

"We don't need an introduction, do we Sheila?" Julie asked sweetly and Sheila raised an eyebrow. "Congratulations on snagging my brother." She smiled and Betty Jean thought, perhaps she could see what Sheila described after all.

Sheila eyed her would be sister-in-law and knew she'd have to get the rules established quickly with little sister. She'd been warned about Julie's sharp tongue and thought it best to put out a few warning signals of her own. She wrapped her hands around Cyron's upper arm. When her ring twinkled in the light, she snuggled close. "Surely, you didn't come alone tonight, Julie? Our party of five would have been better balanced had you brought a man of your own with you. Somebody to occupy your time and attention." She smiled smoothly.

The brothers coughed and choked back laughter at Sheila's defense. Betty Jean stepped into the show down hugging Cyron. "Congratulations, Cyron!"

"Thanks." He grinned, amused by Betty Jean's sacrifice. She was being civil to him hoping others would follow suit with each other. Byron's little cutie was trying to make certain everyone buried their hatchets and hopefully, not in anyone else's back. At least for tonight. He grinned wanting so badly to tease her, but refraining. "We've been kicking around honeymoon ideas."

"Really?" Betty Jean led everyone into the living room.

Sheila looked up in surprise, wondering what Cyron was about. They'd scarcely discussed the wedding, let alone the honeymoon.

"Yeah, it's hard though. We don't know if Sheila will be able to get the time off." His eyes shined. "Her boss is a real stickler," he said smiling down at Betty Jean.

"You mean you still plan to work once you become a de Monbleau?" Julie accepted the glass Byron handed her, but ignored the look he threw her way.

"Why wouldn't I? I've always supported myself. I'd contribute to my household just the same way." Sheila sat next to Cyron, who picked up her hand. He held it in his against his thigh on the couch.

"Because most people who married into a family worth just under two point eight billion dollars wouldn't see the need to - What did you say? Oh, yes." Her smile was still sweet. "*Contribute to the household.*"

She sipped from her glass.

Byron dropped the one he was holding in his hand.

Betty Jean's froze midway to her lips.

Sheila turned to stare dumb struck at Cyron, who sat immobile listening to the blood pounding in his ears.

The doorbell rang and the scene came to life again. Byron reached for Betty Jean, who leapt away to answer the door. Passing Julie, he pushed the back of her head and she turned to glare at him, frowning.

"What? What!" Julie shrugged, lifting her shoulders as though completely innocent.

He's a billionaire. Betty Jean felt foolish for being concerned about his financial well-being. Hell, he was the one slumming! Her six figures had to be a joke to his what? Nine or ten? How many zeroes were in a billion, anyway? Without bothering with the peephole, Betty Jean jerked the door open. She was so surprised she could only stand in the doorway and stare. She opened her mouth, but no sound came out.

He knew she was surprised.

He smiled. Calmly lacing his hands together behind his back, he stood waiting. She was a little shocked. He'd give her a second to adjust before saying anything. That course of action usually worked well enough.

"Betty Jean," Byron called coming around the small corner and into the entryway. "Honey?" He questioned, seeing she still framed the doorway. Walking up to her, he pulled the door open further revealing the visitor.

Brushing past Betty Jean, Byron was smiling widely. "I knew you'd get here in time!" He pulled the man into Betty Jean's house embracing him. "We've all only just arrived ourselves. Betty Jean—" Byron began, but Betty Jean interrupted him.

"I'm going to go out on a limb here and say this is your brother Ayron."

"How'd you guess?" Ayron leaned over to lightly kiss the back of her hand. "What gave me away?"

"Byron told me you had hazel eyes." She said it as though his eyes were the only indication she had to his identity. Ayron laughed, liking her instantly.

"Come on, man." Byron pulled him forward. "Julie's already let off the first round of fireworks."

"She didn't waste any time, did she?"

"You know your sister." Byron ushered Ayron ahead.
**

"Two point eight billion?" Sheila folded her arms leaning against the sink in the bathroom in the hall. She glared up at him.

"Somewhere around there." Cyron shrugged. "It's the net worth of the entire company, though, not just our family. My family's personal wealth is probably somewhere around three or four hundred million.... I think. Hell, I don't know, but I know it's no where near a billion. That money belongs to the company."

"Your family owns the company, though, right?" Sheila asked dryly, implying there was no difference in the point he was trying to make. If his family owned the company, his family owned the money, as well, as far as she was concerned.

"Yes. My great grandfather started it. My grandfather expanded it and made it grow by leaps and bounds. Lumber and shipping. We only operate out of two ports in the US right now, Oregon and Pennsylvia, but Ayron has been thinking about taking the company abroad. But the money isn't mine, Sheila. It belongs to my family, yes, but not to me. That's not what I wanted. I can't sit behind a desk for sixteen hours a day to earn my living and I couldn't live off money I didn't earn." She looked down at her ring and he covered her hand with his. "*I* bought your ring. Not DMB Shipping. Cyron. The only one of us in my family's business is my brother, Ayron. The rest of us do our own thing. Even Ayron only lives off his own salary; not the company. I do well for myself. I'm comfortable as hell, but I'm not a millionaire. I have a number of relatives who are, but not me."

"Why didn't you tell me?"

"Because I'm not DMB Shipping and that's not the lifestyle I'm offering you. I'm offering *me*. Plain ole Cyron." He pulled her towards him, kissing her neck. "Is that okay? Am I enough?"

"Mmm." She made a noise in her throat as if to contemplate his questions. He bit her neck lightly and she yelped. "I guess so!"

They returned to the living room to find Ayron talking with Jules, who seemed confident she'd found an ally.

"What the heck are you doing here?" Cyron asked hugging Ayron.

"I'm leaving right back out in a few hours. I just flew in, so—"

"What?!" Julie asked, outraged by the brevity of his visit.

"Yep. I'm only here over night. I have business to take care of this week. I just thought I'd fly down and congratulate Cyron in person. See for myself who snagged you." He was looking at Sheila when he gave his response. His usage of *snag* didn't sound nearly as offensive as when his sister used it and the way he was looking at her made Sheila blush. *Cyron with hazel eyes.* "Maybe see if she had a sister or two for me."

"Whatever, man!" Byron put his arm around Betty Jean. "There's no one here for you tonight. The only sister's face you'll be smiling into will be your own."

Everyone laughed and Jules rolled her eyes at them all. "It's not so bad a face. You could do worse."

Ayron looked at her sour expression and smiled, wickedly. "Brandon's Brat."

Looking betrayed, Julie rose to add ice to her drink.

"What's she been up to?" Ayron made himself comfortable on the couch.

"Telling the family secrets," Byron said, crossing over to make Ayron a drink.

Ayron smiled, looking from Betty Jean to Sheila. "Who's she trying to scare off?"

"She likes me." Betty Jean smiled, sipping her drink and Sheila made a face at her.

"I never said I didn't like Sheila," Jules piped from the side bar. "I don't know her enough to form an opinion. And that's my problem with you two getting married," she said addressing the engaged couple. "I don't think you know one another well enough to form an opinion, either."

"Look here, Jules—" Cyron set his drink down on the coffee table preparing to tell his sister what he thought of her opinion, but Sheila touched his arm. She gave Julie a hard look.

"Don't get upset because your sister is being honest. It's better than blowing smoke up my ass."

Encouraged, Julie reclaimed her seat in the living room. "I mean, you guys are moving kind of fast, don't you think?"

"Hell, no, we don't think!" Julie raised a brow and Cyron stammered on realizing what she'd made him say. "Not that bullshit, we don't!" Cyron held Sheila's hand. "*We* think we've wasted too much time as it is. *We* think we should be on our honeymoon by now. *We* think you should shut the hell up and keep your opinion to yourself!"

"Don't be like that Cyron. She has a right to be concerned about her brother." Sheila turned her attention to Julie, but spoke to the room. "I love, Cyron.

No, I don't know his favorite color, how he likes his coffee in the morning or what it takes to really piss him off. I don't know if he swears in front of his mother, remembers to put the seat down on the toilet or if he gets enough fiber in his diet. Hell," she said, shrugging. "I didn't even know his family had a net worth until about twenty minutes ago. I don't know a lot of things and I'm not worried about a lot of things. We have the rest of our lives to get to know one another. Ask me those same questions ten years from now and I'll know the answers. All I know right now, in this second, is that I love Cyron de Monbleau. He loves me and we're going to cut out the middle man of Time Wasted."

"Who's to say you'll be around in ten years to ask? Who's to say you won't decide you were wrong in six months and be gone?" Julie asked, staring Sheila in the face.

"Oh, honey, trust me, ten years from now, it'll only just be getting *really* good. I love Cyron and it would take me longer than six months, six years or six lifetimes to stop. But even with all that, tomorrow is promised to no man, woman or child. I'm not about to waste time getting to know him better just to please the crowd." She paused briefly, staring pointedly at Julie. "Regardless to whomever's in the crowd. This is about me and Cyron, not us and the multitude. We're in love. We're getting married. We refuse to wait and anybody who doesn't like it can kiss our behinds on the way out."

When she stopped speaking the room was quiet. Jules smiled slowly, reading the truth in Sheila's face. Pushing her glasses up, she raised her drink in salute. "Hell, I say you're a de Monbleau already!"

Sheila looked at Julie not certain if she'd just been tested or not. She wasn't even certain the toast had been sincere. She felt Cyron's arm around her neck and she fit herself into the comfortable curve of his body, not really caring. She was marrying Cyron, not his family.

The rest of the evening passed with the sextet eating, drinking and laughing while the siblings told war stories from their youth.

When Ayron asked Cyron how he injured his hand, Julie started laughing. Cyron glared at her as he figured she knew his mind had been on Sheila when he was attacked by his office safe. He'd been telling everyone it was the result of an accident at work, not giving much detail, but Jules knew. She'd seen his struggle when he'd tried to let Sheila go. She knew he was in love with Sheila before he did, having been at his home and not doped up on pills at the time of the revelation.

Cyron countered her humor by revealing a story to Ayron he was certain Julie had not rushed to call and tell him about. All in all, the evening was a success.

That night when Cyron dropped Sheila off at her front door he held her. "I've told you burgundy. Black with two heaps of sugar. It takes a whole lot as I try not to sweat the small stuff. Lightly, but never hard core, I couldn't do it even on a bet. Up, because I live alone and it doesn't matter, but I can learn to lower it. And lastly, I generally stay pretty regular, so I suppose my fiber intake is okay."

Sheila leaned against his chest smiling. When he first started speaking, she was confused, but she understood now. He was answering her questions. Stating the things she told his sister she didn't know about him. He'd answered each question as she'd presented it. She closed her eyes squeezing him tight. Standing on her porch, she smiled into the darkness listening to her future husband's heartbeat.

Chapter Twenty

W hat about me and you?" Byron stroked her hand.

"What about me and you?" With a smile, she threw back his words.

"Do you see wedding bells, baby carriages and station wagons in our future?"

Betty Jean laughed softly. "I doubt if Sheila sees station wagons in her future. I doubt if Sheila would even get in a station wagon, let alone drive one."

Byron squeezed her hand. "Sheila is Cyron's concern. I want to talk about us."

Betty Jean turned so that her cheek rested against his shoulder. "What about us?"

"Oh, no." He shook his head against the pillow. "You're the ring leader here."

"What do you mean?" Betty Jean asked, looking up at him. "You started this discussion, not me."

"I love you, Betty Jean." He said the words for the first time ever, holding tight to her hand. "I know you have some things you're trying to work through and I'm giving you the time and space to do it. Don't I always let you throw me out after you've had your way with me?" He smiled to show he only teased her. "I know there's a reason why I can't stay the night and watch the sunrise on your face. Why won't you let me hold you?" This time his words were soft and serious with no trace of a smile in them.

Betty Jean ducked her head, rubbing his shoulder with her cheek. She closed her eyes saying in a low whisper, "I'm not strong enough to be held, yet."

Byron slid his arm around her waist and pulled until her upper body was draped across his and he could see into her face. "What do you mean?"

"I'm not strong enough to stand on my own two feet, yet. To stand alone. So, I can't afford to lean on anyone else."

"What's so terrible about leaning on me? I have enough strength for the both of us."

Betty Jean looked into his eyes, smiling sadly. "I have to have my own strength, too, Byron. Anything, even a couple, is only as strong as its weakest link. If I'm too weak to support myself, I sure can't stand to brace someone else up. I'm too weak right now to be any good to anybody." He just looked at her and Betty Jean continued, fighting to make him understand.

"When two people are together, they're basically leaning upon one another, right?" He nodded his head once and she plunged on. "I don't want to lean on anybody until I've learned how to stand on my own two feet, you know? And I'm not there yet. I don't have any energy to spare right now. What good am I to one man, when I'm still dreaming about another?"

"Wait! What?! I'm sorry, but I don't know anything about you dreaming about other men." He propped an arm behind his head to better observe her. "Who are you dreaming about?" As though he didn't know.

"More nightmare than dream. I finally made it to the other end of the rope. Ezekiel's holding it."

"What's that mean? You're going back to him or something? The rope's an anchor to tie you to him or something? There's still strings between you? Or what?"

"No. I'm not sure what it means. Maybe it's a warning. A reminder of what loving someone can do."

Byron was angry at the comparison, however slight, between him and her no good ex. "From what you told me, that man didn't love you."

"What?" Byron's sudden temper surprised her.

"Love is not bullshit and games. All he was giving you was bullshit and games. He didn't love you. He loved himself and loved the fact that you did too. That's all there was to that."

"Oh, really? Because you were there? You know Ezekiel Johnson? He may have had his faults, but—"

"Look at you!" Byron flung. "*He may have.* You can't even admit his faults to yourself! Even now!"

"He loved me." She completed her sentence on a note of steel.

"You were a fix for a weak junkie just like any other drug. He was hooked on your admiration and devotion. And his own."

His words stung and Betty Jean tried to rise from the bed, but he stopped her grabbing her wrist.

"He had his faults, but he loved me." Betty Jean stared straight ahead at the wall, refusing to look at Byron. "He may have cheated on me—" She took a deep breath. "He cheated on me, but he loved me."

"He loved himself," Byron repeated, disgusted with her show of loyalty. He was sitting up and Betty Jean sat sideways between his legs with her legs hanging over the side of the bed. "He lied to you. Cheated on you. Hurt you and misled you. He had a good woman who loved him and what man doesn't want that? Even if you had stayed where you were or brought him with you out here, nothing would have changed. You accepted what he was and let him be that way. That knowledge would always have been in the back of his mind, ready on a whim. Trust me. And it would have afforded him an easy excuse when he was ready to step out on you again and he would have been ready sooner or later."

Betty Jean was crying. Silent tears slid down her cheeks and Byron felt like an ass. It didn't stop the words from flowing from his mouth, though. "Anybody can cheat and step out on their partner. It's not that difficult a thing to do really. But when you love someone you stop and think about the effects of your actions. What would the one I love think about me having sex with someone else, you ask yourself. And it's the answer to that question that makes you turn and walk away. You put the one you love's needs before your own wants. The walking away is the love. His *love* for you would have kept him from hurting you repeatedly the way he did."

She closed her eyes against the unwanted truth of his words. It's one thing to heal from a broken love that just didn't work and something else to recognize the waste of six years. Instead of being loved, you'd been used because you were foolish enough to love the wrong person. And worse, it was obvious enough that others could not only see it, but point it out to you from a distance!

Byron sat quietly for a moment, seeing the effect of his words on Betty Jean. "I'm sorry. I didn't have to be so brutal." He kissed her temple. "I love you, Betty Jean. There's nobody else I'm checking out or trying to spend time with. I don't hesitate to let women know I'm involved with someone. We don't live together. We haven't even made any kind of commitment to one another, but I'm willing to give that to you. I love you." He pointed to his own chest. "If I'm waiting, I want to be waiting for a good reason. I don't want to be holding on, waiting while you secretly pine away for some guy that never deserved you."

He slid his leg from beneath Betty Jean and stood to dress. Betty Jean sat quietly on the edge of the bed watching him. She wanted to say something, but his words were still ringing too loudly in her ears. She was still smarting from his stinging comments.

When he finished dressing he grabbed Betty Jean's hand and led her down the hall to the front door. Stepping onto the porch, he turned. "Don't paint the past so pretty that you can't even recognize it for what it really was." He leaned in to kiss her softly on the lips. "Lock the door, Queen Bee," he said, pulling it shut behind him.

**

Betty Jean spent the remainder of the week with the ringer off on her home phone. She made herself unavailable at work by arriving extra early, then locking herself in her office. She emailed Sheila advising that unless the building was verifiably on fire, as in, Sheila could see flames with her own eyes and was choking on the smoke, she was not to be disturbed.

Concealed in her office Betty Jean worked through lunch and past five o'clock. She worked like a demon reducing the workload on her desk by two thirds. It was after eleven when she left work Thursday night and she was back behind her desk by six fifteen Friday morning.

She was able to tear through her work because she threw herself into it mind, body and soul. In her impressive office, buried beneath mounds of paperwork, she didn't have to think about anything else, except the job at hand. There was no Ezekiel. No Byron. No empty, lonely house that silently screamed at her. She didn't have to get to know herself again or try to psychoanalyze her feelings.

In fact, she'd learned that if she worked herself to just this side of exhaustion, to the very brink, she didn't even dream. She'd fall dead across her pillow and stay that way until her alarm sounded.

**

Saturday morning, Betty Jean woke early and went jogging. She hadn't been on the trail in a while and was certain she'd probably collapse before she could get any real exercise done, but she surprised herself.

She was so deep in thought, she put two and a half miles beneath her running shoes before she even got winded.

Stopping to drink some of the water she carried in a pouch on her side, like a gunslinger, she sat on a rest bench beneath a tree. She looked out at the children playing in the park and tried not to envy them their carefree existence.

She knew Byron had been trying to reach her since their last conversation. She was even aware that sooner or later, she was going to have to talk to him. She just wanted to get things more together in her mind without the outside interference of someone else's thoughts and opinions, first.

She'd left the south seeking peace and wasn't certain she'd encountered it yet. Sometimes she thought she was going at it the wrong way. Maybe peace wasn't something that could be sought. Maybe it had to just come to you of it's own accord. She squinted into the sunlight thinking of the times she stood still allowing peace a chance to find her and she frowned a little. She guessed coercion didn't constitute as *of it's own accord.*

Her mind drifted to Byron and she smiled a little. Byron was a good man. She could see herself being in a relationship with him, but she didn't know about the love and marriage part. Maybe she was still too raw from Ezekiel, she didn't know.

Thinking about Ezekiel she shoved the pain and bitterness aside, a bit surprised that she was able to do so, so effortlessly. Maybe she had healed more than she thought. Advanced more than she'd given herself credit for. She was able to look at the man himself and their relationship without it hurting her so deeply. There was only a mild discomfort in her chest when she thought of the way she connected with Ezekiel. She'd never had that with anyone before, not even Byron.

She cared about Byron a lot, in time she might even love him, but she didn't feel connected to him like she had with Ezekiel. Ezekiel was hot passion and fire. He was a ride in the dark on a roller coaster that twisted and turned. The air between them fairly crackled with electricity and it wasn't just sexual. It was mental. It was emotional. It was difficult for her to explain, she shrugged thinking. They were just connected.

Byron was more of a nice stroll on the beach. Nice, calm, tranquil. They sizzled together in bed, but without the wild ride getting there.

She sighed. What's good to you, isn't always what's good for you. Betty Jean smiled, conceding the thought to her apparent tendency to favor bad boys. *Bad boys*, she shook her head on the thought. What she needed was a grown man, she mused, rising from the bench. Which Byron was.

She stretched a little then resumed her jog, wondering if Byron had been right. Had she painted her relationship with Zeke so rosy she couldn't even recognize it now? She maintained that they were perfect together. His cheating was the only flaw in their relationship. Had there been more she blinded herself to about Ezekiel that she still couldn't see?

**

Sitting on the couch, she tucked her feet beneath her. She'd just taken a quick shower and felt refreshed. She'd ordered Chinese food for her movie and was waiting for the delivery guy to call. When the doorbell rang she was slightly surprised. They always had to call her for directions once they entered her subdivision. She was going to tip extra to whomever had found her front door unassisted.

Smiling, she jerked the front door open, but the smile froze on her face when the light from the hallway fell on Ezekiel. This was no dream. She was flesh and blood and so was the man standing before her on the porch. Their eyes met and he smiled a little. It was a curious smile. A questioning smile and Betty Jean answered the request. In a daze of confusion, she hesitated briefly, then stepped aside to allow him entrance.

As he passed a prickle of uncertainty played across her mind, but she shook off the sudden feeling of unease. It was just Ezekiel. Full of shit, most likely, but still just Zeke. She closed the front door, turning the lock.

Chapter Twenty One

She came into the living room folding her arms across her chest. Ezekiel had his back towards her observing the room. He turned in a slow circle nodding his head in approval. He stopped, staring at Betty Jean. She had on loose Joe Boxer pajama pants and an A frame tee shirt. Her hair was pulled back in a ponytail and he could see that some of the ends were damp. She'd just taken a shower or a bath. Knowing her the way he did, he would guess it was a bath. She liked soaking in warm bubbles. His eyes fed on her hungrily. She was still sexy as hell.

"You look good, Betty Jean," he said, breaking the silence.

"What are you doing here, Ezekiel?"

He smiled. "Come on, BJ. Give me a break." He spread his hands wide signaling he came in peace.

She relaxed marginally, but repeated her question.

He shrugged his shoulders. "I was in town on business." He saw the doubt and speculation in her eyes and hurriedly added, "I'm putting together the training manuals for a computer software company or at least, I was. The job is finished and I'm flying out tomorrow morning. Heading back home."

She remained silent and he talked to fill the void. "I've been staying at the Regency." She kept staring and he said, "Room 208" on an embarrassed cough. The Regency wasn't the best hotel in town. It wasn't nearly as fancy as the hotel she'd stayed in on her trip to the coast last year, but it was more in line with his budget. "Say something, BJ, please. If you want me to go. Say it. Put me out of your house. Just say something," he pleaded.

She stood a moment longer in silence then lifted her shoulders. "What do you want me to say, Ezekiel?" she asked softly.

"I don't know, just say something. I can't stand it when you just stand there like that. You know that. I still can't handle whatever goes on in your head when you aren't talking."

"You want me to tell you about my struggles to put my life back together?" she asked conversationally, lifting her shoulders. "You want to talk about the problems I'm having with intimacy and trust? How I try to keep real emotions at bay and other people at arm's length? Should I tell you that I can't even have peace in my sleep? That I can't escape the tragedy of our relationship for even a few hours."

"So, I did all that?" he asked skeptically.

"And more." Betty Jean was calm assurance.

"If I tore your world apart, why don't you give me a chance to mend it? To put it all back together again."

Betty Jean stared at him, blinking, wondering if she'd heard him correctly. Deciding that she had not, that she couldn't have, she frowned. "Excuse me?"

"Don't be twisting your face all up like that, like you taste something sour."

"I did. Our relationship left a considerably sour taste in my mouth."

"We weren't so bad," he said in a deep voice and Betty Jean knew where he was going.

"How's Carla? Does she know you're here?"

"Carla was in my past the last time I came to you, back at our house, before you left." There was no point in mentioning the two or three times he tried to get her back over the past year. Whenever he was between women, he'd give Carla a call. And each time he did, she shot him down. Uninterested. It was cool though, because her subsequent refusals had only led him right back to where he never should have left. Right back to the beginning, to Betty Jean. Nothing was the same without her and he needed her back at his side. "Its always been about you Betty Jean."

"Even with Sasha? Was it about me then, too?"

Ezekiel looked at her blankly. The name meant nothing to him. Who the hell was Sasha?

Reading his expression, Betty Jean laughed without humor. "My God, you don't even remember her name, do you?" she asked, breathlessly stunned.

"Who—"

But she kept going looking at him in wide-eyed wonder. "The first time I left you, I left you because of Sasha. I tried to call you one night and you must have answered your phone by accident, because I heard you. I heard you making love to Sasha."

"I never made love to anyone but you, Betty Jean," he corrected. "I don't know what you may have heard, but you never heard me making love to another woman. The only person I've ever loved is you and that's on the real." He was adamant in his conviction. "Everyone else was just—"

"Oh, what's it matter? You stuck your dick in her. Her thighs circled your fucking head! It's all the same thing. You had sex. You made love. You fucked. It was still someone other than me. Someone you had to lie to me to go see and now you can't even recall the woman's name!"

He got a vague outline of big, full lips, but that was all that came to mind with the name Sasha. Maybe he had been with her, he shrugged mentally. "Look how long ago that was, BJ. And even you admit, I don't remember the woman. She can't have meant too much to me. It's been a year and I still can't get you off my mind."

She shook her head at his logic. "Do you have any idea what it was like listening to you with someone else? Unspeakable pain. You would hurt me so deeply over someone who *can't have meant too much*," she mimicked his careless disregard. "Then on the same note have the audacity to try to convince me how much you care about me."

"Betty Jean, none of the other women I was with meant anything to me. None of them."

"Everyone of them meant the world to me Ezekiel."

He saw the tears shining in her eyes and took a step towards her.

"Don't do it," she warned, stepping back. "I don't need or require your comfort, Ezekiel. I don't cry over you anymore."

"Betty Jean—"

"Just go, Zeke." She shook her head at whatever he was preparing to say.

"You're upset. I just want to—"

She waved off his words and her tears. "This is just residue. Closure."

"Give me a chance to make this better. Come back to me and—"

"I did. I gave you a chance to make it better after Sasha. I gave you a chance to do right by me and stop stomping on my heart and my intelligence and my self esteem. And you gave me LaDonna, Sharon and Carla. I'm sure there were more that slipped beneath my nose. If I know of three or four there's bound to be two or three I don't know about, but we'll just concentrate on the four for now."

He never liked her sarcasm. A muscle jumped in his jaw. "That's behind me now."

"Behind you, beneath you, in front of you, on top of you. It no longer matters to me, Ezekiel. Whoever has you can have you. You're hers with my hearty blessing."

He could see that she meant what she said and his temper flared. He had not come all the way to the West Coast for her to be tripping over the past, especially when she wasn't pure and spotless herself. She came to California and opened her body up for a stranger. And she still was, if he guessed right from his observations of the past few weeks. Something was going on between her and old boy. He was willing to forget her transgressions, why was it so impossible for her to do the same for him?

"Betty Jean, I—" The phone rang, cutting him off and she moved to answer it. "Don't." His tone was firm and she froze automatically.

"What?" The phone rang again. She moved towards it again. With surprising speed, Ezekiel stood between her and the phone, shaking his head.

"I want to talk to you some more."

"So, talk. I need to answer the phone."

"Why?"

"Because it's my—" Betty Jean snapped her mouth shut. She'd been about to explain to him about the delivery guy with her food, but changed her mind. She wasn't obligated to explain anything to Ezekiel. "You need to leave."

"Leave?"

"Yes. Now please." She turned to lead him to the front door and he grabbed her arm, turning her to face him.

"I'm not leaving until we talk."

"You're leaving my house now," she said and he grabbed her ponytail jerking her head painfully skyward. He twisted her arm behind her with his free hand, pushing it upward until she cried out.

"That's always been a problem of yours, BJ. Your fucking mouth. You want to throw me out, hun? You already did that. You didn't give me a chance to talk or say anything then either, but I'm going to get my fifteen minutes of attention today," he said in her ear, jerking her arm up a little higher. "That's your man on the phone, isn't it? That's why you suddenly don't want to talk to me. That's why all of a sudden I have to leave."

Betty Jean swallowed pass the pain in her neck and arm. "I want you to leave because I've said all I have to say to you."

"You always were a stuck up bitch when you set your mind to it," Ezekiel hissed, angry that his plan wasn't coming to fruition as he'd envisioned. "So, you've said all you have to say to me?" he asked into her ear again. He licked the lobe, then shoved her towards the couch where he pushed her face into the cushions. She always thought she was so high and mighty. "I still have a lot to talk about." He pulled the band from her hair, letting it fall around her shoulders as he ran the fingers of his free hand through the thick mass.

"I can't breathe, Zeke," Betty Jean said into the couch and he eased his weight off her, allowing her to turn over.

She had such a pretty face, he thought. Why couldn't she smile and welcome him back? But then he knew why. She was choosing someone else over him. He'd come to win her back, only to find she'd already forgotten about him and moved on. He clamped his jaw shut, getting angrier. While their separation stayed on his mind, she'd picked up and moved on like he'd been nothing, but he was still willing to forgive her, he thought looking into her eyes.

When she turned, he kept her arm pinned at her back, so that it was beneath her on the couch. He kept the other one at her side, while his free hand slid up her tee shirt. He fondled the nipple of her breast with his fingertip and it hardened. "See? You still want me. Your mouth may be finished talking, but your body has something to say and it's telling me it missed me." He bent his head to suck at her breast through the fabric of her tee shirt and she tried to come off the couch.

"Yeah." He struggled, trying to keep her pinned down. "Fight me. Be able to say I forced you when your man wants to know why you won't give him none later." He kissed her stomach.

"Stop it, Ezekiel! What's wrong with you?!" Betty Jean thrashed around trying to dislodge him and his hands from her body.

"I get to sit in my little car, night after night while you fuck Mr. Suburban. You can give him what belongs to me, but I have to fight you and beg. I never had to beg you before Betty Jean! What's up with that?" He pulled at the waistband of her Joe Boxer's and Betty Jean started fighting in earnest.

She was able to get her arm from beneath her and struck out wildly at Zeke's face. "Get off me!"

He pulled and she heard cotton tearing. Tears spilled from her eyes as she fought to get from under his weight.

"Zeke, stop, please!" she screamed, crying.

More fabric tore away and she felt cool air on her legs. "Please don't do this!" she screamed trying to get two hundred and twenty two pounds of determination off of her.

He bent to kiss her and she bit him. He slapped her hard across the face and she felt her teeth sink into the pink tissue of her mouth. His face twisted briefly and he slapped her again. She tasted blood. Something Ezekiel said pulled at the back of Betty Jean's mind. How did Ezekiel know Byron drove a Suburban? He'd called him Mr. Suburban. And what car had he sat in night after night?

He'd unfastened his pants and was pulling at her under wear when she wrenched her arm free and swung at him again. He was caught off balance and fell backward allowing her the opportunity to roll from beneath him. She slid from her position and tried to scramble away, but he grabbed her around the ankle, pulling her back. Her exposed knee burned on the carpet. She kicked wildly at his face, but he dodged the blows. Clamping down on her swinging legs, he closed his fist and punched it into her face. He repeated the action and a line of blood escaped Betty Jean's nose and she stopped kicking. Her hands covered her face.

"Why are you fighting me? Damn this can be just like it was." He gritted out. "Watch," he said pulling himself free from his pants. "It's going to be just like before. Just like it used to be, I promise. I know you remember what we were like Betty Jean." He pushed her underwear aside, no longer bothering to get them down and shoved his fingers insider her. "See there? Talking about you don't want me. You're already moist and everything. Wet and ready, like always. See, there! You want me."

"Please don't do this," Betty Jean wept as he slid himself into her body. He pressed further and further until she cradled every inch of him within her.

"Shit, BJ," Ezekeil said, breathing hard and closing his eyes. He braced himself against her shoulders and pulled himself up. He was fully imbedded in her and her walls felt so warm and good wrapped around him. God, he had missed her. He tried to hold himself still, to savor the moment, but his hips began to circle and grind against her. She cried out, but he barely heard it. He was lost in his own pleasures and he would leave her to her own for a moment longer.

He moved his hips a little more allowing himself to fall deeper into her with each stroke. He wished he had taken the time to pull her clothes off completely. He wanted to feel her ankles on the small of his back again. He felt her hands pushing at his arms in her impatience and he pulled her arms above her head continuing to stroke her. A cry escaped her lips again and he smiled, plunging on. He knew she wanted him. Trying to act like she didn't. She felt so good, he could already feel the pressure building. He was going to cum soon.

His eyes were closed, enjoying the bliss of her body, but he wanted to see her face. He remembered the way she would look at him with her eyes damp and glazed when she rode him and he opened his eyes wanting to look at her when they climaxed. She had to be close, too. She kept moaning and whimpering. He opened his eyes, straining to keep up the rhythm and hold his climax back.

Seeing her bloodied face, he closed his eyes again.

He hadn't come to attack Betty Jean. He just wanted her to love him again like she used to. He'd never once struck a woman. There'd been plenty who deserved it, but he'd never succumbed. Not once. Until now and it was against Betty Jean. He buried his face in her hair and she turned her head aside, as best she could. He moved slightly feeling his seed begin to pour into her body and she moaned again. The noise was clearly a sob born of pain and not pleasure, but it didn't matter. He was too close to stop himself or hold back any longer and he spilled himself inside of her. Quietly, he collapsed on top of Betty Jean, feeling himself fall soft. Limp he slid from her body.

"I love your hair. I've always liked the way it felt against my skin when we made love." She didn't respond to his soft words and he sighed. "It's so long and pretty." He rubbed his cheek against its softness and Betty Jean stared at a spot beneath her sofa, saying nothing.

The phone rang again and they both lay on the living room floor listening to it until it stopped. Ezekiel slid off Betty Jean and stood straightening his clothing. "I'm sorry. I didn't come here for this. I'd been think-ing about you lately, that's all. I even sent you a bunch of flowers a few weeks ago to let you know you were still on my mind. That's why I'm at the Regency." He smiled, a bit self-consciously. "I can't afford anything better. Money is a little tight right now. Those flowers cost a small fortune." He shrugged. "But you're worth it."

Betty Jean curled herself into a ball on her side, still saying nothing.

Ezekiel bent to kiss her cheek. "I'm sorry, if I hurt you. I didn't mean to." Stepping across her he finally left her house, closing the door behind him.

Chapter Twenty Two

Betty Jean?" Sheila called from the front door. "Betty Jean?" she called again, entering the house fully. She closed and locked the front door behind her looking around curiously.

She frowned looking into the living room. Something was definitely wrong here. "Betty Jean?" she called again, almost fainting at the sight of the fresh blood staining the living room carpet.

"Betty Jean!" Sheila called, racing down the hall to Betty Jean's bedroom.

"Betty Jean?" She entered the room, flicking on the overhead lights. Betty Jean was not in the bedroom and Sheila chewed down the panic she felt rising in her throat. Slowly, she walked over to the bathroom door that stood ajar and pushed it open with her fingertips. "Oh, my God," she said, walking into the bathroom.

"Oh, Betty Jean," she said yet again as tears sprang to her eyes. She walked around Betty Jean, who stood at the bathroom mirror with a bloody face. Tears streamed down her cheeks, mingling with the blood that dripped from her chin. She stood in a puddle of her own hair, cutting savagely at the rest of it. Crying and struggling to get the scissors through her thick hair, she seemed not to notice Sheila, who reached out removing the scissors from her trembling hands.

Betty Jean leaned back against the wall for a moment, then slid down it too weak to keep standing. She came to rest against the floor, crying with her face in her hands. Great sobs racked her body and she drew her knees up tighter to her chest, curling in upon herself.

"Betty Jean," Sheila said and tears ran down her face, as well. She knelt in the mess on the bathroom floor, pulling Betty Jean against her. The injured woman came willingly, wrapping her arms tightly around Sheila's neck. Together the two friends held one another and cried.

"You have to tell me what happened, Betty Jean," Sheila said rocking her back and forth, some time later. Betty Jean continued to cry and Sheila stood away from her to wet a towel. Wiping gently, she knelt before her friend cleaning her face. By the time she stopped wiping Betty Jean was ready to talk. In a jumble of words and tears, she explained to her friend as best she could the events of the night, but her mind was stunned. Sheila could only make so much out of the confusion. What she could understand, she didn't like.

"I thought he was the Chinese food," Betty Jean cried bursting into tears all over again.

Sheila rubbed her back. "Shh! This is not your fault. You couldn't control what he did. You just opened your front door."

"And let him in," she cried. "I even felt something when he came in. I felt something strange, I even dreamed about it, but still I let him walk into my house. I let him right in, Sheila! Like the Devil," she rambled. "He can't come without an invitation!"

"You didn't know, baby. You didn't know."

"I knew. I dreamt. I was warned."

"No, baby." Sheila shook her head. "That's a coincidence. You couldn't have stopped this."

"I responded to him, Sheila. He said I did. He said I felt—" She hiccupped, cutting off her words. "He touched me and my body responded to him. I must have wanted him, just like he said. I let him in. I wanted him."

"You can't control something like that, Betty Jean."

"I did this to myself. I—"

"Stop it!" Sheila said, shaking Betty Jean by the shoulders. "Ezekiel Johnson did this shit, not you! You understand me? If a man is sucking on your tits and fingering you, I'm pretty damn positive that unless you're a stone, some part of you is going to respond! It doesn't mean you liked it, invited it or wanted it. It means you're human!" Sheila said, brutally honest. "But you did not do this, Betty Jean Carlson. Your body's involuntary response isn't you wanting him. Your saying *no, get out*, isn't you wanting him. Your bloody fucking nose, damn sure isn't you wanting him!"

Ten minutes later, Sheila had Betty Jean lying in her bed. She was on her side hugging her pillow and Sheila stepped out the room. On her way to the kitchen, she dialed Cyron's number on her cell phone. When he answered on the second ring, her voice broke and tears clogged her throat. "Cyron," she said crying.

**

The young man slipped the money into his pocket and knocked at the door. "Room service."

"What?" came the muffled response.

"Room service!"

Looking out the peephole, he saw a hat with the hotel's logo on top and nothing else. The hat consumed the peephole's view. He opened the door. "I didn't order room service."

"Sure you did." The door was unceremoniously shoved open further.

"Hey!" Ezekiel said, at the intrusion as two men pushed past the bellboy, who was now backing out of the room. "Hey!" Ezekiel called again, this time at the bellboy's sudden desertion.

"I'm sorry man, but I have a sister, too. I don't know what you did to theirs, but—" he said in way of explanation and left the room, bowing to a stunned Ezekiel as he closed the door.

"Have a seat," one of the two remaining men said, turning a chair to face Ezekiel.

"Who the hell are you?" In answer, he was shoved down into the chair by the second man in the room. He raised his hands in peace. "Is this about someone's sister? I haven't done anything to anybody's sister. I don't even live in town," he tried to explain. Betty Jean never crossed his mind. He may have upset her a little before he left, but he hadn't really done anything wrong to her. Nothing she hadn't wanted, too. His mind was blank at what could warrant the intrusion into his hotel room. "Was that other guy on staff here?" he asked, thinking he was probably going to sue the hotel establishment.

"Nope," said the only one of the two who had spoken.

Ezekiel looked back and forth between the two men. He hadn't put on his glasses when he answered the door and was only just now noticing the resemblance between the two giants. Twins? His head swiveled between them for a moment. It was like looking from one mirrored image to the next. He didn't know any twins and didn't know anyone who did. They had to be mistaken. He didn't know their sister.

"He was just someone we passed in the hall and bribed to knock on your door wearing the hat we stole off the break room table." The spokesman of the two was smiling, but the mirth in his voice didn't reach his eyes. His eyes were cold...dangerous. He shrugged nonchalantly. "It wasn't that hard either. That's the problem with cheap hotels. They don't really care what happens to you. Lax security."

Ezekiel looked uneasily to his right where the silent man still hovered. He hadn't said a word since entering the room.

"Did she get any warning?" the only man in the room smiling and talking asked pleasantly.

"What?" Ezekiel asked confused.

Rocking forward a little with his hands in his pockets, he leaned into Ezekiel's face. "Did you give her any kind of warning that you were about to attack her? Any kind at all?" the man asked and Ezekiel looked nervously to the second man who still hadn't spoken and back.

"Attack?"

"See this is going to be a little different. It already is, you can tell?" he asked conversationally, then continued without waiting for an answer. "She received no warning at all. You on the other hand, you have an inkling that something ugly is about to happen." He smiled, all white teeth. "Don't you?"

"Wait a minute!" Ezekiel said, raising his hands again. "I didn't do anything," he said looking at the man before him, who only smiled benignly. Turning in his seat, Ezekiel looked up at the quiet menace who stood just at his side. "I don't know what's going on. I haven't attacked anybody."

The smiling spokesman raised an eyebrow and the answer clicked in Ezekiel's mind. One of these men had to be Betty Jean's Suburban driver. He'd only seen the guy from a distance, but he was sure he was one of these two. They were both large enough. She'd felt guilty about what they'd done and cried foul. Well, he wasn't taking the blame. He turned to address the quiet man. His silence seemed more sane than the other's constant smiling. There was nothing humorous in this situation. It was all a mistake. An awful mistake that he needed to put right immediately, if not sooner.

"I didn't do anything that she didn't want. I never attacked Bett—" He was interrupted by Byron's fist slamming into his jaw. The blow spun him around slightly and he fell out of the chair, but came up swinging. Cyron stepped out of the way clearing a path to

Byron, who was ready for Ezekiel's charge. They hit the desk in the room, knocking the lamp to the floor with a crash.

Byron grabbed Ezekiel around the waist, issuing a multitude of rabbit punches to his kidneys.

Another crash sounded, as the two men fell against the nightstand in the room. They rolled around pummeling one another with Ezekiel getting the worst of it. A few minutes later there was a sharp rapping at the door and Cyron stepped to it and quickly slipped out.

"I've had reports of a disturbance," the young manager said, trying to see over Cyron's shoulder before the door closed. As he was several inches below six feet there wasn't a chance of that happening.

"My brother thought he saw a rodent," Cyron said smiling. He slid his hand into his pocket, as he spoke.

"A rodent? Here at the Regency?" He looked insulted. "We don't have pest here at the Regency." Another crash was heard from the other side of the door. "Now see here." Drawing himself up to his full height of five feet seven inches, he tried to push pass Cyron into the room. A solid rock at six feet four inches, two hundred forty pounds, Cyron stood rooted to his spot, barely noticing the manager's feeble attempts to pass him.

Cyron pulled his hand from his pocket and started counting out one hundred dollar bills, idly. "We're going to pay for any damages we may incur during my brother's pursuit of the little beast. So far only a lamp has been broken and I'm sure you guys have plenty of those in storage. No need to spend any money on anything." He paused after counting out fifteen bills, as if considering. "That is, unless we need our money to post bail. What do you think? Will we need our money to post bail?"

The manager eyed the bills in Cyron's hands and licked his dry lips. "That won't be necessary sir, I'm sure," and Cyron resumed his counting. When the manager had twenty crisp bills in his hand, he put the money in his pocket. "As long as your brother only pursues, but doesn't exterminate we have no problem." He turned to go. "If he does, he'd best take it with him and dispose of the body himself."

He turned and walked back down the hallway.

Cyron was just entering the room when he heard the crunch of Ezekiel's nose breaking. He winced in empathy. Leaning his back against the door, he watched his brother beat the other man unconscious.

**

"No."

"Betty Jean—"

"No."

"Betty Jean—"

"No," she said the word forcefully, on a near shout. "He didn't do anything."

"Betty Jean!" Sheila looked at her friend in open shock.

"He didn't do anything," she maintained.

"What the hell happened to your face then?" Sheila snapped losing patience. She'd watched Betty Jean run bath water in disapproval and was having no luck convincing her to call the police before bathing. She wasn't positive of exactly what happened between Betty Jean and Ezekiel, but from the look of Betty Jean it couldn't have been good. She was certain of what he tried to do, what he intended to do, but wasn't certain if he'd succeeded or not. Since she really didn't want to know the gory details, she hadn't asked for clairity but she still didn't think soaking in a hot tub of water was a good idea. "You're going to wash away any evidence," she said softly, barely able to look at Betty Jean when she said the words.

"Evidence of what?" Betty Jean snapped. "He didn't do anything to me, Sheila. So, he punched me in the face a couple of times. So, what. Who hasn't been punched in the face before?"

She sure in hell hadn't ever caught a fist to the face, Sheila thought, but she let Betty Jean rant uninterrupted sensing her need to vent.

"Ezekiel attacked me. So. I was stupid enough to open the front door without verifying who was on the other side. I had dream after dream, warning me about him, but I stepped aside and let him into my house. He may or may not have had his way with me," she said evasively. "And if he did?" She shrugged. "So, what? How many times have I given myself to him? God, we lived together for years! We were a couple. He got angry and hit me a few times." She shrugged again, thinking of their last fight in California. The brief exchange in her hotel room when they scuffled over the card Byron left for her at the front desk, then of the fight at their house when she jumped on his back. She'd gotten the best of him both times, she thought with hollow triumph. "I just lost this time. I'm not calling the police," she said with finality, walking into the bathroom.

"And if he raped you?"

"He didn't rape me!" Betty Jean screamed charging back into the bedroom. "I knew Ezekiel Johnson like the back of my hand. Eight years, I've known him. How many times have I cared for him? Stood by him? Helped make him strong? I've cleaned his house, *our* house. I cooked his meals and took care of him. Damn good care. I was everything to this man. Mother. Father. Sister. Brother. Secretary. Cook and confidant. Everything. More than he ever deserved. Everything!" Angry tears glittered in her eyes.

What was left of her hair stood out on her head at strange angles and there was still bits of dried blood around one ear, on her neck and in her hairline. Her face was bruised and swollen and Sheila curled her lips inward to keep from crying. "We shared a life together. We were going to get married and have children and grow old together. Ezekiel has held me and loved me too many times over the years. He did not rape me. He did not take—" She stopped speaking and took a deep, shaky breath. "He did not rape me." She stared at Sheila with such strong conviction, daring her to speak against what had been said that Sheila knew without a doubt how far Ezekiel had gotten and that she'd never get Betty Jean to call the police.

She nodded her head in resigned understanding and Betty Jean turned and walked slowly back into the bathroom, closing the door behind her with a soft click.

Chapter Twenty Three

Sheila was walking down Betty Jean's driveway when Byron drove up. When he parked, she walked over to his vehicle.

"Is she okay?" Byron asked jerking his head towards the house.

Sheila shrugged her shoulders, then turned her head to stare down Betty Jean's street. "Nothing happened," she said softly, shrugging her shoulders again.

"What's that supposed to mean?" Byron frowned. "When Cyron called me, he said—"

Sheila shook her head in the negative, turning to look at Byron again. "Those are her words, not mine. Betty Jean looks like a train wreck. I mean, I've never been punched in the face, but—"

"He punched her in the face?" Byron's hand went to the door handle, but Sheila blocked his exit from the truck.

Shaking her head again, she said, "I don't think that would be the best of ideas. She's in a weird place right now." Byron looked at her questioningly and she shrugged. "I left her scrubbing blood out of her living room carpet."

Byron cursed and again tried to get out of his Suburban, but Sheila kept talking. "She took a bath first. I pissed her off and she screamed at me, but once she came out of the bathroom—" Sheila shook her head at a loss for words. She lifted her shoulders again, saying, "She was dead calm. She went and got a broom and dust pan for the bathroom floor."

Byron frowned in curiosity and Sheila held up her hand, saying, "You'll see."

"The next thing I knew she had out buckets and sponges. Cleaners. It was Spic And Span and Comet all over the place. She cleaned the whole house. Like I said, she's scrubbing the living room carpet right now."

"Why'd you leave her like that?" Byron demanded and Sheila frowned at the accusation in his voice.

"She told me to! I didn't just leave! She's been saying, polite as shit, for the past few hours, *you don't have to stay here, Sheila*, but I ignored her. This last time she told me to have a safe drive home and since she held open the front door when she said it, what else could I do?" She folded her arms across her chest.

They both stared in quiet contemplation at the door that was closed against them and worried for the one who was locked on the other side.

"What did Ezekiel say when you and Cyron went over there? Did he admit anything? Confess? Apologize? Weep? Anything?" Sheila asked, recalling that she'd passed on his hotel information to Cyron.

Byron stared at her blankly and she frowned, sucking her teeth. She put her hand on her hip. "Cyron said you guys were probably going to have a word with him. So what was the word?! Honestly, I kind of hoped you'd get a little physical with his ass. Maybe punch him in his fucking face a few times. Let him see how he likes it!"

"The word was Betty Jean," Byron said still looking at the closed front door.

"What?" Sheila asked confused.

"The word was Betty Jean and he said it," Byron stated simply.

"*And,*" Sheila prodded for more illuminating details.

"And I punched him in his fucking face." Byron never took his eyes off Betty Jean's door.

The next morning when Betty Jean raised the automatic garage door, she found her path blocked by Byron's truck. Sighing, she left the Infiniti in park and climbed from the driver's side of the vehicle. She tapped lightly on the window. Byron opened his eyes slowly to see Betty Jean standing next to his truck.

She looked like she was dressed for church in a light blue dress and matching mules. She had a dark blue scarf wrapped around her head, concealing her hair and neck. All she needed was a pair of giant sunglasses to look the part of one of those film legends from long ago when movies were still shot in black and white.

"You're blocking my way," he heard her say through the partially open window. He turned his head noticing the raised garage and her waiting vehicle. Rubbing a hand down his face, he fished his keys from his pocket. Seeing them in his hand, Betty Jean turned to walk back to her car.

Coming more fully awake, Byron frowned at her odd behavior.

She treated his presence as though she found him sleeping in his truck, guarding her house, all the time. She hadn't inquired about it one bit. In fact, she hadn't done anything except inform him that he was in her path. His scowl deepened further. Where did she think she was going all beat up and bruised, looking like a fragile china doll? Unless she actually did have a pair of big sunshades, her scarf wasn't really going to hide anything. Hell, he didn't think the glasses would do any real good either. Sheila was right. His Queen did look like a train wreck.

He sat with the key in the ignition, but didn't attempt to start the truck. When he saw Betty Jean exit her car and head towards him again, he got out.

She stopped walking instantly.

Finding the abrupt action odd, Byron stayed where he stood. He had a feeling that if he took another step, she'd retreat a step or two, as well.

"What's the problem?"

"I slept out in my truck last night so I'd be near in case you needed me. I wanted to make sure you were safe for the night."

A shadow flickered across her eyes for a moment, but she blinked it away, saying nothing.

"Weren't you going to ask me about that? About why I'm in your driveway?"

She lifted her shoulders. "Not my business."

Okay, Byron thought and could see the weird place that Sheila warned him about. It was her driveway, how could his presence not be her business? He changed the topic.

"Where are you trying to go?"

"Why?" she asked, defensively.

Byron raised both hands in surrender, shaking his head. "I'm just worried about you."

"Why?" She snapped at him. "I'm on my way to church, if that's all right with you? No need to worry or concern yourself with me," she instructed, full of sarcasm. He stared at her and she added wearily, "I just need to be in my Father's house this morning."

Byron continued looking at Betty Jean, wishing he had taken Cyron's advice to revive that sorry little bastard last night and beat him unconscious again. Her nose was swollen and her face on both sides of it was discolored. One cheek was bruised and puffy looking and her bottom lip was a little fuller than usual also. Byron slowly shook his head.

"What?"

"You can't go to church looking like that, Queen Bee," he said softly. The congregation would focus more on her than on the sermon. By the end of the day, her condition would become the sermon and it would be on everyone's lips. Nope, she couldn't go to church looking as she did.

"Yes, I can," she said, but without any real fight and he knew she'd probably already surmised the truth herself. "I need to visit my Father today, Byron," she said looking him in his eyes, asking him to understand. Ridicule or not, gossip or no, her spirit was hurt. Her soul was in pain and needed to go where it knew it could heal, where it knew solace could be found. She had to place everything she went through, everything she was feeling, at her Father's feet or Lord Jesus, she wasn't going to make it.

"Sometimes we can't go to the mountain. It has to come to us," Byron said holding her gaze. "I'm sorry, Sweetie, but I don't know how much healing you're going to get if you go to Mount Baptist today. People care about you and will be concerned. They're going to want to know what happened, so they can see justice done and set things right for you. I don't know how you feel, but it might be a little too fresh in the wound to have people start poking around at it, you know?"

Betty Jean turned her head, but Byron still saw her quickly brush away a tear with the back of her hand.

"I know a place where He makes house calls," Byron said on impulse and Betty Jean turned back, looking skeptical. "Do you want me to take you?" Her face changed a little and Byron hastily added, "Or you can follow me in your own car. Whichever you prefer."

Betty Jean gave him a considering look. He'd sensed her hesitation to go with him and she felt a little bad about it. Byron had never done her any harm. But then neither had Ezekiel and look what happened there. Please! She thought, switching sides to argue against her previous statement regarding Ezekiel. Pain was pain. Mental. Emotional. Physical. If it hurt, it hurt. She'd had plenty of pain from Ezekiel. It just finally spilled over into the physical.

She shook her head, closing her eyes against the argument in her head. She was developing multiple personalities. She'd be lucky if she didn't end up like Sibil by the time this shit was over!

Byron misunderstood the reason she shook her head and said in an injured voice, "You don't have to be afraid of me, Betty Jean."

Sheila's words came back to haunt Betty Jean and she felt ridiculously reassured, then angry with herself for requiring assurance. She was fine. Nothing had happened. She was making a mountain out of a molehill.

"It's fine Byron. We can go in your truck." Her words were brave, but her voice was a bit wobbly. "Just let me get my things from my car."

"Do you think it would be all right if I used your bathroom really quick?" he asked, hesitantly. He didn't want to spook her, but he desperately needed to wipe his face and freshen up a bit. He felt like he'd slept in his truck last night, which he had.

Betty Jean paused then tried to cover the action by turning her back and walking to the door that led from the garage to the house. She unlocked it, waving him in. "I'll be out here when you're ready."

Five hours later, they sat out on an overhang of cliff looking out at the vast Pacific. Betty Jean was barefoot with her knees drawn up to her chest. She sat in quiet reflection looking out at the water, as she'd been doing for over two hours.

She hadn't spoken much and Byron hadn't tried to make conversation. When he first led her up the path to the protruding rock, she'd been quiet and a tad tense, but once they stood looking out at the water, he'd felt her tensions and anxieties ebb away. He'd felt the same sense of awed peace when he first stumbled across the secluded spot himself years ago and understood her next actions completely.

She'd whispered, "It's beautiful." Then sank down to the sand, lost in the calming peace of the view. The ocean opened up before her, boundless and deep and she sat before it, silent, letting the tranquility heal her.

Chapter Twenty Four

Sheila lay curled on her side with her head on Cyron's chest. She'd been quiet most of the day and sensing her concern for her friend, Cyron had respected her silence. He idly stroked her arm and shoulder, while they watched television.

"Do you think she's okay?" she asked quietly, still watching the commercial.

"Anybody or anything intent on Betty Jean will have to get through Byron first and I don't see that happening. She's safe." He gave her shoulder a gentle squeeze. Silence resumed and Cyron asked, "How about you, Leggs? How are you holding up?" Sheila looked surprised by the question when she lifted her head to stare at him and he elaborated. "I know how close you and Betty Jean have gotten and I can only image what a shock it must have been yesterday when you found her in her house. Byron has her now and we don't have to worry about her, so I can focus all my care and concern on you."

"I tried to call her a few times yesterday. She was in such a pensive mood the last few days that I got worried and dropped by thinking she might need one of our sessions together. I don't know why I turned the knob. The front door was closed and when she didn't answer I thought to leave, but I reached out and turned the knob. It was unlocked. I was so scared Cyron, my heart was beating a mile a minute. I kept calling for her. Just walking through the house calling her name over and over again, but she didn't respond. Then I saw the blood on the carpet—" Her words were choked back by the emotion that was thick in her throat. "I was so scared, Cyron. I didn't know what I was going to find in that house after that," she sobbed out.

"Shh," Cyron soothed when she started crying.

"I thought something bad had happened to her." Cyron hugged her and she gave a strange little laugh. "Hell, something bad *had* happened to her! My God, her face, Cyron."

"Don't keep going through it in your mind," he began and she cut him off.

"I should have just gone straight over there when I couldn't reach her that morning. I shouldn't have waited all day and night like that. I could have been there and—"

Cyron gathered her close. "Stop it, Leggs. Had you been there he just would have waited and struck another time, when he knew she was alone. Just like he did. Didn't you say he was watching her house or something? He would have simply altered his plans and waited. I guarantee it. Your being at her house yesterday would only have postponed the inevitable, not prevented it."

"I just feel so terrible, Cyron. I knew this man. I've joked with him. Laughed with him. Talked to him," she said, shaking her head in wonder. "Who knew what he was capable of doing?"

"Not you and not Betty Jean." Clicking the television off, he reached for Sheila's hand. "Come on."

"Where are we going?"

"Out for ice cream." He stood, pulling her to her feet. "Ice cream will help with your morose musings. No one can think dark thoughts with a double scoop of tutti fruiti before them."

"I don't want any ice cream." Sheila resisted the tug at her hand.

"Good. Then you can watch me eat mine." Smiling, he pulled her upright.

**

"I don't feel good just leaving you here," Byron said pulling into the driveway at Betty Jean's house.

She looked from him to her house looming in the background and lifted her shoulders. "I'll be fine," she said with little aplomb.

"What if I dropped you off at Sheila's house? Would that be better?"

Betty Jean turned her head, looking out her side window. She thought for a moment then shook her head in the negative. "She's probably with Cyron."

She continued to stare out at her neighbor's shrubbery and he continued to frown at her house. He sat for a moment longer, then put the Suburban in reverse and backed out the drive.

Betty Jean glanced at him once, then returned her gaze to her window. She was going to ask him where they were going, but changed her mind. Oddly, she didn't really care.

Byron was right about the spot he'd taken her to that morning. It was indeed the place for God to make house calls and she'd sat there until after the sun set, laying all her burdens at His feet and placing herself in His hands. There was nothing else she could do but wait and see.

She closed her eyes, suddenly tired. When she opened them, Byron was pressing the release button on her seat belt. She looked around, confused for a moment, before realizing they were parked in Byron's garage.

"Come on," he said, quietly leading the way into his house. He led her up the stairs and down the hall to the bedroom across from his. "Are you sure you aren't hungry?" he asked, flicking on the overhead light in the ceiling. He'd asked her on their ride back from the ocean, but she'd declined, as she was doing now.

"If you need anything, I'm right across the hall, okay?" Byron asked, looking into her wide eyes. "I'll get you a tee shirt or something to change into." He left her standing in the middle of the room and crossed the hall. He searched for a clean tee shirt, but couldn't find one, then recalled that doing the laundry had been on his agenda for the afternoon. Giving up his tee shirt search, he looked for something else suitable for her to sleep in and by the time he returned to the guest bedroom, she was lying on her side on top of the covers. She'd slipped her shoes off, but her clothing and head-dress remained in place. He pulled a blanket from the chest at the foot of the bed and placed it over her.

She shifted a little in her sleep, frowning deeply. Byron stood watching her for a moment hoping, not for the first time that day, that he hurt Ezekiel Johnson really, really bad. He put the clothing he'd brought for Betty Jean in the room's only chair, turned off the light and left.

When the phone rung early the next morning, Byron reached to answer it, but Betty Jean's head weighed down his arm when he tried to lift it. Blinking in surprise at the sight of her curled in a ball atop his blankets, he snatched the phone up with his other hand when it rang for the second time.

"Hello?" he asked softly, trying not to disturb Betty Jean.

"Turn on the news."

He reached for the remote, clicking the on and then the mute button. There was only one station still show-ing the news at eight twenty six in the morning and he turned to that channel. "Well, well, well," he said softly at the crowd in front of the Regency Hotel. There was an ambulance in the background loading someone in on a stretcher. "What's he saying?" he asked, as the young manager's name was flashed onto the screen and a mic was shoved under his nose.

There was a pause on the other line, then a chuckle. "He said when he last saw Room 208, he was fine and in excellent health. He knows the man was in town on business, but not the nature of it. He realized 208 should have checked out Sunday afternoon and found him when he went to inquire about the additional night. Now they're saying there looked to be a scuffle of some sort in the room, but the kid is saying he didn't see anyone with 208 or in his room at any time. He's repeating his surprise that the *fellow* hadn't checked out yesterday. Now they're saying there will be an investigation and the extent of the man's injuries are not known at this time."

"So, let 'em investigate. I've never been finger printed. They won't find shit. Besides, it was worth going to jail over, even if they do find me."

"Us," his brother corrected even though personally he hadn't laid a hand on Ezekiel Johnson. They'd have to prove that he didn't.

"Find us, then. In fact, I'll turn myself in, if I can have about ten more minutes with him."

Cyron laughed. "I doubt if it'll get that serious where you'll have to turn yourself in. The little prick is still unconscious and no one's going to give a shit soon. Hell, no one cares now, except the news people and that's just because it's today's story. Tomorrow he'll be just another black man that got jumped on if anyone still gives a shit enough to still be talking about him. We should have planted money on him and made it look like a drug deal gone wrong. Maybe even some anti-gay literature and shit. This is San Francisco. They could have beaten him up."

"Get help, Cyron," Byron said softly into the phone, secretly entertained by both thoughts.

"How's Betty Jean doing?"

Looking down at her, Byron said, "She's not frowning so deeply anymore," observing her nearly smooth brow.

"As long as you know what that means, man, I won't press it," Cyron said. "I've gotta run, though. I just caught that on the news and thought you'd be interested."

"Yeah, thanks, man."

"No, problem," Cyron said disconnecting the call.

"What time is it?" Betty Jean asked softly from Byron's side.

"Eight thirty."

Betty Jean sat up and a hand went instantly to the scarf still secured around her head. She'd changed into the things he'd left in the chair for her and retied her scarf, but hadn't removed it.

Byron's eyes followed her hand to the dark blue scarf and remained there for a moment as he wondered what was hidden beneath it. Something told him it wasn't her usual rich, thick hair. His eyes traveled from the scarf to her face where they met hers, before she dropped her gaze and slid to the far side of the bed.

"I need to get to work," she said, but failed to move pass swinging her legs over the side.

"Sheila said she'd bring home any files you absolutely needed and she'd let them know at HD you'd be working from home for a few days."

"Yeah?" Betty Jean asked. Bless Sheila's heart. She didn't really feel like going into work today and she hadn't even looked in the mirror, yet. She knew she wasn't to the point where make up would hide—She stopped herself from completing the thought.

She wasn't trying to hide anything.

She didn't have anything to hide.

Standing from the bed, she said, "I need to get dressed." Before Byron could form a thought to detain her, she was out the room and across the hall.

A few moment's later he heard the door to the hall bathroom close and cursed under his breath. He threw the covers back, rising from the bed to dress. He knew she'd be ready to go home when she came out of the bathroom.

**

"Congratulations!"

Sheila looked up from her typing to see a hand-some man of indeterminate years standing before her desk. The silver and white hair gave the man a dashing look that failed to undermine the power and strength that exuded from him despite his age.

She smiled at the man in familiar recognition as he lifted the lid from the candy dish on her desk and removed a handful of peanut M & M's, as he did nearly every morning when he passed her desk. Then she frowned, wondering at his congratulations.

"That ring must still be awful freshly acquired if you've forgotten about it already or is it old news by now?" he asked, with twinkling eyes and good cheer.

Sheila blushed, embarrassed. "Don't be coming down here trying to see if you can turn my cheeks pink, Charles. I've already told you, you can't!" she said, laughing at the man who stood at the helm of Hurstwode and Donovan. The man responsible for bringing aboard Betty Jean and inadvertently herself, Charles Hurstwode. She had never met Richard Donovan. The word around the water cooler was that no one had ever met him, spoke to him, or seen him in the distance for that matter. Sheila had her own doubts as to whether the man even existed.

"It only makes you lovelier. My mother always said, only marry a girl who still knows how to blush." She smiled at his words and he said, "See? Lovely." He complimented her again, in that same confident manner people used to tease and flirt with in the days before sexual harassment overtook the workplace.

"I thought I *blinded you* with it last week?" she asked repeating his words of praise from the previous week.

"Oh, well," Charles said munching his candy. "I'd thought you'd rid yourself of that young swain and give ole Chuck a chance, but since I see we're in week two and the diamond is still attached to your dainty finger, we can assume the match will still take place."

"Yes, we can," Sheila confirmed, smiling. She loved his eloquent speech. Charles Hurstwode was a time-less gentleman. A throw back to the days of courtly manners.

"Is she busy?" he asked, stepping around the curve of Sheila's desk to enter Betty Jean's office.

Sheila shook her head at the man, looking stern. "You have to learn how to check your voice messages and email, Charles," she admonished gently.

"That kid genius on thirty two came up and showed me how to get my email right off my desk top," he said proudly. "It's a snap. I just haven't checked it. It's a supreme nuisance," he said cheerfully. "As for the voice mail, Susan tells me what I need to know and I've yet to see my assistant this morning. I keep her busy. Any day, I fully expect her to request I hire an assistant for her!"

Sheila laughed. "I don't doubt it. Ms. Carlson is working from her home office for a few days," she said evasively. She wouldn't go into depth unless asked and even then she planned to lie about Betty Jean being under the weather and contagious.

"It wasn't too important." Charles turned away from the door. "I have something coming up soon and I wanted to know if she's interested in me throwing it her way. It's a little different from what she's been doing, but I think she'll shine none the less."

"Again, I don't doubt it."

Charles Hurstwode had been married in his youth, but his wife passed away young. He never married again and had no heirs. Sheila believed he scoured the country trying to find someone to eventually hand over the reins to his part of Hurstwode and Donovan. Betty

Jean thought she was insane, but Sheila was certain that was the reason why he wanted Betty Jean to work for him. To groom her for his position.

"Anyway, it can keep until her return. Tell her I said to take as much time as she needs. No point in rushing back to work and infecting us all." He assumed illness was the cause for Betty Jean's absence. "I'm not too certain these old bones have much fight left in them; especially, to combat some nasty virus."

Sheila took in the healthy glow in his cheeks and the nice way he looked in his dark pinstripes and made a face. The man was probably going to out live them all.

"I'll let you resume your work." Snagging a few more M & M's from the dish, he walked away waving. Sheila smiled after him for a moment before she dropped her gaze to the computer monitor once again.

**

Betty Jean sat at her kitchen table staring into the living room. She missed sitting on her living room carpet in front of the television set like she did when she was a child. She missed the comfort of her sofa. She'd always liked the openness, the accessibility of the room, but now it was closed to her. There might as well have been a flashing neon sign hanging from the ceiling that screamed EZEKIEL.

He was in that room.

He owned that room.

She saw him stamped everywhere. He was in the furniture. The carpet. Her curtains. She stood up slowly from the table and entered the front room of her house. She grabbed hold of the curtains made from Italian lace that she'd hunted for three months to find, the curtains that matched her furniture perfectly and gave them a vicious yank.

She saw him in the paint on the walls.

She moved to the next set of windows.

Snatching down the drapings, she balled them in her fist tearing at them blindly.

Ezekiel was in her house, *her home* and she wanted him gone. Gone. Gone. Gone. She ran from one window to the next, six in all, pulling down the curtains and shredding them in her hands.

Tired, she sank to the floor crying, hugging the ruined finery to herself. She cried until hiccups replaced her sobs, then sat up, blinking at the destruction done to the room. Her pretty curtains were in shreds all over the floor. She could still see the faded blood in the carpet and she still felt Ezekiel watching her from the walls.

"You can't have my house!" she hissed, closing her eyes as she clamped her jaw shut. She was not going to be a victim. He was not going to make her weak. With new resolve, she raised her head. Giving the room a final look, she retrieved the phone and dialed information.

When Sheila arrived at Betty Jean's home a few hours later, her knock went unanswered.

Betty Jean was gone.

Chapter Twenty Five

W hen Byron arrived at her house a few hours behind Sheila, he entered the living room to find Betty Jean in overalls and a painter's cap. He could tell she had a bandanna tied around her head beneath the cap. She was standing on a ladder marking the walls and outlining the windows with blue painter's tape.

Byron looked around curiously at the naked room. "How'd you get all the furniture out?" he asked in the way of greeting.

"I donated it."

"Don't you have to make an appointment for a pick up day?" He was genuinely curious. He didn't know the laws of recycled furniture, per se, but it didn't seem likely they'd rush right out the moment someone called.

She shrugged. "Not if you say you'll give the furniture to someone else or throw it in the trash or volunteer to pay for the pick up. Any of those will speed up the process, especially the monetary donation." Climbing down from the ladder, she surveyed her work.

"What's the plan?" Byron asked leaning his shoulder against the entryway wall.

"No plan. I just want a new look for this room. I didn't like the old one anymore. I'm repainting, getting new furnishings and thinking about taking the carpet up and having hardwood floors in here, too.

Her words caused Byron to look at the carpet and he wished he hadn't. It was his first time really being inside her house since the attack. He was glad he hadn't been there to see what she'd scrubbed out of the carpet. The stain that remained stood out as though it were still dark crimson in his mind.

He could see where she lain bleeding on the floor and he wanted to take her in his arms and hold her. He wanted to make everything right for her again. He stared at the spot, blinking back the water that blurred his vision and hoped, beyond hope, that he'd put her ex into a coma.

"I've been known for my carpentry skills," he volunteered, trying to clear the husky emotion from his voice.

"I don't need anyone's help." Betty Jean regretted her sharp tone almost instantly. She dropped her head, closing her eyes. She stood in the quiet for a moment, seeking strength. "I'm sorry." Her eyes remained closed. "I just want to do this myself. I *need* to do this myself." She took another deep breath, then opened her eyes. What he saw broke his heart and the desire to hold her grew stronger, but he wouldn't deny her the valiant attempt she was making to stand strong.

"Understood," he said, nodding once. "Can I at least help you with that?" he asked, trying to be friendly and not look hurt or disappointed, the way he felt. He wished to God she'd let him be strong for her. Byron waved his hand towards the can she wrestled with and she stood well out of his way when he reached to open it.

Unnecessarily out of the way, in Byron's opinion. When he woke up that morning, she was using him for a pillow, now she was back to resembling a deer in the head lights and he had the uncomfortable feeling that he was the damned truck.

"Moss green," he said, reading the can's label.

"I'm going to do this room over using greens." She spoke in the same flat monotone she'd been using since her attack.

"I can't wait to see it." They stood in silence staring at the paint in the can. "Well, I'd better let you get to it, then." Betty Jean nodded her head in agreement. Walking towards the door, he attempted to sound light and casual. "Call me if you need anymore cans opened."

"I will," Betty Jean promised, but they both knew she lied.

**

It was well after four in the morning when Betty Jean finished dabbing the last bit of moss green paint onto her living room wall. She had hoped the exercise would encourage sleep, but no such luck.

She was tired, feeling both weary and drained. Her body was exhausted and wanted to lie down to the comforts of her bed, but her mind was still turned on and filled with thoughts, ideas and images, despite the disappearance of energy.

After soaking her brushes in turpentine and paint thinner, she placed them in a bucket in the garage then went to her bedroom where she stood just inside the doorway frowning.

She walked over to the CD rack that covered nearly half of one wall and began shifting through the CD's. There were over five hundred in her collection, but she kept them alphabetized so in no time at all her fingers closed around the disk she wanted and she placed it in the open arm of the stereo.

Accepting the CD, the arm slid shut and she could hear the slight sound the disk made as it began to spin. If music did indeed soothe the savage beast, maybe it would relax her mind enough to slow down and rest, if not shut off completely, so she could get some sleep. Picking up the remote, she curled up at the foot of her bed and pulled a multi colored afghan across her body.

She closed her eyes and pushed play. When lyrics from the gospel soundtrack poured from the speakers in her room, her eyes sprang open. She'd unconsciously selected the wrong CD, but didn't feel like getting up to replace it, so she let it play. Closing her eyes, she listened to the lyrics and the song brought to mind all the things she'd been taught about faith and belief.

She was a child held in God's loving hands.

There was no hurt, pain or hurtle that He could not help her get through.

All she had to do was lay all her hurts and pains before Him and be healed.

Life happened according to God's will.

Presently she wasn't so certain about that, Betty Jean thought turning her cheek into the mattress, letting it absorb the tears that slid down her face. If everything was written and happened according to His will, then why...

She shook her head trying to understand what couldn't be understood.

Oh, she knew that God was indeed the Master Builder, the plan was His, but somehow the blueprints had been stolen ...corrupted...destroyed and made to go awry. None of this could possibly be God's plan.

Betty Jean squeezed her eyes shut, trying to keep the tears that threatened from falling. Surly not all things happened according to His will.

The song built in tempo and expression and a river ran from Betty Jean's eyes to pool beneath her cheek and soak the sheet where her head lay.

**

"Where's my little buddy?" A cheerful Carol appeared at the corner of Sheila's desk. Her hair was set in tight little spiral curls that bounced around her face appealingly whenever she moved her head. The spirals were a new look for her and she liked them.

They made her feel giddy and young.

Sheila looked up from her paperwork, then shook her head. She'd canceled or rescheduled all of Betty Jean's appointments, but had forgotten about her lunch date with Carol. "I'm sorry. It's my fault. I was supposed to call you to let you know Betty Jean couldn't make it."

Carol's eyes narrowed on Sheila's face and Sheila quickly dropped her head back to her desk. The lawyer in Carol sprang to the forefront sensing something was amiss.

"What's going on?" Carol's sing song voice matched her bubbly mood.

"Nothing." Sheila busied herself, refusing to look up. Carol's sweet face was a facade. She had a killer instinct that was rarely wrong and a sharp penetrating gaze that could pluck the feathers from a chicken, then the meat from the bones. Sheila had always thought it a pity that Carol hadn't gone into criminal law. How many confessions could that look of hers have garnered? "She's just out for a few days." Sheila shrugged, hoping she sounded calm and normal, but knew she didn't.

"Mmm, hmm." Carol observed the aerial view of Sheila's bowed head. "When will she be back?" She was casually studying her fingernails.

"I'm not really certain, right now. Maybe by the end of the week or early next week." Sheila pretended to search through the papers on her desk.

"Mmm, hmm." Carol's blue eyes calmly took in Sheila's busy appearance.

Sensing Carol was about to ask another question, Sheila hurriedly explained. "She's not feeling well, that's all, Carol. No big story."

"Okay." Carol was still bubbly and bright, the picture of innocence. Turning from the desk she said, nonchalantly, "I'll drop some soup off from the deli. She'll like that. The Soup King on Rosedale has the best homemade chicken soup."

Quickly, Sheila patted the stack of manila folders that sat on the edge of her desk for visual effect. "I have to take these files to her later today." She was lying. She didn't have a single word, sentence or paragraph for Betty Jean to look at, let alone an entire stack of files. "I'll take the soup to her for you and save you a trip out there."

"Oh, that's okay," Carol said sweetly, turning to face Sheila, who was beginning to feel like a ball of yawn to a kitten. "I have some errands that I might as well take care of now since our lunch date was canceled and it'll be no trouble to shoot by Betty Jean's while I'm out and about." She smiled. The Cheshire cat. "I'll drop those files off for you in you like, save you a trip," she offered with an arched brow of challenge.

Sheila's eyes locked with Carol's and she cursed to herself. Damn Carol's insightful eyes!

"You shouldn't go over there," Sheila said softly.

"Oh, really?" Carol slid back up to the desk.

Sheila groaned, rolling her eyes at having been caught in Carol's web. "If I said she was contagious?" she ventured, hopeful, still not quite ready to divulge her secrets.

"I'd say I have a box of surgical masks with matching latex gloves and a bottle of penicillin in my car." Carol smiled happily, fairly bouncing in anticipation. Her instincts were never wrong! She knew something was afoot.

"If I said—" Carol cut her off, shaking her head slowly back and forth.

"I'd be able to counter anything you can think up. I'm ready for any contingency. Graduated top in my class. Trust me, you can't win." She was still smiling and Sheila rolled her eyes, accepting what she said as the truth.

Damn her eyes!

**

Betty Jean was sitting on her back deck when the intercom buzzed. She sighed heavily and made her way through the house to the front door. She could have answered from the intercom out back, but she didn't want to speak blindly without knowing who stood on her porch. She tip toed slightly to see out the peephole and was somewhat surprised by her visitor.

She was debating what she should do, if she felt like company or not, when the door was firmly knocked upon. "Open, open. I've come bearing gifts."

Deciding there was no point in delaying the inevitable, she would have to meet the public sooner or later, she took a deep breath and opened the door.

To her credit, Carol's smile remained in place and she showed no outward sign of being effected by Betty Jean's appearance. "Come on, step aside. The soup is getting cold." Betty Jean stepped behind the door, allowing her entrance.

Passing the empty, but recently painted living room, Carol preceded to the kitchen table where she placed the brown paper bag she carried in the center of it.

"Why are you bringing me soup?" Betty Jean asked carefully.

Carol turned to face her, planting her closed fists on her hips. "Because your assistant attempted to convince me that you're ill and under the weather. So, I brought soup!" She smiled.

"*Attempted to convince me*, doesn't sound very successful." Betty Jean folded her arms across her chest.

"Oh, that's because she wasn't." Carol was still as blithe as ever.

"Then why the soup?" Betty Jean stared hard at the other woman.

Carol tried to hold Betty Jean's steady gaze, but couldn't. A hardened attorney, she felt sick at the sight of Betty Jean's face. There were four or five different colors fighting for room on her face. Purple, yellow, red...She lifted one shoulder in a quick shrug. "Chicken soup for the soul?" she offered. Betty Jean raised a brow. "My instincts tell me Sheila fed me a little piece of the truth." She held up two fingers a bare fraction apart. "She said you were attacked by your ex." Carol raised both her shoulders this time in a slight shrug. "I wanted to see if you needed me." Looking again at Betty Jean's battered face, she added, "Or Paul." She wondered at the scarf wrapped securely around her head.

The scarf that should not be able to neatly conceal the volume of Betty Jean's hair, but was managing to do just that...and quite nicely, too. Not a follicle could be seen.

Betty Jean saw Carol's eyes shift from her face to her scarf and she self-consciously fingered the pink silk. "Paul?" she asked, as if she had no idea of whom Carol spoke.

"My husband," Carol teased, playing along, but failed to produce a smile from Betty Jean. "Paul's a great attorney." This time when she looked in Betty Jean eyes there was no humor in Carol's. Betty Jean remained silent and she added, "I'd help you myself, but criminal prosecution isn't my forte. That's Paul's arena." Presently Paul handled mostly family law, but had cut his teeth in criminal prosecution and was still a shark at it.

Betty Jean continued to stare at her and Carol took a seat at the table. She slid the table setting and place mat out of the way and folded her hands together neatly on top of the polished wood. "Naturally, I'm assuming you'll wish to press charges."

Betty Jean frowned. "Exactly, what did Sheila tell you?" she asked, calmly. Too calmly and Carol's radar went off again.

"Only what I already said," she returned, then added, "you know Sheila." She waved her freshly manicured hand in the air. "Loose lips sink ships and all of her boats are still floating securely in the harbor. No chance in hell of ending up at the bottom of the sea. Come sit down," she said pulling out a chair from the table. Instead, Betty Jean picked up the paper bag and looked inside.

"You want some?" she asked, walking towards the microwave.

"I ate," Carol lied, "but you go ahead." She observed Betty Jean as she moved around the kitchen preparing her soup. She looked a bit thinner. She should have brought her some bread to go with the soup. "Are you okay?" She waited until Betty Jean finally sat at the table with the steaming bowl of soup in front of her.

On the verge of saying yes, Betty Jean closed her eyes and took a fortifying breath instead. She was a little shaky when she blew it out slowly a few seconds later. "I don't know." There were tears in her eyes when she looked at her friend.

Carol touched the back of her finger to the corner of her eye where she could feel moisture gathering. As a lawyer she rarely cried at the plight of mankind, but Betty Jean's state was too much. Even for her hardened heart. "Oh, shit." She reached out and covered Betty Jean's hand with one of her own. "Whatever you need me to do, you just let me know. I can make a couple of phone calls and have that son of a bitch locked up by night fall. Or missing," she added serious as a heart attack.

"I just want this all to go away," Betty Jean said quietly. "I was just getting my life back. Just rejoining the living and now, here I am just barely able to breathe and not even sure I want to do that anymore either." Her voice trembled. "I just want to be left alone. I want to grab a corner of the air and pull it across myself like a blanket until I disappear." Her voice finally broke and she put her face in her hands and cried.

"Now that's no good." Carol got up from the table to hug Betty Jean. "We can't let Chaos win, can we?" She squatted down beside Betty Jean's chair. "What happened?"

With graphic detail Betty Jean painted a picture that she hadn't even allowed Sheila to see. She told Carol all, withholding nothing. When she reached up to remove her scarf, it was as Carol suspected. Betty Jean's beautiful hair was gone. It was chopped up and uneven. The longest strands couldn't have been more than two or three inches long. Tears shown in Carol's eyes at the damage and destruction. Not necessarily of Betty Jean's hair, but the damage and destruction done to her peace of mind and security. The pain she must have suffered to make her do such a thing, Carol thought, mentally shaking her head.

"When he said he always loved my hair the only thing I could think of was getting rid of it." Betty Jean touched a hand to her shorn locks.

Gingerly Carol touched it as well. "It's soft," she said for lack of another comment.

"I conditioned it," Betty Jean said inanely, staring down at the table.

"I can bring some supplies over later and we can try to fix it." It was a dubious invitation and they both knew it. What could a white corporate lawyer do for her *girlfriend's* hair?

"Spirals?" Betty Jean tugged at one of Carol's blond curls, a ghost of a smile graced her lips.

"Don't I look ready for the Good Ship Lollipop?" Carol smiled, shaking her head so the curls swung to and fro. She did indeed resemble Shirley Temple with the curls bouncing prettily around her face and Betty Jean gave a little laugh.

Chapter Twenty Six

Okay, well, that's fine then," Sheila said into the cell phone. "I just wanted to call and properly exonerate myself. You know how Carol is. She'll leave no rock unturned until she's ferreted out the truth. She was bee lining to your place regardless to whatever I said."

Sheila laughed as she turned on to Red River Creek. She squinted into the distance and frowned. "Betty Jean," she frowned, interrupting. "Let me call you back, okay? Okay, honey, I'll talk at ya later." Pressing the end call button with her thumbnail, Sheila flipped the phone shut. She slowed her vehicle as she approached her house, examining the tiny vehicle that was parked in her drive.

She brought the Honda to a stop just in front of her mailbox as the driver of the vintage sports car climbed out. Sheila's frown intensified as her visitor approached her car. She pressed a button and her window slid down.

"Hi!" She was greeted cheerfully, but that only made her more leery.

"Hello." The word came out as a question.

"I hope you don't mind, I asked Cyron for your address. I thought we could go over your wedding plans if you have some time."

"Am I hallucinating?" Sheila removed her sun glasses to see more distinctly. Shielding her eyes from the sun, she looked up at the assumed apparition.

Magnanimously acting as a shield, Julie stepped over an inch or two blocking Sheila's face from the sun's glare. Gratefully, Sheila let her hand drop back to the steering wheel, but she continued to frown.

"Nope, it's me. In the flesh. Making a gesture. Extending an olive branch," her would be sister-in-law said in short, simple sentences.

"Why?" Sheila didn't attempt to hide her lack of enthusiasm.

"No reason." Julie was now frowning, as well. "Just because."

"Excuse me." Sheila shooed the other woman away from her car with a wave of her left hand. Julie followed the Honda up the drive and waited patiently for Sheila to park.

Before shutting off the engine, Sheila thought briefly about pulling into her garage and going in the house. A mean thing to do to one's future sister-in-law, but Sheila was pretty sure she could handle the fall out to follow. Sure, ole Jules would be pissed off when the garage door started lowering, but so. She'd be all right. Thinking about Cyron's feelings regarding giving his sister the cold shoulder, she decided against the malicious action and turned the ignition towards herself. One day she was going to get to pull into her damn garage and leave someone standing outside. Sighing, she shut off the engine, releasing the key into her hand. She grabbed the designer bag that matched her ankle boots perfectly and got out of the car.

If she could say nothing else about her brother's choice for wife, Julie had to at least admit that the woman had style. Her long legs were draped in cream-colored slacks that cuffed at the bottom. Soft square-toed boots peaked out from beneath the cuffs. She wore a black and cream-colored paisley print, sleeveless blouse and had a lab coat that matched the pants slung across her bent arm.

On her shoulder, her combination briefcase/purse was the same soft leather as her boots and damned if her dark sunglasses didn't have a paisley print frame. Her hair was long and straight today, stopping just above the waistband of her pants. There was an inch long part in the center of her hair to lessen the severity of the straight style, but she still looked impressive. The hair of course, wasn't hers, but Julie couldn't have told it on a bet if she didn't already know it for a fact.

Julie would need to hire a team of assistants, personal shoppers and hairstylist to look like that. She bet the look came effortlessly to the other woman. She sure carried herself like it did. Sheila had one of those, *I just fell out of bed looking this way* type of demeanors.

Sheila stepped up to Julie on the driveway. "Why are you really here?"

"To help with wedding plans isn't a good enough reason?" Damn, she wasn't supposed to be confrontational. She tried again in a friendlier tone. "I brought along some magazines, too. You probably have most of them, but that's cool." Julie couldn't see pass the tinted lens of the glasses Sheila had replaced, but was pretty certain she was receiving a hard stare. She couldn't see it, but she could certainly feel it.

Sheila casually stared down at the shorter woman. "There's not a cloud in the sky."

"Beg pardon?" Julie reached up to shade her eyes from the sun as well as from Sheila's glare.

Sheila stayed planted where she was. Not feeling magnanimous herself, she made no effort to shade Julie, but removed her glasses again. "You want me to believe its cloudy today, don't you? You're at my house pissing on me. Telling me it's just a little shower that'll pass soon, like I can't tell the difference. I'm saying, there's not a cloud in the sky. I know it's not raining. Just like I know you aren't here to discuss my wedding."

"I came ov—"

Sheila shook her head. "You don't have any interest in my wedding. I fully expect you to have to be restrained just before the preacher asks if anyone wants to forever hold their peace. Right on cue with the speak now part. At least keep it real. You did at the engagement party." Sheila put her hand on her hip. "You had no trouble speaking your mind then. Don't try to sugar coat anything for me now. Don't piss on me and say it's rain."

"Okay, I deserve that."

Sheila raised a brow and pursed her lips. "Why the interest in my wedding? Planning some Jerry Springer shit?"

"No," Julie denied, managing to sound insulted. Seeing Sheila wasn't going to give an inch, she sighed. She'd come waving a white flag, but future kinfolk was having none of it. "Fine." She returned Sheila's hard glare. "You're absolutely right. I don't have any interest in *your* wedding. Nary a drop. Let's be honest, I don't know you. Why would I give a remote hoot about your wedding? However, I do care about *Cyron*'s wedding. Remember him? The groom?" Julie asked folding her arms across her chest. Sheila's eyes narrowed. "*My, my, my* is the only thing dropping out of your mouth. What about *my* brother? Doesn't he get a say in this quickie wedding? Are you pregnant or something? I mean why else—"

"Because I know that was asked out of love for your brother I won't slap your face, but you only get one." In demonstration she held her one lone finger. "That's it. Just one and you already used it, okay?" The look in her eyes said Sheila was dead serious.

"Not that I don't believe you about the slap and all, but Cyron's been abstaining for a long time now. Is the ring—" She hesitated seeing Sheila's right eye narrow a bit further. She intended to ask if the ring was down payment for her favors, but she had no doubt that palm would crack across cheek if she did. She revised her question. "Is he marrying you to sleep with you?"

Sheila's brow raised, but she showed no other reaction. Calmly, Sheila replaced her glasses, moving to go around the other woman. "Get off my property."

Julie stepped in her path. "I don't want hostility between us. That's not the kind of family I have. I really did come here with good intentions." She knew she had far too much attitude in her voice, but couldn't manage to keep the bite out of her tone. "I love my brother."

"So do I." Sheila's tone was as lethal as Julie's.

The two women stood staring at one another.

"This isn't going to work," they said simultaneously.

"What isn't?" Again their words collided.

Eyes narrowed and lips twitched in amusement.

"*This.*" They both started laughing after the third collision, cleansing the air of tension.

Finally, Sheila moved her bag from her shoulder to her hand and Julie uncrossed her arms. "Do you want to come inside?" Julie smiled her answer and went to retrieve her magazines from the passenger seat of her car.

Sheila looked at the vehicle in appreciation. "*This* is not what you were driving that morning when I saw you." Sheila vividly recalled the big BMW.

"Nope." Julie smiled, straightening away from her car. "That was my *serious girl at work* car. *This* is my baby. My out and about. My tooling the town. My let's go eat up some road car." She brushed her hand across the black paint. "My Grampy sent her to me on my birthday a few weeks ago. I have three of them now. Not three of these of course, but three cars. I may start a collection like he has. It's awesome, you should see it one day." A true car lover, she beamed with excitement. They were a passion for her. One aided and abetted by her grandfather. "This is a limited series vehicle. An original. My Grampy detests kit cars."

"Kit cars?"

"Yeah, cheaper replicas of classic cars," Julie explained. "Kind of like toy model cars, you know? But Baby is an original," she said, rubbing her hand lovingly across the vehicle. "They only made a couple hundred of these. Grampy says this was number thirty eight off the assembly line in 1964."

"What is it?" Sheila frowned, looking at the grill. She tilted her head to the side for a different angle view. "It looks like it has a face. A shark or something."

"A snake. A cobra, to be exact," Julie corrected her smiling. She was always happy to talk about her cars.

"No, I think it looks like a shark."

"It's a cobra. See?" Julie pointed at the personal plates that read just that.

"Just because you put COBRA on your plates, doesn't make it so." Sheila still thought the silver and black vehicle looked like a shark with it's mouth open. She could just imagine what it must look like tearing down the highway. Seeing it coming at you from your rear view mirror must be a treat.

"Are you insane?" Julie was in heaven, enjoying the topic. "Look at the head lights. Those are the eyes of a snake. A cobra."

"Is it called cobra?" Sheila was being sarcastic, certain it wouldn't be and ready to drive home her point.

Puffing up with pride, Julie smiled. A proud parent. "It's a 1964 Shelby:427 Cobra original."

"Sounds expensive."

Julie hunched her shoulders in answer. "It depends. A Cobra kit can go for about forty thousand."

"This isn't a kit. It's the real deal. You already said so." Sheila stared at the tiny sports car. "I doubt it had a forty thousand dollar price tag."

Again, Julie hunched her shoulders. "I'm not certain what it cost. My grandfather said he thought of me when he saw it. He likes to go to car auctions and stuff like that. I used to go with him when I was little. I still go, if I can find time to get over there." There being France where her grandfather lives.

"I thought you guys shunned the whole *we've got money thing*." Sheila eyed the car certain it cost a fortune. Julie had the grace to blush.

"Sorry about that" She apologized for her behavior at the engagement dinner. "It was a nasty thing to do. I knew Cyron hadn't told you, yet. You know, about our family. I'm sorry, it was a swing at him, really, but still I didn't have to open my mouth."

"A swing at him for what? Me?"

"I guess." Julie shrugged. "Look, I'm the only girl in a family of boys. I only have a few female cousins. The de Monbleaus are a clan of men. It's usually just me and the fellas, you know? The guys. I have them all to myself. I don't have to share. I know that sounds greedy and possibly pathetic." She held up a hand, waylaying any potential comment when Sheila's lips parted. "I don't want to lose my brothers. It's bad enough Ayron's not here. Now Cyron's going to be gone. Who knows how much longer I'll have Byron. Betty Jean was really nice," Julie said mournfully, looking down at the magazines she held.

"What do you think I'm going to do with Cyron? You make it sound like he's going to fall off the face of the earth."

"He just won't be mine anymore."

"Honey, he isn't yours now. He never was. Hell, he won't be mine either." Sheila waved off the whole idea, rolling her eyes at the thought. "Everything is borrowed, girl. You only hold it for a fraction of a time. Even if Cyron and I were together until the day we die, he still wouldn't be mine. Ownership is not our right to claim. It's all borrowed on a vapor, gone before you can even close your hand around it."

Julie opened her mouth to a question and Sheila shook her head. "Don't start me out here preaching today. I can get real religious when I set my mind to it.

Come on inside, before I climb up to the pulpit." Starting up the driveway to her front door, she spoke to Julie over her shoulder. "You should look at it this way. All these men of yours are going to bring you your sisters and cousins. Instead of losing, you're gaining what you didn't have." She threw another backwards glance to Julie's jeans and tee shirt. "You ought to be sick of all that testosterone anyway. It seems to have had a bad impression on you. It's time for a little femininity, if you ask me."

"What if I don't like what I've gained?" Julie followed Sheila up the path.

"Think *I'm glad I don't have to go home and live with that bitch*, don't purposely aim at the bride when you throw the rice and be happy." Sheila entered the house, pushing the door wide open for Julie.

"You can't throw rice at weddings anymore. It makes the pigeons explode." Julie walked in behind Sheila.

"Well, if you don't like her, you better not try throwing anything at the wedding that *she* might not like, if you know what I mean. No rocks, dog shit or punches. No sense in saving the birds if the bride gets pissed and explodes instead, hun?"

Julie agreed, smiling, certain she'd just been warned.

**

Using her knee to slide the lounge over, she stood back to survey the results of her decorating. She'd replaced the carpet with more carpet, deciding against the wood. There was wood in other sections of the house, but she enjoyed the feel of carpet beneath her toes in this room.

Besides, she thought, burying her toe in the thick jade. The carpet she'd chosen made her think of grass.

The furniture arrived on the heels of the carpet installers departure, so she hadn't had a chance to roll around on it like she'd wanted. The large room was wall to wall deep green and she was reminded of being a child in the spring time. She'd lie out in the grass in the backyard for hours, playing or reading a book. Betty Jean smiled. More often then not, she'd be staring up at the clouds, lost in their wafty freedom. Wondering to where they drifted.

The ringing doorbell startled her out of her reflections and she jumped, abruptly descending from the clouds. She looked out the living room window before crossing to the front door. Expecting to see Byron's face she was surprised at the cold nose that came through the open portal.

"What's this?" The tiny bundle squirmed to be put down and turned loose.

"This is Insomnia." Byron handed her the puppy.

"He's so cute," Betty Jean cooed as the pup tried to lick her face. His pretty gray coat was nearly black in certain spots. "Hello, Insomnia. Why'd your daddy give you such a strange name, hun?" Scratching behind the animal's dark ears, she nuzzled his neck.

Because that cute little bundle is going to grow into something nobody will want to fool around with and anybody with any sense will think twice before coming near you with him around. Because I'm worried sick about you. Because I haven't slept in days. Because a watch dog never sleeps. Because I can't be here twenty four hours a day to protect you. But because he didn't think she'd appreciate the sentiment in any of his *becauses*, Byron kept them to himself.

"I figured you could use the company now that Sheila's gone" He reached over smoothing the puppy's shiny coat.

"Really? He's for me?" Betty Jean's new carpet sprang to mind. Instantly, she was both glad for her deep green carpet and wary for it's safety. Hopefully, the deep color didn't remind little Insomnia of grass, too. She nuzzled the soft fur at his neck, again.

"Wow!" Byron was surprised, looking into the new living room. "I'm impressed."

"You like it?" Betty Jean came to stand beside him with her puppy.

"Yes," he said, lowering his voice. "It almost makes me want to whisper." He stood looking around at all the work she'd accomplished on the room. It looked completely different.

Betty Jean laughed. "Me, too. I felt that same thing a little while ago, when I first stood in the center of the floor."

"It's a calm room." He looked from the living room to her face. Is it working, he seemed to ask and Betty Jean smiled tenuously.

"A bit." She nodded, responding to the unspoken question, instead of the statement. "Let's get you some water, boy." Hugging the puppy to her, she turned from the living room. "I think I can sacrifice a couple of Tupperware bowls to your usage."

"I've got a better idea." Betty stopped, giving him a questioning look. "Let's go spoil the tike. There's a pet store on Windale at Parker. We can take little Insomnia in with us and let him pick out a few chew toys for himself." He scratched the top of Insomnia's head. "No Tupperware has to die a martyr."

"Well," Betty Jean thought hesitating. She looked towards the living room windows then down at Insomnia who licked her hand vigorously. "I guess we can," she said slowly.

He pretended not to notice her reluctance. "Good."

"I'll go change." She turned to leave.

"I'll wait here." He entered the living room to try out the lounge.

"How big do you think he's going to get?" she called over her shoulder, holding up a rather large paw for examination.

Stretching out his long legs, he lied smoothly. "No idea." No need to overwhelm the woman with the semantics. He closed his eyes smiling. Her little Insomnia might not be so cute if she knew that he'd outweigh her when fully grown.

**

She tore down the freeway doing eighty, eighty-five, then ninety.

Signaling for her exit, she shifted gears reducing speed. She drove fast, but expertly, making unnecessary twists and turns until finally reaching the residential area she sought. Here, she drove more sedately, as befit a woman with a clean driving record. She slowed the vehicle and obeyed all the laws dictated to her by the posted signs and the California State Driver's Manual. She didn't want to make somebody's kid a speed bump. Pulling into the driveway, she found Cyron outside checking his mailbox.

Surprised, he walked over to the car. "To what do I owe this pleasant turn of events?" he addressed the occupants of the vehicle.

"We're hungry! Take us to dinner," Sheila said, smiling from behind the wheel of the Cobra.

"You don't think I can get in that, do you? Where will the two of you sit?" he asked, smiling, as he looked at the two-seater.

"No, silly. We're taking your truck." Sheila climbed from the car in shorts and tennis shoes. She was in red, white and blue with all the logos matching on her chest, ass and feet. She looked too damned good and she was all his, Cyron thought looking at her perfectly coordinated Ralph Lauren. He had his arms wrapped around her before she finished speaking. "We just drove this to come get you to pay for our dinner." She kissed him smiling, listing their evening agenda. "The three of us are going to eat, then Jules is driving that beautiful machine home while I spend some QT with my fiancé." Kissing his lips again, she wrapped her arms around his neck. "Then you're going to take me home."

"Or not," Cyron said, kissing her again.

"Or not," Sheila confirmed, smiling into his mouth before returning the kiss.

"God, get a room!" Cyron's garage door was up and Julie entered to lean against the tailgate of his Escalade EXT. "Come on. Let's go. I'm hungry!"

"I'm driving!" Sheila called dashing to the driver's side of Cyron's truck. Seeing the Princess cut diamond twinkle on her finger, Cyron smiled. Damn straight she was in the driver's seat. Walking over to the passenger side of his vehicle, he unlocked the doors and everyone climbed in. Leaning over, he put the key in the ignition for Sheila after digging it out of his pocket, then waited patiently for her to adjust the seat and mirrors to her satisfaction. Pressing a kiss to her cheek, he cranked up the volume on the CD player.

"Let's go!" he said and Sheila backed from the garage at the wail of a guitar. Jimi Hendrix was just asking to be excused so he could *kiss the sky* when she made it to the corner.

Chapter Twenty Seven

How are you doing?"

"What do you mean?"

Byron smiled slowly, displaying white teeth. "Do I really have to explain the concept of how are you doing?" He raised his hands as if to lecture. "See, when one is inquisitive about another's welfare, one asks how are you doing or the less severe, how ya doing? Even the occasional, what's up is acceptable. Either of these terms is satisfactory in building a rapport with someone."

She looked at him blinking for a moment, then squeezed her eyes shut. She grimaced as though in a great struggle and Byron touched her hand on the table. "What's wrong? What are you doing?" Concern, erased all humor from his voice.

"I'm trying to see if I squeeze real tight and try really hard can I make you funny. So far it isn't working. Nope." She expelled her breath loudly, opening her eyes to grin at Byron.

He flung her hand away playfully. "Charlatan."

"Been called worse by better people," she shot back quickly.

"Ouch." He grabbed his heart. "Better than a de Monbleau?" He pronounced the name in heavy, wounded French.

"Imagine that! I was surprised, too."

They laughed softly then sat in silence for a moment before Betty Jean asked, "Did you think I would be after your money? Is that why you didn't tell me who you were?" He looked at her for a moment wondering if she shifted the conversation away from herself intentionally. Deciding to address the issue presented, he looked down at the table.

"I did tell you who I am. I'm Byron de Monbleau," he said knocking at the polished wood softly. When he looked up, Betty Jean was watching him, expecting the truth and her face said she was still waiting for it. He shrugged. "I don't have any money. Well, I do, but not Richter scale like you mean. My grandfather is ridiculously wealthy. As is my father and I suspect Ayron will be one day as well. They deserve it. Each one of them have given blood, sweat, tears and countless hours to that corporation. Hell, it *should* make them rich, but none of that is mine."

He rolled his eyes, trying to come up with the words he wanted. "I'm not saying I'm a pauper or that I couldn't pick up the phone and go, hey, dad, I need.... I could. I just don't want to. I respect my granddad's business, but the boardroom was never my thing. We each had to give a year to DMB, even Jules, but the bug only bit Ayron. The rest of us couldn't wait for our year to be up. I live off of what I earn myself with my own projects. You know about the modeling already. I didn't squander it all away. I knew the runway wasn't for me and I knew I'd need something once I got bored walking it. My family helped me financially, in the beginning, but I paid them back as soon as I started seeing a profit. I'm a man separate from the family dynasty. I'm a man making it on his own. Hell, I'm a man! Some people don't understand that or can't understand it, I don't know. I keep my family connections and my business affairs low key, because it's something I learned to do a long time ago. It's a way of being sure people see Byron the man and not just a de

Monbleau heir. Besides, it's like I said, the money isn't mine. All of us will inherit, of course, regardless to whether we worked at the company, but I'm in no hurry to receive it, if you know what I mean."

Considering someone had to die for him to inherit, she did. "Yeah," Betty Jean said, nodding her head. She understood that he wanted to stand on his own two feet without leaning on the family name and fortune. Since he grew up with the money maybe it didn't seem so astronomical to him. A million here. A billion there. But to just walk away from it... she didn't know. If it were her she'd probably be like Ayron, in the thick of it, making certain to procure herself a place in line. Bug bitten or not, she'd be in the trenches. But then too, she *was* bug bitten. She loved the corporate world, she thought judiciously. The boardroom didn't bore her at all.

"I think I've done pretty well for myself." She knew he was fishing for a compliment. Her validation.

"Mmm, I don't know." A small smile teased her lips and she raised her shoulders.

"You don't know?" He reached for her hand across the dining room table again.

"Well, you can play the piano rather well," she conceded. "But I don't know about anything else." She started laughing when he tugged at her arm. "Wait! Wait! you're going to wake up the ironically named, Insomnia." She giggled, trying not to wake the puppy sleeping contentedly in her lap.

Byron sat back in his chair smiling. Her laughter was like bells in Heaven and he'd missed their ringing. She hadn't answered his initial question, but he guessed she was doing okay.

**

"You know what I just thought?" Julie looked up from the magazine she had spread out in front of her. "Mother is going to kill you!"

"What?" Cyron asked, stepping in from the small deck in his back yard.

Julie's head snapped around. "I didn't know you'd gone outside. I thought you were still in the kitchen. Stop doing that! I'm trying to talk to you. Every time I look up you're gone again. Stop it and listen."

"Okay, but the barbecue is going to burn."

"Like we'd be able to tell the difference."

"There's nothing wrong with my barbecue." She raised a brow and he frowned. "What? What?" he asked again, when she smiled but remained silent.

"I see," she said nodding her head in understanding. "You think us calling you the Char King is a good thing. Albeit it's an endearment and said with great affection, it's by no means a compliment to your culinary skills on the pit. It's just an avid description."

He looked uncertain as to whether or not she could be believed. If he was the family Charcoal King, she was the one most likely to use a forked tongue. She liked messing with people's heads just to see what she could get her test subjects to believe.

"Seriously," Julie encouraged when he continued to look uncertain. "Why do you think granddaddy always says he can tell his boys apart easiest when there's a family barbecue?"

"Because I'm the King!" Cyron brandished the barbecue fork he held in his right hand.

"Yeah, of Char!"

"Of Char*coal*," he corrected.

"No, that's just you hearing what you want to hear. We call you *Char* King. Not the Charcoal King. Grampy said he can always count on you to burn the hell out of everything, Byron to make everything too damned spicy to eat and Ayron's depends on his mood. Too pink or just right."

"What about you?"

"Oh." She smiled, pretending she'd forgotten herself. "He likes mine's the best."

"Whatever." Cyron tossed the towel he had slung over his shoulder at her.

"He does! Don't hate!"

"Whatever. You make a good sauce," he lied, it was really fantastic. She used lemons. "But your barbecue is only all right and sometimes a little bland now that I think about it." Another lie. Her ribs were always tender enough to fall off the bone. She wouldn't tell anyone the secret ingredient in her hamburgers and she cooked the sausages and hot dogs without turning them crunchy...like his sometimes were.

"At least I'm not the Char King. And not the one to answer to Mrs. de Monbleau. You're going to be in trouble."

"For what?" Cyron walked into the living room. He handed Julie a fresh drink before seating himself in a chair.

"Duh!" Julie held up her bride's magazine. "Mother is going to kill you. You know how she likes to plan. To reduce her to a mere invitation recipient. The first wedding, too. Oh, man, are you in trouble." She laughed and he got the feeling that she was enjoying the prospect.

He smiled, too. "I actually spoke with the Mr. and his Mrs., I was supposed to pick them up from the airport a little while ago, but dad declined. You know how he always has to run the show. I would have picked them up, then spent the return trip in the back seat like when I was twelve." He was grinning, noting that Julie looked a little pale. "You all right, Jules?"

"They're on their way here? Right now? You said a little while ago. How little a while?" She was up and had shoved her foot in one shoe, looking around for the other one. "My place is a mess. I'll never here the end of it if Mother sees it in its current condition. She'll fuss then somehow we'll end up shopping for me some new clothes! I—" She stopped abruptly at Cyron's hoots of laughter.

He snorted and her eyes narrowed.

"You bastard," she said tossing the newly located shoe. "When are they really getting here?"

"Don't know." He laughed, gasping for air. "*They're on their way here? Right now?*" he mimicked, laughing again.

"It wasn't that funny."

He nodded vigorously. "Yes, it was. You're afraid of Helen still! You're what now, Jules? A hundred? A hundred and two? But your mommy still makes you quake. *My room's dirty. Oh, no! Mother will ground me.*"

"You're an ass." Julie reclaimed her drink, flopping back down into her chair. He had two big comfortable recliners in his living room. They never failed to lure her to sleep, which was why she never sat in either if she was visiting on a time frame. "So what did mom really say?"

He hunched his shoulders, pulling himself together. "I haven't been able to get in touch with them. I think they're on a boat in the Orient."

Julie rolled her eyes. "It figures. They're always off on one adventure or another. Why not the Orient this week?" Her question was theoretical.

"They deserve it. Dad worked hard for his retirement. Mom said she didn't mind his working so much then because they'd be able to enjoy time together later, remember?"

"Yeah, I remember," she admitted reluctantly. "It would be hard not to, she said it often enough. But I still miss them."

"Me, too."

"I miss Ayron, too."

"Yeah, me too."

"We should all get together. All of us can go home for Christmas or something. I haven't been to Oregon in about three years. Pennsylvania for even longer." They'd grown up between the two states but the family's main home had been the one in Oregon and was where they all generally met up at. Their mother loved the Pacific Ocean and the open airyness of the house in Oregon better than the stuffy formality of the house in Pennsylvania.

He was nodding his head in agreement. "Sounds good to me. We should lay it out for everybody. Plan it up."

"Hell, we have to locate the elders first! I remember Mother saying she couldn't wait to escape and have dad to herself. I'm beginning to think she meant it seriously. I miss them. I miss everybody. I guess I'll be missing you too soon."

"What?" he asked pulled from his thoughts of family.

"Once you're the Mr. in Mr. and Mrs., you won't have so much free time."

"It's not like I'll be tied up, though, either. Sheila and I will be together, but life won't change so radically that my sister will have to miss me when we live in the same city." He reached for her hand and squeezed it in reassurance. "I'll just have to add another steak to the grill." He joked to lighten the mood and she smiled.

They both started laughing and he jumped up, heading for his pit. He'd gotten comfortable and forgotten his grilling food.

"Char King!" Julie called after him, laughing.

**

"Why am I planning a wedding?" Sheila asked, making a paper plane of the magazine she held as she tossed it away from her.

Insomnia barked at the sudden action and went chasing off on plump little legs to find the source of the disturbance. Betty Jean watched him trot away with the besotted look of a new parent. "You told me you love him. *He completes me*, all Jerry Mcquireish."

"I did not," Sheila denied, blushing. "He does complete me and I do love him, but I didn't say that!"

"Why not plan your wedding?"

"Because I don't know if I want the big production, the fanfare, the hoopla."

"You've got to be kidding. The Queen wants to abscond from royal court?"

"Abscond, is it? You read too much. No one says abscond in day to day conversation."

"Now that can't be true, because I just did and besides that, not everyone has the honor of conversing daily with a queen." Betty Jean bowed her head to the royal subject in question. Insomnia bounded back to the lap made of her legs as she sat Indian style on Sheila's carpet and she took the magazine from his mouth.

"Is that a compliment or an insult I'm too dumb to recognize?"

Betty Jean laughed. It was her first social trip since her ordeal with Ezekiel and she was enjoying the day. "Why on earth would I be insulting you, Sheila? I call you a queen merely because you have a regal bearing. You have a lot of admirable qualities that make me secretly think of you as a queen. You befit royalty. If you told me you were marrying a king, I wouldn't be surprised at all."

Humbled by the sincere words, Sheila was silent for a moment. "I just want to close my eyes and wake up married to Cyron. I use to have these grand plans of the perfect wedding. Now none of them matter to me. Screw all of it. Let's hold hands and jump a broom, step on a glass or stand in front of a justice of the peace. I don't care about the outside covering. I want to get down to the specifics. The meat and bones. The potatoes. The this is my husband. The dirty laundry, cooking dinner, paying bills part. The looking in his face for the next sixty years. The essence."

"Sounds to me like you're ready to be married not just wedded."

"That's a good thing, right?" Sheila asked nervously.

"I think so. Too many people can't see past the wedding. They think it's all a fairy tale and are completely unprepared for what being married demands."

"Do you think he'd run off with me if I called and asked?"

"Please. I'm not the only one who views you as royalty. What wouldn't Cyron do for you, if you asked?"

"Whatever." Sheila smiled embarrassed. She looked down at the ring on her finger like she usually did when she had Cyron on her mind.

"That's a *Princess* cut diamond, isn't it?" Betty Jean asked softly and tears sparkled in Sheila's eyes. "A princess for a princess."

"I love him, Betty Jean. I'm so ready to be his queen."
**

"Hey there!" Betty Jean said releasing Insomnia from the newspaper strewn hallway bathroom. He came galloping out only to run back in and nip at her ankles as she gathered what was left of the Saturday paper.

His paws were wet when he batted at her legs, then stood braced against her calf, tail wagging. "Do you step in your water before or after you turn over your dish?" She bent setting the bowl aright. She was glad to see that other than destroying his provisions and the paper she'd laid out for him, the room was basically clean. She only needed to sop up the spilled water and throw the shredded paper into the trash.

They hadn't been at it long, but his potty training was going rather well. Already he knew to go to the patio doors when he needed to go out. Every now and then, he'd leave a small puddle on the floor or the carpet for her, but that was about it. All major jobs went to the back yard.

"You're a smart little one, aren't you, Sweety?" Picking up the pup, she exited the bathroom. She'd been to church that morning and she felt good, at peace. Her scarf and carefully applied make up hid her secrets from the congregation and she was able to sit and soak up a little tranquility, unmolested by kindness and good intentions.

The Lord's calming hands were still upon her when she stepped into the living room. Finding a sun-drenched spot on the carpet, she stretched out in it on her back. She held the puppy aloof, dangling him in the air as he energetically tried to lick at her face. His tail wagged and his paws kicked at the air in an effort to close the distance between his tongue and her face.

The warm sunlight felt nice on her face and she smiled in reminiscence of being a child out in the back yard. She played with the puppy, gazing up at the ceiling wondering what illusions drifted by in the clouds beyond her ceiling.

Chapter Twenty Eight

I'm going in tomorrow."

"Are you sure?"

"Yeah," she said with a shrug in her voice. "I can't escape life forever."

"Yes, you can," he said and she knew he was serious. He would whisk her away in a heartbeat if she asked.

"Maybe, but it wouldn't be wise," she said after some hesitation.

"Why not?"

"You have to stand up and fight. Run once and you keep doing it. It'll get easier each time, until you're in a constant sprint."

"So, there's no escaping life?"

"Nope." She shook her head, as one who'd tried to find a route and failed. "Just have to get up and keep trying."

"Do you only do what's wise?"

"Most times I try," she said quietly. In fact, they both spoke in low hushed tones. She sat near him on the couch and he stretched his arm out to tug at the long scarf that hid her hair.

"Let me see." His fingers touched at the fabric intimately, but he made no move to remove it. He waited patiently on her.

"I—" She stopped. "Why?" Her lips parted in a whisper.

"Why not?" Byron questioned softly. "I want to see you. Without you hiding yourself from me."

"I don't want you to see," she said, and he wondered at what she hadn't said. She didn't want him to see what? Her hair? Her face? The truth about what happened? The extent of it? What?

"Betty Jean." His voice was still whisper soft. The living room was lit by candles and intimate shadows bounced off the walls. He turned her face back towards him with a touch of his finger. "I love you. You don't have to respond or give the words back to me, especially not right now with everything else on your mind, but I do love you lady. Whatever it is that you're hiding from me can come to the light. Such as it is." He smiled at the glowing candles. "You are so beautiful to me. Regardless to whatever has been done to you. You don't have to hide from me. You can put on a steel cloak and armor yourself against the entire world if you want, but not me. You don't have to be afraid with me."

By the time he finished speaking Betty Jean's eyes were shining with tears. Her lip trembled a little and Byron reached out for her. She pulled away and he let his arm fall, but before the first tear rolled down her cheek and splashed on her shirt, she'd turned and buried her face in his chest. Closing his arms around the sudden impact of her body, Byron placed his chin on top of her head and closed his eyes.

"I don't want you to see." He heard her say again and fought back tears of his own. When he'd left and gone home a few hours later, her secret terrors were still hidden beneath her scarf. Still cloaked from his eyes.

**

Having stuffed himself on Chinese take out, Cyron stretched out his long length on the living room floor, sighing in contentment. For the next hour or so, he was full. He was never a big fan of Chinese food, because it never stayed with him long enough, but his sweetie seemed to be slightly addicted to the stuff and he was getting accustomed to her desires. One of which included Chinese food at least once a week. He unfastened the button on his jeans and sighed again as his stomach took advantage of the opportunity to expand it's girth.

He looked up at his bride to be and tilted his head to the side. She sat quietly on the couch. She stared in the general direction of the television, but he could tell she wasn't watching it. She was too quiet. When Sheila watched television, she did so as a fanatic fan. She gave commentary from the sidelines and surfed channels worse than he did. She'd been on the same channel now for an entire show, even through the commercials. Reaching up, he retrieved a few coins from the Chinese take out change that laid on the coffee table. Still lying on his back, he carefully tossed a coin that landed in her lap.

Sheila glanced down, then picked up the copper coin. Her chin was in her hand and her elbow was propped up on the arm of the couch. Her head turned towards him, but remained propped in her hand.

She raised a brow at him and Cyron smiled. "A penny for your thoughts."

She returned his smile and let her arm drop. She changed positions on the couch and stretched out. Her head dangled off the cushion slightly, but she was comfortable. "Betty Jean came to work today." She stared up at the vaulted ceiling. Cyron looked surprised by the news, but she didn't see it. Her mind was on her thoughts. "She was already in her office when I got there. She stayed secluded in there until she left for lunch at ten. She didn't come back. She called about two thirty and told me she was taking off for the day." She smiled a little at the obviousness of Betty Jean's statement. She'd reached that very conclusion when Betty Jean hadn't returned by noon.

"I'm worried about her, but she seems to be doing all right. If that makes any sense. She seems to be getting better, yet I'm still concerned." She turned her head to look at Cyron.

"She's your friend. Of course, you're worried about her. You're going through the pain with her. That's what real friends do. They go through the fire with you. It makes sense that you'll worry until she's one hundred percent again."

"I think it was good that she came to work today. She's getting out, moving around again."

"She left at ten in the morning, though." He only pointed it out because he didn't want her expecting too much too soon from her troubled friend.

"She still made the effort. It's like having the flu and the second you feel a little better you try to conquer the world again, but you can't do it. You have to give yourself time to heal and regain your strength or you'll end up flat on your ass again. It's good, though, that she's trying to heal, to get back up again. It means Betty Jean's not down for the count, yet."

"Is that right, oh wise and noble one." He teased her, wanting to lighten her mood.

Sheila smiled, blushing as she usually did when he teased her. "I'm serious." She smiled wider for no other reason than her love for him. "Be quiet." He hadn't spoken.

Cyron fingered another coin, but she spoke before he could toss it to her. "I'm thinking about going back to school."

"Back?"

"You know nothing about me." She turned until her back was flat on the couch cushion and she was upside down. Her head hung inches above the carpet. Her legs were across the back of the couch and her feet pointed towards the ceiling.

"I have plenty of time to find everything out, Nancy." He waved her off.

She twisted on the couch, but kept her position. "Who? What did you call me? All right, I've already told you about doing that," she warned in understanding.

"I've already told you about saying I don't know you. I know what's important, Shei-la." Making a face on the second syllable, he stuck out his tongue at her.

"You need to find something more interesting to do with that tongue, young man, other than sticking it out at people," she said playfully, then rolled her eyes. "Now *listen* to me. I want to make sure you get your penny's worth. I have more thoughts."

"Okay. Proceed." Cyron folded his hands across his stomach and stared up at the ceiling, as docile as possible.

"I went to college for about three years, then I quit and went to work as an office manager, because I was tired of being a struggling student. I worked here and there doing this and that then I went to work for Betty Jean and the rest is history, but," she said now curling to her side on the couch and looking at Cyron's profile. "I want to go back to school now."

"You're going to get a degree to advance in the business world?" He knew she liked working for Betty Jean, but even he could see there was no career advancement in that. Truthfully, he didn't care if she worked or not. The Chicken Shack brought in more than enough revenue to support them both and he was considering opening more spots in the near future, but thinking of Julie's remarks at their engagement dinner he refrained from saying anything. He knew Sheila would be against the idea of being a housewife. Even if she would have considered it before, he knew thanks to Brandon's Brat, she wouldn't do it now.

"Actually, I've always been interested in the human mind. What makes us do the things we do, that type of thing. With everything that's been going on with Betty Jean lately, it's all just been on my mind again."

"Is that the field you were originally studying?" he asked surprised and intrigued that she'd started out in medicine, not business.

"Yep. Then I stopped going to school. I wanted to earn a little money and then return after a semester or two, but I never did. I guess it was something I always wanted, but not something I wanted badly enough. Now I think I do. I'm a little older now. More settled. I think I can go ahead and get it done now without all the distractions of my youth." She hunched her shoulders.

"I think it's a cool idea. My wife the doctor. Dr. Sheila. We'd be Dr. de Monbleau and Mr. Dr. de Monbleau," he announced formally. "Do they do that? Mr. Dr. So and So?" he asked, thinking out loud. "Mr. Dr. de Monbleau. I like it, already. I can quit my job and be a doctor's husband."

She said nothing, only smiled dreamily into the distance and he tossed another coin. He was just as careful with this toss as he had been with the other, but she'd changed positions multiple times since he'd tossed the penny.

"Ouch," she protested as the nickel bounced off her temple and onto the carpet.

"I'm sorry," he said getting to his knees and crossing the distance to her on all fours.

She picked up the nickel, just as he reached her side. "See? As a psychoanalyst, I'll be able to reason out why people sit and chunk coins at other people," she pouted, rubbing at the offended spot near her hairline. She looked at the nickel, then to Cyron whose face was deliciously close to hers. "You give me one." He leaned over, kissing her temple with infinite care.

"Now you." She smiled as though she needed to be persuaded further. "Come on." Cyron nibbled at her mouth. She could feel his breath on her freshly wet lips when he spoke. "Nickel for a kiss and you're holding my nickel, woman."

She tilted her head further back, then rolled from her side until she lie flat on the couch again. Pulling Cyron to her, they kissed softly. Once. Twice. Then once more. Their lips clinging a little longer with each gentle impact.

He pulled back, looking into her eyes. He held up his right hand. Pinched between thumb and forefinger, he held up one thin dime and smiled. Sheila glanced from his face to the dime and back, as a smile spread across her features recalling what a dime purchased. "I love you." Cyron kissed her again. This kiss turned hungry and when Cyron pulled away, his heart beat fast and his breath was ragged.

He dug his hand into the pocket of his jeans, then the other. Seeing his search, Sheila frowned. "What are you doing?"

"Searching for more nickels so I can take your advice."

"What advice? To get help?" she asked, teasing.

"I'm going to find something decidedly more constructive to do with my tongue." The look he gave her was a hot one and Sheila felt her insides melt and liquefy.

"I said something *interesting.*"

"Oh, it'll be interesting," he said, still looking.

"I thought you were digging for a condom or something," she said remembering the hunger in his kiss and he stopped patting his pockets.

"A condom? My, my, my, but the future Mrs. Dr. de Monbleau has a dirty mind."

"I was just thinking of your sister," she defended herself. He raised both brows. "Nothing."

He knew it was something and teased, "Don't you want to have my children?" He leaned in kissing her navel through the cotton of her shirt.

"Yes, but they better not be conceived too close to the wedding date."

"You think Jules'll be counting backwards from nine in the waiting room?"

"She asked you, too, if I'm pregnant?"

"Nope. I just know my sister."

"Humph," Sheila said offended anew. They'd agreed to bury the hatchet and all, but just then none of Sheila's burial sites would have been sister-in-law friendly approved sites.

"Wa-la!" Cyron said, digging a nickel from his pocket finally and brandishing it before her triumphantly.

"Come here." Sheila cupped the back of his head and drawing him down to her. "This one's on the house." Her lips parted in invitation under his.

**

"You didn't call me so I assumed you survived."

"You assumed correctly."

Noting her voice, he asked, "Too many well wishers?"

"No. I don't think anyone even knew I was there other than Sheila. I slipped in early, about six thirty." There was a pause on the line before she added, "Slipped out early, too. I was gone before lunch."

"Everything was okay?"

"Yeah, I guess. Outside everything was fine, but I don't feel right inside my skin anymore, you know? Or maybe you don't. Maybe I'm not explaining it right. Or—"

"Maybe you should run away with me. I'm still tired. Still in need of a vacation. We can go visit Rania in the Maldives, or Altamer, Anguilla. The Seychelles. Barbados," he said rattling off various destinations. "Maybe Aruba. We can fly down to Palm Island and have a tropical adventure."

"I don't know if I'm up for any adventures. Tropical or otherwise."

"Well, come along for the ride and keep me company. I hate flying alone."

"Come along for the ride, is it? Like I can sit in the car and wait while you run into the Bahamas real quick. You going to bring me out a soda?"

On the other end, Byron smiled. "Okay, so maybe you'll have to do more than ride shot gun. It'll be worth it. We can both use the rest."

"I can't go anywhere. Sheila and Cyron's wedding is coming up."

"They haven't even set a date yet."

"But you can't deny that it's coming up."

"Eventually, doesn't count. You can't hold an argument with it."

"Insomnia needs me. I don't want to put him in a kennel. He'll pick up bad habits from the other dogs."

"We can get him a plane ticket, too. He'll love Key West."

"I don't know, Byron. Let me think about it."

"What's there to think about? The Cocomos are beautiful this time of year."

She laughed. "You've named about a dozen different places. What happened to Palm Island or the Maldives?"

"We'll get there. *Eventually*. I want to take the scenic route."

"At the route you're taking by the time the destination is reached, it'll be time to turn around and come home."

"Okay, maybe we can shorten it a teeny bit."

"A teeny?"

"Yeah, but nothing more. We can have your people call my people in the morning to set it all up."

Betty Jean laughed. "Sheila's the only people I have. She's my whole network and if you call her with such an itinerary, you'll be buying three tickets instead of just our two. There's no way in hell, she'll be left behind. She'll beat us to the tarmac."

"What about Insomnia? You forgot about his ticket just that quick? I'll have to purchase four tickets."

"Well, you might as well buy Cyron a ticket, too. If Sheila's going he's bound to tag along as well!"

"The four of us are going plus the dog?! Jules won't be left behind. None of us would be able to come back!"

"She'd hop a plane and join us."

"After calling Ayron to tell that we tried to leave her, first!"

"Hey, he's welcomed to come along, too!"

They both laughed. It seemed the whole world was going along for their great escape.

Chapter Twenty Nine

It was barely six a.m. when Charles Hurstwode exited the elevator, heading towards his office suite. Under his arm were tucked three newspapers. None were in English. None were from the United States. He had his eye on the international market and checked its pulse first thing each morning. In his hands he carried a bag of donut holes, his favorite and his own special coffee blend. He always enjoyed a cup with his donut holes as he read his papers.

Turning the corner, he was only mildly surprised to see he had a visitor. Surprised, only because he rarely found someone perched on a seat in his waiting area, but not so surprised that the visitor was Betty Jean Carlson.

She put in nearly as many hours as he did. Probably more. He stopped competing months ago, conceding the title of Most Tireless Worker to her youthful hands. He knew Betty Jean to work hard and early, but it didn't bode well that she was sitting in the near dark waiting on him.

"If you will get the pastries, I will get the door." He greeted her as though nothing were out of the ordinary. Betty Jean stood from her seat and took the bag from his hand while he unlocked his office. Once unlocked, he pushed the door open and she preceded him into the large office.

He indicated a couch for her to sit on and placed his newspapers on the coffee table. Betty Jean sat while he prepared his coffee. Knowing her penchant for cocoa over coffee, he held only one cup when he returned to take his place across from Betty Jean on another comfortable couch. There was a desk in his office, but no chairs sat before it. Charles Hurstwode preferred the personal touch in his business dealings and always saw desk seating as a power play. He already knew he was a powerful man, as did most people that made it to the confines of his office, his personal space. He saw no reason to shove it down anyone's throat.

"Have some?" He picked up the white bag, offering it to Betty Jean who declined. "Well, you must forgive me, my dear. I'm too weak a man when it comes to all things sweet." He popped one in his mouth and smiled.

Sipping his coffee, he looked at Betty Jean who sat quietly with her hands in her lap. "Okay, I'm ready now." He bit into another sugary sweet, leaning back on the couch. "Let's have it." He might be old, but he was no fool. She wasn't in his office before sun up just to decline donuts and sit.

He chewed a little less industriously and felt the wad grow thick in his throat as he tried to swallow. Was she resigning? Had someone stolen her away from him as he had done to her previous employer? Who? He'd offer her more money, he decided, preparing himself for the battle ahead. He wouldn't give up her expertise, diplomacy, grace, charm, talent and hard work without a fight. He searched a long time for Ms. Carlson. He wasn't about to give her up so easily.

"I'm ready," he said again, rising to the edge of the couch, ready to bargain. He sipped more coffee and beckoned with his free hand. "Come on. Talk. Lay it on me."

And she did.

After she made her request, they both sat in silence. Again, he held out the bag to her and this time she accepted, removing two holes from the bag. She ate them and accepted more. Together the two polished off the bag.

Charles rose and walked over to the mini refrigerator he kept in his office. It was too early in the morning for soda, so he extracted a bottle of orange juice. He picked up a coffee stirrer to serve as a straw and went back to the couch. He shook the bottle of juice before handing it to Betty Jean.

She drank her juice and he sipped his coffee. Another ten minutes or so slid by in silence before he finally spoke. He freshened his coffee, took a sip and grimaced. It needed sugar. With his back towards Betty Jean, he said, "I don't have a problem with you taking a leave of absence." He reseated himself, arranging the suit jacket he'd forgotten to remove. He sipped the sweetened brew. "I do have a problem with you not coming back."

Betty Jean was taken by surprise. She expected to be terminated, released from her duties with her request for leave. Indeed, she'd come to terms with it over the course of the night. Having made her decision, she was prepared to be gracious when he made his. She was prepared to fight for Sheila's position with the company. She shouldn't suffer for Betty Jean's personal choices. She was not prepared for his reaction anymore than he was prepared for hers when teardrops fell on her folded hands. She'd been gripping them together and hadn't even noticed when the tears began to roll down her face.

Apologizing for her tears, she wiped away at them.

Charles removed the carefully folded handkerchief from his suit pocket and handed it to her. She took it apologizing again when more tears followed the first. Embarrassed, but unable to stop the flow, Betty Jean buried her face in the silky cloth, apologizing with her whole heart for the unexpected display.

Once again Charles Hurstwode leaned back against the cushions on his leather couch. Meditatively, he sipped at the steaming coffee. He had little experience dealing with crying women, other than his late wife, Ellen. When Ellen cried, she either wanted to be held or left alone. As he could not hold the young woman seated across from him, he reached for one of the newspapers on the coffee table. Crossing his legs, he opened the paper to the business section.

He would wait.

She would stop crying and they would discuss the terms of her leave. He knew what everyone employed by him was working on. Betty Jean's workload was diminished because of the hours she'd put in prior to her illness and he'd purposely left it that way, gearing her for something else.

As he said, he didn't have any real problem with her leave as long as she guaranteed him it was only to rest and recoup and that she was coming back. He'd gone through a lot of trouble to find Ms. Carlson and he didn't want to lose her without at least having a chance to persuade her to stay. And he would persuade her too, even if it meant disclosing the true reason behind his hiring her.

Wishing she could click her heels three times and fly away home, Betty Jean folded the damp cloth and took one final trip across her face with it, grateful she wasn't a woman prone to wearing a bunch of makeup. Sitting across from her boss bawling into his handkerchief was mortifying enough without coming away from it looking like Bozo the Clown with makeup running down her face. While she refolded the piece of cloth, Charles refolded his newspaper. Things were looking good in London and Tokyo.

"I'm sorry." She shook her head at a loss for words.

"You have nothing to apologize for. I've weathered rougher storms in my day, young lady. Your few drops were small in comparison. I apologize that the law dictates I do nothing to offer comfort to you when you are clearly in distress." He looked at Betty Jean for a long moment with a soft look in his brown eyes. "What can I do for you? Name your terms and conditions. Tell me about your lovely assistant. Will she be taking a leave as well?"

"We have one or two small details that might need to be covered or taken care of, but I don't see anything that will spill over into next week. It wouldn't be a problem if she did." She hunched her shoulders, shaking her head. "I suppose it'll be up to Sheila whether she would prefer to be temporarily reassigned to someone else or sit it out and wait on my return. She could use the time to plan her wedding, I guess."

"Wait on your return? So there is definitely going to be a return? You're just taking some time for yourself, which is quite understandable. Everyone needs some time away from their regular routine every now and then," he said conversationally, then added for assurance, "This isn't you saying goodbye?" He watched her intently and Betty Jean sighed, heavily.

"I don't know what to tell you, Charles. I want to come back. I plan to come back. I truly do. But I don't know." She lifted her shoulders, then dropped them. She turned to look out his windows at the early morning sun.

"I left the south running, trying to reach the sunshine." She stopped, not knowing what she was going to say. "I went through an ordeal recently that let me know a couple of things. The first being that I didn't run far enough. The second is that no where is far enough. I could circle the globe twice over and not have covered enough distance." She stopped again, not having meant to have disclosed so much to her boss.

"Are you lacing up, getting ready to do some more running?" Charles asked genuinely concerned for her. Despite all his lofty plans for his company and her place within it, he liked Betty Jean as a person. She was smart and ethical and cared about her people, he thought, thinking of her handling of Grailton. That cranky old man turned to mush in her hands.

"Just searching a little bit," Betty Jean said. "I've been looking and looking, but I can't seem to find me anymore." She knew she sounded like a nut, but she spoke the truth. Looking at Charles Hurstwode, she thought she saw in him a kindred spirit. Someone who would understand what she was saying even if she was getting the words all wrong. Her meaning was felt.

Charles sat quietly thinking of a time when he too had to run and hide to lick his wounds in private after losing Ellen. He didn't know what pain Betty Jean was trying to soothe and rub away, but he well understood the need to run and do it.

When their business was concluded, he stood taking her hand in his. He looked into her eyes and smiled. "I remember my Momma holding me and rocking me. I was thirty six years old at the time, but she held me in her arms like I was a babe. I'd just buried my Ellen and thought never again to be consoled. I hurt so bad. It was painful trying to breathe, but Momma held on, rocking me. Rocking her baby and she just kept saying, *This too shall pass, son.*"

Betty Jean tried to blink away the shine in her eyes and he continued. "Momma was right. That terrible, ugly hurt did pass and every day it gets a little easier to breathe. I carry a little bit of the pain with me every day, but it's just a dull ache now. Whatever this thing is that seems like a mighty beast right now will diminish in strength until you'll be more than able to conquer it. Until then," he patted her hand, "you just remember what Momma said."

**

"Let's do it." Sheila snapped the magazine closed.

"What's that, honey?" Concentrating on the television screen and the rapidly moving yellow chomping dot, Cyron gave half of his attention to his intended.

"Let's get married." She shoved the glossy magazine away from her until it slid smoothly across the carpet.

"I thought that's what we were doing. You were saying how's this, this and that and I was saying great, fantastic and no way in hell I'm wearing that."

Sheila sat up directly in his line of view. "We were planning our wedding. I said let's get married. There is a difference, you know."

Gaining his full attention, she held his eyes. A frozen Pac Man was stung repeatedly by various colored ghost until Cyron's game ended unheeded. "So, what are you suggesting, Leggs?"

She sat back rubbing her hands nervously down her thighs. She licked her lips. "I think I'm suggesting that we elope."

"You're kidding, right? My Princess doesn't want the whole Cinderella shebang wedding with the twelve foot long train, the footmen in lively attire and a four tiered cake?"

"Why would you think I wanted all that?" He raised a brow at the absurdity of the question and she blushed slightly. "Well, so," she said, folding her arms across her chest. "That doesn't mean anything. I may be a bit high maintenance, but that doesn't mean my wedding has to be the ball of the season."

"The ball of the season? Would that make you the Belle of the ball?" he teased and her eyes narrowed. "Be kind." He held up a hand in mock self-defense. "I'm just a little surprised, that's all."

She scooted across the floor until she came to rest by his legs. Wrapping an arm around them, she laid her head against his bent knee. "I want to be your wife. I want to come home and cook dinner. I want to sit and be comfortable knowing we're both at home.

No one's leaving. I want to get to know you. Really, really, know you. The kind that comes from years of sleeping next to somebody. Where you can complete their sentences. I want to look at you and know what you're thinking. Laugh at something you said, when you haven't said a word." While she spoke he stroked her head. She'd taken out the extensions and it was her own hair he softly caressed. She closed her eyes enjoying the pampering. "I want to carry your children beneath my heart. Hold them in my arms. I want to see if our little boy will remind me of you."

A few moments passed in silence and she whispered, "I'm ready to be your wife, Cyron."

"Are you ready to be a mother, too?" he asked softly. He wanted to have children, but he wanted Sheila to himself for a while too, before they both succumbed to the demands of parenthood.

Sheila hesitated before answering. She smiled slowly, thinking of the children they would have. "Yes, I'm ready, but," she said quickly, "I'd like to wait before we started trying to build a family. I know it's going to sound pretty selfish, but I want you all to myself for a time. Maybe a year, maybe two. I don't know. I can wait a bit for motherhood, but I think I'll lose my mind if you don't hurry up and marry me."

Cyron smiled, pleased that she was so anxious. "Come here," he said, pulling her up and into his arms. "Let's see if I can take your mind off any rash decisions you may be having."

"This isn't rash. I've been—" Her protest was cut off by Cyron's kiss and she melted into it. Turning her body, she straddled him, deepening the kiss. She told him she loved him and felt him grow hard beneath her at the words. "Penny for *your* thoughts," she said smiling and he captured her mouth in another searing kiss.

Chapter Thirty

Turning the water off, Betty Jean stood in the shower for a moment with her eyes closed. She was young, having seen less than thirty-five years on this earth. In fact, she'd only just reached thirty-one, but Lord she felt so old. If science was correct and the world really was millions of years old, she felt like she'd been around and lived through each day of it.

Reaching for the baby oil, she poured some into her cupped palm. Rubbing her hands together she smoothed the oil down one wet leg then the other. Pouring out more oil, she repeated her ministrations until her entire body was baby oil smooth. Stepping from the shower, she used a large fluffy towel to gently pat away the excess moisture.

Standing in front of her wall mirror, she stared hard into her eyes trying to recognize the stranger that looked back at her. There were lines in her face that shouldn't be there. She traced them with a fingertip and the sad eyes in the mirror followed her stroke. She stepped closer to the mirror until her breath puffed a small circle of fog on the glass.

With a critical eye, she pointed out every flaw in her face. Retrieving a pair of tweezers, she repaired what she could. She tidied up the arch in her eyebrows and plucked out the few stray hairs that stubbornly insisted upon sprouting on her chin.

She puffed a little air into her cheeks watching as the barely discernible lines in her cheeks disappeared. She released the breath from her cheeks blowing hard on the mirror as she did so, obscuring her face from view momentarily.

When she came into focus again in the fading mist, the stranger's eyes were still upon her. Backing from the mirror she again observed her full length. Here she could not be so critical. Here she was no stranger. The body was hers, though it had followed another's command. If her eyes were those of a stranger, revealing nothing, then the body that she knew intimately revealed too much. When she looked at her form in the mirror it was Ezekiel she saw. What he had been to her before and what he'd become.

She saw the things that Ezekiel did to her that night. She looked at her breast and remembered his touch. She could feel his hands on her hips, pushing himself into her warmth. She could feel him throbbing inside her. No. Her body was not a stranger to her. It was a vivid reminder. Even her hair would not let her forget or deny her experience. It still stood out on end as she couldn't figure out what to do with it.

If she went to a stylist she'd have to explain how it got in it's current condition. She wouldn't have to explain, but they'd wonder and whisper when she left. She could try to do something with it herself, but as she'd always had long hair, she had no idea what to do with the few inches that remained. She could hack it off, but she was no stylist and she was through with scissors. Sheila came to mind, but that would just bring up that night to both of them and that would be too awkward.

So, she was stuck with it until she could figure out what to do with it. She rubbed moisturizer between her hands, then ran them through her hair. She retrieved her blow dryer. Without bothering with a hairbrush or sectioning her hair, she turned the dryer on maximum power.

All the while the stranger's eyes were upon her and she tried to figure out a way to help herself. She needed to erase Ezekiel Johnson from her mind, her body, her soul, once and for all. She couldn't look in the mirror everyday and see him.

She couldn't keep hurting. She was tired. Turning off the light in the bathroom she walked naked into her room and lie across the bed. She stared up at the ceiling wondering what to do.

**

It was just after three in the morning when Byron pulled into his driveway. From his cell phone he tried to call Betty Jean's, but there was no answer. He didn't know if that was a good thing or not. Good, she was asleep and didn't hear the phone ringing or bad that she was awake, but ignoring the ringing phone. Sighing, he got out of his truck. Letting himself into the house, he debated on calling Betty Jean again. He'd been trying to reach her since about seven.

Sheila told Cyron that Betty Jean was taking a leave of absence from her job and he wanted to know what she was planning. He'd throw the keys to both his clubs to Cyron and be buckled into the seat next to her. Plane, train or automobile, he was there.

He picked up the phone and pulled his shirt over his head at the same time. He needed a shower. He only allowed smoking out on Rufio's back terrace but he always seemed to smell like an ashtray when he came home. One day he was going to ban smoking at his clubs all-together. He was just about to punch in Betty Jean's number again when he changed his mind and tossed the receiver on his bed. He'd get with her first thing in the morning.

Walking to the den, he retrieved a bottle from the bar, then went to the kitchen for a glass. Two fingers of alcohol splashed into the glass and he made a face at the first sip. Going back into his room, he removed the rest of his clothes, scratched lazily and took another swig from his glass. He poured a little more liquid into the glass.

Placing it on the marble counter in the bathroom, he stepped under the massaging jet of water in the shower, while steam filled the glass cubicle then floated out to drape across the bathroom. After showering and shampooing his hair, he stepped from the shower, wrapping a towel around his waist. The blue terry cloth fell to the middle of his calves and he quickly pressed it against whatever skin it touched. The rest of the water was left to dry as it would from the drops that still glistened on his body.

Exiting the bathroom, he picked up his glass, then the remote control to the television set and stretched across his bed. He turned on the television, then pressed mute a bare second later. Cocking his head to the side, he sat up listening.

Nothing.

He waited a moment longer, but it was only his imagination and he turned up the volume again. Standing, he muted the set again and left his bedroom. Entering his living room he kept an ear out for the noise and was only vaguely startled when it came again. Walking quickly and without sound, he crossed the entry way and unlocking the door, he pulled it open. Huddled in a baseball cap, oversized shirt and sweat pants, Betty Jean stood on his porch.

"May I come in?" She brushed past him and into the house. Crossing the dark house, she followed the silvery trail made by the television set in his room. After locking the door, he traced her footsteps to where they ended at the side of his bed.

She picked up the glass and drank from it. Sitting on the side of the bed, she slowly removed her clothes. The cap stayed on her head as she stood again, reaching for the towel wrapped snugly around Byron's waist.

When he was naked, she stepped up to him and circled his body with her arms. Her cheek rested against his warm chest and she sighed, closing her eyes when his arms came up around her. She tilted her head up and he kissed her. Soft and sweet. There was a slight hesitation, a question in his initial contact, but it was soon forgotten and he pulled her tight against him and backed her to the bed.

She was beneath him but maneuvered until he was beneath and between her thighs. She broke the kiss and sat up until she was looking in his eyes. She saw no questions, only expectancy and she reached up, removing her cap.

She felt the soft in take of his breath, but nothing else betrayed his emotion. He sat up until he could reach her face, then pressed his lips to her forehead. Slowly, with painstaking care he sought out each feature at random and gently placed a kiss upon it.

The whole time from the first kiss of her forehead to the last kiss of her lips, he held her face between his hands. She could feel the tips of his fingers just barely caressing the edges of her hair, tears came to her eyes and she closed them.

Byron shook his head and hers a little bit. "Open your eyes, Betty Jean." He moved his hips a little. "You feel that?" She nodded her head. "Good." He lifted her slightly until he was poised at the entrance to her body.

"Did you come here tonight for me?" Again, she nodded her head. "Good." Slowly, he eased her down until he penetrated her. When she would have closed her eyes again, he said, "No, Sweetie. Keep 'em open." His voice was strained and she felt good hugging him within her. He swallowed hard. "I want you to see me. I want to be the only person occupying your mind. The only memory you have, okay?" He moved his hips and watched as Betty Jean's eyes glazed over.

"Okay." Her voice was as strained as his.

"Okay, what?" He pressed deep.

"Okay, Byron."

"You want me, Betty Jean?"

"Yes," she said, a tortured whisper.

"Come on then, Queen and let me see." He plunged deeper again, but Betty Jean was with him and parried with a thrust of her own.

He continued to move, but was soon made aware that it was Betty Jean's show. He alternated between holding on to her and grabbing the sheets or bedpost for support. She rode him hard before shuddering and convulsing above him. He spilled his seed seconds later and through it all, her eyes never left his face.

**

Lying on his side in the bed it was the darkest part of night just before the sky gives way to the first fingers of light. He should be asleep, but he was not. Even the warm body curled next to him had not managed to lure him into the unconscious realm of sleep.

Slowly his hand reached out until his fingers curled around the glass he'd placed on his nightstand hours before. Raising himself slightly, making an effort not to jostle the bed, he brought the glass to his lips and sipped, then swallowed it's contents in one big gulp. He shuddered a little as the warm liquid coursed a hot path down his throat to explode in brilliant color in his stomach.

Turning on the bed without all the quiet care of his first movements, he kissed the bare shoulder nearest his nose and the recipient of his affection snuggled deeper into his side and smiled in her sleep.

He kissed her shoulder again biting down lightly and flung the covers back, all at the same time. He smacked her behind when she tried to burrow away from his intrusion of her rest. He nipped her shoulder again, then her ear.

"Wake up! Put on some clothes and lets go get married!"

**

Lying flat on his stomach with his head half buried in his pillow, he pretended sleep. It was the darkest hour of night just before the inky blackness relinquishes it's hold on the sky and the first colors of day can be seen. He should be asleep, but he was not. He'd come awake when the warm body beside him slid from the bed.

Silently he watched her dress in the near tomb like darkness of the room. Heavy drapes hung at the windows to block out unwanted light. She was aided in her dressing by the small amount of light coming through the open bedroom door from other areas of the house. The muffled rub of fabric told him she was dressing to leave more clearly than his eyes could.

She paused for a moment after dressing and he wondered if she was going to kiss him goodbye. He lowered his eyelids to mere slits hoping he looked lost in innocent slumber if she did. He needn't have bothered with his deception. She stood beside the bed a few seconds longer, quiet and still. He felt it when she turned and walked from the room.

He opened his eyes fully, knowing his ruse had no chance of being discovered. She wasn't coming back.

He lie quiet for a moment thinking about the woman who had just left his side. The woman he'd wanted to reach out for and comfort and hold. The woman he'd let leave without saying a word. He was going to get up to lock his front door when he heard the faint mechanism of the garage door raising echo softly through the still house. A few moments later the sound came again as the garage door was lowered.

He reached for the glass on his nightstand, trying to fathom the amount left in it. Satisfied with his deduction, he lifted the glass to his lips and drained the contents.

**

Arriving home she sat in her car for a long moment. She turned the engine off but left the key dangling in the ignition. Often times it was her mother she missed, but of late she found herself craving her father's presence. Malcolm Carlson was a big bear of a man, but he was too friendly to intimidate anyone for too long. If his smile didn't win a stranger over his pleasant disposition surely would.

Betty Jean closed her eyes, put her forehead against the steering wheel and hugged it. She could sure use her daddy right now, she sniffed, feeling every bit of five years old and not caring.

Her head jerked up from the steering wheel and she looked around quickly.

Either she was really in touch with the spirit world and her daddy was trying to communicate with her, she'd spooked herself thinking of ghosts, though that had never happened before, she wasn't afraid of her parents, dead or alive, or the last and most unpleasant choice... she wasn't alone in the early morning darkness.

Retrieving her cell phone from the glove compartment, she peered out her car window trying to discover the source of the noise she'd heard. The intelligent thing to do would be to just simply park in the garage, but she wasn't going to let herself be bullied about. She shouldn't have to pull into her garage if she didn't want to and damnit she was just going to have to be brave and brazen it out.

After pretending to dial, she placed the phone to her ear. Unlocking the car door she laughed into the receiver. Keeping up a conversation all the way to her front door, she tried to appear casual and unconcerned about what lurked in the semi darkness of the near morning.

"Well, come on by. I'll be here," she said loudly, shutting the door on another manufactured giggle. Expelling air, she sagged against the door. She really was losing her mind. Talking to herself on the phone. What was next? She'd be at the firing range with a pistol in her hand if she wasn't careful, she thought frowning as she pushed away from the door to head down the hall. She couldn't keep being afraid of things that went bump in the night.

"Hey, Mommy's mini dog," she said, turning on the bathroom light and watching Insomnia stretch himself into wakefulness. She scooped him up and headed for her bedroom. Holding the puppy to her chest she lay on the bed, pulling the afghan across them both. She yawned, suddenly sleepy. She'd rest for a moment then get up. There was plenty to do before they left.

She woke up nearly eight hours later to the sound of her own voice.

Frowning in confusion, she stared around the sunlit room. There was a beep, followed by a voice vaguely similar to Sheila's.

"I'm going to need new stationary," her friend laughed breathlessly into the phone. "Stop!" She giggled and Betty Jean's frown deepened. *Stop what?* "I'm throwing out all that old shit with Sheila Cooper on it. Leave my ear alone." Betty Jean's eyebrows shot up into her hairline. *What the hell was Sheila doing?* "As of a few hours ago, my name is legally Sheila—" By this time Betty Jean was sitting up in bed with Insomnia perched right beside her.

"de," Sheila said and Betty Jean leapt off the bed frantically searching for the phone. Thinking she wanted to play, Insomnia sprang up after her nipping at her feet.

"No, no, Insomnia." She tossed clothes, bedcovers and shoes aside, as she searched for the receiver.

"Monbleau. Stop it!" Sheila laughed from the machine, as Betty Jean finally located the phone.

"Hello!" she said into the receiver, but only caught the distant tingle of Sheila's happiness as the other woman hung up the line laughing in the background. "Curses and double curses," Betty Jean said, disconnecting her end of the call.

Sheila and Cyron were married. She put the phone on its charger base, called for Insomnia to follow her and started for her bedroom door. She stopped walking and Insomnia's wet nose smashed into her calf. Sheila and Cyron were married! A smile spread slowly across her face lighting her eyes. Sheila was Mrs. de Monbleau. She turned back to the phone wanting to call someone with the good news, but there was no one she could tell.

There was Byron and his sister, Julie, but the newly weds would probably want to break the news to their family themselves. Resuming motion, she left her room with the puppy on her heels. Sliding open the patio door, so Insomnia could slip out, she thought of someone she could call. Leaving the door slightly ajar for his return she picked up the phone in the kitchen and dialed. Plopping down on a bar stool she waited for the ringing to be answered.

"Carol Shipley's office."

"Why are you answering your personal line like that?"

Smiling at the familiar voice, Carol relaxed in her seat. "Until I can get caller ID here at work, I never can be too careful. Some days I have to answer the phone sounding like my assistant."

"Why if it's your personal line? It's supposed to be a limited access number for a reason. How many people have your direct number?"

"A few. One or two. Maybe three or four. Who knows? The point is just because a caller has my number doesn't mean I have to feel like talking to them every time they call. I could be busy."

"Are you?"

"No, but again, that's beside the point. As I said, I may not always want to chat, even with Paul. There's no exceptions."

"Should I hang up?"

"No, you're okay. Answering in my assistant's voice is just a precaution. Even though Paul says I never fool him, that I don't sound anything like Gena."

"You don't."

"I do so. Everybody says so."

"That's because you're answering your own line pretending to be her. Of course, everyone is going to say you two sound just a like."

Carol considered Betty Jean's words, then laughed. "Hell, I guess that would do it, wouldn't it? What's up, doll face?" she asked liked a detective from a 1940s B movie.

"With me? Nothing." Betty Jean grinned, trying to sound evasive.

"With me? Of course with you." Carol squinted her eyes as though she could see across the distance separating them. "Okay, what gives?"

"With me? Nothing." Betty Jean looked down at her nails. They looked like shit. She could really use a good manicure. Her cuticles stood out like spikes. She stretched her leg out in front of her and wiggled the toes on her right foot. A pedicure wouldn't be too bad an idea either.

"I'm way over here and I can smell the shit!" Carol beamed, hot on her trail.

"With me?" Betty Jean asked innocently dropping more crumbs.

"Hell, no. I ruled you out with the second eyelash bat and *Who me? Nothing,*" Carol said with a flutter of her lashes and a hand splayed across her chest.

"I did not, nor have I ever batted my eyelashes," Betty Jean cut in with solemn dignity.

"I'm going to explode if you don't tell me what's up!"

"I don't know now." Betty Jean examined her other foot. She placcd all ten toes side by side and wiggled them. Seeing the motion Insomnia ran in from the deck to bite at them. She stopped wiggling and tucked her feet out of his reach on the stool's highest rung. Losing interest, Insomnia went back outside.

"Betty Jean—" Carol was cut off mid warning.

"Let's go celebrate."

"Sure," Carol assented, ever ready to party. "To what are we raising our glasses?"

"Umm," Betty Jean hedged enjoying the ill concealed excitement in Carol's voice.

"Betty Jean!" Carol whined spinning around in her desk chair, full circle, with her head thrown back in dramatic fashion. "My natural nosiness is killing me and my spidey senses are tingling out of control! Tell me what's going on or put a bullet in my head and close the coffin!" Carol said with great drama. *Yet another calling missed.* "But either way put me out of my misery!" She spun around in the chair again.

"What's today's date?"

"The eighteenth why?"

"We'll need to know for the engraving."

"What engraving and your answer better not be another MFing enigma."

"MFing, Carol?"

"Yeah. Paul's been at me again about my usage of the more colorful words in my repertoire. They're like cigarettes for me. I'm trying to cut back a little at a time and since I noticed this isn't CA, stop evading my questions."

"What's CA?"

"Cursers Anonymous and unless you want to know why I had to join, I suggest you spill it now. We're going to celebrate the eighteenth and have it engraved for what purpose?"

"To give to Sheila and Cyron..." Betty Jean said slowly then paused.

"Damnit!" Carol huffed into the phone when the silence stretched her nerves to the point of snapping and she thought it would be nice if Betty Jean's neck would follow suit.

"de Monbleau," she finally completed her sentence.

"What? de Monbleau? What the hell is - Wait a minute! Sheila and Cyron - Oh my God! Am I understanding you correctly?" Carol asked, sitting rock still in her chair.

"I don't know. What do you think I said?" Betty Jean asked slyly, enjoying her power.

"I believe you just said Sheila and Cyron de Monbleau. Which leads me to believe the happy couple are a happy couple. If you get my drift."

"Yes ma'am, I get your drift. And you are correct. Apparently, they exchanged vows a little while ago."

"How did they - I mean, why - Oh, hell! I mean that's great! It's fantastic! They eloped! I knew Sheila wouldn't make it to the church on time!"

"It's romantic and sweet," Betty Jean added thinking about her conversation with Sheila.

"Share the details."

"I haven't any. She called but I couldn't find the phone in time. By the time I answered, they were hanging up. I'm as clueless as you are, this time."

"Sheila got her man. Hot damn!" Carol said and clapped her hands together loudly. "This calls for a celebration. Where is she? Do you know?"

"You know, I haven't even thought about it? I figure wherever they are, they probably don't want any company."

"Hell, I wouldn't," Carol said thinking of her own wedding night with Paul. "The first person to knock at my door would get shot! So, what's the plan Stan? Margaritas and jello shots? Tequila, lime and a worm? Should I tell Paul to have our bail money ready? And does my car need a full tank of gas?"

"What are you talking about?" Betty Jean asked trying to rid her lowered foot of the returned bout with Insomnia. She made as if to stand and he scampered off out of arm's reach. She reclaimed her seat, raising both feet to the top rung again.

"Celebrating and the depths of said celebration. Are we staying just this side of legal or are we going full Thelma and Louise? We won't need bail money if we can out run the police. That's why I asked about the full tank of gas."

"I don't think I want to celebrate with you anymore," Betty Jean laughed. "You sound a little dangerous."

"Okay, White Bread and Vanilla Ice Cream. Plain. Plain. Plain. So, what's your idea of fun?"

"For starters, not requiring bail money. Hopefully, I'm not being too risqué, but I want strong hands on my feet and a little color on my hands."

"Your hands already have a little color on them," Carol cut in, grinning at her cleverness.

"Remember our last trip to the projects in Oakland?" Betty Jean warned.

"We've never been to any projects in Oakland," Carol said frowning.

"Want to take a trip?" Betty Jean asked, and Carol laughed.

"Are you threatening me, Betty Jean?"

"Are you through getting cute?"

"Course not."

"Course not for me too, then." They both laughed. "Now, as I was saying before I was so rudely interrupted...how's lunch, a drink or two for Sheila's sake, no worm for me, though, then a pedicure and manicure at the spa?"

"No bail money or tank filled with gas?" Carol's tone was as disappointed as a giftless child on Christmas morning.

"I'll let you keep the jello shots and throw in a deep tissue massage," Betty Jean bargained.

"It's not the same as being finger printed and a high speed chase, but I guess it's okay. What time?"

"Call me when you're ready."

"Sure thing. It may be a late lunch, I have a couple of contracts to explain to the folks upstairs."

"That's fine. My calendar is clear."

"Oh, and Betty Jean?"

"Yeah?" she asked in the middle of hanging up.

"I think you would have liked the worm."

"Goodbye, Carol." She hung up the phone, laughing.

Chapter Thirty One

She stepped from the shower in Cyron's bedroom toweling the edges of her hair. It was pinned up out of the way, but some loose tendrils had still gotten damp and Lord knows the last thing she needed was to get her hair wet and have to fool with it. Especially, not right now when she was without the necessary toiletries to mend it properly. She retrieved another towel from the cabinet and wrapped it around her body. Exiting the bathroom, she clicked off the lights and joined her husband in the living room. He pulled at her towel and she giggled sounding like a love struck girl. Which was only fitting, as that's how he made her feel.

"Stop that." She swatted at his hands without much convincing.

He pulled her towards him and she smiled, returning his tender kiss. "I love you."

"I've always loved you." Looking into her eyes, he saw the truth in her fanciful words.

"Kiss me again."

She did and he squeezed her tight.

"Again."

She complied and his hands tugged at her towel again.

"Behave." She swatted again, stepping from his arms. "I thought you were hungry."

"Hell, I thought I was proving that."

"What do you want to eat?"

He raised a brow and gave her a wicked smile.

"You are the limit." She turned to leave, blushing.

"You asked," he called out smacking her behind as she passed him. "Sexy self," he muttered and she gave the rump beneath the towel a little shake. "Be kind and put a robe on for my sake, woman. I can't get at you all day, you know. At least let me rest for an hour or two." Sitting on the couch, he snapped the newspaper open on her indignant gasp. Chuckling, he buried his nose in the business section.

**

Getting out of the vehicle, she closed the door.

"Stay right there!" he ordered.

Turning, she smiled as he hurried over to the passenger's side. Flexing the fingers newly released from the splint, he grinned. "Come on." He made as if to scoop her up. She stepped out of his reach, shaking her head.

"Had you not just done that," she said mimicking the flexing gesture he'd made with his hand. "Turn around," she ordered and he presented his back to her. She jumped up and he grunted, buckling his legs slightly. She slapped his shoulder. "That's not funny!"

"I guess I should get used to this position...you on my back."

She slapped him lightly again. "Now that one's never going to be funny." She kissed his neck. He shivered slightly at the contact.

"Let's get in the house first," he said, heading up the path. "Hang on." He shifted her slightly to get the key in the door. She giggled sliding down his back a bit.

"Cyron!" She laughed, barely clinging to him as they crossed the doorway into the house.

"Cyron!" Another feminine voice echoed in alarm, pulling at the sash on his bathrobe.

"Mother?"

"Cyron!" A deeper voice boomed.

"Dad!" Cyron shifted Sheila's weight on his back.

"Sweetie!" Helen said, finally moving from the paralyzing embrace of first discovery.

Sheila slid from Cyron's back as the older couple hurried towards them. After they exchanged excited hugs and kisses, Cyron reached for Sheila's hand.

"Mom, Dad, this is Sheila. Sheila," he kissed the back of the hand he held, "my mom and dad, Helen and Brandon de Monbleau."

"It's so nice to meet you, darling. I've heard so many good things about you." Helen embraced Sheila in a warm, friendly hug. "Let's look at you. Isn't she adorable, Bran?" She beamed at Sheila, hugging her again.

"Yes, Helen, she's darling," Brandon drawled out and Sheila noticed he was nearly as large as his sons. Maybe even larger.

Still speechless, Sheila returned Helen's hug. Her mother and sister-in-law bore a striking resemblance to one another. Remove thirty years on one end or add it on another and you'd have either's face. Grown Up Julie was hugging her, welcoming her, she thought standing in her mother-in-law's embrace. Just when she thought she was sure to faint, Cyron rescued her suggesting they all step out of the entryway and into the living room.

"When did you guys arrive?"

They looked at one another for confirmation, then shrugged in unison. "A few hours ago," Brandon said.

"We caught a cab here from the airport," his mother, cut in to add.

"It was too early to drag anyone out to the airport—"

"But no one was here when we got here anyway, so you were already up and about—"

"We knew if we called, one of you kids would be sure to meet us at the baggage claim—"

"No, they wouldn't have. There were no bags to claim!"

"Yeah, but nobody knew it at the time—"

"Yes, that's true—"

"Even us."

"That's true," Helen agreed again. Sheila sat looking at the two of them in a daze. Did either of them ever get a chance to finish a sentence with the other around? "Can you believe they lost our luggage?"

"Pity," Cyron said solemnly. "I know how you hate to shop."

"Don't get sarcastic in front of your lovely fiancée, Cyron. She might change her mind about marrying you."

"No chance of that, Mom," Cyron said, smiling at Sheila, as he perched on the arm of her chair.

"Don't be so certain, Mr. Cocky," his mother admonished. Focusing on Sheila she said, "We came as soon as Ayron got word to us about you two getting married."

"Why didn't you guys let Ayron fly you in?"

"We were over there in East Nowhere, seemed easier to just hop on a plane that was already there."

"Had we known they'd lose our luggage, we would have waited for Ayron," Helen added, then turned back to Sheila. "Ayron had nothing but glowing remarks to say about you. Knowing Cyron, I knew we'd better get here straight away. He's always had this absurd notion that if we miss him doing something, we can always catch the next two acts, as he puts it. Absurd. We wouldn't have missed this for the whole world!"

"How was Ayron able to get in touch with you when nothing I tried worked?" Cyron looked from one parent to the next.

"Did you try calling your grandfather?" His mother asked, turning her attention to him.

No, he hadn't, but didn't want to say so.

"You know that man does not hit brick walls. I don't know how he walks on water, but every time I look up, he's standing out in the middle of the ocean doing just that! Whenever you can't reach us, try calling Papa Smurf," she said, as only Helen was allowed to affectionately call him. "He can find us."

"Only if it's an emergency, though—" Brandon added from her side.

"One of my boys getting married is important, even if it isn't an emergency. Do you know how long I've waited for this?" she asked, thrilled.

Brandon teased her. "Longer than any mother should have to."

She took him at his word. "Thirty five! I didn't think any of them were ever going to settle down and do the right thing. And give me grand babies!" she added on an excited note. "I can't wait! A nice big wedding! Have you set a date yet?" she asked, beaming from one face to the other. "You two are so handsome together. The wedding pictures are going to look lovely. Two beautiful people. My grand babies are going to be the cutest babies in town!" Her lower lip quivered a little at the thought of her own baby getting married and her eyes sparkled.

"Uh, Mom," Cyron began, preparing to tell her that she'd have to catch the next act this time, too. That him and Sheila were already married when Sheila cut him off.

"We can't decide on a firm date. Everything seems too far away."

"Yeah, we want to do it as early as yesterday," Cyron said. "Or this morning," he added beneath his breath to a blushing Sheila.

Watching the two, Brandon shifted his gaze between them as if to reason something out. Seeing her flush, Sheila's unwitting mother-in-law smiled. "You behave Cyron. Don't be over there trying to convince Sheila to do wrong. I see her blushing! What did you say to her?"

"Now, mom, I don't ask you what Brandon says to make you turn pink in the face. I didn't even ask him what he was doing to that robe, or trying to do to it, when we came in."

"You'd better not either," Brandon warned.

"Oh, all right. Keep your secrets then. We were just about to eat when you guys came in. Sheila you'll come help me in the kitchen? There's enough for all of us." She stood from the couch, tightening the robe.

"Yeah, Leggs, go help in the kitchen, but be careful. Don't be in there spilling the beans all over the place."

"Boy! Nobody's cooking any beans!" his mother said striding from the living room with Sheila trailing.

"You already married that young lady, haven't you?" Brandon asked as soon as they were alone.

"How'd you know?" Cyron couldn't stop himself from smiling.

"How'd I always tell you boys apart from day one?" Brandon countered shrugging. "Don't know, just did. That and the fact that you're about as subtle as a sledge hammer. It's all over your face every time you look at her. You might as well stamp a Mine brand right in the center of her forehead!"

Cyron chuckled a little at his father's words. "Are you going to tell on me to Mom?"

"Now you know I wouldn't do that, son." Brandon smiled just as Helen called them into the kitchen.

"What's so funny?" Cyron asked as Brandon stood up. "You're going to screw me over, aren't you Dad?"

"Me? Hell, no. I was on a plane at the time the incident occurred. You did it to yourself. "

"How?"

"Why, you can't claim your wife now, until after your mother hears you say your vows, dip stick. Looks like you're going to get married twice." He clapped a hand to Cyron's shoulder and made the young man walk beside him from the living room, as hc chuckled.

"Good and trapped yourself this time, didn't you? Married man, sleeping like a bachelor."

**

Betty Jean had barely returned from her jaunt with Carol, fed Insomnia and changed clothes when the phone rang. Hoping for Sheila, she rushed to answer the phone.

"You left your baseball cap when you fled from the ball, Cinderella."

"Yeah, I know. I couldn't find it in the dark. Thanks."

So that's what she'd been doing. Standing around in the darkness trying to locate her hat and he thought she was going to kiss him. "Why didn't you at least wait until first light?"

They'd had jello shots before their massages and she felt too relaxed to go into anything heavy, even a discussion. She could think of nothing to say and was reluctant to lie to him, so she held her tongue.

Sensing he wouldn't get an answer, he pressed on without it. "My parents are in town, staying at Cyron's. I'm heading over there, but I can drop off your hat later if you want."

"Your parents are here? That's great! They must have found out about him and Sheila."

"I think Ayron told them."

"Ayron? How'd he find out, so fast? Well, I guess he received a phone call, too." She answered her own question.

"What do you mean? Ayron - Hold on a second." He clicked over to his other line, returning a few seconds later. "I have to call you back, Queen."

"No problem. I'm about to stretch out across the bed for a little while."

The house was completely dark when she woke again to a ringing phone.

"Betty Jean?

"Mmm, hmm?" Propping the phone up to her ear, she refused to open her eyes.

"I need you to help me plan my wedding."

"Hun?" She puffed out air, frowning in confusion. "Sheila?" she asked, waking up some. "I thought you were married this morning?"

"I was."

"Cart behind the horse, or what?" Betty Jean asked, still sleepy.

"Cyron's parents came to town." She sniffled. "His mother is so nice, I didn't have the heart to disappoint her. She came to help with the wedding!" Sheila wailed into the phone and Betty Jean's eyes sprang open.

"Tell me, again."

Sheila repeated the events of the day and Betty Jean began to giggle. "So, you're going to have a wedding whether you like it or not and no man and wife until then? You're in your zip code and he's in his? Oh, this is too much." She laughed some more.

"No, it isn't! Well, yes it is! This *is* too much! I don't want to get married. I'm already married!"

"Well, look at the bright side."

"I hardly see the bright side in this non laughing matter, Ms. Carlson."

"Sure, there's a bright side. You'll have two wedding dates. Which means two anniversary dates. Two gifts. Each year demand that Cyron recognize both dates. You guys can have a private affair for the two of you, like you did this morning then have the big blow out for family and friends on the second date."

"Well, I guess we could do that," Sheila said, only slightly mollified.

"Sure you could." Betty Jean propped herself up in bed. "Now give me the juice. How'd you guys get hitched?"

**

She came awake impatiently brushing the hair from her face that was hanging over into her eyes. She swiped again when it fell back across her view belatedly realizing it was her twisted headscarf, not her hair that bothered her.

Her hair was gone.

She rubbed a shaky hand down her clammy face while searching in the darkness for the clock. Three o' eight. She fell back against the pillow, frowning at the damp moisture that greeted her bare skin. Sighing, she flipped the pillow over to the dry side, then lay against it again to stare up at the ceiling.

She'd been running through complete blackness. Woman or beast, she did not know. The darkness surrounding her had been absolute. In the darkness, she hadn't known which direction to take. She was lost and in her haste she hadn't cared if it was foot or hoof that took her into the light, as long as she put distance between herself and the night.

The crease between her eyebrows deepened causing the scarf to slip down her head again. She reached up and snatching it off, she tossed it on the floor. How the hell was she supposed to out run the night?!

Huffing with great indignation, she flounced to her side. She was getting really tired of being the resident soothsayer and wished to hell her dreams or visions or whatever they were that plagued her, would just go away and leave her sleep undisturbed.

It wasn't like having them did any good anyway. How many times had her unconscious mind tried to warn her about Ezekiel? Did it do any good? No. She'd still been victimized, she thought sourly, bitterly despising the word and it's association to herself.

For years she'd allowed herself to be Ezekiel's victim, his patsy, then finally she'd gathered all her courage and strength and left. She'd put Ezekiel Johnson, his bullshit, lies and countless string of other women in her rear view mirror.

Literally.

She'd left him standing on their old porch and she was certain that had she looked at the time, he would have been center focus in her mirror, but she hadn't looked. She said goodbye and everything else she had to say before she got in her car and drove away. There hadn't been any point in looking back.

At least not then.

She'd spent nearly the entire part of her first year in California, facing away from the Pacific. The West Coast had been her goal, but once obtained all she could focus on was the south and what she'd left behind. It took Sheila kicking her in her head to get her to wake up and see that she was just floating through life. She was going down for the count.

But she got up, Betty Jean thought sighing. Or at least she'd tried to rise before Ezekiel threw that rope around her neck and drug her to the ground. She didn't know if she was interpreting her dreams correctly or not. She was no psychoanalyst and unlike Sheila, never had a desire to be one, but lately she'd been thinking of her attack as the rope forewarned about that was going to land around her neck like a noose.

She'd only just begun to live a little bit again and taste freedom when it was snatched away from her. He was no better than a thief, she thought, hugging her pillow tight. Now she had to decide what to do. Stand and fight for her peace of mind or run and hide? But fight whom if she dared to stand and hide where if she chose to run?

Again, she turned, flopping heavily to her other side. She had her leave from work, but what was she going to do with it? She wanted to get herself together and was really disappointed it was taking so long. Why was she so shell shocked and distraught over what happened? It was Zeke, not some stranger who attacked her. It wasn't like she'd been jogging in the park, gotten conked over the head and drug into the bushes.

It was Ezekiel.

She shook her head against the pillow sighing. It did no good. Regardless to how many times she thought it was just Ezekiel, her mind couldn't wrap itself around lessening the gravity of the charges against him. In fact, whenever she thought the words there was a small defiant voice in her head that gleefully told her that knowing her attacker as she did made it worse. She should not have had to defend herself against someone she once shared a life with.

What was she going to do? The words paraded across her mind over and over.

Stand and fight? She was tired of standing and wasn't certain she had too much fight left in her. She was tired of fighting, too. Run and hide? Hell, she was tired of running. She'd fled in more instances than when she stood and fought. She was *really* tired of running. And the places where she could hide, even from herself, especially from herself, were getting fewer and further between. She sighed again, glancing over her shoulder at the clock. Four fifteen, the clock told her in neon red. *Way past time to forget you,* the line from the poetry book flashed before her mind and she sighed again, too lazy to get up and look for her book. Too tired to read, anyway.

She should be asleep.

Knowing that she shouldn't disturb him, he was probably asleep, she did it anyway. Placing her tongue against the roof of her mouth, she whistled low, once, twice, then Insomnia bounded across her and onto the bed. He licked her face then curled next to her, putting his head on the pillow that her arms were still locked around.

She didn't think she'd be able to nod off again, but when the morning sun entered the room and fell across the bed, it dawned on two sleeping forms.

Chapter Thirty Two

You look like I could crack an egg and fry it right there on your forehead. That's what my mama used to say...*Stay outta your daddy's way, you can fry eggs on his forehead*! That meant he was mad. Really mad."

Sheila gave Carol an ugly look and the blond reared back as if struck. "Whew! Make that madder than the Devil when the A.C.'s blowing." Sheila frowned and Carol's eyes narrowed a bit. "Look it's only so much I can do without the cursing. I was born and raised in the back woods of Kentucky, believe me it's going to get real interesting before I finish." As she spoke, she developed a country twang that deepened with each word. "Why so glum, chum?" she asked in her normal voice. "Damned if I'd run off, get married, then return to work although my boss is on leave and I'm supposed to be on one, too."

"My in-laws are in town."

"And that has what to do with tea in China?" Carol questioned, drawing a blank. "The relevance of the comment is completely lost on me."

"I can't hang out with my husband. I might as well come to work and hang out here," Sheila said crossly.

"Why can't you hang out with your husband?"

"Because we're not married, yet."

"Grapevine has it different."

"Well, grapevine doesn't always have up to the minute details," Sheila snapped. She knew she should apologize for biting off Carol's head, but she didn't want to. She felt surly and inclined to stay that way.

"What's the caption going around the bottom of the screen read? You can't get anymore up to the minute than that."

"Cyron and I eloped on the eighteenth. We said screw waiting on a big shindig, we're ready. We're doing it now. We flew to Vegas and got married in this really cheesy spot. It was ridiculously corny." She smiled remembering the makeshift chapel decorated with pink and purple flamingos. "We flew home and were surprised by his parents and now we're trapped."

"Why did you guys come back? You were already in Vegas. Already gone and married. Why not just go on to your honeymoon or stay in Vegas for a while or something?"

"We just sort of woke up and said let's do this. There was no thought out itinerary plan or anything. We did think about just leaving from Vegas, then we got to thinking about what we left hanging here. Cyron needed to make sure Byron had time to keep an eye on his club. I needed to check in with Betty Jean and Charles." She shrugged, miserable. "We thought we'd come back, tie up the loose ends, pack a bag or two and ride off into the sunset again. Simple. So very, very simple. Now that's all shot to hell and I'm looking at bride magazines again!"

"Your in-laws are excited, hun?"

"Jules came by with her mother yesterday and we went to lunch together. During lunch we picked out the bride's maids dresses and again his mother, Miss Helen, asked if we've set a date."

"Did you tell her the eighteenth?"

"Do you want me to keep talking to you?"

"I'm sorry. I see it's too soon to joke. So, what are you guys going to do, have a wedding? Pretend the

deed hasn't already been done? Sounds a little adolescent to me."

"So, you really don't care if I speak to you or not?"

"Hear me out," Carol said, raising her hand. "The
thing is you and Cyron love one another. You've
demonstrated that love by exchanging vows. Everyone
missed it? Oh, well, catch the anniversary show then.
You guys didn't want to wait. Why wait now?"

"Everyone missed it, like you said. They shifted
plans to be here. They'll be all disappointed," Sheila
said grudgingly.

"Well, it's like my Momma said, you miss the boat,
you gotta swim." Carol turned away from Sheila's desk.
"In other words—" She lowered her head looking at
Sheila to complete the thought that she couldn't.

"Tough shit?"

"Exactly. Go claim your husband, girl," Carol called,
walking away.

**

"Should I be concerned?" Byron asked walking into
Betty Jean's garage. Her Infiniti was backed in and
she was struggling to lift a suitcase into the truck. She
hadn't seen his approach and jumped at the sound of
his voice.

"Hi," she said excessively cheery, feeling as though
she'd been caught in the act.

She straightened and Byron felt a smile of his own
stretch across his face. Her scarf was gone. Her hair
was styled like Halle Berry's pixie cut with short tufts,
spikes and licks. The cut fit her face, accentuating her
high cheekbones and arched eyebrows.

Cut short her hair was still a riot of multiple shades
of brown, but the ends seemed lighter than usual. His
smile widened. His Queen was slowly making her way
back to the throne she belonged on.

She shifted the suitcase, balancing it on her up-
raised knee and he rushed forward to take it from her.

"I'm nervous. Should I be helping you load your car with suitcases."

"It's just the one. A big one, but just the one."

"Yeah, but should I be helping?"

When the suitcase was nestled securely in the trunk of her vehicle, she closed the hood. "I can't imagine why you shouldn't help me. You're a gentleman aren't you?" she asked, walking back into the house.

"I can't ever recall having made such a claim." He entered the pantry off the hall, closing the door that led to the garage.

She cut her eyes at him laughing. "Good, because I'm not certain you'd be telling the truth."

She threw him another look and his stomach somersaulted. Was she flirting with him? How long had it been since she'd flirted with him in any capacity? "What's in the suitcase, other than your body weight in stones?"

"My body weight? My suitcase wasn't that heavy."

"Hell, your body weight isn't that heavy." He was rewarded by an instant flash of her naked above him. The same image must have popped into her mind, too.

"You'd be the one to know." She turned the corner, entering the kitchen.

He stopped at the bar stools, propping himself up against one. Insomnia rushed over to meet him and he scratched the pup behind his ears causing him to wag his tail in exuberant pleasure. "Hey, there boy," Byron said looking down at the dog. "Do you know why your momma's packed her bags and put them in the car? You going to tell me so I can stop her? Hun, boy?"

"He won't tell my secrets. You can forget it," Betty Jean said, rinsing out the glass she'd used earlier that day, so she could refill it.

"What's that?" he asked letting Insomnia lick his hand and wrist enthusiastically. "You want me to come, too? Well, I'm supposed to be a gentleman so I'd better

MBridges

wait to be invited. Oh, you're inviting me along?" he joked, looking at Betty Jean from the corner of his eye.

"Byron, do you want—"

"Yes!" he answered cutting off her question.

She smiled. "You don't even know what I was going to ask you."

"Insomnia, told me you were going to invite me along, so naturally I assumed—"

"See what happens when you listen to dogs?" Her smile grew. She placed a fresh glass of ice and a can of coke before him on the counter, then refilled her own glass with orange juice.

Exiting the kitchen, her arm was caught as she passed his stool and he pulled her into the v made by his parted thighs. "Seriously, Queen Bee, where are you headed?"

She looked into his face for a moment before finally shrugging. "Just out." She smiled into his face.

"Just out?"

She nodded. "Just out. No particular place to go. I have a leave of absence from Charles. I'm going to take it and hit the road for a bit."

"Going where?" he asked looking into her eyes. The humor was gone from his face, but she still smiled at him, happy with whatever decision she had made.

"Honestly, Byron, I don't know. I'm flying by the seat of my pants here." She smiled a little larger and suddenly it looked to him like she was placing support beams under a collapsing roof. Grabbing her hand, he stood from the barstool and pulled her into the living room. "You're forgetting your coke."

"So. I never wanted it."

"I asked you if—"

"I thought you were going to ask me to go with you."

"I'd forgotten," she said, as he reclined on the chaise lounge. "You were listening to the dog."

"Actually, I was anticipating our getaway. Montego Bay. Palm Island. Altamer. Remember?"

She was on his lap or what was left of his lap once he lay back. Instead of reclining against him, she remained sitting up, resting her spine against the bit of armrest behind her. "I don't know if you'll want to travel with me, Byron. I'm a little strange lately. Some days I smile, some I cry, rant and rave through, and on others I'm quiet as a pin drop. I don't know if you'll want to deal with all that."

"Yeah, well, I'm like that myself." She smiled at him. "No, really. I am. I'm a complex man. I know you look at me and it's hard to see pass the pretty face, but I'm really complex. I don't know if you'll want *me* along," he said turning his face away from her.

"You're so crazy." She shook her head at his antics.

"About you," he said easily, turning his gaze back to her. Their eyes locked and he stared into hers for a long moment. "Silly, crazy. Head over my heels, crazy. Getting more insane by the second, crazy about you." He'd said the words in fun, but he'd never been more serious about anything in his life. He reached up tracing the outline of her face with his finger. "I love your face, Betty Jean Carlson." He saw something flicker briefly in her eyes. A shadow of some doubt and he touched a hand to the back of her head pulling her towards him. "Kiss me."

She leaned forward and he sat up a little to meet her halfway. "I like your hair," he said as they broke away.

"I made an appointment and had it done this morning. It's a little different," she fingered the curls, "but I'm getting used to it."

"Long or short, it's fine," he reassured, never taking his eyes from her face.

"Why do you want to go with me?"

"Why not? I'm tired. I need a vacation, too. I want to spend some time with you. Why can't I come? Are you running from something? From me?"

"Not today." He raised an eyebrow and she smiled. "Not today," she confirmed her comment. "I told you with me everyday is a surprise. There's no telling what emotion I'll pull from my cornucopia of feelings each morning. Today isn't so bad. I feel like getting out and getting away but I don't feel pursued. Not today. I just feel the need to have a breeze in my hair and wind at my back, if that makes any sense at all."

"Can I come along?" Byron asked watching her face. "You don't have to be in love with me, Betty Jean. It's okay, we don't have to discuss it at all during our trip. We don't even have to share a room if you don't want, but I'd really like to go with you, to spend some time with you."

"But I don't even know where I'm—"

"It doesn't matter. My business can run itself for a while. I'm tired. I just want to get away, lay on a beach and hold you in my arms for a little bit."

"I can't promise—"

"Then don't," he cut her off. "Don't promise me a thing, Queen Bee and I won't expect anything. Let's go lie on the beach and watch all our troubles drift out to sea. We can pile them all up on the shoreline and just let the tide take 'em. What do you say?"

"I say you'd better get home and get packed if you're coming with me." She smiled and he hugged her to him before jumping up from the lounge and unseating her.

"Let's go!"

"Where am I going?" She laughed as she was pulled behind him and led down the hall.

"I have to go pack and give Cyron my keys." He was pulling her from the house and into the garage. "You're packed right?" he asked, as they passed her car.

"Yes. Why? Where are we going?"

"I already told you. I have to pack and give Cyron my keys. I don't want to let you out of my sight until we leave. You can't be trusted."

"What?" Betty Jean asked as he opened the door of his Suburban for her. He slammed it on her indignation and trotted around to the driver's side. Climbing in, he put on his seat belt and started the engine. Backing out of the drive, he said, "Oh, yeah, you didn't know? Can't be trusted for a moment. What would have happened had I not shown up when I did today?"

"I would have sent you a post card," she said smiling in excitement at the spontaneity of their actions. Is this how Sheila felt when she and Cyron eloped? Like there was no yesterday or tomorrow? Like the only thing on earth that mattered was the moment that they were standing in and everything else could go twist in the wind?

He gave her a dirty look. "You would be evil enough to send a wish you were here card after leaving me behind purposely."

"No, not purposely."

"Betty Jean, did you call me to say you were leaving? Would you have called me to say goodbye?" She remained silent as they sped down the street and Byron laughed. "I rest my case."

**

"But where is this funny?" She folded her arms across her chest, the very picture of petulance.

"I'm sorry, baby," he said, making little effort to sober up and be serious.

"At least pretend to mean it, Cyron," she pouted and he put his arm around her shoulders across the back of the purple couch.

"Where are we going to live?"

"Looks like you'll be at your house and I'll be at mine."

"C'mon Leggs, cheer up," he said squeezing her arm a bit with his fingers.

"I don't want to cheer up," Sheila said, turning her head aside to look up at the ceiling.

"Okay, you win. I'm sorry."

"I don't want to win," she pouted, continuing to look at the ceiling. She readjusted, pulling her folded arms tighter across her chest.

"Then what do you want? Tell me what to do to make this better, Leggs. What do I have to do to make you smile again?"

"I don't *have to* tell you anything, just like you don't *have to* do anything to make this better or to put a smile on my face," she said to the ceiling, emphasizing each have to.

Cyron turned her towards him and slowly unfolded her arms to place them around his body. He pulled her to him until her head rested on his shoulder and he reclined against the cushions with her in his arms.

"I don't want you to have to go home tonight," she said into his neck and he frowned, confused at the statement.

"Then I'll stay the night."

"You can't. You—"

"Why not?" Cyron raised a brow. The insipid little man she allowed to take her to dinner and a movie leapt to his mind and he added, "Mrs. de Monbleau."

"Because of the other Mrs. de Monbleau. I don't want your mother to think you're buying the cow be-cause you're getting free milk from it."

"Buying the - I already bought the cow." He smiled, squeezing her to his chest, but Sheila wasn't joking.

"She doesn't know that. I don't want your mother thinking I'm a slut."

"My mother knows I'm not a choir boy. I've been home before ten every night since they got here. They knew that wouldn't last long. They were bound to wake up and not have me at the breakfast table sooner or later. Besides you see how they are together, all touchy feely and nasty looks? They've always been that way. If they even notice my absence, I'm sure they'll appre-ciate the privacy."

"And have your mother counting her fingers and toes when the baby's born along with Julie?"

"Fingers and toes? Damn Leggs, it won't take but nine fingers, ten at the most, hun? If we need fingers and toes to count the length of a pregnancy, we've got bigger issues than the date of conception to worry about."

She raised her head to look in his eyes. "Again, I ask, where is this funny?"

His smile fled. "And again I ask you, what to do to fix it? I want that beautiful smile I love seeing so much," he kissed her quickly, pecking her lips as he spoke, "back where it belongs."

Sheila looked at him a moment then dropped her head to his chest. She sighed deeply and squeezed him tight before speaking. "I'm being silly. Every woman wants to be a bride with a beautiful gown and wedding cake and people fussing over her. And we're already married, even if no one else knows it. So, it's not like it's a really big deal, right? It'll be cool to have our little secret. We can tell everyone the truth after the wedding, that way no one's feelings will be hurt. We'll just wait, that's all. We're married and that's what we wanted. The families get what they want and I don't know what I was thinking, Roslyn," Sheila said, referring to her mother, "would kill me. She's been planning my wedding since I was six. And daddy would be so hurt not to have finally gotten the chance to give me away. He joked about it a lot as me and my sister got older, the giving away part. I just need some patience. My daddy will be the first to tell you that and Roslyn the second. Yeah, its better like this, no one has to be sad or hurt. Everyone can be happy."

Cyron frowned. She sure as hell didn't sound happy. He kissed the top of her forehead and squeezed her a little tighter. It had been her idea not to tell his parents that they were too late for the wedding, but Cyron was beginning to think the charade was too much for her.

All she'd wanted was to be married, to live as man and wife. That's all he cared about too, that's why he woke up in the middle of the night to elope. He'd wanted her for his wife right then and for always. Now he was back to staring at the ceiling at night wishing she were beside him. He felt like a teenager sometimes when he woke in the morning with Sheila on his mind, the evidence of his thoughts on his body and his mother singing in the kitchen while she fixed breakfast.

He had to admit, he did find the situation amusing at times. It was just as his father had said. He was good and caught in a trap of his own making this time. He sighed. It wasn't just about him anymore. He had to think about someone else and presently, she found no humor in the ironic situation at all. Her morose rambling hadn't fooled anybody, least of all him. He doubted if she'd done too well a job on herself either and could think of only one thing to do about it.

He stood from the couch, pulling her to her feet along side him. "Let's go."

"Where?" she asked, barely cooperating.

"To get ice cream."

"I don't want any ice cream."

"Yes, you do," he said cheerfully, all but dragging her to the door.

Chapter Thirty Three

This is not Baskin Robins," Sheila said as the Escalade pulled to a stop in front of Cyron's mail box.

"Yeah, I know, but I need to get something. Come on inside," he said climbing from the truck's cab. He started up the drive, leaving her to follow.

Sheila looked out the truck's window, rolling her eyes at Cyron's retreating back. She knew she was being rude to whichever of her in-laws that was inside the house, but the last thing she wanted just then was to get out, go inside and make polite conversation about a wedding she didn't want. In her current mood, she'd end up hurting someone's feelings, so it would be best if she just sat in the truck and waited for his return. She was just about to open the door to tell Cyron just that when the front door opened and Julie stepped out onto the porch.

Sheila sucked her teeth and turned her head in the other direction, changing her mind. He'd get the picture sooner or later without her comments. Folding her arms back across her chest she sighed irritably.

"Hey," Jules called, greeting Cyron on the stoned path that led from his driveway to the porch steps. She tiptoed, kissing his cheek. "I was just leaving. I swear if mother drags me shopping again! Three days in a row, Cyron!" She illustrated her point with three fingers raised in the air. "I can't do it! I don't know how

she and Sheila can slide from department to department putting together these bad ass outfits. I'm feeling
more like a bum that should be carrying their bags
every day!"

When she stopped for breath, Cyron was laughing.
"You know mom's always been like that. You don't
remember how you used to complain about having been
kidnapped as a child when she'd take you shopping
with her all day?"

Her smile grew and she crinkled her nose. "Well, it
was true. She did kidnap me. We'd leave the house
before nine and wouldn't return until after dark. My
whole Saturday gone and wasted trying on clothes."

"Surely you couldn't have thought my Leggs would
be any different?"

"I suppose not," she said frowning then she smiled
as an idea occurred. "At least now the two of them can
shop till they drop together and I can finally be freed.
If I never step into another mall or department store
again, it'll be too soon." She looked towards the
Escalade parked at the curb and waved. Sheila didn't
respond and she let her arm fall. "I don't think she's
looking this way," she said to Cyron. "I guess you're
just in and out."

"I don't know. It might take a minute to get this
done."

"Why is Sheila in the car still? You told her it would
be quick or is she already hiding from the de
Monbleaus?" Julie grinned devilishly, as though people
often hid from her family.

"She's not sitting in the truck." He said the words
so matter-of-factly, Julie's head snapped back to Sheila.

"She looks pretty settled in to me, big brother."

He waved her observation aside. "She's getting out."

Again, Julie's attention shifted to Sheila who
remained just as still as before in the truck. "Okay.
Whatever, Cyron." She clapped a hand to his forearm,
making to move around him on the path. "I'll see you

guys later. I made the great escape when Mom went to put her packages up. She'll probably be in your guest room for the next six months, trying to find a place for all her purchases." She shook her head in wonder. "I swear it's like she doesn't think her luggage will ever show up. She needs to call 1-800-I-Shop-2-Much. Maybe you should suggest it." She smiled broadly at the prospect. "Well, see ya!"

"Wait a minute, Jules. Come back inside with me for a second."

"Are you crazy?" Her eyes grew wide. "Mother wants to go look at shoes tomorrow. We haven't set a time and unfortunately I will be unavailable until it's much too late for us to go. I've already stood here talking too long. Nope, sorry." She shook her head. "Not going back in there."

"Okay, I just had something I wanted to get said, but I guess mom and dad will do. Go ahead then." He gave her a little push in the back. "Don't let me and my problems hold you up."

She frowned suspicious of his motives. "What problems? Are you and Ms. Thing breaking up or something?" Her head swiveled to Sheila. "Is that why she's not getting out or returning my wave?"

"She is getting out and I thought you said she didn't see you?"

Julie hunched her shoulders, pursing her lips. "You never know, do you?"

Cyron frowned. "Never know what?"

"What's really in a person's mind? Maybe she saw me wave, maybe she didn't. Maybe she's sitting in the truck mad, maybe she's not mad at all and she plans to get out eventually." She hunched her shoulders again. "As I said...you never know. Anyway, what's going on? Tell me real quick, so I won't have to go inside and get caught."

"It's not something I intend to have to keep repeating, Jules. It's no big deal, though, go ahead and burn off." He gave her another slight push in the back.

She looked into his eyes for a few seconds trying to fathom his secret. Failing, she rolled her eyes at him and reversed directions on the path. "Oh, you make me sick! You could just tell me now, out here, without me having to go shopping for shoes in the morning!" She marched back up the path and into the house, muttering and frowning.

Cyron took his cell phone from his pocket and dialed.

The number he'd called rang once.

Twice.

Three times.

"Why?"

"Come here."

"For what purpose?"

"Do I need one?"

Sheila turned in her seat to look at Cyron over her shoulder.

"Well, do I?" he asked softly into the cell phone and Sheila's eyes narrowed across the distance.

"Will we be long? I don't really feel like making nice right now."

"So, I see. Speaking of which, Jules thinks you saw her waving."

"I didn't," she said, dryly, giving him the impression that it would not have made any difference even if she had.

"I love you," he said staring at her.

"I love you, too, Cyron," she said softly. Looking at him a fraction longer, she hung up the phone. Putting her cell phone back in her purse, she got out of the truck. Halfway, to where Cyron waited for her on the stoned path, she looked around as Byron's Suburban pulled into the driveway next to Julie's car.

Some of her annoyance slipped away when she noticed Betty Jean on the passenger's side of the truck. She saw that a huge smile was stretched across her friend's face and couldn't help but respond in kind. It did her heart so good to see it.

"Hey, honey!" She hugged Betty Jean as soon as the other woman climbed down from the truck. "Look at your hair! Girl, I know Manuel had fits when he saw it!"

"Actually, he surprised me. He said he loved my hair long, but always thought I'd look cute with shorter hair. He says it opens up my face. He did his magic and I've felt beautiful ever since I rose from the chair in his shop."

"You are beautiful!" Sheila said, hugging her again, still smiling at Betty Jean's smile.

"He said he may have to throw Stephen out for me." Betty Jean giggled thinking about her hairdresser's flamboyant boyfriend.

"I was wondering what was taking you so damn long," Cyron said, watching Byron approached him.

Taken back, Byron frowned. "What are you talking about? I just dropped by to leave the keys to Rufio's with you and to ask you to keep an eye on the place for me for a minute or two. What was taking me so long?"

"I left you a message to meet me over here a little while ago."

"I didn't get any - Wait a minute! That was you? I couldn't make heads nor tails of whatever the hell you were saying." He demonstrated by making a bunch of low hissing noises.

"I was whispering," Cyron said, offended. He waved off Byron's next remark. "It doesn't matter. You're here now. Come on inside." He turned but Byron didn't follow.

"We're kind of just trying to slip in and slip out. Kind of real low key, you know? I'd rather not go inside and get delayed. We've got places to go, people to see."

"Man, look. I just had to twist Julie's arm to get her in the house. Don't make me have to get rough with you, Byron!" Cyron snapped in irritation, throwing his hands up in the air. "What is it with everybody today? Why doesn't anybody want to just freaking cooperate? What's wrong with my house?"

"Well, I always thought you could use a few flowers out front myself," Betty Jean said smiling, walking up the path with Sheila. "Hello, Cyron."

"Hey, Cutie." Cyron kissed her cheek. "It's nice to see you out and about."

She nodded her head in agreement. "It's nice to be out and about."

"Can we all just go inside now? Please?" Cyron spread his arms wide with exasperation, he led the way up the path. Leery of another outburst, Byron followed quietly.

"Is that Ayron?" Cyron asked entering the living room. His parents were seated on the couch and Julie stood with her back to them whispering furiously into the cell phone. Her head snapped around at his question.

"Yes and we're not talking about you so don't start. What? No, it's Cyron being paranoid," she said into the phone, turning to fully face the room and was surprised at all the additional people. "Actually, every-one is here now except you. Even Sheila and Byron's friend, Betty Jean. Hey, Betty Jean! Hi, Sheila," she called waving to everyone. "I don't know what's going on either. Let me call you back. Oh, all right, but be quiet. Don't be asking questions until it's over." She turned with the phone at her ear to look expectantly at Cyron who stood holding Sheila's hand.

The room was silent and they all looked around waiting for Cyron to speak.

He took a deep breath then squeezed Sheila's fingers. "Mom, Dad, Sheila and I are really pleased that you two cut everything you were doing short to come be with us and offer your help, support and guidance. Everyone has been asking us when we'll set a date for the wedding. Well, we finally have." He paused, looking around at everyone's face. His mother's beamed. His father's was meticulously blank. Julie and Bryon's were expecting and Betty Jean's was hard to read, but her eyebrows were knitted together in curiosity.

He didn't read Sheila's expression, because he addressed the room again without looking at it. He'd seen her expression for the last few days and was certain it hadn't altered unless she was wearing a mask now for the others.

"The eighteenth of this month, next year, Sheila will finally get to walk down the aisle."

His mother and his siblings were excited at the news, but Betty Jean's face remained the same and his father's matched it. Cyron shook his head and raised a hand for silence. "Sheila will walk down the aisle in a year, but it'll be for our first year anniversary. We'll be repeating our vows for the benefit of our families and friends."

There was shocked silence, broken by the gentle rumble of Brandon's chuckle.

"But the eighteenth? But - What do you mean your first anniversary?" Helen's head went from her son to her husband and back. "What's going on here Cyron? Stop laughing Brandon!"

"Shhh! I said don't ask questions!" Julie hissed into her cell phone.

"I asked Sheila to marry me, but we couldn't come up with a date because we didn't want to wait. Everything was too far away. A week. Two weeks. Two months. Too much time gone. I asked Sheila to marry me because I wanted her as my wife, not my fiancee. I got tired of coming home to an empty house after leaving her every night. I wanted my girl here with me, but not just my lady, I wanted my wife." He felt Sheila's fingers tighten and squeezed back. "In fact, we'd just come back from being married the day you two arrived. We were just supposed to be in and out. I was coming to drop off the keys to the Chicken Shack to you." He turned to his brother, thinking Byron was there to do the exact same thing. "Tie up a few loose ends and be gone."

"But we were here," his mother finished for him. "Oh, we're so sorry, Cyron. Spoiling your romance like that!" She looked genuinely sorry, too.

"We're sorry for lying to everyone and wasting your time," Sheila finally chimed in, now that the weight had been lifted from her chest. "We just didn't want to hurt anybody's feelings."

"But that didn't seem to be working." Cyron was looking down at his wife. "Feelings were being hurt, anyway."

I love you, Sheila mouth the words and Cyron hugged her close.

Thirty minutes later everyone was seated around Cyron's living room and Ayron had called demanding to be put on speaker phone so as not to be excluded. Julie kept shhhing him on her phone and he couldn't hear well enough to participate.

"Is the honeymoon waiting until next year's wedding, too?" Julie sipped a coke giving her brother and his bride a mischievous look.

Cyron looked at Sheila. "Well, we hadn't actually had time to discuss it yet. We were going to take a few days away, but we hadn't planned out an actual honeymoon or anything." The question was repeated in his gaze and Sheila turned hers to Betty Jean who looked surprised.

"It's not up to me. You have the leave, use it as you choose."

Jules turned to her mother. "Sheila works for Betty Jean," she explained.

"Which brings me to my own announcement. We've got to go, if we're going to make our flight," Byron said to Betty Jean.

The speaker phone was the first to ask, "What flight?" Everyone laughed.

"I've been twisting Ms. Carlson's arm for some time now and she's finally agreed to take a vacation with me. We have a flight to catch to destinations unknown."

The room was quiet as everyone looked around absorbing this new bit of information. Could there be two weddings next year?

"What have *you* been up to lately, young lady?" Brandon boomed at Julie who jumped and looked innocent. "We might have to start looking at real estate in this area. These children are out of control," he said looking at his wife and everyone laughed again.

Byron and Betty Jean were the first to stand up.

"You guys are welcome to set up residence here in the meantime. We've been trying to figure out whose house to live in. Either way, we'll have one just standing empty," Cyron said smiling. He was a man who believed in owning real estate, so they'd be keeping both of the houses. He stood, pulling Sheila with him. He kissed her hand. "Me and the Mrs. are going on our honeymoon!"

Sheila threw her arms around his neck and Ayron said from the phone, "I can send the jet and the four of you can use it." The suggestion was met with silence. "It can be to you guys in a few hours. Let me know something, so I can go shake a stick at the pilot."

Byron and Cyron looked at one another like *why not?* and they both smiled. Byron shrugged saying, "It *is* your honeymoon, man. You might as well do it right."

"You cut your hair." Helen had her head tilted to the side, looking at Betty Jean.

"Excuse me?" Betty Jean assumed she'd misunderstood the older woman's comment.

"In the picture at Byron's house, your hair is longer. I didn't recognize you at first."

"The picture - What picture?" They were standing to the side while the brothers discussed their plane arrangements with Byron and Cyron trying to figured out who best to shift their duties to since the other would be unavailable.

"I was at Byron's desk sending an email to a friend and I noticed your picture by the computer. I believe it may have been taken at his nightclub, but I wasn't sure. I've only been there once or twice"

"I never—" Betty Jean began then stopped. She was going to say she never took a picture with Byron then she remembered that she had. It was a year ago, on the night they first met at Rufio's. They'd taken photographs. Her and Byron and the two women she'd met while waiting in line. Ariel and Tamara!

But how'd he get the picture?

She remembered intentionally leaving it on the bathroom counter in the ladies room and felt her face heat with embarrassment. Obviously, someone recognized Byron in the photo and returned it to him. She glanced over at Byron wondering why he'd kept the picture. Recalling her current conversation she smiled a little shyly. "Yes, ma'am, I sure did cut my hair. I guess it is me in the picture after all."

"You didn't know he had the picture?" Helen asked astutely reading Betty Jean's expression. Betty Jean shook her head in the negative and Helen patted her hand. "Don't worry. My boys will do that. The unexpected. They get it from him." She jerked her head towards Brandon who turned his head towards her as though she'd called his name out loud.

"Well," Byron said loudly after hanging up the speaker phone. "We have a few hours to kill before our flight arrives. How about we all go to dinner? My treat."

"Sounds good to me." Brandon rose, stretching. "I've been starving for hours and the food is always better on someone else's dime."

"Fine with me." Julie used Brandon for support to pull herself up.

"Where'd you get those sandals?" Helen asked Sheila, joining the group heading towards the front door. "It's almost a shame you won't be here tomorrow. Julie and I are hitting the shoe stores bright and early. I like to be there when they open, if I can, before all the good stuff gets picked over and pulled out." Julie groaned rolling her eyes at the ceiling, but Helen ignored her. Placing her arm around Sheila, she stepped out the door.

Julie punched Cyron hard in the arm, then stormed out behind them.

On his way out, Brandon stopped in front of Cyron and stood nodding his head as though pleased with the appraisal. "I knew you'd come through. I knew you'd stand up, make me proud." He hugged his son. "You did good. I feel good about you two. See the way she lit up like a Christmas tree when you claimed her? I hadn't seen her looking like that since she rode in on your back the other morning." He nodded his head again. "You did good, son." He turned to the door clapping his hands together. "Let's eat! I'm hungry!"

Betty Jean smiled. Brandon de Monbleau reminded her of Malcolm, her daddy. Her smile turned whimsical and expanded a little further.

Byron placed his hand in the small of her back. "So, are you ready?"

Ready for what? The next second, the next moment, the next hour of her life? The next phrase, chapter and book? The next thing she laughed about, cried over or shouted at? Betty Jean was quiet for a moment. She stood smiling a small secret smile that grew a little bit the longer she held it, until it spread out into a full fledged toothy grin.

"Yeah, I'm ready." Still smiling, she turned and crossed the open threshold.

Coming Soon

Life Happens

Chapter One

"A s I live and breathe." The fashionably clad woman rubbed a hand down the round, mound of her unborn child, smiling warmly at her friend who sat across from her on the sun drenched patio of Chicas Mexican Cafe. She shook her head and her ponytail swung gently. Her smile grew. "I still can't believe you're here."

"Neither can I," the other woman concurred the sentiment. She looked around with a small smile touching her lips. "It's good to be back."

A sadness surfaced briefly in the pregnant woman's eyes, but she blinked it away, dabbing at her eyes with her finger tips. Her friend noticed the action and sat up in her chair frowning with concern, but before she could speak, her concern was waved back.

"Ignore me. It's the condition," she said, once again unconsciously rubbing her stomach. She stared hard at the other woman who sipped at her ice tea. "When I read your letter, I wanted to come."

Though the letter in question had been sent years before, her friend knew exactly what she spoke of. "It's okay. I understand. I didn't intend for you to drop everything and fly half way around the world just to hold my hand."

"You shouldn't have been alone." The other woman reached over squeezing the slender hand that lay casually on the table.

"Yeah, well." She hunched her shoulders and looked off across the busy plaza.

"He wanted to come; to be with you. He wanted to just hold your hand, I think."

"Yeah, I know. He called and asked." She shook her head a little at the memory. "I told him not to, to stay away."

Maybe it was her impending motherhood that made her want to fix and heal everyone's problems, so she nudged, "He loved you. He would have been there for you."

"But he didn't need to be. It wasn't his—"

"I know you know him better than that," she cut in, saying. "It didn't matter to him that—"

"It mattered to me," she said a bit more aggressively than intended, swinging her gaze back to the table.

"How are you doing? Are you okay?"

"Sweetie, I'm fine. All of this was a long time ago. A lifetime. I've dealt with it. Cried my tears over it." She shook her head again. "I'm all right now. Honestly."

"Yeah, I know, but you know me. I have to be sure."

"Sure as certain?" she asked, borrowing one of the other woman's favorite sayings.

"Exactly. Sure as certain. And I could never be certain you were okay with you so far away. I don't want to dredge up old things to hurt you, you know that," she said squeezing the other's hand again. "It's just my first time seeing you and I have to kiss and hug each boo-boo."

She smiled, slowly. "Each boo-boo?"

A beautiful smile spread across a dark face. "I think it's the influence of that loon I'm married to." She smiled, affectionately smoothing her belly. "I want to be certain you're all right. I don't want you to feel like I'm flaunting myself in front of you."

Her companion's eyes widened. "Flaunting yourself because you're living? I'd never think such a thing.

I'm happy for you and anxious to see my God child. Don't worry about me really. These are all old scars that we're picking at. I learned to accept quite a few things while I was overseas. I accepted my pregnancy before I even left. I accepted the fact that I was going to be a single parent whether I wanted to be or not. I settled into my life in Tokyo and was prepared to do what needed to be done to raise my child." She hunched her shoulders slightly. "Then I lost it." She looked down at the food on her plate, but didn't really see it. "Premature labor. The baby wasn't strong enough to survive on it's own yet and he didn't make it," she said, shrugging in acceptance.

"I'm sorry."

She hunched her shoulders again. Raising her gaze, she said simply, "Life happens." There was a momentary pause before she added, "or doesn't," thinking of her child.

"I know this sounds like an asshole's question, but," she began, then paused briefly, looking into the eyes of her closest friend. "How did you feel when it happened? I mean," she said quickly, trying to clean up her question. "How did you...*feel*?" she repeated, sheepishly, apologetically, but her friend understood what she was asking and took no offense. She was seated across from the one person in life she could always speak the truth to regardless of what she had to say.

Without any pretensions at all, she shook her head slowly from side to side. Tears sparkled in her eyes suddenly when she opened her mouth to speak belying her adamant insistence that their conversation was of all things past. "I don't know, Sheila. I honestly don't know. I'd be lying if I said there had been any joy in me when I found out I was pregnant. I was on vacation supposed to be having the time of my life and...Well, I don't have to explain all that to you, you were there. So, I won't lie about it, but there was this little life growing just beneath my heart and I couldn't stop myself from caring about it."

Unconsciously, Sheila's hand stilled for a moment in its ministrations, then resumed it's stroking as Betty Jean resumed speaking. "I'm not all honorable, though. I accepted my fate, but there were still times when I couldn't put to bed my hurt and anger at what had happened. There were days when I wanted to find Ezekiel Johnson and—" She closed her eyes and held them that way for a silent moment, letting the anger drain from her. When she opened her eyes again the fire was gone and she looked placidly across to her friend.

"I don't know what I felt. Hurt that my child was gone. I'd grown to accept the pregnancy and the baby, then that too was snatched from me. I was sad that a life had been deferred. Relieved of a burden. I wanted children, but not like that. Guilty. Ashamed of the way I felt. Glad that Ezekiel wouldn't be the father of my son. Hurt that my son was gone, but glad that his was, too. It didn't matter that they were one and the same. He didn't deserve to be a father. Even if he would have never known about the baby, he didn't deserve it. A special gift for what he did to me?" she asked shaking her head in the negative.

"I felt like a monster for so long. Just chewed up with guilt. I hurt because I'm human and regardless to the circumstances of its conception, I lost my child, but Sheila I swear every other emotion I felt outweighed the hurt and sadness of the loss."

They sat in silence for a moment, each digesting the conversation along with her enchiladas, beans and rice.

"I wish I could have been there."

"I put what happened into a letter for a reason. I could have called."

"I did wonder about that."

"I was just trying to do my own thing. In my own way and come to terms with everything that was happening. I just wanted to give myself a little time to grieve for Phoenix in private."

Sheila raised a brow at the name and Betty Jean blushed. "It's the nickname I started referring to the baby as. My little Phoenix. One day we were going to rise from the ashes, you know? Me and Phoenix. Now it's just me to rise from the ashes alone."

"I'm sure you will, too," Sheila agreed softly with love in her voice. "And you won't have to do it alone."

Betty Jean caught her meaning and offered a small smile herself. "Anyway, I knew you would be there in a heart beat if I whistled for ya," she said, lightly. "You had classes and the wedding and your own life buzzing around you. I was okay. It was a difficult time, but I pulled through okay."

"I'm glad to hear it."

"Glad to be able to say it. Thank you for looking after my house for me," Betty Jean said, changing the subject.

Sheila waved her off and sunlight danced off the diamonds in her wedding ring and tennis bracelet. "No trouble at all. It was just standing empty and it was great to have a place to throw all our wild parties and not have to worry about cleaning up."

"Ha! Ha! Ha! Very funny!" Betty Jean said smiling, then frowned. "So, that's what happened to that table."

"What table?" Sheila asked alarmed, then laughed. "You aren't funny."

"I had you for a second there. You were ready to confess all sins," Betty Jean said wagging a finger at her friend.

"Only the stuff that'll make you blush. Heck, some of it brings a little color to my dark cheeks, too, and you know that's saying something."

"Never mind," Betty Jean said waving her off. "I don't need to know anything that's sinful enough to make *you* blush."

"What's that supposed to mean? I'm respectable and married now. My wild escapades are behind me. I've changed."

"Married, yes, but respectable?" She raised a brow in doubt.

"I've changed," Sheila insisted with a smile.

"Your underwear...if you're wearing any."

"With this load? I have to." Betty Jean raised a brow and Sheila laughed, chewing on her straw. "Okay, maybe not all the time, but I am right now."

"TMI," Betty Jean said, wrinkling her nose. "You really should find out what that means one day."

"I have a problem with *too* and *much* running concurrently with one another. There's simply no such phenomenon and I refuse to wrap my mind around the possibility."

"It's good to see some things never change." She raised her glass in salute. Making an arch she encompassed Sheila's wedding ring and full belly. "And some things do."

Sheila smiled down at herself, watching the diamonds sparkle in the sun as she stroked her child. "Can you believe this? Married with a family. Me."

"Sure I can. It's plausible," she said and an emotional Sheila sniffed. "But if I hadn't seen it with my own two eyes...."

Sheila looked up, smiling. "I am such a mess. Mood swinging from tree to tree."

"Not branch to branch?" Betty Jean asked smiling.

"Girl, no. My swings are wild and varied," she said wiping at the corner of her eyes. "Damn that branch, shit. I'm going from tree to tree, since I've been pregnant. I can laugh, cry and curse you out all in the space of five minutes. My mood flips just that quickly!"

"How can you tell the difference between pregnant mood swinging Sheila and regular Sheila?" she asked innocently.

Sheila smiled. "Again, not funny. What do you do, run corporate America by day? You should keep that job. It's a good one for you. Mild Mannered Comedian Girl isn't working. Let it go."

"How are the classes coming?"

Sheila beamed. She was starting her internship soon where she'd be working in an actual clinic setting. In no time at all she would be Dr. de Monbleau, psychoanalyst. Smiling she held up her thumb and forefinger. "I'm just this close to having the credentials to prove Cyron's insane. This close."

Betty Jean laughed. "Let me know if you need a signed affidavit."

"I keep telling him he's the only reason I'm interested in this field of study! Girl, I need some schooling to understand his brand of insanity."

"With Cyron, I don't doubt it."

"And you shouldn't doubt, none's required. So, when do you step back into HD's offices?"

Betty Jean shrugged. "I have a couple of weeks until I'm due to report in. You know, Charles. *Take your time. Get settled in. Breathe a little bit.* I'm sure it's one of those last chance type things. I'll probably be up to my neck in alligators when I get back. I was intending to rush back, but—" She lifted her shoulders again. "I might as well take my leisure now, especially if I'm looking at twelve hour days for the next few months. Sixteen without super assistant."

"That's right. You will need someone now, won't you?"

"*That's right*...oh please!" Betty Jean smiled waving Sheila off. "Like you forgot you got married and started a fabulous life and ditched me!"

"I didn't ditch you!" Sheila laughed as she picked at the remains of her lunch. "Had you not gone off to Tokyo, I would still be working for you. Assisting away."

"I doubt that. You have school, a husband, shoot a whole family now," she said nodding at Sheila's stomach. "Working for me, too, would have really been too much."

Sheila sipped at her water. Frowning she shook her head at Betty Jean. "What did I just finish saying? *Too* and *much* should never meet. There's—"

"No such phenomenon," Betty Jean said in unison with her friend and they both laughed.

"It is so good to have you home."
**

Betty Jean pulled into the driveway of her house and turned the engine off. She sat behind the wheel of the big Mercedes, but made no move to exit the vehicle other than removing her seat belt. She looked around at the perfect yard, the lush landscaping and allowed herself a small smile. Sheila had taken care of everything it seemed. The lawn was so well manicured no one would guess that the house had been standing empty for over five years.

Betty Jean sat staring at the house, but her focus along with her thoughts, was on the past. She'd told Sheila that she'd moved on and didn't dwell on bygones, but it was a half-truth. Mostly a lie, but still a half-truth since there was a kernel or two of honesty in the statement. For the most part, she'd put the ugliness behind her, but it's memory would sneak in every now and then to disturb her as it had done last night.

She'd driven to her house from the airport, but after sitting in her car for half an hour clutching the steering wheel, she'd backed out the drive and gone to a hotel. It wasn't that she was afraid to enter her house, after her long flight she just wasn't up for any ghost busting and she wasn't sure just how much she'd have to do upon entering her home.

Home.

A word that had always been elusive for her and still was. If anything the word had become synonymous with pain. Her first and true home had been destroyed and taken away with her parents sudden and unexpected death. The next home she'd tried to build with Ezekiel Johnson was ripped and torn asunder by his constant cheating. She'd left him and come to the golden state to rebuild and start her life again, but pain and misery had followed, leading Ezekiel straight to her where he could ruin and disrupt another home for her.

She sat in her car staring out at the house contemplating selling it. She chewed her lip worriedly. If she did that, would he be winning? She shook her head slightly at the thought, tired of thinking in terms of wins and losses. She just wanted to *go home*. That safe fortress that buffeted one from the harshness of the outside world. The place she'd only just realized she'd been searching for since losing Belle and Malcolm. The place she was parked in front of.

Placing her hand on the door, she opened it. She slid her left leg out, but didn't follow it. She stared up the path to the front door and remembered Ezekiel sitting in his car stalking her. How many times had he sat much the same way, patiently watching and waiting? A silent threat, waiting to strike.

"Shit," she said out loud, exasperated with herself. "It's just a damned house and Ezekiel is no where around." Even as she said the words, her eyes swept the perimeter and she glanced in her rear view mirror.

Irritated by the action, her right foot finally joined her left on the driveway and she exited the car. The walk up the drive to the front porch was slow. Betty Jean took her time looking around at her neighborhood. She felt like a stranger in a foreign land. Finally standing on her front porch, she inserted her key. Unlocking the door, she pushed it open. Peering inside, she could see everything was still covered in dust cloths waiting her return. She wished she would have let Sheila open the place up and air it out as she'd wanted to do, but Betty Jean hadn't wanted to burden the other woman further and had declined the offer.

Staring at the white sheets from the doorway, she wished she had someone with her. Sheila. Insomnia. Anyone to keep her from walking in alone. Anything to distract her mind from what she was doing, what she was feeling. She hadn't known returning would be so difficult.

"Hello? May I help you?"

Betty Jean turned from the doorway to see a petite woman in an oversized straw hat, holding a huge pair of gardening shears. Betty Jean smiled. The shears were nearly as big as the woman holding them. "It's okay, I live here."

"Is that so?" The woman asked, coming a little closer. "Are you sure about that?" she asked skeptically. "I happen to know the lady who lives here and—" She was cut off when Betty Jean came down from the porch and stepped into the sunlight.

"Anne?" Betty Jean questioned trying to recall the woman's name.

"Abby," the much shorter woman corrected, lowering her shears and snapping the lock in place to keep the blades from opening again. She walked over to Betty Jean, meeting her on the path. "I don't wear my glasses when I'm gardening, ironically enough. I'm sorry I didn't recognize you."

"Oh, it's all right. I'm glad to see my house was so well protected in my absence."

The other woman waved away the kind words. "We're neighbors. It's what we do."

They stood in awkward silence for a moment. They had just begun being cordial and friendly to one another when Betty Jean left for Tokyo. Being such, their repertoire of things to say to one another wasn't that impressive.

"Looks like you were gone for more than a year or two," Abby said, stating the obvious.

"It took longer to establish the overseas offices than we originally thought," Betty Jean said, struggling for conversation. If Abby left she'd have to go inside and face her house.

"It must have been something living in Japan for all that time. Stan, my husband, and I visited a time or two, but nothing so extensive as that."

"It was a unique experience," Betty Jean said, smiling. "I have tons of pictures. You'll have to come by and see them some time."

"Yes, of course. Maybe when I'm less dangerous," she said, brandishing her shears. "I won't keep you. I'm sure you have lots of things to do to get back into the swing of things."

"Right now, I'd settle for just getting into my house," Betty Jean responded automatically.

Unaware of Betty Jean's troubles, Abby misunderstood what she was saying and apologized. "Here I am running off at the mouth. How rude. You must be tired and anxious to get inside. You go ahead and we'll talk more later." Abby turned, preparing to leave.

"No," Betty Jean said, putting her hand out to stop the other's exit. "I didn't mean it like that. I was just looking inside before you came over and the whole *draped in sheets* thing was looking a bit daunting to me, that's all. I need a ponytail like *I dream of Jeannie*, then I could have everything cleaned up and set aright in no time."

"Like that," Abby agreed, snapping her fingers. "Well, how about if I help?"

Betty Jean was shaking her head. "No, you don't have to do that. I wasn't lobbying for assistance or anything," Betty Jean said, laughing.

"Well, I'm volunteering my services." Abby removed her straw hat to wipe her forehead. Shiny, red curls fell to the middle of her back and she looked like a teenager. But at four feet ten inches tall, weighing ninety eight pounds and having flawless skin, her appearance routinely denied her forty-two years. She left her gardening shears on the lawn and started up the path. "We're mere mortals, but it shouldn't take us too long to snatch the sheets off the furniture, hun? No ponytails, but nearly as quick and painless."

"What about your gardening? I don't want to pull you away from anything," Betty Jean said, hoping she was protesting enough that Abby wouldn't feel taken advantage of, but not enough to make the other woman want to leave.

She need not have fretted. She was in the presence of a drill sergeant. Abigail Jackson had raised two daughters and three sons. She knew the fine art of wanting help, but not wanting to ask for it. Betty Jean's languid objections were dually noted, but ignored, as Abby continued up the path with her task in mind.

"My garden will still be there. Lord knows the weeds will! I swear I can't rid my rose beds of them! Besides, I've been out there a couple of hours now and straw hat aside, I need a break from the sun. At this rate, I'll be one giant freckle in the morning!"

Betty Jean laughed as she joined the red head on the porch. When she'd gone down the path minutes before, she'd left her door standing ajar and Abby pushed it open further. With a grand flourish she spread her arm wide towards the house's interior and said solemnly, "Welcome home," as Betty Jean crossed the threshold for the first time in five years.